THE NOSY NEIGHBOR

Also by Fern Michaels
in Large Print:

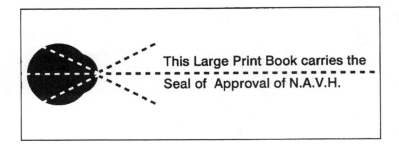

This Large Print Book carries the
Seal of Approval of N.A.V.H.

FERN MICHAELS

THE NOSY NEIGHBOR

WHEELER PUBLISHING

Published in 2005 by arrangement with Pocket Books, an imprint of Simon & Schuster, Inc.

Wheeler Large Print Hardcover.

The text of this Large Print edition is unabridged. Other aspects of the book may vary from the original edition.

Set in 16 pt. Plantin.

Printed in the United States on permanent paper.

Library of Congress Cataloging-in-Publication Data

Michaels, Fern.
    The nosy neighbor / by Fern Michaels.
        p. cm.
    ISBN 1-59722-014-0 (lg. print : hc : alk. paper)
    1. Swindlers and swindling — Fiction.   2. Criminals — Fiction.   3. Large type books.   [1. Lawyers — Fiction.]
    I. Title.
PS3563.I27N67 2005
    813'.54—dc22   2005009135

THE NOSY
NEIGHBOR

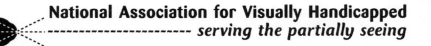

As the Founder/CEO of NAVH, the only national health agency solely devoted to those who, although not totally blind, have an eye disease which could lead to serious visual impairment, I am pleased to recognize Thorndike Press* as one of the leading publishers in the large print field.

Founded in 1954 in San Francisco to prepare large print textbooks for partially seeing children, NAVH became the pioneer and standard setting agency in the preparation of large type.

Today, those publishers who meet our standards carry the prestigious "Seal of Approval" indicating high quality large print. We are delighted that Thorndike Press is one of the publishers whose titles meet these standards. We are also pleased to recognize the significant contribution Thorndike Press is making in this important and growing field.

Lorraine H. Marchi, L.H.D.
Founder/CEO
NAVH

* Thorndike Press encompasses the following imprints: Thorndike, Wheeler, Walker and Large Print Press.

Prologue

Lucy Baker stared across the room at the twelve empty jury seats. She wanted to scream with frustration. What was taking them so long? The judge said the jury had signaled they had a verdict, but that was forty-five minutes ago. She dropped her hand to her side and crossed her fingers. *Please, God, let the verdict be guilty. Please, please, please.*

She tugged at the hem of her skirt. Lucy's brother Steven — sitting second chair on this case — leaned over and smiled confidently. His expression clearly said, don't sweat it, our client is going to walk out of this courtroom a free man. We did our job, and our bank account is now five hundred thousand dollars more robust.

Her brother was right — Justin Riley was going to walk because she had put up a superb defense. Unparalleled and unequaled, according to the press. That same press had followed her career and dubbed her Lucky Lucy along the way. What it all meant was she'd never lost a case. Yet. A guilty verdict was wishful thinking on her part. Nonetheless, she started to pray, saying the words she'd learned so long ago in catechism class and now had all but forgotten. Today, for some reason, she feared that God wasn't listening to her heartfelt plea. Why was that?

She felt rather than saw her client jerk to attention. Her brother followed suit. The judge was about to enter the courtroom.

The bailiff walked to the front of the judge's high desk and said, "All rise. The Honorable Sidney Blake presiding."

A hush fell over the courtroom but not before someone coughed. Papers rattled, feet shuffled on the hard wooden floor. Someone else cleared their throat as the jury filed in and took the same seats they'd sat in for the past three weeks.

The judge banged his gavel. Lucy sat up straighter in her chair. This was the moment when her blood always ran cold.

The moment.

The judge turned to face the jury. "Ladies and gentlemen of the jury, have you reached a verdict?"

"We have, Your Honor." The foreman of the jury, a retired schoolteacher named Abner Scribner, stood and handed a folded sheet of paper to the bailiff, who in turn handed it to the judge. Lucy watched as the judge unfolded the sheet of paper, read the contents, and folded the paper to return it to the bailiff, who then passed it back to Abner Scribner.

"Will the defendant please rise."

Justin Riley rose to his full six-foot-four-inch height. He was trembling. The thought pleased Lucy. Lucy stood, then moved to the side to take her place alongside her client, with Steven on his opposite side. *Please, God, let this scumbag be found guilty. Please, please, please.*

Abner Scribner cleared his throat and focused his attention on Justin Riley. "We find the defendant, Justin Riley . . . not guilty."

The courtroom erupted in joyous outcries. Justin's courtroom fan club, his parents, the media, his brothers and sisters, all shouted with glee. Lucy felt herself being squeezed, then pummeled on her arms by Justin's fists. Thank God it was Steven who was hugging her. "I have to get out of here!" she hissed into her brother's ear. "Now!"

"But —"

"You deal with the press," she interrupted, not wanting to hear anything he had to say. "I'm going to the office, then

I'm going home. I never want to see Justin Riley again as long as I live, and no, I am not going to any celebratory gathering, so don't even ask."

Lucy motioned to the bailiff, and whispered, "Can you get me out of here and to my car before they attack me?" The bailiff, an older, kindly gentleman, smiled and nodded. Lucy tugged at the jacket of her charcoal gray Armani suit, knowing hundreds of eyes were following her exit.

Lucy faltered once when she heard Lorraine Sumpter, the victim's grandmother, shout, "I hope you rot in hell, Lucy Baker!" Lucy didn't look back. There was no need. She could see Annie Sumpter's grandmother behind closed eyes. She even dreamed about the little old lady. Now, she would probably have nightmares about Annie's grandmother.

It was six-thirty when Lucy rode the elevator to her suite of offices on the eighteenth floor. The lighting in the hallway was dim. Like she cared. She fit the key into the lock, opened the door, and walked inside. One long arm reached out to shove the dead bolt home. She dropped her briefcase on the floor. Angrily, she kicked it across the reception area before she slid out of her shoes. Her shoulders slumped as she walked down the long hallway to her private office. There, with the door closed, she could cry. She could scream and yell and vent to her heart's content. If she wanted to. *To what end?* she asked herself.

Lucy sat down in her ergonomic chair, which was surprisingly comfortable, and looked around at the luxurious office. Everything was tony, high-end, and shrieked of billable hours. That was what the law was all about — billable hours.

Lucy was off the chair a moment later, padding through the meadow of sea-green carpeting that hugged her ankles, to the minifridge, where she withdrew a bottle of wine. She carried it and a Baccarat wineglass reserved for clients back to her desk. It took her a full five minutes to work the corkscrew. She poured till the wine sloshed over onto her desk. Two gulps, and it was gone. She poured again. Two more gulps. Her eyes teared up when she poured the third glass. Big mistake. She hadn't eaten today because she'd been a basket case, knowing the verdict was coming in.

"I can't do this anymore."

"I don't *want* to do this anymore."

Tears rolled down her cheeks as the telephone console on her desk lit up, every

11

line, including her private line, blinking. *They can blink from now till the end of time, for all I care.*

Lucy brought the wineglass to her lips and sipped. Tears kept running down her cheeks. Bitter tears of victory. She blinked away her tears to see her brother standing in the doorway, a look of something she couldn't define in his expression. Wariness, fear, anger? Whatever it was, she didn't care about that either.

Steven's voice sounded jittery when he asked, "Are you all right?"

Lucy eyed her handsome brother and was reminded of Justin Riley. They were both tall, preppy, handsome, the type of man women drooled over. Both of them knew how to take advantage of that particular characteristic. She continued to watch as Steven shuffled his feet. He didn't, however, cross the threshold. No one ever entered Lucy's private office unless invited.

"Do I look like I'm all right, Steven?" Even she was surprised at how slurred her words sounded.

"You look . . . drunk."

"That's because I *am* drunk. If I'm drunk, I have to look like I'm drunk." To prove her point, she reached for the bottle and upended it.

"I think you've had enough, Lucy. Come on, I'll drive you home."

Lucy looked around the office again. She had to squint to bring the room into focus. The rich mahogany paneling, the custom-made cherrywood desk, the wine-colored Naugahyde furniture, the custom book-shelves with the leather-bound law books, the thick carpeting, the lavish drapes, all courtesy of billable hours. "I don't want to do this anymore, Steven."

"You always say that after a verdict, Lucy. Go home and sleep it off. Things will look different tomorrow." His voice was pleading — he was worried. Yes, his sister always said she wanted to quit prac-ticing law after a verdict, but she had never gotten drunk after a verdict. Even he knew that this time was different. He wished he had the guts to step into her office.

"It wasn't till closing arguments that I knew that bastard was guilty. Afterward I accused him of being guilty, and do you know what he said, Steven?"

"No. What did he say, Lucy?" Steven asked, knowing he wasn't going to like the answer.

"He didn't answer. He laughed at me instead. His eyes said it all. The State's case was circumstantial. Justin Riley is a pedophile and a murderer. I don't care how good-looking, or how preppy he and his rich, influential family are. He is what he is. And I got him off. Me and you. Do you hear me, Steven? We sold ourselves to the Rileys for five hundred thousand dollars. And you know what else? The Rileys paid us in full — their account is current."

"The jury said he was innocent," Steven reminded her. "We did our jobs. We gave him the best defense possible, and we got lucky. That's what defense lawyers do. The law says justice was served. Mr. Riley Senior said he's giving us a bonus of a hundred thousand. That's not shabby, Lucy. We followed the letter of the law. We did what we were hired to do."

"Steven, read my lips. The guy killed that little girl. I know it, and you know it. He is now walking free to do it again because we did such a damn good job. I haven't been able to sleep since he laughed at me. I can barely eat. I wasn't absolutely sure until that precise moment. I saw it in his eyes. Do you want to know something else? His sister and his mother believe he did it, too. His sister Sally told me the things he used to do to her when she was little. And to her little friends. Don't take that bonus. That's an order, Steven."

"All right, Lucy, I won't take the bonus. But it's a mistake not to take it because we earned every damn dime of it."

Lucy brushed at her hair to get the spiky bangs off her forehead. Fashionable hairdo or not, it was annoying her. She couldn't remember the last time she had been so tired, so drunk. She slugged from the bottle, and, when nothing came out, she said, "Ooops, gotta get another bottle. Don't even think about telling me I can't, Steven. Go home. I'm going to sleep here on the sofa tonight. I have a lot of thinking to do."

"You can't possibly think with your snoot in a bottle. Come on, Lucy, let me take you home. We can get some coffee and talk all night if you like." Home was a brownstone on East Forty-ninth Street that he and Lucy had inherited from their parents. The bottom floor was rented out to two doctors for enough money to pay the taxes and utility bills. Lucy lived on the second floor, Steven on the third. It worked for all concerned.

"I'm talked out, little brother. Didn't you hear what I said? I don't want to do this anymore. I've had it with the criminal justice system. I need to get a life. I'm sick and tired of working ninety hours a week so some jerk can go out there and mutilate a little girl because of some sick — Go home, Steven, and leave me alone."

"They're just about ready to announce your appointment to the bench. Are you giving that up, too?" Steven asked uneasily.

Lucy yanked at the cork, and both cork and corkscrew flew across the room. "Wow, did you see *that?* The answer is yes. I told you to go home."

"All right, I'm going."

" 'Night, Steven!" she bellowed.

When she finally managed to weave her way back to the ergonomic desk chair, Lucy could see that the telephone console was still lit up. The blinking red light indicated there was voice mail on her private line. Only four people had her private number. Steven, the mayor, her housekeeper, and Jonathan St. Clair. She pressed the button to hear the message.

"Lucy, it's Jon. I just flew in this afternoon and heard about the verdict on the news. I was calling to invite you to dinner, but I guess you're out with your colleagues celebrating. Congratulations. They said you were the best of the best, honey." His carefully modulated voice turned intimate, and Lucy had to strain to hear the words. "I could have told them how really wonderful you are, but they didn't ask me. I'll call you in the morning. Sweet dreams, my darling."

Lucy eyed the newly opened wine bottle with a jaundiced eye. Did she really want to drink more wine? Of course she did. She tilted the bottle and watched the wine splash into the glass and over her desk. She sat down and propped her feet on the desk.

Jonathan. Jonathan with the infectious smile and crinkly eyes. Jonathan with the wicked sense of humor. Jonathan the consummate lover. She'd known Jonathan for a year, having met him on the tennis court at the City Racquet Club. One thing had led to another, and they'd ended up a couple. She thought she loved him. He said he loved her. Sometimes she found that hard to believe. She flipped the pages of her day planner to confirm what she already knew. In the year she'd known him, she'd been with Jonathan a total of twenty-two times. Either she was tied up in a court case or he was traveling on business. There had been one, wild, delicious four-day weekend where they'd both professed their love. Then she hadn't seen him for a solid month. Phone calls and e-mails were not the most satisfying kind of interpersonal communication for a woman going on thirty-eight whose biological clock was ticking. And yet their relationship worked for both of them.

Lucy slurped from the wineglass. She felt like crying all over again because she knew she was drunk and had just missed out on spending an evening with the man she adored. Talk about stupid, bad luck. Hers was running at an all-time high. As she made her way to the couch, wineglass in hand, she couldn't help but wonder if her parents were spinning in their graves over her decision to abandon the practice of law.

Both her parents had been attorneys. Her mother had been in family law, her father in corporate law. They'd built the firm. Then, nine years after her mother died, her father had retired to roam the world and she and Steven had taken over. At the height of his retirement while he was exploring the Amazon, he'd contracted a jungle disease she couldn't even pronounce and died within two weeks. Baker, Baker, Wong, and Lickenstein was one of the most prestigious firms in the city. There never had been a Wong or a Lickenstein. Her father had thought it was more impressive to have four names on their letterhead when he started the firm.

Lucy couldn't ever remember a client asking for Wong or Lickenstein. What she did know for sure was that with her and Steven at the helm, the firm had one of the best criminal practices going.

Lucy moved over to the couch and plopped down. In the morning she was going to have the Queen Mother of all hangovers. She reached for the pillow one of her first clients had crocheted for her. It was tacky, with its gaudy colors and equally tacky fringe hanging from the corners, but she loved it. A moment later she was sound asleep.

1

Six Months Later

Lucy Baker shoved her tennis racquet into its case, waved to her tennis partner, and proceeded to jog across the high school field to the track where she would run her daily five miles. A roll of thunder caused her to pick up her feet and sprint. When she reached the track, she tossed her canvas bag onto the bleachers and took off running.

Tennis, and a five-mile run every day regardless of the weather, had become a routine for her in the six months since she'd stopped practicing law.

Lucy kept one eye on the threatening thunderclouds overhead and the other on the track. She picked up her speed, not wanting to get caught in a thunderstorm. Off in the distance she could hear hard, rolling thunder, which seemed to be getting closer. One more lap to go. If she pushed it into high gear, she could pass the other runners, who looked like they were dragging. It was always this way on the last lap, she thought smugly.

She loved passing the muscle boys, shouting out words of encouragement. They were slugs compared to her. In all fairness, not that they needed to know, she'd run track in high school as well as college. She'd hurdled, too. Best on her team. She had the medals to prove it. Of course, they were locked away in one of her trunks. One didn't show off medals. At least *she* didn't. It was enough for her that she'd earned them, had them, and could look at them anytime she wanted to. Sometimes she needed to remind herself that at one time she'd been the best of the best.

Her coaches had said she was good enough to go to the Olympics. She had thought so, too. But life got in the way, and she'd had to bow out. She didn't have any regrets. Taking care of her mother during the last two years of her life had been more important than bringing home the gold.

Lucy whizzed past the bleachers at the south end of the track. She couldn't help but notice two men in dark suits, their arms crossed over their chests. She wondered which one of the guys on the track they were waiting for.

Sweat dripped down Lucy's face, soaking the tank top she was wearing. Her muscular arms glistened. She was hurting. She'd pushed too hard, too fast on her last lap. "No pain, no gain," she muttered over and over as she flew down the track. She saw the bleachers beckoning her. For one wild moment she thought she was at the wrong end of the track when she saw the two men approaching the north side bleachers. They must have run at her own speed to get there at the exact moment she came to a stop, bent over, with the palms of her sweaty hands on her knees as she took deep breaths. They looked as if they were in great physical shape under their dark suits. She wondered again who they were waiting for.

When her breathing was almost normal, she walked over to the end of the bleachers away from the men and did leg stretches. Out of the corner of her eye, she could see them approaching her. Lucy looked around to see if anyone was paying attention. Her heart kicked up a beat. This was suburbia, nothing happened in suburbia.

Lucy was about to reach up to the second row of seats for her gym bag when one of the men handed it to her. "Lucy Baker?"

"Yes. I'm Lucy Baker." She waited. They could have passed for twins. Frick and Frack. Yin and Yang.

"Special Agent Harry Conover. This is my partner, Larry Smith."

"What does that mean? Special agents of what?" She could feel an itch settle between her shoulder blades.

"We're from the Federal Bureau of Investigation." Two badges were suddenly shoved under her nose. Lucy backed up a half step and reached for the men's credentials. She read them carefully before she handed them back. She waited, her heart thumping inside her chest.

"We'd like to talk to you for a minute."

Lucy looked up at the darkening sky. She could still hear the thunder, now directly overhead. It sounded more ominous for some reason. "Why? I haven't done anything wrong. I pay my taxes on time and never cheat. I never even got a parking ticket. It's going to pour in another minute. Like I said, why?"

"We could sit in our car and talk."

Lucy snorted. "I-don't-think-so!" No sooner were the words out of her mouth than the sky opened up. Within seconds she was soaked to the skin. "As you can see, I'm already drenched. If you want to get those nice suits all wet, oh, well," she said with false bravado. Why did the FBI want to talk to her?

23

The agent named Harry said, "We'd like to talk to you about your fiancé."

Lucy gaped at the two men. "Jonathan? Why? Oh, God, did something happen to him?"

"Not yet," Larry said. "We'd like you to tell us about your relationship with Mr. St. Clair."

Lucy relaxed. The rain was coming down harder. Before long it would be like a waterfall. "I'm going to marry him. We're engaged." She waved her ring finger to show off her three-carat diamond.

"We already know you're getting married next year, on Valentine's Day. You have your gown. Let's see, you purchased it at Bethany's Bridal Shoppe. They're doing the alterations as we speak. The invitations have been ordered. You're holding the reception at the Ritz-Carlton. I believe there are 250 guests expected. Dinner is a choice of lobster or filet mignon. The salad is an arugula medley. Vegetables are baby carrots, peas from the Emerald Isle, potato-apple fritters, and flaky croissants. Dessert is wedding cake. Cristal champagne will flow endlessly," Agent Smith said, his expression as flat as his tone.

Lucy didn't like what she was hearing. There was nothing like an FBI check to put the fear of God into a person. There was shock as well as fear in her eyes as she backed up one step, then another. They followed her.

"A pretty pricey wedding for a girl who graduated at the top of her law school class, quit a thriving criminal law practice, and now makes popcorn balls and sells them through a catalog."

Well, they had one thing wrong. She wasn't the one who made or sold the popcorn balls. Lucy eyeballed the two agents. "I make an honest living, and I pay my taxes. Listen, I have to go home. It was nice talking with you gentlemen. If you want to talk to Jonathan, call him or go to his apartment. He doesn't leave for work till around nine-thirty when he's in town." She knew for a fact that Jonathan wasn't in town. Let them spin their wheels.

The agent named Larry wiped the rain from his forehead. "If we wanted to talk to Mr. St. Clair, we would have gone to see him. We know his habits as well as we know yours. Agent Conover and I would like to talk to you."

"What do you want to talk about? If it's about Jonathan's business, I'm afraid I can't help you. I don't know anything about it."

It was raining harder now. Since she was already soaked clear through to her skin, what did it matter? "Furthermore, I don't have to talk to you. The last time I checked, this was still a free country. Now, if you'll excuse me, I have to go home."

"Miss Baker." It was Agent Conover talking now. "It's imperative you not tell Mr. St. Clair about our meeting this morning. By the way, Jonathan St. Clair is not your fiancé's real name."

Lucy whirled around. "What are you talking about? Of course it's his real name. Jonathan is Jonathan. You must have him mixed up with someone else." Overhead, thunder boomed, followed by a streak of jagged lightning ripping across the gray sky.

"If you talk to your fiancé, it will jeopardize the case we're working on. We can take you into custody if we want to. In order to avoid that, we're asking you to cooperate with us."

Take me into custody. Jonathan isn't Jonathan. I'm having a nightmare, and I'll wake up any second now. She pinched herself. She felt the pain.

"All right, I won't say anything to Jonathan. Now can I go?"

"We'll know if you break your promise,

Miss Baker. Do you know what obstructing justice means?" Agent Conover asked. "Of course you do; you're a lawyer."

"Of course."

"We'll talk again, Miss Baker."

"No, Agent Smith, we will not talk again because there is no need for us to talk. I cannot help you with whatever it is you're doing or investigating. I told you I would not say anything to Jonathan, and I won't. That's the end of it."

"Where was your fiancé born, Miss Baker?"

"Winchester, Virginia, but then you probably already know that."

Both agents threw their hands up in the air. They looked like they were catching rain by the handful. "You see, wrong again. Your fiancé was born in Akron, Ohio. Do you want to know his real name?"

His real name. They were making Jonathan sound like some kind of criminal. Lucy could feel her shoulders start to slump. Her voice could barely be heard over the rumbling thunder. "What is it?"

"Leo Banks. His friends used to call him Lucky Leo. Does that ring any bells for you, Miss Baker?" Agent Smith asked.

Lucy looked at both agents. She hoped they would freeze in the rain, just the way she was freezing. They'd just invaded her life and turned it upside down. She thought about the thousands of seed pearls that were being sewn on her wedding gown. The FBI agents had made a mistake. Of course, this was all a mistake.

"I never heard the name before. I'm telling you, you have the wrong person. Jonathan is not this . . . this Leo Banks person. I would know. I saw a picture of the house he grew up in. The house is in Winchester, Virginia. I know the street and house number, but I can't think of it right this minute."

"Were you ever there, Miss Baker?"

This was all wrong. This shouldn't be happening. But it was. "No, I've never been there." Both agents raised their eyebrows.

She sounded desperate when she said, "Jonathan is incredibly busy. We just couldn't find the time to get down there. Winchester is a bit of a drive."

"The house in Winchester belongs to one of Leo's friends."

It's all a bunch of lies. It has to be all lies.

"Did you ever meet your fiancé's parents?"

"How could I meet them? They live in Spain. If we couldn't find the time to go to Winchester, Virginia, how could we find the time to go to Spain, or Chile, where his sister lives? He has no brothers, just one sister. I'm leaving now."

"How convenient. We'll talk again, Miss Baker," Agent Conover said.

Lucy ignored both men as she jogged off, her feet squishing inside her sodden sneakers. She needed to go home, where it was warm and toasty, so she could think. Hot, black coffee was a must. What had just transpired was too preposterous for words.

"One more thing, Miss Baker," Agent Smith called out. "Be careful, your life could be in danger."

Lucy raised her right hand and gave the agent a single-digit salute. She wondered if he saw it through the pouring rain. She'd heard his words, though. Until that moment, she'd never been colder in her life. Or more frightened.

Twelve minutes later, Lucy bolted up the front steps, body-slammed the front door, barreled through, and headed straight for the downstairs shower, where she stepped in — clothes and all — to let the steaming water wash over her. She shook from head to toe. The stink of her own fear clogged her nostrils until she thought she was going to choke to death.

Lucy reached for the shampoo bottle

and poured some over her long, tawny hair. The same hair Jonathan liked to run his fingers through after they made wonderful, satisfying love. Jonathan.

No, not Jonathan St. Clair. Leo Banks from Akron, Ohio.

It had to be a lie. Otherwise, the relationship she thought was so wonderful was all a lie. It couldn't be! Not now, when the seed pearls were being hand-sewn onto her wedding gown.

She knew a thing or two about the FBI. Actually, she knew more than she wanted to know. Dogs with bones. They never gave up. They always got their man.

Lucy was finally warm, so she kicked off her sneakers and peeled off her clothes. She continued to stand under the needlelike spray, knowing she was going to need at least half a jar of body lotion for her skin once she toweled dry. Did she really care? Maybe she needed to care because Jonathan said her skin was like silk and satin all rolled into one. Yes, she needed to care.

Instead of drying herself off with a towel, she reached for a thick, thirsty robe that Jonathan had bought for her at the Ritz-Carlton when they'd vacationed on Amelia Island.

Even though the heat blasted from the registers and the steam was still fogging up the bathroom, Lucy shivered.

In the kitchen, she did everything automatically. She filled the coffeepot, plugged in the toaster, took bread out of the wooden bread drawer, reached for the jam, which was nestled behind a quart container of orange juice. She poured. She softened the butter in the microwave and reached for the vitamin bottle. The beginning of a new day. Something she always looked forward to.

Rain beat against the kitchen window. Lucy brought her clenched fist up to her lips to stifle a cry that was about to erupt from her soul.

Two men. Awful words. And her world as she knew it was changed. How could that be?

Lucy poured coffee, buttered her toast, then spread the strawberry jam on it. She carried both the coffee and the plate to the table, along with a napkin. She eyed the glass of orange juice but didn't move to pick it up. She knew she wasn't going to eat the toast either. How could she? It would stick in her throat like wet straw and strangle her. Instead, she gulped at the coffee, burning her tongue and throat.

She'd forgotten the cream and sugar. She detested black coffee, but Jonathan loved his black, the stronger the better.

She needed to think. Instead, she let her gaze slide past the kitchen doorway to the dining room, where a pile of wedding invitations waited to be addressed and stamped. She'd started writing them out two days ago. She knew in her gut she would never mail them. Not now. Probably not ever.

Tears puddled in her eyes and rolled down her cheeks. She made no move to wipe them away. She continued to sip at the scalding coffee as she sniffed and sniffled.

The FBI agents had been wrong. She didn't make popcorn balls, nor did she sell them. She did, however, work three hours a day for Nellie Ebersole, a delightful elderly lady, who supplemented her income doing just that. All she did was process orders on the computer because the old lady had bad eyesight and didn't want to learn the intricacies of the computer. It was something to do to fill the hours of her days until she decided what new direction she wanted to take in her life.

She'd moved here to Edison, New Jersey, almost six months ago, exactly two weeks after Justin Riley walked out of the courtroom a free man. She'd rented the house she was living in for a month, then purchased it, bought new furniture, and settled down to vegetate. Sadie, her golden retriever, loved the huge backyard, and was happily digging a tunnel to the next yard so she could visit Clueless Cooper, a hundred-pound golden Lab. Coop, as he was known in the neighborhood, was tunneling on his side of the fence, too. Sooner or later they were going to meet somewhere underground. She hoped the meeting would be everything Sadie wanted it to be.

Lucy groaned when she saw Sadie run up to the deck and slam against the sliding door. She was covered in mud. She inched the door open and squeezed through. Damn, the temperature must have dropped twenty degrees since she'd gotten home. "You know the drill, Sadie," Lucy said as she slid back the cover of the hot tub. The retriever hopped onto the bench and into the tub, where she splashed around until she was clean, then hopped out. She shook off the excess water as Lucy shocked the hot tub with chemicals, turned on the jets, and replaced the cover.

She was almost to the door when she heard someone shouting. She cocked her head to peer around the corner to see a dark-haired man dressed in a business suit jumping up and down by the fence. "Hey, you! You with the dog! Do you think you can keep that mutt of yours inside when my dog is outside?"

Clueless Cooper's owner. He hadn't come over and introduced himself or welcomed her to the neighborhood in the six months she'd lived here. He only yelled at her from the other side of the fence about her dog. A couple of times during the summer she'd caught him peering nosily into her backyard. What a jerk! "Why don't you try keeping your mutt inside when *my* dog is outside? What do you expect me to do, stand by the door all day and watch to see if your dog is outside? Get real, mister," Lucy snarled. Like she needed a confrontation with her nosy neighbor today of all days.

"You're going to be a hard-ass about this, aren't you? I can tell by the sound of your voice you're a troublemaker," the man on the other side of the fence challenged.

Lucy chewed her lower lip to keep from laughing. She offered up a parting salvo before entering the house. "Try sitting on a pointy stick for a while, you . . . you . . . lawyer." She knew he was a lawyer, a commercial litigator with a firm in New York because Nellie Ebersole had told her all about the neighbors. She'd referred to Coop's owner as a delectable hunk of beefcake who couldn't seem to hang on to a woman. Crazy hours, crazy dog, she'd theorized. She'd gone on to say that if the neighbors didn't take pity on him, he'd starve to death and that he stank up the neighborhood when he tried to grill. The summary on one Wylie Wilson by the neighbors was that he was as clueless as his dog, a shark in the courtroom, and one handsome fortysomething dude. Just what Lucy needed.

Sadie bellied across the carpet in the family room, her eyes soulful as she looked up at her mistress as though to say, you take the fun out of everything. Lucy tried to ignore her as she padded barefoot into the kitchen to pour more coffee. She was scanning her grocery list when Sadie reared up and raced to the sliding glass doors, her bark so shrill the hair on the back of Lucy's neck stood on end.

There on her deck was Clueless Cooper, covered in mud from head to toe. Obviously, he'd finished the tunnel from his side of the yard. A second later the door slid open, thanks to Sadie's paw on the latch, and Coop was in the house. All one hundred pounds of him. Lucy watched in horror as the huge dog hopped on the beige sofa, then onto the matching chair, before he hopped down and rolled over and over on the beige carpet. Lucy shrieked and shouted to no avail. The dogs raced through the house leaving a trail of mud that was going to take her all day to clean up.

"Damn!" she said succinctly, just as the doorbell rang.

Lucy knew who it was even before she opened the door. He looked sheepish, she had to give him that. He looked good, too, and he smelled . . . sexy. "I hope you brought your work clothes, because I'm not cleaning up after your dog," she shouted, to be heard over the sound of the dogs' barking.

"Listen . . ."

"No, you listen. Your dog tunneled over here. That makes you culpable. He is your dog. He's trying to make out with my dog, which is an exercise in futility because Sadie has been fixed."

"Cooper's fixed, too. I'm sorry. I'm running late this morning. I didn't know about the tunnel. I guess he's been digging it for some time. It's usually dark when I get home. I guess I should have seen it, but I didn't. What do you want me to do? I have to be in court by ten o'clock, and I just missed the train." He whistled sharply for his dog, who ignored him completely.

"Sadie!" Lucy bellowed. The retriever ignored her, too. Angrily, she stomped her way down the hall to the last room on the right, where she stared in horror at the bedroom she'd spent weeks decorating. The champagne satin comforter was streaked with mud, the matching chair was so dirty it looked like it had come from the garbage dump. Both dogs sat up straight, their rumps on her satiny pillows. Sadie had the good sense to slide off the bed and wiggle under it, knowing full well Lucy couldn't reach her. Cooper stared defiantly at his owner and his hostess.

"I'll make this up to you, I swear I will," Wylie said, his voice desperate-sounding. "Look, I'm going to have to drive to the city. I really have to go, or the judge is going to fry my ass. When I get home tonight, I'll come over here and help you clean up. I'll pay for any and all damages."

"You expect me to leave all this till sometime tonight when you get home. In your dreams, mister!"

"Yeah. Yeah, I do. I don't have any other

options right now." Wylie had his hand inside Coop's collar and was dragging him off the bed. Lucy took a small amount of pleasure in seeing some of the mud rub off on her neighbor's pant leg. She grinned as he cursed under his breath. At the door he turned, and sniped, "That remark about the pointy stick was uncalled for." The moment the door closed behind her neighbor, Lucy shouted for Sadie, who continued to ignore her.

If nothing else, Sadie and Cooper's romp had driven the ugly thoughts concerning Jonathan and the FBI agents from Lucy's mind.

An hour later, Clueless Cooper was back on the deck demanding to be let into the house. Wylie Wilson must have a doggie door. It was cold, and it was still raining. A heavy sigh escaped Lucy's lips when she let herself out onto the deck. She moved the cover of the hot tub, and said, "Get in; then you can come in the house." Clueless Cooper, whom she now knew for certain to be as clueless as his owner, jumped in, paddled around, then hopped out. He looked up at her with puppy-dog eyes that melted her anger. "Okay, come on. You can keep Sadie company." The house shook as Coop beelined through the rooms in search of his friend.

Jurisprudence was never this interesting, she thought as she leafed through the yellow pages to call Disaster Master Cleaning Service. She was told they could accommodate her in three hours for the sum of four hundred dollars. She was no fool; she snapped up the offer and clicked off the phone. Wylie Wilson was going to be four hundred dollars poorer by this evening.

Lucy stared down at the emerald-cut diamond on her finger. Tears burned her eyes as she wondered if there would ever be a matching band on that finger. The FBI was wrong. They had to be wrong. Jonathan was Jonathan, not that Leo Banks or that Lucky Leo person. It was all some big misunderstanding. It had to be. It just had to be.

2

Lucy's thoughts turned dark as she found herself staring down at the emerald-cut diamond on her ring finger. Suddenly, she saw the gaudiness of it, the look-at-me statement it seemed to be making. The moment Jonathan had placed it on her finger she'd been reminded of the square solar lights that lined her driveway. She'd always wanted a marquise diamond, but Jonathan had wanted to surprise her and had picked out the ring himself. The thickness of the gold band plus the heaviness of the stone weighed down her hand. Suddenly, it didn't feel right. She slipped it off her finger. Where to put it? Finally, she dropped it into the toe of one of her sweat socks and rolled it and its mate into a ball. Jonathan had made a point of telling her he'd insured the ring. She wondered if it was true.

Five minutes later she was dressed in a navy blue sweat suit and sneakers. She rummaged in the vanity drawer for a rubber band for her ponytail. For some reason she was having a hard time getting warm. She was almost to the door of her bedroom when she realized how quiet the house was. Tiptoeing down the hall, she looked into the guest bedroom to see both dogs asleep side by side on the queen-size bed. *Even animals need friends,* she thought.

Carrying a cup of coffee, she walked through the family room, where she tried not to stare at the muddy furniture, and turned the corner and walked up the steps to the room over the garage that she used as an office.

The frog, or as the Realtor called it, the finished room over the garage, was a room of built-ins. Built-in desk, built-in book-shelves, built-in entertainment center, and built-in storage. The bathroom was small, with a toilet, tiny sink, and an equally tiny built-in shower. Sometimes she came up with Sadie just to sit and veg out with the TV. Maybe it was just to say she used all the rooms in the big house. Sadie loved running up and down the steps. Sometimes she would hide her toys and chew bones under the comfortable sofa.

Lucy sat down and hugged her knees to her chest. She really needed to think about what the FBI agents had said to her. Really think about it. She was a lawyer, so that had to mean she was smart enough to figure out what was going on where her fiancé was concerned.

For starters, how much did she *really* know about Jonathan St. Clair other than she'd turned her heart over to him. Jonathan, with the wicked sense of humor; Jonathan, with the laughing eyes and crinkly smile. Jonathan, who was never shy about telling her how much he loved her. He'd spun a tale for her about how wonderful and rich their lives would be once they got married. He'd said he planned on cutting back on his traveling so he could be home more because he wanted to be a hands-on husband and father. Four children, he'd said with a wicked grin. And he wanted them all to look like her.

Was it Jonathan St. Clair or Leo Banks who had made all those promises? She wished she knew. She also wished there was a way to call her fiancé, not to tell him what the agents had said, but just to hear his voice.

Her thoughts drifted to the last time she'd been with Jonathan. It was such a wonderful three-day getaway at a little inn on the Chesapeake that was private and secluded. Three whole days, half of which were spent in bed, the other half walking along the shore, holding hands, staring at one another as they both whispered promises they swore they would never break. He was the consummate lover, gentle, kind, considerate, passionate. A satisfying lover.

Jonathan was a true romantic, something that had surprised her in the beginning. He loved giving her silly little gifts, then stunning her with a diamond bracelet that almost blinded her. She pretended to love the bracelet, which she did, but she loved the snow globe more.

Once he'd surprised her by scattering rose petals on the sheets when they made love. The scent of the roses and the loving words he'd whispered had been a heady mix as he caressed her in all the right places. Over and over, he'd professed his love, promising that life together was going to be wonderful. She'd believed him.

Then, of course, there was the wine. Very, very good, expensive wine. Way too much wine. Now that she thought about it, those trysts were always a little blurry in her memory. Maybe the romance and the sex were colored by the wine, and she was too stupid to know the difference. Her brother said she was one of the smartest people he knew. She assumed he meant professionally. She was convinced now that where men were concerned she really was stupid.

When it had been time for him to leave the last time he'd visited, she'd cried. She never cried. Well, hardly ever. All that expensive fine wine had been the culprit. Jonathan had cupped her face in his big hands as he'd whispered more endearing words, then kissed away her tears. He'd called her ten minutes later just to say he loved her and to make her laugh, which she did. Knowing how alone she was feeling, he'd continued to call her every ten minutes for the next few hours until he boarded his flight.

"Bastard!" was all she could think of to say. And now this . . . whatever this was.

In all the time she'd known him, he'd never once given her his travel itinerary. His home base, such as it was, was a small one-bedroom apartment on East Seventy-ninth Street. She knew she could call the number at the apartment, leave a message, and sooner or later, most often days later, Jonathan would return her call. At least that's always the way it had been. For some reason, she knew things weren't ever going to be the same again.

Jonathan was in Guatemala. At least that's where he said he was going two weeks ago. He'd promised to be home for Thanksgiving, which was a week away.

Jonathan did not have a key to this house, and she didn't have a key to his apartment. *Now, where did that thought come from?* she wondered. She'd never been to the apartment. There was no need really. When she'd met him, she'd been living in the city at the brownstone on Forty-ninth Street, right around the corner from the United Nations Building. He'd always preferred to go to her place, claiming it was bigger and more comfortable than his apartment. Now, she felt an urgency actually to *see* where her fiancé lived.

If the Disaster Master people arrived on time, she could leave them to do their work while she loaded the dogs into her sports utility vehicle and drove into the city to Jonathan's apartment, pick the lock, and be back by dinnertime. Early in her career she'd represented a client named William Fogerty also known as Three-Fingered Willie who had been accused of multiple burglaries. She'd gotten him off. To show his thanks at her skilled representation, he'd spent hours showing her "the tricks of the trade," which she'd actually enjoyed learning. When Willie said he was confident she could pick any lock as well as he could, she'd felt pleased. Willie had been so happy with his acquittal, he'd given her

her very own lock picking kit. She'd doubled over laughing, knowing she'd only have occasion to use it when she accidentally locked herself out of her own home, but still, she'd kept it, and now she was glad she had brought it with her to New Jersey. *If* she believed what the federal agents had told her. Well, there was only one way to find out.

Jonathan brokered business deals and received a commission for his efforts. He'd intimated that he was a multimillionaire. He looked the part, dressed the part, and acted the part. She had to admit she didn't know what kind of deals he brokered, and when she had inquired, he'd wagged his finger playfully under her nose and said his business was the same as hers, confidential and client-privileged. She'd never asked again, but she had discussed it with her brother. Between the two of them they'd finally decided Jonathan was the man who brought the money boys together. A sheik in Saudi Arabia who wanted to buy some high-end real estate in New York without anyone being the wiser. Or, as Steven put it, anyone who wanted to conclude a high-stakes business deal without the facts leaking out to the opposition called on Jonathan St. Clair. And for his efforts, Jonathan was rewarded with a percentage of the deal.

What could Jonathan possibly have done to make the FBI place him and, as a consequence, her, under their microscope? And why would her own life be in danger? Did the agents think she knew something damaging about Jonathan?

Lucy finished the coffee in her cup. She herself was a free agent. Again. Nellie Ebersole, the popcorn lady, was leaving for Fort Myers, Florida, over the weekend, where she would reside until the end of March. That meant Lucy was out of her part-time job until the first of April. By April 1, she would be back from her honeymoon in Greece and be ready to settle down to being Mrs. Jonathan St. Clair. She shivered when she thought that the first day of April was April Fool's Day. Tomorrow night was the going-away potluck supper for Nellie that the neighbors were throwing. Her contribution was to be Swedish meatballs. She wondered what Clueless Cooper's owner would bring.

If she wanted to, she could drive to Jonathan's apartment in New York and take a look around. She could also drive to Winchester, Virginia, tomorrow. If she left at dawn, she could scout out the area and make the return trip home on the same day. How hard could it be to locate the house Jonathan said he grew up in? She could take the picture with her since it was in her album. She supposed she could fly to Spain if she had to. Checking out Jonathan's parents shouldn't be that difficult. She could go to the American embassy and ask for help. Or, maybe she could call the embassy for the information she needed.

Why am I thinking like this? "I have to prove them wrong," she muttered. "I know they have Jonathan mixed up with someone else."

Lucy bounced off the sofa and walked over to the window. The rain had turned to sleet. It was a horrible day for horrible thoughts.

I would know, Lucy thought, *if my fiancé was some kind of criminal. I don't know any such thing. Why am I so willing to take the word of two FBI agents? Because . . . because . . .*

There *were* a few things. One slight disagreement she'd had with Jonathan a few months before Jason Riley had walked out of the courtroom a free man. Jonathan had been in town for five days. He'd begged her to take the case of a friend of his. She'd turned him down flat. He'd been perturbed but had tried not to show it. She couldn't even remember what the case was about. Another time he'd said he could get her all the business she wanted. High billables on each and every case. She'd told him she had all the business she could handle, and she didn't ever want to mix business with pleasure. He'd said he understood, but things had changed after that. Subtly, but still they'd changed.

Then, a few weeks later, she'd told Jonathan that despite how unusual it was for a criminal defense lawyer to be considered for a judgeship position on the state supreme court, she was up for one. His attitude had changed again. He'd been practically euphoric at the news.

But then had come the Justin Riley case and her decision to stop practicing law. When she had told Jonathan, he'd called her stupid, though he'd apologized immediately.

Damn, did her decision to stop practicing law have something to do with what was going on? How could it? Her career or lack thereof didn't affect Jonathan. Or did it?

Lucy was staring intently at the bust of Blackstone sitting on her desk when the phone shrilled to life. She almost jumped out of her skin. Should she answer it? What if it was the FBI agents? Maybe it was Nellie Ebersole or her brother, Steven.

She reached for the phone and said hello cautiously.

The voice on the other end of the phone sounded just as cautious. "This is Wylie Wilson, your next-door neighbor. I called Nellie, and she gave me your number. I'm calling to apologize again and to tell you I will help you clean your house. And, I'll pay for any damage."

Relief washed through Lucy. "Okay. The Disaster Master people will be here shortly. They said it would cost four hundred dollars. If they can't clean my satin bed comforter, I'll buy a new one and give you that bill, too. I think you should know your dog is here again."

"What?" the lawyer squawked.

"I said your dog is here. Obviously, you must have a doggie door or else you left your back door open. He came through the tunnel. I made him jump in the hot tub to clean up, and he's sleeping right now in my guest room. Hello. Are you there?"

"I'm sorry. I should have thought about the doggie door. I was in such a rush this morning I wasn't thinking clearly. Listen, I'll find a way to make all this up to you. I promise. Coop really is a good dog. His problem is he's lonely. I think he lives for the times you let your dog out. He pines by the door and waits. It's sad."

"You're breaking my heart. Stop it. Let's not make a habit of this, okay? Don't worry about your dog while he's here. Is there anything else?" she asked coolly.

"Well, there is one other thing. When you pick up whatever it is you're taking to Nellie's potluck supper, could you pick me up some seasoned wings? That's what I'm supposed to bring. I'll pay you, of course."

"Do you think I'm some kind of maid service put on this earth for your convenience?" Lucy squawked indignantly. "I'm cooking my contribution. You are supposed to cook it, not buy it. The neighbors say no one eats the store-bought stuff."

"Oh. I guess I won't be attending then. I won't have time to make anything. Can you feed Coop? I didn't have time this morning. He loves meat loaf. He has a stomach condition, and it's the only thing he can eat. I have to go now. I'll see you later. Thanks again for watching Coop."

"You expect me to make your dog a meat loaf?" Lucy asked incredulously as she stared at the buzzing receiver in her hand. She replaced the phone just as the stairs started to shake with Sadie and Coop bounding up the steps. The frog was new territory for the Lab, and he had to

51

smell every inch of it, his tail, like a weapon, swishing furiously. Sadie sat back on her haunches, her eyes adoring as she watched her new friend frolic in the space that was originally hers.

Lucy snapped her fingers, and said, "Sit!" Coop looked around. Since his new best friend was already sitting, he took the command to heart and sat. He waited for approval, and Lucy was lavish in her praise. He licked her hand, whined softly, and lay down at her feet. Sadie followed suit.

Lucy dropped to her knees and tussled with the two dogs, who barked and rolled over and over, then on top of one another. They jumped on her, sat on her, tugged the rubber band out of her ponytail, and stretched out for a nap. Giggling, Lucy went downstairs to make fresh coffee.

Maybe she should leave the dogs in the frog when she drove into the city. She could leave dry dog food and water, lock the door so they wouldn't bother the cleaning crew and the cleaning crew wouldn't bother them. It was doable.

All she had to do was wait for the Disaster Master people.

Ahead of schedule by an hour, the crew arrived with a ton of cleaning equipment.

Lucy spent ten solid minutes explaining what she wanted done, locked up the dogs, gave instructions to the bonded crew on how to lock up, and left the house for the forty-five-minute drive into Manhattan.

It was twelve-forty-five when she parked the car in her brother's spot at his building and then took a cab to Seventy-ninth Street. It was going to be tricky. Jonathan had told her once it wasn't a doorman building, but there was an elevator operator. And he was on duty. He glowered at her as she stepped in, and said smartly, "Seventeenth floor please."

Lucy hoped the operator didn't wait to see if whoever she was visiting was home. He didn't. Sighing with relief, she walked around the short hallways until she spotted Jonathan's door. A business card was taped to the front door. Three locks. Customary and not out of the ordinary for New York City. Not a problem. She could pick a lock with the best of them, thanks to her old client, Three-Fingered Willie.

The moment all three locks snapped free, she opened the door and stepped inside, carefully locking the door behind her. She'd expected to see lavish furnishings because Jonathan loved fine things. For some reason she thought an interior decorator would have done the job. Her jaw dropped when she looked around the living room. A chair and a floor lamp were the only furnishings. A phone and an answering machine sat on the floor. There was no blinking red light, so that had to mean there were no messages.

There were no towels, no carpets, and no soap in the bathroom. The room she surmised to be the bedroom had a chair and a table with a small lamp on it. The only thing in the closet was a windbreaker that smelled like Jonathan and a pair of running shoes sans shoelaces.

In the kitchen, she opened the cabinets. Blank space stared back at her. The refrigerator that was plugged in and running held two bottles of Evian water and a tray of ice cubes. Nothing else.

Had Jonathan moved and forgotten to tell her? Had Jonathan ever lived here? Was this just an address for business cards? What? When she sat down on the chair, a puff of dust swirled upward. She stood immediately. Did *anyone* live here? Unlikely.

Now what? she asked herself, looking around.

If she hadn't leaned up against the wall by the door, she probably never would have seen the small mailbox key hanging on a nail at the side of the door. She recognized it because she'd had one just like it when she'd lived on Forty-ninth Street.

Lucy felt light-headed at the mere thought of going near Jonathan's mailbox. Tampering with the United States mail was a federal offense. She wanted to cry at what she was thinking and feeling.

She'd been a criminal defense attorney long enough to know she'd screwed up by running here to Jonathan's apartment just hours after her meeting with the federal agents. She knew without a doubt that someone, probably Frick and Frack, had followed her into the city. How could she have been so stupid? She'd just given them another reason to suspect her. Of what, she didn't know. They probably thought she was either tearing up stuff, burning it, or trying to hide it. That's exactly what she would think if she was in their place. There was a lot to be said for suspicious minds.

Lucy looked longingly at the mailbox key but knew she wasn't going to touch it. Touch it. What had she touched? Doorknobs, the cabinet doors, and the refrigerator handle. That was it. With a tissue from her purse, she wiped everything she'd touched, then let herself out of the apartment. She relocked the door with the aid of one of

Willie's picks, walked over to the elevator, and pressed the button.

She was back home in her own house at three-thirty. The house sparkled. The crew was worth every cent she'd paid them. By three-forty-five she had her hands deep into a meat loaf mixture. Clueless Cooper's owner was paying for this meat loaf, too.

Damn you, Jonathan, what are you involved in? A fat tear rolled down her cheek.

The phone rang, but she didn't answer it because her hands were full of egg, bread crumbs, and hamburger meat. Whoever it was would call back.

Five minutes later, Lucy covered the roasting pan and slid it into the oven. She looked around and knew that the dogs had to go out, but the yard was too muddy, which meant she would have to walk them. She found an extra leash of Sadie's, put on her coat, and left the house, the dogs literally dragging her. The slush on the road had turned into a sheet of sheer ice. She picked her way carefully, the dogs now walking just as gingerly. As she struggled along behind them, she couldn't remember when she'd had a more miserable day.

When they had gone about a half mile, Lucy announced, "Okay, guys, come on, time to head home." The words were no sooner out of her mouth when her feet went out from under her, and she was on the ground. She felt a sharp pain in her foot and ankle, an even sharper pain behind her right ear. Stunned by the fall, she stared around groggily at the dogs. She'd let go of the leashes when she fell.

She saw it then, the wire from the utility pole skittering across the road like a skinny snake. A live wire. Her heart pounded in her chest when she saw the high wind whip the wire in her direction.

She struggled to get up, rolling over so she could get to her knees when she felt Coop put all his hundred pounds against her back to steady her, and yet the wire swiped her rubber boot. She felt the electrical shock from her foot all the way to her head. With Coop's help she rolled over again, out of reach of the wire. Sadie yipped her approval until Lucy was on her feet. The golden Lab stared up at her. *This dog loves me,* Lucy thought crazily. What was even more weird, she realized she actually liked, maybe even loved, Clueless Cooper. She was glad now that she'd made a meat loaf for him.

Steadying herself on one foot, her vision blurry, Lucy bent down to hug the wet dog, who whined his approval. *I'm alive,* she thought. *I wasn't electrocuted.*

Their leashes dragging on the road, the two dogs separated and walked alongside Lucy until they were back at the house. Inside, she hopped around as she found towels to dry off the dogs and herself. She was exhausted by the time she built a fire, which blazed within seconds. The dogs immediately lay down by the hearth and went to sleep.

Lucy poured herself a glass of wine, kicked off her shoes, and settled down on the sofa. She tried not to think about the pain in her ankle or the weird feeling inside her head. She gingerly touched the peanut-sized bump behind her ear. The aspirin she'd downed would take some of the edge off the pain. When she was a kid, she'd fallen off her bike and sprained her ankle. To her mind, the pain and the swelling looked the same. She could move her foot, so that had to mean nothing was broken. Later she'd soak it, and the next day an Ace bandage would help. *I'm living under a black cloud,* she thought as she finished the wine in her glass. She poured a second glass.

This is nice, she thought. *Sitting here all cozy and warm while bad weather beats against the house. The two dogs close by, dinner roasting in the oven. What could be better?* A man maybe, someone to hold her hand, to curl up against. Jonathan? Jonathan wasn't a warm and fuzzy kind of guy. He was passionate, though.

She thought about her neighbor and wondered what kind of guy he was. He had to be at the very least her own age, possibly a few years older. Since it was obvious he lived alone with Coop, he had to be a bachelor. Maybe he was divorced. Maybe he was engaged. Did she care?

Lucy closed her eyes and was asleep within seconds. She didn't wake until the timer on the stove buzzed. She rubbed the sleep from her eyes as she hobbled to the kitchen to remove the meat loaf from the oven. It smelled good. While the meat loaf cooled, she slid some frozen peas and carrots into the microwave oven, along with two scrubbed baking potatoes. She debated making a salad but scratched the idea when her ankle started to throb in tune with the throbbing inside her head.

The front doorbell rang just as Lucy finished mixing the peas and carrots into the meat loaf for both dogs. She looked at the clock — 7:10. It must be her neighbor. She called loud enough over the barking dogs for him to come in. "I'm in the kitchen," she shouted. The dogs barked louder.

Wylie appeared in the kitchen doorway, a check in his hand. "Smells good," he said hopefully.

Lucy called the dogs and set the bowls on the floor. "Help yourself. I made some baked potatoes in the microwave. They won't be crusty, though. No salad either. I sprained my ankle," she said, holding out her swollen ankle, "while I was walking the dogs. I gave my head a good clout, too. I also got clipped by a live wire. Coop saved the day, though. He helped me get up on my feet. The stuff is in the vegetable bin if you want to make a salad. I guess that means I'm inviting you to dinner. What exactly is wrong with Coop that he can only eat meat loaf?"

"It's a long story. Coop was really sick for a long time and was slowly starving to death when I found him during a really bad storm. God only knows how long he was out there on his own. I took him to that vet on Oak Tree Road. He had to have some stomach surgery, and even when he came home it was still touch-and-go. I started to feed him little bits with my fingers, and he started to eat again. I appreciate your taking care of him and making him the meat loaf. I usually do it on Sunday. I make a whole batch of it, but I ran out this week. He won't eat the deli kind if I buy it. He just wants mine. Looks like he likes yours, too. I'll make the salad, and thanks for inviting me."

"You'll have to walk them after they eat. The yard is too muddy to let them out. Do you always talk so much?"

"It's the lawyer in me. You remind me of someone. Did we ever meet?"

Lucy stared at the tall man cutting up her lettuce. She wanted to say, if I had met you, I would remember you. And then she did remember meeting him years earlier when he was a prosecutor. She'd gone up against him and won. She hated lying to her neighbor, but lie she did. "I don't think so." What was the point in telling him she'd looked different back then in her designer, high-powered court suits, fashionable flaming red hairdo, exquisite makeup. Today her hair was back to its natural tawny color. The high-powered suits had been replaced with jeans and sweat suits. She looked exactly like what she was, a suburbanite.

"Maybe you have a twin out there somewhere. Everything looks nice and clean. I guess you were satisfied, huh?"

"Yes, they did a good job, and, no, you don't owe me any more money." He was good-looking. Dark brown hair and brown eyes. Five o'clock shadow, but that was okay. Good suit, so well made it fit him perfectly. She looked down at his Brooks Brothers loafers. A nice shine. His tie, loose at the neck, was nice, too. Obviously, he knew how to dress. To her eye, he looked like a runner or a jogger. On the other hand, maybe he simply worked out at a gym in the city on his lunch hour the way her brother did. Whatever he did in the way of exercise put him in good physical shape. She felt disloyal to Jonathan just thinking about Wylie.

Lucy rubbed at her throbbing temples as she struggled to keep up with her end of the conversation. "How is it that you know how to make meat loaf? I realize it isn't rocket science, but most men would opt for steak or chicken or go with takeout. That's what my brother does. Of course, he doesn't have a dog."

"I was married for ten years awhile back. My ex-wife had no expertise in the culinary department. I realized if I didn't want to starve, I would have to learn to cook. She was a lawyer climbing up the ladder. When she got where she wanted to go, on my back, she divorced me. She turned around, married a newscaster, and lives in Scarsdale. She now has a cook, a housekeeper, a gardener, and a chauffeur. Guess that was more than you wanted to know. Couldn't think of any other way to let you know I'm available. If you were looking that is." His expression was sheepish yet hopeful.

"Oh," was all Lucy could think of to say.

"Yeah, oh. I wouldn't marry a lawyer again if they paid me my weight in gold."

"Oh," Lucy said again.

Wylie chopped a skinny cucumber and dumped it into the bowl. His movements were deft as he cored and sliced a tomato. He tossed the salad, uncapped a bottle of blue cheese dressing, and placed everything in the middle of the table. "Do you think I should walk the dogs now, or should we eat first? Do you mind if I take off my jacket and tie?"

"No, I don't mind. I think you should walk them now. I'll set the table."

"No, don't do that. Wait till I get back. You need to stay off your foot. I'll make you a good foot bath after dinner. You probably should see a doctor. If you hit your head, you might have a concussion."

When Wylie returned he was wearing

jeans and a heavy sweatshirt. Obviously, he had stopped at his own house to change. He looked even better in casual clothes. Nice thighs under the jeans.

Lucy enjoyed dinner despite her throbbing ankle and head. She let Wylie do most of the talking.

"So, what are you, independently wealthy or what? The neighbors say you're home all the time and only work a few hours a day for Nellie. Great old gal, isn't she? I miss her in the winter." He peered at her across the table as he waited for her reply.

"I have a . . . nest egg. I live frugally," Lucy said by way of explanation. "I got burned out and moved here to the burbs. End of story." All she could think about was Wylie saying he would never marry a lawyer again.

"Where's that eye-popping ring you were sporting this morning? Are you engaged? You don't strike me as a person who would wear something that ostentatious. Costume jewelry, huh?" Wylie said, pleased with himself at his assessment of Lucy's engagement ring.

Lucy shrugged as she sipped at her coffee, relieved that Wylie was satisfied with his own answer.

An hour later, Lucy marveled at her spotless kitchen. "You do good work," she said, laughter ringing in her voice.

"My mother's upbringing. She taught us to clean up after ourselves and always to offer to help out. Otherwise, she said, no one will invite you back. There were nine of us, so we had to learn how to do our own laundry, make beds, clean, and cook. You should see the hospital corners on my sheets. So, do you think you'll invite me back?"

"There is that possibility. My mother always said we should be neighborly."

"Mothers are great people. If you can make your way into the living room, I'll build up your fire and fix that foot bath I mentioned. By morning, you'll be right as rain, a little tender, but you'll be able to get around. A bucket will do."

Lucy explained where everything was and made her way into the living room, where both dogs were sitting on the sofa. They waited to see if they had to get off. When Lucy sat down, they relaxed, their heads on their paws, the picture of contentment.

Lucy sat up to put her bare foot into the steaming bucket of water. "Ohhh, that feels good. What's in it?"

"Just you never mind what's in it. It's an

old secret family remedy my mother came up with for all us kids. We were forever breaking or spraining something. I should be going. I have to be in court early tomorrow morning. I can't afford to have the judge chew my ass out again. Thanks for dinner and thanks for taking Coop. I'll be sure to block the doggie door so he doesn't do an encore."

Sadie slinked off the sofa and tried to be invisible, as did Coop. Lucy knew exactly what they were doing and where they were going. Sadie was going to show Clueless Cooper her hiding place under the bed, where no human had gone before.

"C'mon, Coop, let's go. Time to go home."

"You're too late. They've gone to ground. Coop wants to stay with Sadie. Right now, I can guarantee they are both under my bed. They won't come out either. It's okay, he can stay the night," Lucy said generously. Suddenly she realized she liked this new neighbor of hers. And she really liked his dog, too.

"What about tomorrow?"

"I'm not going anywhere, so it's okay if he stays. I have one more pound of hamburger meat, but after that you'll have to take him home. By the way, you better pick up something for me so *you* can take it to the party tomorrow night. I'll call Nellie and explain what happened. Press the button on the lock, and the door will lock itself on your way out."

Wylie looked dubious. "Are you sure?"

"I'm sure. He really isn't any trouble. I kind of like him. It's obvious he likes Sadie, and if Sadie is happy, I'm happy."

"You are a nice lady, Lucy Baker." He pronounced her last name, Bay-cur. "Did I tell you I was available? My hairline is not receding like most men's my age. I work out, know how to cook and clean house. I come from sturdy stock, and my cholesterol is normal."

Lucy blinked. In one breath she knew more about Wylie than she knew about Jonathan. "I will store all that other information aside for a time when I might need it." In spite of herself, Lucy burst out laughing. *Bay-cur.* "How did you know my last name?"

"Rachel at Number 12 told me who you were when you moved in. Seems she knows the Realtor who sold you your house. She said your name was Lucy Baycur, and I remembered it."

Lucy didn't bother to correct the way he pronounced her last name once she realized seventy-five-year-old Rachel Muller with her German accent was the one who'd told him her name. That was another reason why Wylie didn't connect her to the ace criminal defense attorney she'd once been.

" 'Night, Lucy."

" 'Night, Wylie."

The moment the door closed and locked behind Wylie, both dogs thundered down the hall and leapt onto the couch. Lucy laughed again.

A fitting end to an awful day.

3

Two things happened simultaneously the next morning when Lucy woke up on the couch with the two dogs. The phone rang, and the doorbell rang. She struggled to a sitting position and reached for the phone. She said hello as she hobbled to the front door, thinking it was Wylie who'd come to walk the dogs. It wasn't Wylie, but he *was* walking up the driveway. Frick and Frack stood in front of her. She sighed, then her heart took an extra beat when she recognized Jonathan's voice coming from the phone that was pressed to her ear. "Can you possibly call me back in a few minutes? I sprained my ankle, and my neighbor is here to walk the dogs, Sadie and his own. Yes, ten minutes is fine," Lucy said as she ushered the men into the foyer and watched as Wylie loped up the driveway and into the house. Both dogs barked a boisterous greeting.

Lucy swiveled on one foot to reach for the dog leads hanging on the coatrack by the front door. Wylie's eyes were full of questions as he gazed at the two men, who stepped aside to permit the dogs to take center stage. His expression clearly said most people don't get visitors at six o'clock in the morning. When he realized Lucy wasn't going to introduce him, he fastened the leashes onto the dogs' collars so he could lead the pair down the driveway.

"Looks like a nice guy," one of the agents said.

Lucy eyed the two gray suits, hoping the fear she was experiencing didn't show on her face. "He's my neighbor. I sprained my ankle yesterday. As you can see, he came over to walk the dogs. Isn't it a little early for a visit from the FBI? What do you want?"

"We stopped by the tennis court and track, but you weren't there. We thought something might have happened to you."

"Something did happen to me. I slipped on a patch of ice yesterday and sprained my ankle. I also gave my head a good crack." She fingered the bump on her head and winced. "I repeat, what do you want?"

Instead of answering her question, the second agent said, "Was that Mr. Banks on the phone?"

"I don't think that's any of your business, Agent Conover. Why are you here? I told you yesterday I don't know anything about Jonathan's business. If I don't know anything, how can I possibly help you?"

Lucy wondered how two men could wear identical blank expressions.

"Then why did you go to his apartment yesterday? Did you leave him a note or a warning? That's another way of saying we don't believe you."

Pretend outrage rang in Lucy's voice. "You followed me!"

"Why did you go there?" Agent Conover asked a second time. "You said you had never been to Mr. Banks's apartment, but all of a sudden, after we spoke, you suddenly wanted to visit your fiancé's apartment. I guess you were a little surprised to see that it was empty."

Conover had her there, and she knew it. Lucy motioned to the two agents to follow her into the kitchen. She nodded as she watched the water drip through the coffeepot. She turned on one foot and reached into the cabinet for a cup. One cup. There was no way she was going to offer these two a cup of coffee. She tried unobtrusively to sneak a look at the clock on the range to see how much time she had before Jonathan called back. A precious few minutes. "Since you know the apartment is virtually empty, I hope you had a search warrant when *you* entered."

The agents ignored her comment. "We have it on good authority that Mr. Banks will be joining you for Thanksgiving. That's six days from now. We were going to ask you to come into our office in Manhattan, but seeing as how you're slightly incapacitated, we can have our superiors come here. We need to talk, Miss Baker. We want you to help us."

The words sounded so ominous that Lucy felt herself cringe. What exactly did they mean by *help?*

"How many times do I have to tell you, I don't know anything about Jonathan or his business. Yes, I was upset yesterday after we spoke. I didn't believe what you said about my fiancé. That's why I went to his apartment. In case you don't already know, I picked the lock. I don't know why there isn't any furniture other than a few chairs and tables. Maybe Jonathan doesn't like the area, or maybe he can't break his lease. He's only in the city a few days at a time. Perhaps he likes staying at a hotel where everything is done for him. I simply don't know. There's nothing I can do to help you because I don't know anything. What right do you have to come here and turn my life upside down this way?"

Agent Conover looked pointedly at his watch. "We'll call you to set up an appointment. Be sure to answer your phone, Miss Baker."

The moment Lucy opened the door to usher the two men out, Wylie and the dogs blasted through. She would have slammed and locked the door if not for Wylie and the dogs. Wylie unhooked the two leashes and hung them on the peg on the coatrack. Lucy thanked him and waited to see what he was going to do. Instead of leaving, he followed the dogs to the kitchen. She groaned as she locked the door behind the two agents.

In the kitchen, Lucy watched as Wylie handed out chews to the two dogs, who trotted off to the living room. It irritated her that her neighbor was making himself so at home.

"Talk about your steely-eyed whoever and whatever they are. Those guys looked like CIA wannabes to me. Are you okay, Lucy? You look worried. Is something wrong?"

Lucy brushed at the hair that was falling over her forehead, aware suddenly of how she looked and what she was wearing — a faded plum-colored sweat suit. The phone rang at that precise moment. Answer it, not answer it? Lucy opted for the latter.

"It's just my brother. He calls every morning before he goes to work. That old sibling thing. With eight brothers and sisters I'm sure you understand what I'm talking about." She hated the sound of desperation ringing in her voice.

"Well, sort of. No one calls to check on me except my mother, and she only calls on Sunday afternoon. Two o'clock sharp, and woe is me if I'm not there to answer. Can I have a cup to go? Listen, I'll be home early to walk the dogs. Please don't even try going out. The roads are sheets of ice."

Lucy grimaced. "Okay, *Dad.*"

Wylie laughed as he made his way to the front door, coffee cup in hand. He waved, then shouted, "Take good care of my dog."

"Don't forget to pick up some stuff for Nellie's party." They sounded like an old married couple, Lucy thought.

Back in the kitchen, Lucy looked at the small four-cup coffeepot and decided to make another pot. When the phone rang, she sucked in her breath, and, with as much enthusiasm as she could muster, said, "Hello!" It was Agent Conover calling to say the meeting would be at three o'clock that afternoon.

Wonderful, one more thing to worry about! The phone rang a second time just as she poured fresh coffee into her cup. This time it was Jonathan with an edge to his voice. Another time, another place, and the hardness might have bothered her. "Where are you, Jonathan?" she asked, not sounding completely friendly herself. The question surprised him. She could tell by the gap in the conversation.

"Buenos Aires. Why?"

"Just curious. I thought you were in Guatemala. Sometimes you remind me of a phantom. You're here, you're not here; then you're there, and you're not there. Whatever will you do when you don't travel as much?"

"Spend all my time with you. You sound different this morning. I tried calling you a few minutes ago, but there was no answer." To Lucy's ears, the statement sounded accusatory. Normally, she'd fall all over herself with an explanation as to why she hadn't answered the phone. Just then she didn't feel like acting normal. She was also feeling a smidgen of guilt about Wylie. "I sprained my ankle yesterday, Jonathan, as I told you. My neighbor came to walk the dogs, and I had to be hospitable because tonight is Nellie's going-away party. Are you in a hurry or something? It seems to me you're always in a hurry when you call me." She knew he would be able to detect the anger she was feeling in her voice. She didn't care.

"No, I'm not in a hurry. It just wasn't like you not to answer the phone. I like knowing you're sitting there waiting for me to call. I'm looking forward to seeing you. Are we eating in or going out for Thanksgiving dinner?"

"I'll leave that up to you, Jonathan, but tell me now if you want me to cook, so I can order the turkey from the butcher. Are you going to be staying here or at your apartment?"

"With you. I'll stop by to pick up my mail and repack my suitcase. I'm heading off to Madrid when I leave on the Sunday after Thanksgiving."

Lucy knew a lie when she heard it. Almost to a man, every client she'd ever had lied at some point. Even her brother lied sometimes. She wondered if Wylie was a liar, too. More likely than not, Jonathan would get a phone call the day after Thanksgiving and off he'd go. It was his pattern. "You're only staying for a few days! When will you be back?"

"For Christmas. For ten whole days.

Let's try to get away for a few days? How does four days in Aruba sound? Or we could go back to Amelia Island and get in some golf."

"Sounds wonderful," Lucy said. She wondered when he was going to ask her about her ankle or the bump on her head. Did she tell him about cracking her head? She couldn't remember, and in the end, what difference did it make? He wasn't going to ask her how she was, that was the bottom line.

"Lucy, I have a client who could really use your services. I'd take it as a personal favor if you'd come out of your self-imposed retirement to represent him. It's a million in legal fees easy. I want to talk about it when I get there for Thanksgiving."

They'd had this conversation so many times, Lucy had lost count. She wasn't in the mood to go three more rounds with Jonathan, not with the FBI spying on her. They were probably listening to her phone conversation at that very moment.

Jonathan took her silence to mean he'd finally worn her down. "Any more news on your appointment to the bench?"

Actually, there was news, but she wasn't about to share it with Jonathan. She'd been dropped from the list of possible candidates.

"No, not really. Why do you ask?"

"Because I'd like to see you wearing a black robe. Preferably with nothing on under it." He chuckled at his own wit. "Seriously, you earned it, Lucy. I don't want to see you do something you'll regret later on. Besides, I think it will be a real hoot to introduce you as, my wife, the judge." He laughed then. His laugh wasn't half as nice as Wylie's laugh, Lucy decided. She felt disloyal all over again.

Lucy thought about all the seed pearls for her gown and the wedding invitations on her dining room table.

"I'm being paged, Lucy. I have to go. I'll see you on Wednesday. Let's eat in. Just you and me. Promise you'll dream about me."

"Oh, I'll dream about you, all right, Jonathan. Have a safe trip home," Lucy said curtly.

"I love you."

This was where she was supposed to return the sentiment. She couldn't force the words past her lips. She pressed the button to disconnect the call. In doing so, she hoped this wasn't one of those things she'd come to regret later on.

It wasn't until she showered and washed her hair that she started to feel strange.

The bump on her head seemed to be smaller than it was the night before, the size of a peanut. She wondered if she might have a concussion. When her head hit the road it had been almost incidental compared to the pain in her ankle. She wondered if the electric current that ran up her side had anything to do with the ferocious headache pounding behind her eyes. She'd been more concerned with her ankle than the dull, throbbing headache that had just blossomed into a full-blown, mind-bending headache. Lucy washed down a handful of aspirin and crawled into bed. Maybe if she slept for a few hours in her own bed, the headache would let up.

When she woke, it was noon. Lucy's ankle felt better, but she still had a dull pounding inside her head. She lay quietly for a few moments, trying to identify the sounds she was hearing. The television must be on. If not, someone was in her house chattering up a storm. She made her way to the bathroom to swallow more aspirin, then headed for the kitchen, where she ate a bowl of cereal. She shrugged when she realized the television wasn't on.

Lucy let the rambunctious dogs out into the backyard, satisfied that the ground was frozen and they wouldn't return full of mud. Five minutes later they scampered back in and immediately ran down the hall to the guest room, where Sadie kept all her junk. Lucy headed for the couch, walking gingerly to avoid putting pressure on her ankle. She called Nellie to explain the situation and express her regrets about not being able to attend the going-away party.

Lucy realized she had nothing to do until three o'clock, when the FBI agents would arrive.

She finally admitted to herself that she was bored. The law had been her life. Maybe she needed to think about going back to the firm and taking on only those cases where she was convinced her client was innocent. As if that were even possible.

Lucy leaned her head against the back of the sofa. Her ears were starting to hurt. She wondered what that meant. Maybe she was coming down with a bug of some kind. It was almost three o'clock. Time for her visitors. If she didn't help the agents, they could charge her with obstructing justice. When they got done with her, she'd never practice law again. *Oh, God, Jonathan, how could you put me in such a position?*

To pass the time, Lucy made herself a grilled cheese sandwich with a small green salad. She barely tasted what she was eating because her brain was going ten miles a minute as she tried to figure out what was going to happen to her life. Her thoughts were so scattered she felt like a kaleidoscope was inside her brain. In brilliant color. She had to keep blinking her eyes to ward off the blurriness.

After she tidied up the kitchen, Lucy made her way to the living room to wait for Frick and Frack's "superiors" to show up. Before she sat down, she threw some logs on the smoldering embers and watched the fire spring to life. She felt just like the fire, like her body was crackling with something . . . *electricity.* To prove her point, she ran the palm of her hand up and down her arm and heard the little snicks that told her she was right. Again, she wondered what it meant.

Precisely at one minute to three, both Coop and Sadie raced to the door. A second later the bell rang. Lucy calmed the dogs as she dragged her injured foot across the carpet. At one point, she thought she saw sparks on the carpet. *I must need glasses,* she thought as she opened the door. Coop reared back and howled. Sadie barked her disapproval. Neither dog moved, but both of them tucked their tails between their legs. A clear sign to anyone who knew dogs that meant don't mess with me or anyone close to me.

The two men and one woman stopped in their tracks as they eyed the two golden dogs. "Stay," Lucy said to Sadie. She knew Clueless Cooper would do whatever Sadie did. She motioned for the trio to follow her into the living room.

Lucy offered them nothing more than a place to sit. "Let's skip the small talk and cut to the chase. I told your two agents I know nothing about my fiancé's affairs. I don't see how I can possibly help you. What is it you want from me? Just so you know, I am not one bit happy with what is going on. Until yesterday, I had a nice life, and you and your agents are turning it inside out."

The agents stared at her, obviously paying little if any attention to what she was saying. "Allow me to introduce myself," the tallest of the three said. "I'm Agent Harry Mason, this is Special Agent Sylvia Connors, and the man on my left is Agent Thomas Lawrence. Fine animals you have here. Very protective, I see. That's a good thing when a woman lives alone."

Lucy nodded. She wasn't giving up anything, even if it was the mating habits of dogs. She stared across at the agents with unblinking intensity, wishing Mason would get on with it so she could take a nap. She blinked, then rubbed her eyes. For just a second the room was fuzzy, slightly distorted. *Concussion.* The thought made her heart race.

"Miss Baker, Agent Conover's report indicates he's explained our suspicions concerning Leo Banks. You, of course, know Leo Banks as Jonathan St. Clair. I'd like you to look at these photographs and tell me if the man you know as Jonathan St. Clair is the man in the photographs."

Lucy reached for the eight-by-ten black-and-white glossy prints of her fiancé. How handsome he was. She nodded. "Yes, that's my fiancé."

"Now, I want you to look at these pictures. This is Leo Banks at his high school graduation, his college graduation, random pictures taken over the past three years by one of our agents. Do you agree they are pictures of one and the same man?"

Lucy sucked in her breath. There was no denying the likeness. She nodded again, biting down on her lip so she wouldn't cry. As hard as she tried, she couldn't help but stare across the room at the dining room table. The female agent followed her gaze and looked at her with pity in her eyes. Lucy felt faint with the realization that the agents hadn't lied to her.

Anger at her circumstances rippled through her. "A lot of people change their names for a variety of reasons. That doesn't necessarily make them criminals. What is it you *think* Jonathan has done?"

"Do you want the long or the short version, Miss Baker?" Lawrence asked coolly.

Lucy brought her hands up to massage her temples. "I want you to tell me everything," she whispered.

Lucy almost jumped out of her skin when the reply came firm, hard, and cold. "Murder, drug dealing, money laundering. None of which we can nail him with. The list is very long. Your boyfriend is a very arrogant, respected, sophisticated businessman. He has his fingers in a lot of different pies. His legitimate enterprises are a front for a very sophisticated money-laundering operation that no government has been able to penetrate until now. In the last five years we suspect he's moved three billion, that's billion with a *b*, through his legitimate businesses.

"Where did you get the money to buy that ten-million-dollar house in the Watchung Mountains, Miss Baker?" Agent Mason demanded.

All Lucy could do was gape at the agent. "What ten-million-dollar house? I've never been anywhere near the Watchung Mountains in my life. This house you're sitting in right now is the only property I own." Before she could blink, a property deed was thrust under her nose.

Lucy skimmed the contents. Her throat constricted, making it difficult to swallow. "This isn't mine. There must be some mistake. It's not mine," she said again, this time more forcefully. "I don't care what that deed says."

Agent Lawrence stared at Lucy with a jaundiced eye. "Mr. Banks leased that property for a number of years. It's his home base. It's where he goes when he's here in the States. A little over a year ago, he bought the property outright and transferred the deed into your name. Without a doubt, it is a valuable piece of real estate. The security system alone is worth hundreds of thousands of dollars. The whole place is loaded with motion sensors, laser trip wires, and tremor plates. Terrorists and drug dealers use devices like that. Now, to our way of thinking, if you're a normal person who just safeguards his privacy, that's one thing, but systems like the ones installed on that property make us wonder what Mr. Banks is hiding. Or what you're hiding since the property is in your name. In addition, there are a half dozen very-high-end vehicles parked in the six-car garage. Six-car garage," the agent repeated sourly. "They're all in your name, too. A Bentley, a Mercedes, a Porsche, a Rolls-Royce, a Lamborghini, and a 1965 restored Mustang convertible. Not to mention the fleet of cigarette boats he has stashed in Florida. They're in your name, too. Those cigarette boats raise your net worth considerably."

"I don't care. They aren't mine. I don't even know what a cigarette boat is. I think I heard the term once when I watched *Miami Vice* on television, but that's all I know. I didn't know about the cars until this moment. I drive a BMW. I make payments every month. It's a leased vehicle, for God's sake. I'm telling you the truth." Lucy cringed at the desperation in her voice. Fear, unlike anything she'd ever experienced, rushed through her.

"What about these?" Special Agent Connors asked. Lucy watched in horror as brokerage statement after brokerage statement slid out of the manila folder Connors had been holding. Goldman Sachs, Prudential, Merrill Lynch, Smith Barney, Charles

Schwab, and a few more she couldn't read because they were upside down. "Your name is on every single one of these accounts. The account total in case you're interested, is 21 million dollars. These statements make you a very wealthy lady, Miss Baker."

A scream built in Lucy's throat. "They aren't mine! I can't even begin to comprehend 21 million dollars. Check the signature. I never opened any of those accounts. It's all a big mistake. You can check my income statements. What are you people trying to do to me?"

Another sheaf of papers fell out of the manila envelope. An amended tax return — bearing her signature. Agent Lawrence ignored her stunned expression when he said coldly, "We're trying to get you to help us. Do we have your attention now?"

Lucy clenched her teeth. "Yes, you have my attention. I want a lawyer."

Special Agent Connors snorted. "You are a lawyer, Miss Baker. All we're doing is asking you questions. If you want to lawyer up, that's going to make us think you might not be telling the truth. You don't want to mess with an OOJ charge, now do you?"

Lucy felt light-headed. No one wanted to mess with obstruction of justice charges. At least no one with even minimal intelligence. She shook her head so hard she thought she was going to pass out from the pain.

"Good." Special Agent Connors smiled.

"By the way," Mason continued, "Mr. Banks, who began using the name Jonathan St. Clair a good many years ago, is the beneficiary on all those brokerage accounts. The real Jonathan St. Clair, by the way, died as a child, before children got social security numbers. So it was simple for Banks to steal his identity and get seemingly legitimate documents in the St. Clair name. He's also the beneficiary on all the life insurance policies in your name. Twenty-five million that we know of. We don't know for certain, but we suspect he has a quit-claim deed, signed by you turning the house over to him for the sum of ten dollars, all ready to go on the house in the Watchung Mountains in case . . ."

"In case of what?" Lucy snapped. "I only have a fifty-thousand-dollar life policy. I make quarterly payments. It's a whole life policy. Prudential Insurance. You're crazy, you're all crazy!" Lucy snapped again. Although it didn't seem possible for her head to pound harder, it was. *I'm going to explode right here in front of these people,* she thought.

"Your untimely demise."

It was a nightmare, pure and simple. Things like this didn't happen to people like her. They happened to other people. The sick feeling in the pit of her stomach was working its way up to her throat. The pounding inside her head was unbearable. She was going to wake up any minute and realize she was having a terrible dream. She pinched the inside of her arm but felt the pain. She was wide-awake, and this was no nightmare. *Your untimely demise.* She shuddered at the words, and a chill washed over her.

Lucy's eyes snapped open. The three agents were staring at her with pity in their eyes. Agent Lawrence pointed to the pile of papers and the photographs on the coffee table. "We can make this all go away if you agree to help us."

Lucy snorted. It was blackmail pure and simple. Her legal brain kicked in. "I want to see that in writing. My brother can handle the legal work. It's that, or it's no deal. You do not have my legal signature on any of those documents. Those are forgeries and you damn well know it. Yes, you can drag me down, but in the end, I'll win because I didn't do anything wrong." Brave words that meant squat. She knew it, and the agents knew it.

The agents stood as one. "You look tired, Miss Baker," the third agent said quietly. "We'll be in touch. Soon. Don't get up. We can see ourselves out."

A sob caught in Lucy's throat. "Take your junk with you," she said, pointing to the pile of papers and photographs.

"They're for you, Miss Baker. We want you to study them so when we contact you again, you'll appreciate what a precarious position your fiancé has placed you in. We want you to think about what has happened and what can still happen. We'll be in touch," Agent Lawrence said, just before the door closed behind him.

Lucy cried then because she didn't know what else to do. In the whole of her thirty-eight years, she'd never been so miserable. Lucy thought about Jonathan's quick little visits, the weekend getaways, the little gifts he'd given her, the way he'd whispered in her ear, the way he'd kissed her. There had been no bells, no whistles, no breathtaking moments. She'd always been contented after sex, though. Her blood didn't sing when she was around him. Did she love him? She thought she did. She liked him, or at least she had. Now, she couldn't abide hearing his name mentioned. And yet she was going to marry him. Why was that? Because her clock was ticking, because her friends were all married. Because there wasn't a line of men outside her door begging for her hand in marriage. Because it was time to get married. Well, she didn't have to worry about that any longer. She wasn't getting married to Jonathan or anyone else!

Her head pounding, her ankle throbbing, she hobbled into the dining room, every expletive she'd ever heard in her life spewing from her lips. With a sweep of her arm, she sent the pile of wedding invitations flying across the table and onto the carpet. The dogs twirled and pranced as they tried to catch the swirling invitations. When Lucy saw that there were four invitations left on the table she was like a maniac as she ripped and tore at them.

Both dogs, uncertain if this was a fun thing or not, jumped back into the fray, romping on the cream-colored invitations, then chewing at them.

Satisfied that the invitations were ruined, Lucy pivoted around on her good foot and hopped her way back to the living room, where she collapsed on the sofa. She was suddenly chilled to the bone, more proof that she was probably coming down with a bug of some sort. She reached for the colorful afghan Nellie Ebersole had made her for her birthday and snuggled under it.

The dream, when it came, was springtime in the Watchung Mountains. She was hosting a gala soirée to celebrate her appointment to the bench. Off in the distance, as she brought her champagne flute to her lips, she could see a man dressed in camouflage fatigues pointing a high-powered rifle directly at her. She screamed when the flute shattered in her hand.

Did the marksman miss?

Was it a warning?

Lucy opened one eye. "Sadie! Don't bark in my ear like that. Oh, God, now what?" She rolled off the couch and hopped her way to the door. Expecting to see the federal agents demanding to be let in, she was stunned to see Wylie, his arms full of packages. Takeout for Nellie's party. "What time is it?" she mumbled.

"Almost six o'clock. The party was canceled. Seems like everyone on the street has the flu or something like the flu. We're going to have to eat all this stuff ourselves. You look like you have it, too. Do you?"

Lucy did her best to focus on her neighbor, but her vision was too blurry. He was so cheerful, she wanted to slap him. "I think I'm catching something; but worse than that, I think I might have a concussion. I must have hit my head harder than I thought. If that's not what it is, then that electric charge did something to my body. My vision is all blurry. It clears up, then the blurriness comes back. My ears hurt, and I have a killer headache."

"Do you want me to take you to the doctor? There's a good one right down the road. He's a GP, and everyone on the street goes to him. He'll make a house call if you need it. Do you want me to call him?"

The concern in her neighbor's voice pleased Lucy as she hobbled to the kitchen. Her voice was apologetic when she said, "I think I'll wait till morning, and if I don't feel better, I'll make an appointment. Is he open on Saturday?"

"Yeah, he has hours from eight to noon on Saturday."

"By the way, I didn't make a meat loaf for Coop. I think there's enough left from yesterday if you mix it with something."

"If you want, I can take the dogs to my house, or I can stay here and take care of them. I can make us some dinner and a meat loaf for Cooper. I can fetch and carry for you, too. Are you running a fever?"

"I don't know. Probably. I had chills a while ago. Yes, please stay. I'd appreciate it,

Wylie. I'm sorry I never made an effort to introduce myself after I moved in. I guess life just got in the way. I like your dog. I really do."

Wylie jerked at his tie and tossed it over a kitchen chair. His suit coat followed. "I like making myself at home. I'll borrow your slicker to walk the dogs," he said, pointing to the coatrack by the back door. "When I get back, I'll make you some hot tea. Do you have any cognac? My mother swears by hot tea and cognac. Makes you sweat. Go back on the couch and don't do anything. I'll replenish the fire. You can thank me some other time." Wylie grinned as he bustled about.

Even as bad as she felt, Lucy took a moment to marvel at how sexy her neighbor looked in his white dress shirt, the collar open, the sleeves rolled up to his elbows. She admitted she had a *thing* about white dress shirts on certain men. Men like Wylie. Jonathan in the same attire did nothing for her. How weird was *that?* She pushed the thought away. She had enough on her plate just then without thinking about a sexy neighbor she'd met only the day before.

Grateful for the help and attention, Lucy tottered back to the living room and the sofa that beckoned. She leaned her head back and closed her eyes. She heard the door open and close before she drifted off to sleep . . . again.

On his return, dressed in jeans and a fleecy sweatshirt that said GEORGETOWN on the back, Wylie set to work in the kitchen. He worked swiftly and cleaned up after himself as he mixed up the meat loaf, slid it into the oven, and removed the contents from the take-out restaurant onto plates. While he worked, he talked to the dogs, who watched him intently. "I'm probably a better cook than I am a lawyer." He looked down at Coop and felt a pang of something he couldn't identify. His dog was in love with another dog and her owner. Where did that leave him in the mix? Standing on the sidelines, that's where.

As he waited for the water for Lucy's tea to boil, he set about adding kindling and logs to the dying fire in the living room. When he was finished, he dusted his hands and walked over to the sofa where Lucy was sleeping. He put his hand on her forehead the way his mother would have. She didn't seem overly warm to him.

He stood back to watch her. When she was asleep, she looked vulnerable, and so very pretty. He was almost certain he'd met her someplace, somewhere before, but he couldn't recall where or when.

He bent over the coffee table to shuffle the papers and photos back into the manila folder lying on the floor. If there was one thing Wiley hated, it was a mess. He wasn't being nosy, he really wasn't but he'd never seen so many brokerage accounts in one person's name in his life. Nor had he ever seen so many zeros. He barely looked at the arrogant-looking, elegantly dressed man in the photos. He was about to replace everything in the folder when he thought better of it. He left the papers and photos just the way they were and headed for the dining room where he saw the litter on the floor.

Wylie gaped at the chewed-up invitations, knowing instinctively that Coop had had his teeth in the shredded mess. He sighed heavily as he picked up everything and placed it on the dining room table. He wondered what *this* was going to cost him.

His shoulders slumped as he walked back to the kitchen, where he made the tea and drank it himself. His lovely neighbor was getting married. Just his dumb luck. Damn, he really liked Lucy. He'd even dreamed about her last night, and he'd almost killed himself getting to her house that afternoon.

"Story of my life," he muttered to the snoozing dogs.

4

Lucy woke at eight o'clock, when she felt a cold wet nose nudge her chin. Through sleep-filled eyes, she did her best to focus on Sadie and her surroundings. She felt groggy and cranky at being disturbed. When she opened her eyes wider, she saw her neighbor sitting across from her. He looked like he belonged in the chocolate-colored chair. He even looked like he belonged to the room. She wondered how that could be. "It's eight o'clock," she mumbled, looking down at the watch on her wrist.

"Yep, it's eight o'clock," Wylie said cheerfully. "Are you hungry? I was starved, so I ate when I fed the dogs. I kept yours warm. How do you feel?"

Lucy massaged her temples. "Don't ask. Did anyone call?"

"Your phone rang four times, but I didn't answer it. I assumed you had voice mail, and it would pick up your messages. So" — he clapped his hands — "do you want dinner or not?"

"I'm not really hungry, Wylie. Maybe

later. Thanks for taking over. I feel so . . . so awful. I feel like there's a Chinese fire drill going on inside my head. It's like a hundred voices all talking at once, and yet nothing is clear. It's starting to scare me." Tears of frustration puddled in Lucy's eyes.

Wylie was off the chair and on his knees by the couch in a heartbeat. Papers crunched beneath his knees — the brokerage statements.

"Hey, it's all right. I'll take you to the doctor in the morning unless you want me to phone now for a house call. If it's really bad, I can scoot you over to Emergency at Kennedy. Do you still have the headache?"

"Actually, no. But my head is . . . busy. I'm hearing stuff. My God, maybe I'm having a nervous breakdown." She shook her head, hoping to clear it of the noise. "I can wait till morning."

Wylie inched upward so that he was sitting on the coffee table. "You are not having a nervous breakdown. However, you might have a concussion. You were fine before the fall, weren't you?"

Lucy nodded, her gaze going to the dining room, where she'd destroyed her wedding invitations. *Maybe she's one of those people who have telekinetic powers. A* moment later, she said, "I am not one of those people with telekinetic powers, Wylie, so get that idea out of your head. I can't even predict rain when there are storm clouds overhead."

Wylie's jaw dropped. "What are you talking about?"

"You just said I must be one of those people who have telekinetic powers."

"No, I didn't. I didn't say a word."

"I heard you, Wylie." *I should scoop her up right now and take her to the hospital.* "I'm not going to the hospital, either, so get that out of your head, too. Oh, my God, your lips aren't moving!" Lucy burrowed deeper into the corner of the sofa. Her voice was full of panic when she said, "I just read your mind, didn't I?" A scream built in her throat. "I did, didn't I?"

Wylie stood up and moved back to the chair he'd been sitting on earlier. He had to say something. "Yes," he croaked.

. . . statements . . . too many zeros . . . married. "I'm not getting married. You saw the brokerage statements. Were you snooping? You were thinking other things, but they aren't coming across clearly. You moved away. Oh, God, oh God, oh God! There's something wrong with my brain. Maybe it was that electric wire. I don't

want to read your mind. Don't think. Please, don't think. Make your mind blank. I didn't hit my head that hard. That wire touched my shoe, but I wiggled away. I did feel a shock run up the side of my body, but then Coop boosted me up, and I got out of there. That live wire was dancing all over the road." She was babbling, and she knew it. "You aren't thinking, are you?"

Don't think, Wylie. How was that possible? A person had to think. He lied, and said, "No, I'm not thinking." Wylie struggled for a diversion because this was beyond bizarre. "Listen, Coop got into your invitations and chewed them up. I'll pay for them. I'm sorry about the bank statements. I was trying to tidy up, but I thought you might think I was snooping. I wasn't. I left everything the way it was. I did clean up the invitations though." He was babbling just as she was. "Listen, I have to think. If I don't think, I'll go nuts."

"Maybe you should go home. Coop didn't do anything. I'm the one who ripped up those invitations." She *heard* fragments of his thoughts again. *Klutz . . . this is scary. . . . maybe a CAT scan or an MRI.* "Are you scared because of me or because you're a klutz? Or am I the klutz?

You're right, I need to see a doctor about my head." Lucy's voice was full of panic when she said, "You don't think this is fatal, do you?"

Wylie rubbed at the stubble on his chin. He suddenly felt like Clueless Cooper. "No, of course not. Just a little glitch of some kind. I'm sure there's a pill or shot for it. Maybe a shrink . . ." He knew it was the wrong thing to say the minute the words shot out of his mouth.

"You are crazier than I feel right now if you think that! Even I know there's no pill for something like this. If I go to a shrink, they'll lock me up and throw away the key. I'll be a freak. Promise me you won't tell anyone, Wylie. I need to think. Really think. Go out to the kitchen and let me see if I can . . . read . . . *hear* your mind at a distance. Promise first."

"Well sure. Whom would I tell? Maybe you're just stressed. Sometimes it helps if you talk about things that are bothering you." He didn't mean to look at the dining room table, but he did. "The ring is gone from your finger. You did say you weren't getting married, so I have to assume something went awry. Maybe that's what's stressing you out."

"You're a lawyer, right? I want to retain

you. Here," Lucy said, fishing in the purse that was on the table behind the sofa. "Here's five bucks for my retainer. Everything is now privileged, and you can't talk to anyone about me. Correct?"

"Well, yeah. Okay, you're my client." Wylie pocketed the five dollars. "I'm not going to like this, am I?" he said as he made his way to the kitchen.

"No," Lucy whispered, "you are not going to like this at all. Think!" she shouted.

"All right, I'm thinking!" Wylie bellowed from the kitchen. "Can you hear me?"

"I can hear your voice but I can't *hear* your thoughts," Lucy shouted again. "Keep thinking."

Ten minutes later, Lucy called a halt to the experiment. "Obviously, in order for me to *hear* you, you have to be reasonably close." As she hugged her knees to her chest, both dogs pressed against her sides. "I'm scared, Wylie. I don't think I've ever been this scared before. I don't know what to do."

"I have an idea, Lucy. I'll warm up some dinner for you, make you a cup of tea, and we can talk. I have all night. Since tomorrow is Saturday, I don't have to go into the city. I'll help in whatever way I can."

All thoughts of the legal brief he had intended to work on during the weekend flew right out of his mind.

Lucy took a moment to reflect on what she was doing. Who was this man she was literally trusting with her life? A neighbor whose dog had moved in with her so it could be with her dog. A neighbor she had only seen once or twice and had never even spoken to until a day ago. Maybe she really was crazy and needed a shrink. *No,* she told herself, *Wylie is okay. He's warm, compassionate, and he loves animals. Putting my trust in Wylie is not a mistake.* Childishly, she crossed her fingers.

Lucy walked out of Kennedy Hospital on Saturday afternoon with Wylie at her side. Surprisingly, her head was quiet. The CAT scan, the MRI, and all the other tests she'd undergone had showed no abnormalities. As Dr. Schlesinger put it, "You're golden!"

Wylie cupped Lucy's elbow in his hand. "I don't know about you, but I sure feel relieved. You must be exhausted. Why don't you wait here while I get the car. It's still pretty icy, and this light snow is masking the ice patches."

"Okay, Wylie. I really appreciate your

coming with me today. I owe you."

Wylie yanked at the baseball cap on his head. He turned the brim to the back before he loped off to the parking lot.

Lucy stepped under the overhang as a family of four exited the building. She strained to pick up their thoughts as they discussed the new baby they'd just seen. Nothing came back to her. She frowned. Maybe she could only *hear* thoughts if the person was stressed, excited, or angry. Maybe she herself had to be stressed, excited, or angry. She'd certainly felt that way last night. She was calm now that a team of doctors couldn't find anything wrong with her after five hours of testing. Maybe the whole thing was some kind of crazy fluke. She was glad she hadn't told any of the doctors about the Chinese fire drill going on inside her head. She was relieved also because she wouldn't have to seek out a shrink and bare her soul.

Wylie pulled alongside the curb in his Land Rover, reached across, and opened the door for her. The heater was blasting warm air. Lucy buckled up and leaned her head back against the headrest. "Are you thinking, Wylie? Because if you are, I can't *hear* you."

Wylie grinned. "That's a relief. Listen,

how do you feel about going out for some Chinese? While you were being tested, I did all my Saturday errands, made Coop his meat loaf, fed the dogs, picked up my dry cleaning, and did my week's grocery shopping. I even washed some clothes. My evening is free."

"Chinese is good, but let's take it home. The weather's pretty ugly. I'd rather sit by a fire and eat. I miss the dogs."

"That's doable. You sure you're feeling okay?"

"Pretty much so. My head isn't a war zone at the moment. What if it comes back? How am I going to deal with that?"

Wylie stopped for a traffic light at the corner of Grove and Oak Tree Road. "I don't know, Lucy. I think you should try and figure out why this happened to you. Stress does some really strange things to people. If you want to talk about it, I'm a good listener. You paid me a retainer, so you might as well get your money's worth."

Lucy laughed. "You have a point. Do you want me to call and order the food?"

"Good idea. Get some of everything. Do you like Chinese beer?"

Lucy looked across at Wylie. "I love Chinese beer. Do you?"

"Yeah, and Japanese beer, too. I like

eating hibachi food with a good bottle of Sapporo. How about we go tomorrow night? Little Tokyo has the best." Wylie waited, holding his breath, for her answer. If she said yes, that meant they had a date. If she said no, that would mean she was still hung up on the guy who gave her the headlamp for a ring. A ring she no longer wore.

Lucy weighed the question. She thought about the federal agents, about Jonathan and what was going on in her life. She adored Japanese food. "I'd love to go to Little Tokyo with you, Wylie."

Well hot damn! She must like me, he thought.

She must like me. Lucy turned to look at Wylie. "Why wouldn't I like you after all you've done for me?"

Wylie slammed his foot on the brake and turned into the parking lot of the grammar school on Oak Tree Road. After the Rover came to a complete stop, he turned to look at her. "I didn't say anything, Lucy. You just read my mind. *Again.*"

Lucy stared at Wylie as she struggled to digest his words. Her head wasn't hurting. She felt fine. Even the pain behind her eyes and ears was gone. "Are you sure you didn't say anything?"

Wylie yanked at his cap. "I'm positive. I was thinking how great it was and that maybe you liked me after all. I was excited."

Lucy tilted her head for a better look at her companion. "Maybe that's part of the answer. You were excited. Are you thinking now?"

"Yes, of course."

"Well, if you are, I don't have a clue as to what you're thinking. This is crazy!" Lucy dropped her head into her hands and started to cry.

Wylie looked across at Lucy, uncertain what to do. If there was one thing in the world he hated, it was seeing a woman cry. For a moment he was tempted to lie and say he'd spoken aloud just so she would stop crying. "Listen, Lucy, we're going to figure this out. I have a friend who's on staff at Duke University. He studies parapsychology and stuff of that nature. I can call him. It won't hurt to ask questions. I'm thinking this is just a temporary kind of thing, something you're going to have to live with till it . . . till it goes away. You said yourself you were feeling better, your head is clear, nothing hurts. You did have all those tests. Physically, you're okay."

Lucy raised her head and wiped her eyes with the back of her hand. "Okay," she murmured. "Are you still thinking?"

"Yes. My brain is going a mile a minute. Can you hear me?"

Lucy shook her head. "Okay, I was going to call the restaurant. We can talk about this later."

"Sounds like a plan to me." Wylie jammed the baseball cap back on his head. "Make sure you get some hot mustard."

By ten o'clock the kitchen was clean, Wylie had walked the dogs, replenished the fire, and poured a fresh glass of beer for both himself and Lucy. He carried a tray loaded with munchies to snack on.

This was what he liked, what he had hungered for when he was married to Allison. It hadn't happened because Allison wasn't into home, hearth, dogs, and Chinese out of a carton. The only time she'd ever curled up on the sofa was when she had the flu. She didn't like a fire because it bothered her cat-green contact lenses. She didn't like beer because it bloated her. Chinese and Japanese food made her sleepy. The only time she came alive was when she went shopping or they dined at a five-star restaurant.

"Do you want me to go home, Lucy? I don't mind sleeping here on the couch. I don't think you should be alone."

"No, Wylie, please stay, but you don't have to sleep on the couch. I have a spare bedroom. I don't think I want to be alone."

Wylie heaved a sigh of relief as Coop bounded onto his lap. He did everything but purr so Wylie would rub his belly. His owner obliged.

Sadie snorted her jealousy and started to paw the carpet. She let loose with an ear-splitting bark. Coop leaped off Wylie's lap and raced down the hall after his girlfriend. Lucy laughed. "Dogs are so funny sometimes."

Wylie stretched out his long legs, his eyes on the dancing flames that were so mesmerizing. He risked a glance at Lucy, who was staring at him intently. He wanted to say something, but the words stuck in his throat. The decision was taken out of his hands when the phone rang. He could see the panic in Lucy's face when she debated if she should answer the phone.

"I always get nervous when the phone rings after nine o'clock," Wylie volunteered.

"Yeah, me, too." Lucy picked up the phone, her greeting strained and cautious.

She listened to Special Agent Connors ask how she was feeling before she agreed to a meeting at noon on Monday. "Fine," was Lucy's comment before she hung up the phone. She was jittery. That meeting, she knew, would be where the rubber met the road.

"Is something wrong?" Wylie asked. "What? You look scared to death. Tell me. Listen, I have a gun. I'm not a great shot, but I can shoot. I have a permit, too. What? Talk to me, Lucy."

Lucy debated for all of five seconds. "Okay, come over here," she said, pointing to the sofa. Wylie needed no prompting. He walked over and sat beside her.

Lucy pointed to the stack of brokerage statements. "Those are just the beginning." She talked nonstop for twenty minutes, ending the conversation by pointing to the shredded remains of the wedding invitations on the dining room table. "I'm going to sell my gown on eBay!"

Wylie stared at his neighbor. "That's . . . that's spook stuff."

"No, spooks are what they call CIA agents. FBI agents are just cold, steely-eyed people with no hearts. They believe I know all about this. I swear to God, I don't know a thing. They're ruining my life. Remember that man in Atlanta who they thought had something to do with the bombing at the Olympics? They ruined his life. That's what they're going to do to me."

"Only if you let them. You said that's not your signature on the brokerage accounts. That will hold up in a court of law. As your lawyer, I know how to get down and dirty if you want me to."

Lucy pressed her knuckles against her eyes so she wouldn't cry. "Wylie, the signature on those papers is mine. I've been racking my brain, trying to figure out how all this happened, and now I remember. They have me dead to rights. That's why they were so smug when I kept saying my signature was forged."

Lucy lowered her head, her eyes full of shame. "About a year ago, Jonathan and I were celebrating some big deal he'd put together. I don't even know what the deal was, just that it was big, and he'd made a bundle of money. We were at my place in New York and had had several bottles of wine. The truth is, I was pretty tipsy. I thought Jonathan was, too. Out of the blue, he opened his briefcase and pulled out all these papers and asked me to sign them. Most of them were blank, you know, the last page on a stapled document. He said his attorneys were putting my name on some of his holdings so if anything happened to him, I'd benefit. He cited how things happened with airlines after 9-11, and he wanted to make sure I was taken care of. I signed everything he put in front of me. I never gave it another thought until those agents showed up. I was going to marry the man, so why wouldn't I sign the papers? I wasn't thinking like a lawyer at the time," Lucy said defensively. "It is my signature on every single piece of paper, and it is my word against Jonathan's. I feel so incredibly stupid. I knew better, and I still did it. I guess he had me bewitched."

"That's not good, but then you already know that. What exactly does the FBI want you to do?"

"That's just it, I don't know. They're coming back on Monday at noon. I guess you need to be here since you're my lawyer now. Like I said, I just kept telling them I didn't know anything. I don't, not really. They want me to help them. With the FBI hounding me and what's going on in my head, I don't know if I'm coming or going.

"Jonathan duped me, Wylie! It wasn't like I was desperate to find a man, to get married. I wasn't. He came along, a nice guy, he knew how to flatter me and treat me as if I were special, and I fell for it. Dammit, he isn't even who he says he is,

112

and he's coming here on Wednesday. That's only four days away. How am I supposed to act? What am I supposed to say?"

Wylie stared at Lucy, a helpless look on his face. "I guess the agents will tell you what to do and what to say. I can make a pest of myself if that will help."

"There's one other thing, Wylie. I probably should have told you earlier, but I didn't know you. I don't mean that I know you now . . . this isn't coming out right. Look, I didn't exactly lie. I just didn't . . . what I didn't do was . . . you *do* know me. You prosecuted a case in which I was the defendant's attorney. I'm Lucille Baker, not Baycur. Rachel Muller has a strong accent and pronounces my name wrong. Please, don't hold that against me. I moved here to New Jersey because I was burned out. I needed to fall back and regroup. People as a rule have a very jaded opinion of lawyers. I didn't want anyone to know what I did. We can talk it to death, but I would prefer not to."

Wylie slapped at his forehead. "I knew I knew you. You look different. Didn't you have very short red hair back then? Man, you were hell on wheels in that courtroom. I almost didn't mind losing to you. I did, but it was a pleasure watching you strut

113

yourself. You just walked away, eh? Just like that."

"Yes, just like that. And now this. You aren't angry with me, are you?"

"Nah. I understand. I have six sisters. I know how women think and act. Are you giving up the law altogether? What's your feeling now about the guy you were going to marry?" He hoped his voice sounded casual.

"No, I'm not giving up the law. I was just thinking the other day about how bored I was. I'll probably go back to the office after the first of the year. If I'm not in jail, that is. As for Jonathan . . . I don't know how I feel about him — aside from angry. It's over, that's for sure. Will I pine away for him? I doubt it. I thought I was in love with him. Maybe I was in love with the idea of love."

Her voice was so pitiful-sounding, Wylie grinned. He knew all about that. His mother was forever telling him stories about his sisters and the bums they were going out with. Fear of becoming old maids, she'd said. He needed to say something to wipe away the awful look on his neighbor's face. "I don't think that's necessarily a bad thing, Lucy. How much do you think you can get for your gown on eBay? I have a bunch of junk I'm thinking of selling," Wylie added, his curiosity aroused.

Lucy burst out laughing. Wylie joined in at his own expense.

She's free. Maybe that means I have a shot. Been a long time since I met anyone I like half as much. We have a lot in common, we're both lawyers, even though I said I would never again marry a lawyer. She loves my dog. That might be a plus. Lucy lowered her gaze to her lap. There was no way she wanted Wylie to know she was hearing his thoughts. Especially thoughts like these.

"You aren't reading my mind, are you?" Wylie asked uneasily.

Lucy shook her head. "I think I'm going to go to bed. Tomorrow I'm going to drive to Rutgers and use their library. I want to read up on what's going on inside my head. You're welcome to come along."

"Well, sure. Good night, Lucy. I can make us eggs Benedict in the morning to earn my keep if that's okay with you."

"It's very okay with me. I love eggs Benedict."

"Oooh, it's so beautiful," Lucy gasped as she walked over to the sliding doors to let the dogs out into the yard. "I can't believe it snowed five inches during the night. Before Thanksgiving no less. It looks just like a winter wonderland. The dogs are having so much fun." She watched as both dogs raced the length, then the width of the yard, barking and yelping at the strange phenomenon.

Wylie chuckled at Lucy's exuberant tone as he, too, looked out the kitchen window at the cavorting dogs. He looked up when Lucy entered the kitchen. She looked surprised at what she was seeing. "I borrowed your apron since I'm a sloppy cook. I went home earlier to shower and shave and to turn up my heat. I've been up since five o'clock. Did you sleep well?"

Lucy sat down at the table. Wylie looked so at home in the kitchen. *Her* kitchen. Jonathan had an aversion to kitchens. She couldn't ever remember if he'd set foot in the kitchen of her brownstone when she'd lived in New York. Most times she'd brought him a cup of coffee or a drink. She'd never cooked for him, though. Thanksgiving would be the first time.

"I hope this tastes as good as it looks," Lucy said, unfolding her napkin. "I feel like I'm taking advantage of you, Wylie. But, to answer your question, I slept soundly."

Wylie raked his fingers through his unruly hair. He squinted at his neighbor, a suspicious look on his face. "You are not taking advantage of me. I'm glad I can help. I haven't had this much excitement since I broke my ankle. That was six years ago. You aren't reading my mind, are you?"

"No, I'm not. I wish I could explain how it works, Wylie. Right now I can hear a jumble of voices. There's nothing clear, nothing distinct. Once in a while a clear word will surface, but it has no meaning. I guess right now it's because all the neighbors are outside shoveling snow and talking to one another. Are you thinking now?"

"Yes. I was wondering if you want me to call my friend at Duke. You didn't answer me when I asked you yesterday. Are we still on for the Rutgers library?"

"I am if you are. You have four-wheel drive, right? Let's see what we come up with at the library, if anything, before you call him."

Lucy was clearing the table when the phone rang. She looked at Wylie, who was on his way out to clear her driveway with his snowblower, and he looked at her. He shrugged. Lucy saw him wince when she said, "Oh, Jonathan, I wasn't expecting your call."

Wylie's face darkened as he used his index finger to offer up a salute.

"Lucy, are you there?" Jonathan's voice was sharp. "Did you hear a word I said?"

"No, Jonathan, I did not hear what you said," Lucy responded coolly. "We had a snowstorm last night, and your voice keeps fading in and out. Wet wires, I assume." Her voice was even cooler when she said, "What did you say?"

"I said, I'm not going to be able to join you for Thanksgiving after all. I called to apologize."

The relief Lucy felt was immeasurable. "Perhaps that's a good thing, Jonathan. I think I'm coming down with the flu. It seems everyone in the neighborhood has it. My brother will probably come here and bring dinner with him. Is there anything else?"

"You sound like you're trying to get rid of me."

The chuckle on the other end of the phone didn't sound sincere to Lucy's ears.

"No, no, Jonathan. I know how busy you are. I was looking forward to seeing you," she lied. She wondered if her tongue would fall out. When she was a kid her mother had scared the daylights out of her and Steven. She'd told them their tongues would fall out if they told a lie or even a little fib. Lucy remembered walking

118

around with a mirror in her pocket to make sure her tongue was still there.

"I really miss you. I hate this traveling. I can't wait till we get married so I can cut back. Eat an extra slice of turkey for me, sweetheart. I have to run now. I love you, darling."

Lucy didn't bother to respond. Instead, she pressed her finger down to break the connection. There was no way in hell she was going to tell Jonathan St. Clair she loved him. No way in hell. Right now, right this very minute, she hated the suave, sophisticated man she was supposed to marry. The most she could say about him was that he was decent in bed. Not great but okay. She didn't know how she knew, but she knew that Wylie would be spectacular between the sheets. Her body grew warm at the thought. She chastised herself immediately. She'd just met the man, for heaven's sake, and here she was thinking about how he'd perform in bed. Better not to think about things like that. Her life was messed up enough at the moment without adding Wylie to the mix.

The ride down Route 27 with Wylie driving his Land Rover was mostly spent talking about the weather, snowplows, and the newscast predicting even more snow later in the day. "Not to worry, Lucy, this baby can handle anything," Wylie said confidently referring to his Rover. "I hope we're still on for Japanese this evening." He took his eyes off the road for a minute to look across at his companion. She looked wonderful this morning, dressed in a sky-blue winter jacket with matching wool slacks. A snow-white wool hat covered her hair. He liked the way little tendrils escaped by her ears.

"I'm looking forward to it. So, you really like driving a truck like this?"

"Absolutely. The gas mileage isn't that great, but I wouldn't give it up for anything. It's five years old. My friend, the one I was telling you about who works at Duke, has the big Range Rover. Of course he needs it, with four kids. He loves to go four-wheeling with his family. Jake is my best friend. We've known each other since our college days, when we were in the same fraternity. Do you have a best friend?"

"Not really. I was pretty much a bookworm, and beyond the necessities for professional contacts, I'm not a joiner. You know how it is with the law. If you're a lawyer, you're married to the profession.

There isn't much time for a social life. Tell me about your friend. How did he get into parapsychology?"

"I'm not really sure. I can give you the version he hands out to most people. Seems he and his mother both have what he calls extrasensory perception. When we shared an apartment when I was at Georgetown Law, he was forever cautioning me about doing or not doing things. He was usually on the money. The guy is a pure whiz. He's got his doctorate and an MBA.

"His wife was Miss North Carolina in the Miss America pageant ten years ago. She was the first runner-up. Nice lady. She's always trying to fix me up with one of her friends," Wylie said hoping to get a reaction from Lucy. When nothing was forthcoming, he said, "I know you'll like him. The truth is, it's impossible not to like Jake," and focused on the snowy road ahead of them.

Five minutes later, they arrived at the library. "Let's split up. We'll hit the stacks, you take one shelf, and I'll take another. We can make notes and check stuff on the Net when we get home."

"Sounds good." Lucy hopped out of the truck and immediately went down on her fanny. Wylie bent down to pick her up and ended up right next to her. He laughed uproariously at their predicament. With their faces just inches apart, vapor from their mouths colliding, Wylie leaned slightly forward, intending to kiss her. Alarmed at how much she wanted that to happen, Lucy moved away from him, and the moment was quickly lost.

Finally, they both managed to get to their feet and into the library. Both of them were huffing and puffing as they shook the fine snow from their jackets. Neither one mentioned how close they'd come to locking their lips together.

"This is a daunting task," Lucy mumbled an hour later. "I've got a list a yard long. We can try the Internet later. Most of what I found are just case studies of people who suddenly get a feeling that something is happening to a loved one and come to find out that whatever it was actually happened. There seem to be thousands of those that are documented. I haven't found one instance where anyone *hears* another person's thoughts."

"Are you hearing anything now?" Wylie asked as he perused his own list.

"Background voices, but they sound far off. Are you thinking, because if you are,

I'm not picking up on it?"

I'm thinking I wanted to kiss you till your teeth rattled, Wylie thought. He watched Lucy's eyes to see if she was picking up on his thoughts. It didn't appear so. "I found a book titled *The Frontier of the Mind.* I think you are receiving some sort of transmissible signal, for want of a better word, from someone else's brain. Like mine, when you *hear* me. I think we will just *borrow* this book and return it later. I'll stick it inside my jacket. Tell me if anyone is looking. We'll bring it back or send it FedEx with a donation. Tell me when the coast is clear."

Lucy's eyes scanned the massive library. "Do it now," she whispered.

"Done! Okay, let's get out of here," Wylie said in a jittery voice.

"You go out to the car, Wylie. I want to walk around here for a while to see if I . . . *hear* anything. Until now, you're the only person I've been around aside from the FBI agents. I want to see if . . . if I have the same unusual ability here as at home."

"Okay," Wylie said as he walked quickly out of the library, the "borrowed" book under his jacket. He knew he'd never make a good thief. His heart was pounding so fast he thought he was going to pass out.

Lucy waited until the door closed behind Wylie before she made her way into the library's main reading room. She walked slowly as she tried to *hear* things. Libraries were normally quiet to begin with, so this was probably an exercise in futility, she told herself as she walked around the seating area. She was nervous, her hands twitching as she concentrated on two students sitting together at a table. She almost tripped on the blue carpet when she *heard* one of the two students' thoughts. *Man, how can I study after last night? She was so hot I thought I was going to go up in smoke.* Lucy clapped her hands over her ears as she pressed forward.

As she meandered around, she heard words, some clear, some muffled. She heard a reference to a washing machine, a thought about a grade that was unacceptable. A whole jumble of words suddenly seemed to come from all directions. The Chinese fire drill again. She turned and rushed to the front of the library. As she passed the librarian, she heard the librarian arguing with herself about whether to tell her husband she was pregnant or wait another month. Lucy wanted to tell her to tell him now but she didn't. Instead, she slammed through the doors and saw Wylie waiting in front of the building. He took her hand and guided her across the parking area to the Land Rover. After she helped him clear the snow from the front and back windshields, she hopped into the truck, buckled up and proceeded to tell him what she'd *heard*. When he laughed, Lucy grimaced. "I bet I could get a job in a circus with this . . . new talent of mine."

Wylie laughed again but he reached over to pat her hand. It felt so comforting. Lucy relaxed immediately.

"Jake can interpret all this for us. I don't understand it any more than you do. He's a real force in his own field, so let's leave it to the experts. You feeling okay?" Wylie asked anxiously.

"Yes, I feel fine. My head is quiet now. When we were clearing the snow away, I had the feeling that the snow was buffering my thoughts. Does that make sense?"

Wylie shrugged. "Listen, Lucy, I don't want you to get upset, but I called Jake last night after you went to sleep. I really called him just to talk. He volunteered to come here. I swear to you, I didn't ask him. He'll be here tomorrow. And, he's staying through Thanksgiving. His wife and kids went to Minnesota because his mother-in-law broke her hip and Jane wants to be with her mother. I couldn't say no. If you don't want to talk to him, that's okay. He's going to be staying with me. I'm just trying to help, Lucy."

Lucy smiled. "I know that, Wylie. It's okay. The feds are coming back tomorrow. Up till now it's been a mind game with them. Tomorrow they're going to bring out their big guns. It might be a good thing if your friend is here. You can both sit in on the meeting."

"With this new . . . ah . . . power of yours, you are now the eight-hundred-pound gorilla. Think about that, Lucy."

5

Lucy woke up to a quiet white world. As she looked out at the yard, which was covered in a blinding pristine whiteness, she remembered that Wylie had taken the dogs when he'd left last night so they could play in the snow.

She wondered if the FBI agents would still come today. Were they like the mailmen, undeterred by sleet, snow, or rain? Thinking about them set her stomach to roiling with fear again. *How could I have been so utterly stupid where Jonathan was concerned?* Because when you were working eighty hours a week having a fiancé in absentia suited you just fine.

Twenty minutes later, Lucy was in the kitchen, whipping up pancake batter and frying bacon, while coffee dripped into the pot. She almost jumped out of her skin when she heard a *thwamp, thwamp* sound at the sliding glass doors. She burst out laughing when she went to the door to see Coop and Sadie, covered in snow from head to foot. Obviously, they'd tunneled from yard to yard and come up through the snow. They barreled through the house to the front door just as the doorbell rang.

"It's a holiday!" Wylie bellowed as he stepped out of his Timberlands. "Hmmm, smells good. I could eat a horse. Or, whatever it is you're making."

Lucy laughed again. "Pancakes, bacon, coffee, juice." This was nice. Good-looking guy, his dog, her dog, her cooking in the kitchen. A roaring fire in the fireplace. Snowbound. The stuff dreams were made of. In this case a nightmare if she carried the thought any further.

"How'd you sleep?" Wylie asked as he made himself at home in the kitchen by setting the table, getting out napkins and silver. "I slept like a log," he volunteered.

"I did, too. I woke up, and it was so quiet. I missed the dogs, though. I can't believe they made it through the tunnel and then up through all that snow."

"Sadie wanted to get home, and Coop was right behind her. They're in love." He guffawed.

Wylie looked really good this morning, in a yellow sweater and jeans that fit him like a second skin. Nice buns and great thighs. Lucy felt like she was sizing up a chicken at the market.

"How's the head?" he asked.

"Quiet. I was thinking when I woke up that maybe this whole thing is just some temporary fluke."

Wylie stared at her. "Lucy, I just don't know. Weather permitting, Jake should be here soon. I checked the airport, and flights are coming in. I hope he can make it from the airport. He told me not to pick him up, that he would rent a car."

Lucy placed a stack of buttermilk pancakes in front of Wylie, then fixed two plates for the dogs.

Wylie looked across the table, wondering if Lucy was tuned in to his thoughts. He didn't ask. It didn't matter to him if she knew he was worried about the FBI's visit. He knew enough about the way the bureau worked to realize that there was no way in hell Lucy was going to get away from them unless she did what they wanted.

While Lucy cleared the table, he watched her and liked what he was seeing. Hell, he liked everything about her. Today she was wearing a long-sleeved pink shirt, open at the throat, and jeans that hugged her slim hips. Nice shape, 110 pounds, he judged. Nice blond hair, too, although today she wore it pinned on top of her head in a knot secured by tortoiseshell combs. He knew his mother would like Lucy. His dad would dote on her.

Wylie's cell phone chirped. He rummaged in his pocket and flipped it on. "Where are you, buddy?" he asked when he recognized Jake's voice. "You're standing in my driveway! Hot damn. Come next door, and we'll cook you some breakfast.

"It's Jake. He's here! I don't believe that guy! He eats like a truck driver, just so you know. Guess that's him knocking on the door."

Coop and Sadie made it to the door before Wylie. Both dogs barked happily, but they reared back when they heard a bark coming from the bag hanging on Jake's shoulder.

"I had to bring Lulu. My mother-in-law is allergic to dogs." Jake shrugged as he lowered the canvas carry-on to the floor and unzipped it.

Coop and Sadie skidded backward when a five-pound Yorkshire terrier dressed in a pink sweater with matching bow in her hair pranced out of the bag and started to yip and yap as she sniffed and pawed at her new surroundings.

Lucy stifled a laugh as she extended her hand. "Lucy Baker," she said.

"Jake Parsons. This little stick of dynamite

is Lulu. My four-year-old twins named her. They also like to dress her up. Cheaper than buying Barbie clothes. She's trained," he added as an afterthought.

Lucy eyed the studly-looking shrink with the sparkling eyes behind the trench glasses. He looked like a movie star with curly, dark hair.

"How are the roads?" Wylie asked, leading his friend toward the kitchen.

"Horrendous. Don't go out unless you have to. As I was leaving the airport they announced they were closing it. And LaGuardia and Kennedy, too." He bent down to scoop Lulu into his arms.

Lucy started to whip up more pancake batter, while Wylie meticulously placed bacon into the fry pan. This movie star type couldn't possibly help her. What could this hunk who traveled with a miniature dog do for her? She turned around to see the Yorkie squirming to be put down on the floor. "If you're worried about the dogs hurting her, don't." She looked up to see both dogs in the doorway. Both looked like they were poised for flight.

"Coop thinks Miss Lulu is a wind-up toy. Watch," Wylie said as he took Lulu out of Jake's arms and set her down on the floor. She yapped immediately, the pink bow in her hair jiggling with excitement. Clueless Cooper advanced tentatively into the kitchen, then stopped in his tracks while Sadie hung back, her tail tucked between her legs.

Miss Lulu did a little dance, her tiny feet skittering this way and that, all the while yapping her head off.

"Nah, they aren't going to hurt her. Coop will figure out she's real when she nips his feet." Wylie grinned.

The trio watched as Coop bounded over to the yapping dog, bent down to sniff her, then circled her, his weaponlike tail swishing furiously. A second later, he had the pink sweater bunched in his teeth and was trotting off with his prize. Miss Lulu looked around, undecided if she was being rescued or captured. She let out a joyful bark as Coop romped down the hall.

Lucy shrugged. "I think it's a good thing. That little gal looks to me like she can hold her own."

"That's the problem. I'd hate to see her hurt Coop." Jake guffawed as he snatched a strip of bacon off the plate. "She can be a dynamo when she sets her mind to it."

Wylie hooted with laughter. Lucy turned to hide her smirk. Sadie did not like other female dogs, especially bossy female dogs.

She might also be jealous if Coop paid too much attention to the little fur ball. Something else to worry about.

Lucy sipped at her coffee while Jake ate his breakfast. The two men talked about the weather, North Carolina, and the dogs. She tried to shift her mind into neutral to see if she could read either man's mind. Nothing was coming through. She finally gave up and started to think about Jonathan. Maybe the reason Jonathan had canceled his trip was because he knew the FBI was onto him. Maybe he would go back to one of the third-world companies he did business with and never be heard from again. Or, maybe he was busy plotting her death, as the FBI had implied. She shivered inside the pink shirt she was wearing.

The minute Jake Parsons finished his second cup of coffee, Lucy cleared the table and turned the dishwasher on.

"That was very good, Lucy. I enjoyed every bit of it. It's refreshing to find a young woman who actually cooks as opposed to ordering in. Now," he said, placing a tape recorder in the middle of the table, "let's get started. I want you to start at whatever you perceive to be the beginning. I only know what Wylie has told me. For now, let's make the starting point the day you decided to give up practicing law."

Lucy looked down at the tape recorder self-consciously. She was nervous, the words tumbling from her lips in her haste to get them out. From time to time she looked across at Jake Parsons to see his reaction, but his facial expression was totally blank. Wylie simply leaned back in his chair and sipped at his coffee, never taking his eyes off Lucy.

Thirty minutes later, Lucy threw her hands in the air, and said, "That's it. The three agents are due today. I imagine they'll be calling soon. The weather may have slowed them down a bit." She looked at the two men, waiting for them to speak.

"Do you want us here when the feds come?" Jake asked.

"Yes. I think I need witnesses. I'm not hearing anything from either of you," Lucy said sourly. She fixed her gaze on Jake, and said, "Maybe it all went away, and I'm back to normal."

"All things are possible. I never close the door to anything. When you do that, you miss all the good stuff."

"Can you tell me if this is a long-term thing, short-term, a fluke? What?" Lucy asked. "Do you know of anyone else who . . . who can read people's minds?"

"No, not personally. As far as I know, there are no documented cases like yours either. However, I have heard of several cases from others in my field. Three, to be exact. All three refused, quite adamantly, to continue with testing, saying they didn't want to be written up, turned into freaks or sideshows. I also know all three are being monitored, but it will never show up in black-and-white. Anxiety, fear, adrenaline rushes, all three can contribute to what you are experiencing, Lucy. In time, you can probably use your new ability to your advantage once you learn how to control it.

"I know you want me to explain how something like this could happen. All I can do is try. There have been many, many papers written on ESP, extrasensory perception, and even professors and researchers at prestigious universities like Duke and Harvard have been persuaded that human beings can actually read the thoughts of others. The evidence presented has been hard as well as statistical." Jake massaged his temples as he tried to figure out how best to explain Lucy's condition in layman's terms. "In the 1930s at Duke University, before my time, there was this researcher named Joseph Banks Rhine, who is considered the father of serious scientific research into the paranormal. He had a colleague named Carl Zener, and they did the first systematic study on the subject of extrasensory perception. It was a colorful card study. He used bright colors and geometric symbols. The subjects he worked with were receiving information from something besides the known five senses when they viewed the cards, so he said it was a sixth sense.

"Rhine defined this sixth sense as ESP. Then he subdivided it into four basic abilities. Telepathy. Clairvoyance. Precognition. And psychokinesis."

It sounded ominous to Wylie. "Which one does Lucy have?" he asked carefully.

"In my opinion, Lucy is telepathic. That's the ability to tune in to the thoughts of others, or sometimes, inject your own thoughts into another's mind. I don't think she has the ability to do the latter.

"Clairvoyance is the power to see things that aren't available to you by the five senses and aren't known by other people.

"Precognition is the skill of looking into the future and seeing events before they take place. Sometimes through the subconscious or when you're dreaming or even daydreaming.

"Psychokinesis is the ability to use the power of the mind to influence matter; moving objects by thought is an example."

"That's pretty scary stuff," Wylie said.

"To you, maybe. I deal with it day in and day out. There aren't that many believers out there," Jake said. "There are, however, a robust number of people with at least one of the four abilities I just told you about. However, our numbers are growing daily, by that, I mean believers. There was even a television show about a man who got a newspaper a day ahead telling him what was going to occur.

"Ordinary people can develop ESP with no logical explanation. It simply happens. One day they wake up and can read someone else's thoughts. I've read some of those case histories, and I've kept an open mind. Still do. They were not cases like yours, however, where trauma was involved. Some small part of your brain was altered when you got that electrical shock would be my best guess. You aren't going to die or anything like that," Jake added hastily. "In time, if your ESP doesn't fade, you'll learn to live with it the way the others do.

"The cases I've mentioned aren't listed by name but by number for anonymity. I remember one in particular had to do with a person who dealt with magnetic fields day in and day out. He gave up his profession and is now a landscape painter. None of the cases were subjected to the traumas that you were is what I'm saying."

Lucy's shoulders slumped. "So what you're really saying is you can't help me."

"That's pretty much it unless you want to become a case history. Even then, I don't think I can help you. You can speak with a psychiatrist or a neurosurgeon if you like. Most people tend to shy away from doing that because, like you, they've been tested medically and given a clean bill of health. If you want to go that route, it's entirely up to you. Like I said, eventually you'll be able to control what you want to *hear* and not *hear.* You'll try not to subject yourself to undue anxiety. Life will go on, Lucy. You haven't been able to hear either one of us since we sat down here, right?" Lucy nodded. "Things are quiet, no one is upset, we're just talking normally. You're fine.

"Right now I see the federales as your immediate problem."

As if on cue the phone rang. Lucy jerked to attention. Was it the feds or Jonathan? She didn't know which she feared more.

When the phone rang for the seventh

time, Jake asked, "Aren't you going to answer it?"

Lucy grabbed the phone. A moment later she growled into it, "One-thirty is fine, Mr. Lawrence. Of course I'll be here." Lucy hung up the phone and looked across at the two men. "It was Agent Lawrence. They'll be here at one-thirty."

"If I might, I'd like to make a suggestion," Jake said. He reached for the recorder and removed the small cassette to replace it with a fresh one. "Tape the agents while they're here. Meet with them in your family room so you can keep the recorder between the cushions. This is way too serious for you not to have proof of what's been said and by whom. I don't think it will be to your advantage for us to stay here for the meeting. I think the agents and Lucy will be more relaxed, more open with each other if we aren't hovering. Those guys get pissy when you tread on their turf. They know we're here as backup, and that's a good thing. The tape recorder will do the rest. Do you agree, Wylie?"

"What are you saying, Jake? Hell no, it is not a good idea. No, no, no, we are not going to leave Lucy here with those agents."

"Get real, Wylie. They are not going to harm Lucy. All they're going to do is talk to her, question her. Everything will be recorded. Will you please trust me on this?"

"Are you sure, Jake? I mean *really* sure? I don't like leaving Lucy alone, period."

"I think your little lady can handle things. She does have this new ability to *hear* things. She also has a cell phone and a killer dog to protect her. She doesn't need either one of us."

Wylie looked like he still wasn't convinced, but he gave in at the mention of the killer dog. "Okay, I'm going to go home now so I can mix up some meat loaf for Coop. I gotta settle Jake in, Lucy. We'll be back for lunch if you invite us. Noon is good for us."

Some nice hot soup with crusty bread would be a really good lunch, especially on a day like this. Lucy whirled around. "I'm not excited. I'm relatively calm. Both of you appear to be calm. So, how come I know you would like some nice hot soup with crusty bread?"

Jake turned, his jaw slack. "I was just thinking . . . I don't have the answer, Lucy. I wish I did. The only thing I can think of is you got upset when Agent Lawrence called you just now. You look . . . *twitchy.*

Are you feeling nervous?"

"Yes, I am. I dread meeting and talking with them because I know they think I'm lying. If they can't get Jonathan . . . Leo, whatever his name is, they're going to get me."

"When the roads clear a little more, maybe we should check out that multimillion-dollar house the FBI says you own. There might be something in the house that will help us figure out exactly what is going on," Wylie said.

Lucy nodded.

Wylie whistled for Coop, who came on the run, Sadie and Miss Lulu alongside. All three skidded to a stop as they tried to figure out if they were going out, staying, or what. Coop galloped to the door when he saw Wylie slip into his jacket. Miss Lulu pawed her owner's leg to be picked up, while Sadie hugged Lucy's leg.

At the last second, after Jake marched ahead of him, Wylie turned, his face a mixture of emotions. He leaned forward, smacked Lucy on the lips, and squeezed her arms. "Call if you need me!" He kissed her again when Jake bellowed for him to hurry up.

When the door closed behind her guests, Lucy felt a little dazed, but in a good way.

Smiling, she took Sadie into the kitchen and offered her a treat. Sadie turned her head, walked over to the sliding door leading to the deck, and lay down, her head between her paws.

Ten minutes later, as Lucy was emptying the dishwasher, she heard Sadie slam herself against the sliding door, her bark loud and shrill. She went into the family room in time to see Coop bound through the snow with Miss Lulu's pink sweater clutched between his teeth, Miss Lulu attached to the sweater. Miss Lulu looked happy as a lark, her pink bow bouncing every which way.

"Guess your boyfriend can't stand to be without you, Sadie," Lucy said as she opened the door. Sadie almost turned herself inside out as she romped and barked with her buddy. Miss Lulu sat on the sidelines watching, her dark eyes sad and forlorn. This time Sadie was the one who nuzzled the little dog until she had a firm hold on the pink sweater. A second later, Miss Lulu perky as ever, went along for the ride. All three dogs trotted through the room, then down the hall to Sadie's lair.

If only life were that simple, Lucy thought as she sat down at the table. Was it a good idea to go to the mansion in the Watchung

Mountains? If there was as much security as the agents said there was, how would she ever get in? Since she was the owner, according to the FBI, she could call the police, give them some story about losing the code or something to that effect so they wouldn't investigate and arrest her when she set off the alarm. *Where there's a will there's a way,* she thought grimly.

Lucy pondered the more immediate problem that was Jonathan. How could she have been so stupid where he was concerned? Why wasn't her heart broken? Why wasn't she feeling anything other than fear?

Her gaze swept to the portable phone on the kitchen counter. She should have called Steven days ago. Her brother, razor-sharp, might have some ideas on how to deal with the feds. If she told him, he'd worry about her and become a pest. Steven had always felt the need to play the role of big brother even though he was her little brother. Wylie was a good stand-in. Why cause Steven grief?

Steven had never liked Jonathan. The truth was, Steven had never liked anyone she dated more than three times. He'd said Jonathan was a phony. At the time she'd thought of it as a "guy thing" and didn't pay attention. Another time, Steven had said Jonathan was a gutter fighter. Just feelings I have, he'd explained. Well, how right he was. Maybe the reason she'd never told him what was going on was because she didn't want to hear him say, I told you so.

Lucy bolted out of her comfortable chair when the phone shrilled behind her. Sucking in her breath she reached for it, her greeting cautious. "Steven!" she said in relief when she heard her brother's voice.

"I'm just calling to check on you," a deep voice said. "How's the weather in Jersey?"

"Pretty much the same as in New York, little brother. Did you open the office?"

"I'm here but that's about it. Listen, sis, I'm calling to ask if you mind if I don't make it for Thanksgiving. A couple of the guys want to go skiing. Your fiancé isn't one of my favorite people as you know. You two won't miss me at all."

"Actually, Jonathan can't make it, so I'm having dinner with a neighbor. It's fine, Steven, don't give it another thought. Don't go breaking your legs. I'd make a lousy nurse, and you'd make a worse patient."

"I'll be careful. I'll call you when I get back. Give Sadie a hug for me."

"Will do. 'Bye, Steven."

Lucy walked back into the living room to get the manila folder lying on the coffee table. Earlier she'd been too panicked to go through the material the agents had left her. Now, though, she needed to look at everything carefully, using her legal brain, not the paranoid brain she'd used thus far.

At twenty minutes to twelve, Lucy stuffed the deeds, the copies of insurance policies, the brokerage statements, her tax forms, and the titles to boats and cars back into the envelope. She closed it securely. She hoped she never had to look at it again.

How in the hell could anyone with a brain believe she was capable of money laundering? How? Angry beyond words, Lucy stomped her way to the family room. On the count of three she was going to toss the whole mess into the fire. Suddenly, she was angrier than she'd ever been in her life. In the end she dropped the envelope behind the wide-screen television set. Since the monster set sat catercorner, it was doubtful anyone would look behind it to the tangled mess of wires from the VCR, the cables, and the new DVD player she'd installed just last week. She didn't know why she felt the need to hide the envelope.

Her eye fell on the stolen library book,

The Frontier of the Mind. Unfortunately, both Wylie and she had closed the book in disgust, with Wylie saying, "Between us, we have two fine, legal minds, and neither one of us can make sense of this brain stuff. You know what I think, Lucy? I think you got it, and you're stuck with it." And she was . . . stuck with it.

Back in the kitchen, Lucy picked up the phone to call her neighbor. Her message was short and curt, "I'm making lunch now."

Lucy's anger stayed with her as she banged pots and pans and slammed the refrigerator door. Anger was better than tears, she thought, as she slapped cheese between slices of bread.

The dogs didn't bother to investigate when Wylie and Jake came through the front door.

Lucy forced a smile as she opened soup cans. She turned back to the business at hand and strained to see if she could *hear* either man's thoughts. Her head felt clogged up the way it did when she had a sinus infection. *She's never going to agree to go to Watchung. She's too pissed. I never saw such a rigid back. She's no match for those FBI stooges. She won't know what hit her by the time they get done with her. If I ever get my hands on that schmuck who set her up like this, I'll strangle him.* The words were crystal clear, but she couldn't tell which man she should attribute the thoughts to. Possibly both of them. It must be Wylie, she decided. She felt pleased that he cared enough to want to strangle Jonathan. Not that he would. Still, the thought was nice.

My mother always served those little white soda crackers with tomato soup. Tomato soup isn't the same unless you have those little crackers. Lucy reached up into the cabinet for a package of the crackers Wylie was thinking about. She turned and plopped them in the middle of the table. He looked at her in awe. She nodded.

Jake stared up at her. "If you can harness that anger you're feeling right now, you just might be able to figure out what the agents have in mind. That's another way of saying work yourself into a frenzy before they get here. Can you do that?"

Lucy threw her hands up in the air. "I don't know. This is all new to me. I tried the other day to . . . to do it, but it didn't work. I was upset, but I wasn't angry at the time. All I can do is play it by ear and hope for the best. You're right about something else, too. They might *look* like the Three Stooges, but they aren't that stupid."

Jake toyed with the silverware in front of him. "You read my mind. I am totally amazed. This is the first direct contact I've had with a person who could actually do it. Reading case histories is not the same thing." Subdued excitement rang in his voice, and it did not go unnoticed by Lucy. She felt herself shivering at the realization that she'd become a freak.

"By the way, we were watching the Weather Channel at Wylie's. The worst of the storm is over, and the roads have been sanded and salted. We can make a try for that house in the mountains after the agents leave if you're up for it. The bad news is there is another worse storm riding on the tail of this one. They've been using the word *blizzard* a lot."

Lucy ladled soup into bright yellow cups. "I'm up for anything at this point," she said curtly.

6

Jonathan St. Clair eyed his expensive croco-
dile luggage with a jaundiced eye. He was
getting damn sick and tired of packing and
repacking his pricey luggage. He was also
damn sick and tired of airplanes and hotel
rooms. It didn't matter if the airplane was
his own private Gulfstream V or that the
rooms were suites in five-star hotels. The
truth was he was damn sick and tired of just
about everything in his life. And today he
hated Chile in particular.

Stepping back, cutting back, whatever
you wanted to call it, wasn't working for
him. He told himself the bottom line was
his own greed, but that wasn't really true.
What he was experiencing, and what he refused to acknowledge, was panic. With
Congress's passage of the Patriot Act, he
was now on the FBI's radar screen, and he
wasn't just a little blip. He knew he was a
very big blip, which meant that travel back
to the States was a gamble. He wasn't sure
he was ready to take that particular
gamble. Not yet, anyway. The bottom line

was he wanted out of the business that was driving him ragged. When you were the best in your field, and people were comfortable with the results you got for them, why would they want to see you retire? They didn't. Instead, they offered to pay you more and more until you couldn't refuse the high-seven-figure commissions. It was that simple. Besides, you couldn't spend money in a federal prison.

A threat was a threat no matter how nicely worded it was. He'd been in the business far too long not to recognize the subtle threats that his clients tossed his way after they upped his percentages to obscene amounts of money. More than he could ever spend in his lifetime.

Those same clients had their lifestyles in place, their money secured, their very lives shielded by layers and layers of protection while he was front and center as he scrambled twenty-four hours a day to make sure he kept both feet two steps ahead of the law. They were just waiting for him to make a mistake, and in his present frame of mind, it was just a matter of time before he slipped.

He knew he had been on the FBI's radar screen for some time, knew it was just a matter of time before they made a move on him. He'd tried to warn his greedy clients, but they'd refused to listen. Because they refused to listen, he'd canceled his trip to the States. If his situation didn't improve quickly, he would probably have to cancel his Christmas trip, too.

He realized that he was sweating even though the air-conditioning was turned to the coolest setting. Now he was going to have to change his shirt again. He thought he could smell his own fear as he ripped at the shirt he was wearing, a simple, fine linen, round-necked shirt that cost four hundred dollars. He was addicted to fine, costly things. It was the reason he worked on the wrong side of the law.

His diamond-studded Rolex watch told him he had just enough time to change his shirt, repack his bag, attach the manacled briefcase that his clients demanded he use to his wrist, and go downstairs to wait for the chauffeured car that would take him to the airport and his Gulfstream.

He was an attractive man, one men envied and women fawned over. Tall and lean, with sharp-chiseled features, penetrating gray eyes that could turn steely as flint, perfect ruler-straight teeth, and a crop of slightly wavy hair that was all his own. He tipped the scales at 180 and was perfectly proportioned for his six-foot height. He wore a year-round bronzed tan that flirted with his graying temples. More than one person told him he could have posed for *Town & Country* or *GQ*, a compliment so pleasing to him that he traded on it when necessary.

Jonathan gazed at his reflection in the mirror as his mind continued to race. Satisfied that he looked his impeccable self, he snapped the cuff onto his wrist, picked up his case, and started for the door. There was no time to wait for a bellhop. He'd cut it a shade too close this time around. He wondered why that was. Maybe because he was jittery, his nerves twanging for some reason. He'd been fine until the last few phone calls to Lucy. His stomach had protested by tightening up after their conversations because he'd heard something in his fiancée's voice he'd never heard before. That was when he'd started to feel uneasy, and the feeling remained with him.

As he rode down in the elevator, Jonathan thought about his fiancée. It wasn't like Lucy to be so careless that she'd fall and sprain her ankle. She was a runner, a true athlete. She was like a gazelle in motion. No, it was unlike Lucy to fall. Her voice had been so cool. On second thought, *cool* was the wrong word. The right word was *strained.* Now why would Lucy's voice be strained? Unless . . . unless someone was around asking questions or somehow she had gotten some notion of the real reason he'd had her sign all those papers a year ago. He needed to call Lucy again to see if he was being paranoid or his survival instincts were on the money.

Jonathan stepped out of the elevator into the marble-and-tile lobby of the hotel. His gaze raked the interior of the lobby until he found the chauffeur standing near the wide double doors. He held up his hand. Within seconds the driver had his bag in his hand and was striding toward a luxurious Mercedes-Benz. A Mercedes-Benz and an experienced chauffeur were always at Jonathan's disposal.

Outside, Chile's humidity slapped Jonathan in the face. Perspiration beaded on his brow as he stepped into the icy-cold air-conditioning of the car. His destination, Zurich, Switzerland, for a nine-hour stay, then on to Mexico, where he would meet with his new client, back to Zurich for six hours, then on to Cairo. Within a week he'd probably have pneumonia. He constantly amazed himself at how he managed to stay hale and hearty with all the traveling from one intense climate to another. Hot to cold. Cold to hot. A good way to get sick. Maybe it was all the airtime or the rich food or . . . something else, but the past week he'd felt unlike himself. Almost as if a bug were creeping up on him in slow motion. He'd been popping aspirin by the handful to ward off whatever it was. Like aspirin could ward off fear.

Five minutes later, his baggage was stowed, his briefcase on his lap. He leaned back and closed his eyes for the 25-km ride from Santiago to Rudahauel, where the Gulfstream was waiting for him. His mind wandered back to his fiancée.

There was no way in hell she could know *anything*. His organization had so many firewalls installed that even he had trouble sometimes understanding the scope of his many operations. He definitely needed to call Lucy again just to satisfy himself that their relationship was on firm ground and it was only his imagination working overtime. The minute the Gulfstream reached its cruising altitude, he would call Lucy, regardless of the time difference.

Fifty minutes later the Gulfstream reached its cruising altitude. Jonathan undid his seat belt and motioned to the lone steward that he'd like a drink and a sandwich. While he drank and chewed his way through roast beef with mustard on fresh-baked bread, he thought about his fiancée and their upcoming wedding. Being married would make him more human in his clients' eyes. He also knew if he wasn't careful, being married could be dangerous. For Lucy more so than himself. Disgruntled, aggressive clients tended to get nasty and from time to time threatened to take out that nastiness on family members. Jonathan shrugged. Life was full of nasty surprises. Getting married probably wasn't one of his better decisions, but once he'd made up his mind, all his future plans quickly fell into place. The fact that Lucy was a top-notch attorney was a plus he couldn't deny. It wasn't written in stone that he had to be in love to get married. He needed Lucy, needed her respectability, her background. And for a while he'd have a woman in his bed. When it was time for her to go, she would go. It was that simple. Would he shed any tears when that happened? Perhaps in public.

Jonathan shook his head to clear his thoughts, but somehow Lucy stayed right there with him. What really surprised him about Lucy was as smart as she was, she hadn't picked up on anything. He chuckled to himself. Maybe when the lovebug bites a woman she doesn't think about anything else.

At best, life with sweet Lucy would be boring, but that was what he needed. For a while, at least. But there was no way in hell he was going to live in that saltbox of a house she had bought in Edison, New Jersey. He'd go out of his mind in twenty-four hours if he had to live in a two-thousand-square-foot house. If the timing was right, and if things progressed the way he wanted them to, he might give serious thought to opening the house in Watchung.

Jonathan thought about his parents, who'd lived in a small house much like the one Lucy now lived in. His father had worked his whole life in the Firestone rubber factory in Akron. His parents had struggled to pay their mortgage, make car payments, meet other household expenses, while still trying to donate 10 percent of their salary to the church. The first chance he got, he moved them to the other side of the world, where they lived in the lap of luxury. He was a good son. He called regularly and tried to visit at least once every two months for a few days.

His fiancée had simple tastes: she wasn't into designer clothing, jewelry, or fancy cars. She considered it all a waste of money, preferring to sock her money into a pension fund.

The dog was going to have to go, though. He would never live in a house that had a dog. That might pose a problem, with Lucy being such a dog lover. He could take care of that.

He'd told Lucy he wanted children, but he had lied. He'd been stunned when she said children were not in her immediate plans. That had clinched the engagement. It didn't hurt that Lucy was a lawyer, one of the best in Manhattan, according to his sources — sources who knew about such things. Her brother Steven was almost as good as Lucy in the courtroom. He remembered how angry he'd been when Lucy had said she was chucking the law. He'd called her stupid that day, and she hadn't really gotten angry. He was going to need her legal expertise at some point. How she could turn down representing some of his clients on the shady side of the law for big bucks boggled his mind. Her knowledge of the law was one of the reasons he'd chosen her. The day he'd met her on the tennis court had been planned in great detail, and she'd never even suspected. Maybe he gave her too much credit for being smart. Maybe his original assessment that she was stupid was spot on.

Jonathan could feel his stomach muscles start to tighten up. Something, somewhere, was amiss. Had he made a mistake? More to the point, had one of his clients made a mistake that could lead back to him? In the twenty years since he'd started JSC Enterprises, he had never before been fearful. He could feel the fear, smell it; it was starting to choke him.

Jonathan unlocked the cuff on his wrist, massaged it gently, then opened his briefcase on the tray in front of him. He withdrew a digitally encrypted satellite phone and speed-dialed Lucy's home number. He listened to the phone ring eight times before her voice mail clicked on. His brows knitted together as he tried to imagine where she was and what she was doing. If she had the flu, she might be sleeping. He grimaced at the thought. The phone was a lifeline to Lucy just the way it was to him. If she was there, she would have answered the phone. It was a long flight, he could always call later.

Jonathan pulled out his laptop, flexed his fingers. While he was by no means a bean counter or number cruncher, he did know what his assets were, down to the penny. He smiled as a blizzard of numbers raced across the screen. It would take him a lifetime to spend all the money he'd accumulated even if he spent a million dollars a day. He might be exaggerating but if so, it wasn't by much.

He hoped he lived long enough to spend it all.

Lucy sat in front of the fire hugging her knees, tears dripping down her cheeks. She needed to get a grip on her life, figure out what she was going to do and stop relying on other people, well-meaning or not, to help her. When the agents arrived, she needed to act like the lawyer she was instead of this wishy-washy person she'd turned into in less than a week. A sob escaped her throat. A second later, the three dogs were circling her, Lulu leaping into her lap. Sadie pressed against her side, Coop's big paws circled her neck. They whined, their bodies shaking at the strange sounds coming from her mouth. She spread her arms to encircle all three dogs, then laughed as she wiped at her eyes on the sleeve of her shirt. "I'm okay. Just a bad moment there. The bridal shop called to tell me my wedding gown is ready for my final fitting. If you stop and think about it, that's pretty damn funny from where I'm sitting."

Fear was for other people, not a savvy, high-priced lawyer like her. In the blink of an eye, she disengaged herself from the dogs and went up the steps, landing with a painful thump on her tender ankle. She ignored the pain as she limped into her bedroom, stripped down, and decked herself out in a long, paisley skirt with a delicious thigh-high slit up the side. She stepped into suede boots, mindful of her ankle, and donned a pumpkin-colored cashmere sweater. A lustrous set of pearls found their way to her neck, as did matching earrings.

In the bathroom she undid the ponytail and brushed her hair till it framed her face like a nimbus. Reaching for the atomizer, she spritzed the air and stood under the fragrant spray. *Now* she was ready for the federal agents.

The dogs followed her down the steps just as the doorbell rang. Lucy made one stop at the sofa to turn on the small cassette player, then placed it between the cushions where she planned to sit.

Through the beveled glass at the side of the front door, Lucy could see the same trio who had grilled her on Friday. They looked like they were freezing. Good.

Lucy glanced at her reflection in the mirror hanging in the foyer. She smacked her lips and wiggled them to distribute her lipstick evenly. She did her best to feather her eyebrows with her pinkie finger, fluffed her hair, and smoothed down her skirt. A wasted minute. She opened the door, her expression cold and hostile as she motioned the agents inside. The dogs sniffed and growled, but they didn't bark. They did follow her to the living room and took up positions at her feet, their eyes wary, their ears flat against their heads. Even Lulu's perky pink bow seemed to wilt.

Her eyes still cold and angry, Lucy crossed her arms over her chest. In body language it meant, take your best shot, but you aren't getting anything out of me because I don't know anything. She waited, staring first at one agent, then the other, and on to the third. The same way she stared at prosecution witnesses in the courtroom. Most of the time it unnerved people.

And then her head started to buzz. She could feel a distinct ringing in her ears, too. The sound was the same as when her brother Steven turned on his electric razor.

She cautioned herself not to panic as she took long, relaxing breaths. She was partially successful. *My anger or theirs?* she wondered.

Then it hit her in a jumble of thoughts. The Chinese fire drill was back but in low gear. She could have been in Madison Square Garden or Shea Stadium, listening to a hundred people all talking at once. *Concentrate,* she told herself. *Don't think, make your mind blank. Listen.* It was hopeless, nothing was coming through, and she suddenly felt stupid because she didn't know what her expression was giving away.

To calm her twanging nerves, Lucy stood up and walked behind the sofa, where she had a good look at all three agents from higher ground. She liked to stand when she interviewed witnesses or cross-examined them. Those seated were always at a disadvantage. The person standing was the power person. "Well?" she said coldly.

There it is, she thought with elation. *Maybe changing position has something to do with it.* She felt like laughing out loud. *No prairie flower . . . she's had time to think . . . hard as nails . . . no backup . . . classy skirt . . . cost more than I make in a month . . . she's not going to cave . . . she looks like she knows something we don't. . . . dogs . . . not killer dogs . . . not guard dogs . . . where's the neighbor . . . I'm never going to get warm again . . . hit her hard . . . right between the eyes . . . no wiggle room . . . give her just enough rope . . . throw out a carrot . . . offer a deal . . . maybe she isn't as dumb as she looks. I wish I was on some warm island somewhere.*

Lucy started to tingle all over. She could hear them thinking, but she couldn't pin down which thoughts belonged to whom. She waited, feeling almost giddy at what she was *hearing.*

"How would you like to cut a deal, Miss Baker?" Agent Lawrence asked.

The chaotic transmissions — that was how she thought of what she was experiencing — suddenly stopped. She felt normal again. It might be a good time to throw all three of the agents for a loop. "I really am smarter than I look, Agent Lawrence. Throwing a carrot my way isn't going to get me to tell you something I don't know. You could toss me twenty miles of rope, and it isn't going to make a difference. I'm a lawyer, and I know my rights. As a lawyer, I am always open to negotiations. What's the deal?" she snapped.

Special Agent Connors reared back in her chair as Coop rose to his feet and growled. It pleased her that all three agents looked stunned. Why shouldn't they? She'd just read their minds. In another minute they'd chalk it up to coincidence.

It wasn't true what they said about male FBI agents being good-looking and manly, not to mention virile. Nor was it true about female FBI agents being beautiful the way they were portrayed in the movies. Agent Mason, who was packing twenty extra pounds around his middle, looked up at Lucy. "We want you to help us set a trap for your boyfriend."

"And I would do so because . . ."

"You would do this because you are a responsible citizen and because we have you boxed into a corner. It's the only way you'll get off the hook." *She'll go for it, I know she will.*

Lucy's head was back in play again. Yahooo. Her voice rang with angry confidence when she said, "You really think I'll go for a deal like that?" The agent looked at her, his eyes popping wide. "I'm off the hook anyway because I didn't do anything wrong. I don't scare easy, Mr. Mason. The burden of proof is on you. I can account for my time, my money, my savings, and anything else you want accounted for during the last ten years, way before I ever met Jonathan St. Clair. You know it, and I know it. We both know you can turn this into a messy circus, but in the end I'll come out whole. Now if you want my help, spell it out, put it in writing, and maybe we can deal. That's my offer. Take it or leave it."

Special Agent Connors stood up to move closer to the fire. She must have been the one who was thinking she'd never get warm again. "We're prepared to consider it," she said. Lulu ran over to where she was standing, sniffed her boots, and barked. "Shoo, go away," Connors said, waving her hands. Lulu continued to sniff and snarl.

"We want you to tell us everything you know about Leo Banks, no matter how insignificant you may think it is. Start from the moment you met him."

This is where she'll trip herself up. She has no clue what we know and don't know. Lucy took a moment to puzzle over what she was feeling. The fire drill and Shea Stadium were gone. Her head was quiet, and her ears weren't ringing. She was reading and hearing their minds. She was actually calm, shooting down everyone's theory about anxiety and anger. "It's not all that interesting, Agent Mason. If you're hoping

I'll trip myself up, think again. Know Your Enemy 101. You're probably thinking I have no clue as to what you know and don't know. Just like you don't know what I know and don't know." Lucy smiled. The FBI agent looked spooked. Good.

Special Agent Connors moved back to her chair, Lulu dogging her every step. The little dog positioned herself at her feet and stared up at the woman with bright eyes, defying her to move again. If she did, the fuzzy boots would go right out from under her. Terriers had a bad habit of sinking their teeth into something and never letting go. It looked to Lucy like Special Agent Connors knew all about terriers.

I hate dogs, especially little ones. This one looks like a rat dressed up for Halloween. Yuk. Lucy almost laughed out loud. She should ignore Special Agent Connors's thoughts, then thought otherwise. "I see you hate dogs, especially little dogs that look like rats dressed up for Halloween. Dogs know when people don't like them. Did you know that?"

Special Agent Connors looked away, a strange look on her face. *Either I'm crazy, or she's crazy, and she's reading my mind.* She turned back to face Lucy, who was smiling. There was no way the lawyer was responding to this thought.

"Yes, I have heard that said about small dogs," Special Agent Connors said. "When I was a child I was bitten rather badly. I've been afraid of dogs ever since," she volunteered.

Lucy turned her attention to the two male agents, her eyebrows raised. She flipped her hand backward as though to say, let's get on with it.

"Tell us about Leo Banks."

"There's nothing much to tell you. I met him about eighteen months ago on the tennis court. He liked me, I liked him. It worked for us because he understood my working eighty hours a week. He traveled constantly. I was lucky if I saw him once a month. He called regularly. He was always a gentleman with me. He was thoughtful, sent me gifts, said all the things a woman wants to hear. We got engaged, were going to get married last year but postponed it. We were supposed to get married in February. That isn't going to happen now. I know nothing about his business except what he told me. He said he brokered business deals between different parties. He was the go-between. That is the sum total of what I know." Lucy's face was devoid of any kind of expression, but she felt alert and wary.

"Okay for now. Maybe something else will come to you later on," Agent Lawrence said.

Agent Mason stood up and took his turn standing next to the fireplace. "Your boyfriend, Leo Banks, popped up on our radar screen two years ago while we were investigating another case that he was involved in. A key player so to speak. Until that time, he was *under* our radar screen. It's not easy for our agents in third-world countries, as you can imagine. Since that time, we've been tracking him. I see no harm in telling you that the man is like a phoenix, he keeps rising out of the ashes. He's here, he's there, he's everywhere. You can do that when you have the network he has. He also has a Gulfstream that ferries him around at a moment's notice. Our people have to fly commercial. We managed to lose him quite a few times, and the bureau is not proud of that. We aren't sure if he's the main man or the main man's right hand. It is what it is.

"Mr. Banks treads on thin ice sometimes. He's as slick as they come, and one almost has to think he leads a charmed life. About six months ago he managed to swindle a Colombian drug dealer who was trying to put together a deal in Florida to gain some legitimacy and got away with his skin intact. We have the dealer in custody minus his money. He told us all he knows, which of his cronies pay Banks megamillions to set up legal businesses." The agent fixed his gaze on Lucy, and said, "The man is a pro at laundering money. Now he's on a hit list with the Colombians. That's a serious hit list. One simply doesn't screw around with those thugs.

"If scenarios like that aren't enough to keep you awake at night, here's another one. He killed one of his clients at point-blank range when the man refused to pay a higher percentage of the deal they were working on. Banks has a bad habit of agreeing to a deal and then, at the eleventh hour, raising the stakes. You're probably wondering how we know this. The man took a long time to die, and he talked. Deathbed confessions are something we pay attention to. Then there was Adam Ligar. Banks killed him, too, but that was a long time ago. I have more stories like these two, but you look a little ill, Miss Baker, so I'll save them for another time."

Not only did Lucy look ill, she felt ill. My God, she was going to marry the man they were talking about. Lucy's mind raced. "If you're so convinced he's doing what you say, why don't you just arrest him? What are you waiting for?"

"The right moment. We need an airtight case. Going off half-cocked gets you nowhere. And the man never asked you to sign a prenuptial agreement?" Connors lifted her eyebrows to show what she thought of that question.

"No. We talked about it. Jonathan said nothing would sour a marriage like a prenup. I was surprised, but he said he waited this long in life to get married, and it would be for a lifetime, and he wanted to share. I don't need his money. I had a career, I have my own portfolio, a pension fund, a stake in a lucrative law practice, and an inheritance from my parents. On my own, I could be comfortable for the rest of my life."

All three agents stared at Lucy, knowing they would be working the rest of their lives until it was time to collect their retirement. Lucy thought she saw resentment in Special Agent Connors's face.

Agent Lawrence chewed on his lower lip before he spoke. "Your fiancé is not a broker. A broker is a legitimate businessman. Leo Banks is a *facilitator.*" The term sounded obscene coming out of his mouth. "If someone wants something delivered or spirited out of the country, they call Leo Banks. Sometimes that *something* turns out to be a *person* or *persons*. Leo is known for getting the job done. In fact, Leo offers up a personal guarantee or he doesn't take that robust seven-figure commission you mentioned. Being a lawyer, you should know the first rule is, *follow the money.* That's what led us to you, Miss Baker. To our knowledge Banks has about fifteen different aliases with passports to match. He's also a master at disguising himself. A little spirit gum, a little latex, different clothes, and he's a different man. Three months ago he flew into Heathrow Airport dressed as a rabbi. Sad to say, we were a little slow to figure that out. Are you following me, Miss Baker?"

Lucy was following him all right, but she was more concerned at the moment with her head going quiet on her. Nothing was coming through. She wondered what would happen if she told them she could *hear* their thoughts. They were waiting for her to say something. She grappled in her mind for something to say. "You . . . you're making Jonathan sound like . . . like James Bond, Hannibal Lecter, and Jack the Ripper."

Agent Lawrence grimaced. "He's got all

the same hardware as Bond. Why does one man need six cigarette boats? Do you know anything about cigarette boats, Miss Baker?" Lucy shook her head.

"Let me bring you up to speed, then," Agent Lawrence said. "They're long and low, usually black-hulled. Very sleek. The low profile makes it almost impossible to pick them up on radar. Now, if the water conditions are right, and if the engine compartment is insulated properly and the exhausts baffled, it wouldn't be detected by infrared sensors. Those babies can do eighty knots with no sweat. A boat like that can outrun anything on the water. It's the boat of choice for drug runners and some arms runners, too. And you have six of them in your name." Lucy started to feel sick to her stomach at the agent's words.

"Why does Leo Banks need a fleet of cars? Why does he use digitally encrypted satellite phones? His laptop is encrypted, and he has enough firewalls installed to drive any encryption specialist to the brink of insanity. None of the above makes our job easier." He asked again, "Are you following me, Miss Baker?"

Lucy nodded, her heart pumping furiously. God in Heaven, who was this man she'd promised to marry?

Special Agent Connors picked up the conversation. "That brings us to the house in Watchung that has your name on the deed. We're a little concerned with the elaborate security attached to that property. Do you know anything about alarm systems, Miss Baker?"

Lucy licked at her dry lips. "I have an alarm system here in the house, but it's standard. Keypad, panic button, all the doors and windows are armed. I put it on when I go to bed at night. My own personal feeling is a dog is the best security in the world. The only reason I have an alarm system at all is to make my brother feel better. He insisted I have it installed. So, to answer your question, no, I know nothing about sophisticated alarm systems. I also know nothing about the house in Watchung. I told you that already." She tried to clear her mind, strained to pick up a word, but nothing was coming through.

Connors acted like she hadn't heard Lucy's words. "I believe Agent Lawrence informed you the other day of the house's unusual security system complete with laser trip wires and tremor plates. But did he mention our experts tell us they suspect there are pressure pads in the house that would activate, and trigger alarms, as well as release an incapacitating gas? This is warfare type of security. Now, our question to you is, why would a person need that kind of security if, as you say, he is a legitimate broker and does business ethically and aboveboard?"

All Lucy could do was shake her head. "What is it you want me to do?" she whispered miserably.

"Help us to get our hands on Mr. Banks. When do you expect to see him again?"

Lucy could feel her stomach start to churn. "Jonathan was supposed to come for Thanksgiving, but he called the other day and said he couldn't make it. He is coming for Christmas for ten days. I haven't talked to him since. And, no, I did not tell him about any of our conversations. If I agree to help you, are you going to make . . ."

"Your immediate problem go away?" Agent Lawrence said. "We'll discuss the matter with our superiors at Justice and get back to you. Tomorrow. This might be a good time for you to explain why you defended José Rafael and Manuel Aroya. Both men are associates of Leo Banks."

"What?" Lucy sputtered.

Mason's face showed disbelief. "You didn't know?"

"No! No, I did not know." Lucy hated herself for saying it, but she said it anyway. "I guess that's why Jonathan was so upset when I said I was giving up the law after Aroya's trial. Then I changed my mind and kept on working. Up until the acquittal came in, I thought he was innocent. Then he looked at me with this . . . this . . . smug look, and I knew he was guilty as hell. I was sick to my stomach. I knew right then I couldn't do it anymore. Steven talked me into staying on. Jonathan was very upset. Then, after my last case, I finally made up my mind to hang it all up. Jonathan has been nagging me ever since to go back to the firm. I swear to you, I didn't know those men knew Jonathan. All either one said to me at the initial consultation was that they had heard I was the best of the best and they needed the best. They had the money to pay my fees, and I don't come cheap. Later on, Jonathan said he *knew of* José Rafael, and Aroya, but did not know either of them personally, and followed the case in the papers. I had no reason not to believe him then."

"They, as in Leo Banks and his people, would have put the squeeze on you if you'd been appointed to the bench. The house, the brokerage accounts, the cigarette boats, all of that would have been used to black-mail you," Agent Lawrence said quietly.

Lucy fought down the bile that was rising in her throat. At the same time she strained to *hear* their thoughts, but to no avail. She looked down at the hands on her watch. How long was the tape in the cassette player? An hour on each side or was it a thirty-minute-sided tape? Would it make a sound when it clicked off? She didn't know.

She had to get rid of the agents now. "I don't think we have anything else to discuss. I'll wait for you to get back to me tomorrow. What that means is this meeting is over." To make her point, Lucy started for the door, the dogs following her.

The moment the door closed behind the federal agents, Lucy locked it and slumped against it. She was definitely in the tall grass now, and the view ahead was not to her liking.

7

The two men sat in Wylie's kitchen staring at one another. Wylie spoke first. "What do you think, Jake?" He didn't realize he was holding his breath until it exploded out of his mouth like a gunshot.

"What I think, old buddy, is you have the hots for your neighbor, and you can't see straight." The parapsychologist shrugged. "Listen, I wouldn't stake my reputation on it, but I think Lucy's condition will fade in time. Right now she's on a high unlike anything she's ever experienced. Plus, she's a woman, and women tend to get emotional, even women lawyers. Now, if her present condition isn't what's bothering you, I bet you're worried about the man in her life who is responsible for all this. Right or wrong?"

Wylie ran his fingers through his hair before he got up to make a pot of coffee. "The bastard set her up," he barked. "Yeah, I like her. I like her a lot, as a matter of fact. You don't think she loves him, do you, Jake?"

"Nah. You know what I think, Wylie. I think she was *relieved* that this happened. That's my own ESP at work. You got anything to munch on?" the handsome parapsychologist asked.

Wylie reached up to the top of the refrigerator and tossed Jake a bag of corn chips. He poured two cups of coffee and set them on the table.

"Coffee and corn chips don't go together, Wylie. Don't you have any Coke or Pepsi?"

"No. The weather's been too bad to go to the store. Just drink the damn coffee already, Jake."

"Testy, aren't we." Jake grinned. "You know, for a guy, this is a cozy, comfortable kitchen," Jake said, changing the subject in the hopes of driving away the intense look on his friend's face.

"My mother decorated the kitchen. She pretty much did the whole house after my ex cleaned me out," Wylie said, waving his arms at the green-and-yellow balloon-type curtains, the matching yellow crockery, and the green plants, one in the corner by the bay window, one hanging over the sink, and one in the corner of the counter. All looked lush and green, with no yellowing leaves. "Mom said I have no decorating sense. She calls me every Sunday to make sure I water and feed the plants. It's easier to follow through than it is to try and explain why they die. Been there, done that. Actually, Jake, I take great pride in my plants," Wylie said defensively.

"Well, good for you. If there was ever a guy who should be married, it's you. You really like Lucy, huh?"

Wylie rolled his eyes. He gulped at the scalding coffee in his cup, his eyes watering. "They should be leaving by now, don't you think?"

Jake fished in the bag for a fistful of chips. He popped them in his mouth, one at a time, and crunched down. "You could check to see if their car is still there. That would be one way to find out."

"Wiseass," Wylie muttered as he sprinted to the living room window.

"You're right, they're leaving," he shouted. "Should we be discreet and wait like two minutes or barrel over there right now?"

Jake shook his head. If his friend wasn't in love, he was about to fall head over heels for his neighbor. "Whatever floats your boat, Wylie."

"I think we should wait ten minutes, or so. I don't want to seem . . . you know, pushy. Yeah, ten minutes is good. What should we do while we're waiting, Jake?"

Jake's face scrunched up in a grin. "When was the last time you got laid, Wylie?"

Wylie pretended horror. "Is that what you think this is all about, sex? Well, it isn't. It's about helping, understanding, being there, my dog loves her, and then maybe sex. Not in that order. Shut the hell up, Jake. Why'd you ask me that anyway? It's none of your damn business."

"We *are* prickly. Relax, Wylie."

"Easy for you to say, Jake. You aren't personally involved!" Wylie huffed.

As soon as the FBI agents left, the phone rang. Lucy was on her way to the kitchen in search of the brandy bottle. If there was ever a time in her life when she needed a drink, this was it. She didn't hurry to answer the phone, thinking it was Wylie. She took a healthy swig straight from the bottle. Her eyes burning, she carried the bottle to the family room and answered on the speakerphone. Her greeting was flat when she said, "Hello."

"Good afternoon, darling," Jonathan St. Clair said cheerfully, his voice coming through the speakerphone loud and clear.

Lucy looked at the bottle she was holding, then at the phone on the table. She felt like pitching both into the fireplace. "Jonathan, I wasn't expecting your call." What an incredibly stupid thing to say.

"I've been thinking about you and missing you. I'm just so sorry I won't be there for Thanksgiving. I just wanted you to know it's tearing me apart. I promise to make it up to you over Christmas, though. I never break a promise, you know that. How are you, darling?"

Once the question would have thrilled her. Now, it scared the hell out of her. An actress she wasn't, but she tried. "Well, Jonathan, I'm sad that you won't be here. I do miss you, and I'm looking forward to spending the holidays with you. Should I wait to pick out the Christmas tree till you get here, or should I get it, put it up, and then, when you get here, we'll decorate it?" Lucy felt sickened at the artificial lilt in her voice and wondered if Jonathan was picking up on it. He was not stupid, as she knew very well.

"I'm not one for tromping through fields to pick out a tree. I can, however, see myself putting the star on top." The chuckle in his voice sounded forced to Lucy's ears.

Lucy swigged from the brandy bottle. "Actually, Jonathan, I was planning on getting the tree from the Sunoco station where I get my gas. They deliver and set it up for a small fee." She was feeling lightheaded. Now, she wished she'd eaten more instead of picking at her food earlier. Drinking on an empty stomach was not a good idea.

"Do you miss me?"

"Of course. Do you miss me?" Lucy asked, in return, hoping that her voice did not give away just how much she did *not* miss him.

"More than you know. By the way, I'm on a plane headed for Switzerland. Would you like me to send you some Swiss chocolate? I know you have a sweet tooth."

"That would be wonderful, Jonathan. You always think of me, don't you?" Lucy took another swig from the bottle. *You're a weasel Jonathan St. Clair/Leo Banks or whoever you are. Like I would really eat anything you sent me.*

"Are you ready to go back to work, honey?"

Lucy looked at the brandy bottle in her hand with narrowed eyes. "Not really." A devil perched itself on her shoulder. "I'm going to sell my interest in the firm to

Steven. I want to be a full-time wife. I am going to take such good care of you, Jonathan," she said sweetly. "I'm going to cook, and bake, and iron, and all that stuff. I'm going to plant a garden. I might extend the deck a little farther and put in a swimming pool. Life in the *burbs!* Doesn't that sound wonderful, Jonathan?"

"It wasn't exactly what I had in mind, darling. We'll talk about it when I get there," Jonathan replied, his voice dropping to somewhere near the subzero level.

Ignoring the coldness in his tone, Lucy continued. "Jonathan, what is it exactly that you do? I know you broker deals, but what kind of deal are you working on now?" As she waited for his response, Lucy took another belt out of the brandy bottle. There wasn't much left. "Jonathan, are you still there?"

"I'm still here, Lucy. Why do you ask? Maybe I should ask why you want to know. You made a point of saying you could never discuss your cases with me, and I told you I can't discuss my clients. I sign a confidentiality agreement before I begin to work for a client. In my business, it's a necessity. You know how that works, don't you?"

Lucy opted to ignore the question. "My gown is finished," Lucy blurted. "The dogs chewed up the wedding invitations. Everything seems to be going wrong. The roof is leaking," she lied. "I'm thinking we should postpone the wedding until June. Maybe the dogs chewing up the invitations is an omen of some kind."

The silence on the other end of the phone was palpable. Now that she had Jonathan's attention, Lucy rolled on. "And, the IRS sent me a notice," she lied still again. "They want to talk to me January 17 at 9 a.m. I am not looking forward to talking with them. I'm always meticulous about preparing my tax forms." The silence on the other end of the phone sizzled. She wondered if she'd gone too far. Lucy felt the need to prod him once again. "What do you think, Jonathan?"

"Routine, darling. I told you to get rid of that dog. Pay extra and order new invitations. Money talks, sweetheart. We are not postponing our wedding. You are mine, and I intend to claim you. Don't even think about it. I have to hang up because we're starting to make our descent now. I'll call you in a day or so. I love you." *Sure you do, you weasel. Well, guess what, I don't love you. Another thing, there is not going to be a wedding in February or June because if I have anything to do about it, you'll be in prison by then. So there, Jonathan St. Clair, aka Leo Banks.*

184

Lucy was prevented from making a reply because she was draining the last of the brandy in the bottle. She clicked the cordless phone to the OFF position and sat down on the sofa. She was tipsy if not outright drunk, and she knew it. She was also scared out of her ever-loving wits. In all the time she'd known Jonathan, she'd never, ever heard him use the tone of voice she'd just heard humming over the wire.

The dogs thundered down the hallway and around the corner to the front door. She could barely hear the bell with all the barking going on. The door was locked. That meant she had to get up and open it. It had to be Wylie and his friend, the parapsychologist.

When she opened the door both men stared at her glassy eyes. It was Coop who nudged her toward the sofa in the family room. Lucy stared around at the room as though wondering how she got there. She rubbed at Coop's silky back.

"Coffee! I think we could all use some strong, black coffee," Wylie said enthusiastically as he pantomimed behind Lucy's back, urging Jake to get Lucy to talk. In her condition he had no idea what would be forthcoming.

Jake propped his elbows on his knees

and leveled his gaze on Lucy. "So, how did it go? Are they going to let you off the hook or what? Did you *hear* anything that will help the situation?"

Lucy fumbled for the cassette recorder, digging between the cushions on the sofa. Jake reached across to take the recorder, his bright blue eyes twinkling at Lucy's condition.

"It's still on, the tape is almost full. Let's see what we have here," Jake said, as he pressed the REWIND button. Lucy leaned back and listened to herself and the FBI agents. When Wylie handed her a huge mug of black coffee, she reached for it with both hands.

Wylie positioned himself on the sofa next to Lucy but not too close. Coop leaped up and wiggled next to him. Lucy and he reached out to stroke the big dog's head at the same time. A jolt of electricity whipped through Wylie at Lucy's touch. Neither one moved. Sadie sat up on her haunches and barked, Lulu yapping at the top of her lungs. A second later, both dogs were on the sofa, and the highly charged moment was gone.

"I guess you didn't remember to turn off the recorder before the phone call, huh?" Jake said.

"No, I guess I forgot. I was pretty wired at that point. Then Jonathan or . . . whatever the hell his name is, called. That's when I finished the brandy." Lucy propped the coffee cup between her knees as she waved her arms in the air. "I lied all over the place to . . . to that man. When I hung up, I was scared. I never heard such a cold tone in his voice before. Do you think I tipped him off?"

Wylie eyeballed the parapsychologist sitting across from him. He shook his head imperceptibly. Jake nodded. "I suppose anything is possible," Jake said. "Since I don't know the man, I don't want to be rash and say yes. Did you *hear* anything significant when you met with the FBI agents?"

"Yes and no. Nothing that's going to help me. I really tried there at the end to *hear* something, but nothing came through. We have to wait till tomorrow for them to get back to me. Do you think my phone is tapped? If it is, they heard my conversation with Jonathan. Are we going to go up to Watchung or not?" Lucy asked, changing the subject.

"Are you up to it?" Wylie asked, concerned. Lucy looked at him and smiled, her eyes lighting up. Wylie thought it the most endearing smile in the world.

Again, Wylie forced himself to look away and locked his gaze with Jake's. He shrugged.

"I'm up to it. The brandy will start to wear off soon. The coffee will help. By the time we get there I should be fine. I'm not a drinker. I hardly ever drink. Well, sometimes, a glass of wine or a beer, but I don't *guzzle*. What about the roads? If we're going, we should go now." She was babbling but didn't know how to stop. Then she heard the click of the recorder again and her own voice as she spoke to Jonathan. Lucy felt herself cringe, and was aware of how still both men had become. Even the dogs didn't move, sensing something was suddenly different.

Lucy threw her hands in the air. "So, I forgot to turn the damn thing off. You can hear Jonathan since I put him on speakerphone. Easier to drink my brandy that way. Are you picking up the change in his voice?" Both men nodded. It was a relief when Jake switched the recorder off. No one said anything.

Wylie jumped up first. "If we're going, let's go." To Lucy's ears, his voice sounded brusque and cold. It bothered her. She didn't like the look she was seeing on Jake's face either.

"Wait just a damn minute, you two. It was a stupid phone call. I was trying to act normal, not to raise any suspicion where Jonathan is concerned. Not that it's any of your business, but I was playacting. And drinking at the same time to make it easier. Read my lips. I do not love Jonathan St. Clair or whatever his real name is. I don't think I ever did. Now, you can run with that in whatever direction you want. I'm also not hearing any of your thoughts. I can be ready in five minutes. I take it the dogs are staying here."

Properly chastised, both men nodded.

"I'm suddenly thinking this is not such a good idea, Jake. If we're going to the house that Lucy allegedly owns, are we going with the intention of breaking and entering? Or, are we doing a simple drive-by? There's a good eight inches of snow out there, and there might be more in Watchung. What's that snow going to do to all that warfare security those agents said was in place? I think we need to fall back and regroup."

Jake slapped at his forehead and cursed under his breath. "Sometimes I am stupid. Wylie, do you remember Mitch Logan?" Wylie frowned but nodded. "He's a Navy SEAL. Remember how he was regaling us with stories at our ten-year reunion?" Wylie nodded again, wondering where Jake was going with all this. "Well, according to the alumni newsletter, he's out of the SEALs now because of a severe back injury. He put together a security company somewhere outside of Washington, DC — Fairfax, Virginia, I think. I'm thinking we should call him and ask him to help us out here. If anyone can help us, it's him. The guy has some big government contracts, so he must be good."

"How do you know all this?" Wylie asked.

"I *read* the newsletters unlike you, who throws them away."

Wylie looked offended. "I don't throw them away. I let them pile up, and eventually I read them. Good idea. You got his number?"

"Not with me. I'm sure you have it at home. Go look. The guy's a fraternity brother. We're supposed to stick together. I'm up for a daylight drive-by and maybe a talk with some of the neighbors."

Five minutes later, Wylie returned with his alumni telephone list. Mitch Logan's name was in the middle of the list along with the name of his security firm, Millennium Security.

Wylie unzipped his jacket just as Lucy made her way into the den. Her eyes were full of questions as she watched Jake punch out a number on his cell phone. Wylie drew her aside and explained what was going on. "You look as relieved as I feel," he said quietly.

Lucy took off her sky-blue jacket and tossed it over the back of the chair. She sighed. "I am relieved we're not going up to Watchung today. I know in my gut if we went there, the FBI would know it within seconds. All this snow would only hinder us anyway."

"How's the head?" Wylie asked, to have something to say.

"I have a dull headache, but I attribute that to the brandy. I took some aspirin. Nellie kept wanting to fix me up with you. She kept saying how nice you were, and I should check you out before I got married," Lucy blurted.

Wylie blinked in surprise. "Nellie was always on my case about introducing you to me. It just never worked out. It took two dogs for us to meet. I guess I owe Coop big-time. Maybe I'll upgrade his meat loaf from ground chuck to ground round." Lucy burst out laughing. Wylie thought it a wonderful sound. He thought everything about the woman standing next to him was wonderful. "Did you mean what you said about that guy you were going to marry?"

Lucy nodded just as Jake clicked his cell phone shut. "Okay," he said, "we're in business. Mitch is going to leave now and drive here. He said he should arrive around eight. First thing in the morning, we'll head up to the mountains. He said he has all kinds of equipment that will locate and disarm any kind of security. I think it's safe to say we're in good hands. At least for the moment.

"I did my part, so you two can make dinner. I'm going to your house, Wylie, and take a shower and a nap. I also want to call my wife. I'll leave Lulu here. You guys okay with that?" Wylie and Lucy nodded.

Spending the balance of the afternoon with Wylie was not an unpleasant thought, Lucy decided as she made her way into the kitchen, Wylie behind her.

Lucy opened the freezer and looked at the contents. She reached for a pot roast that was frozen solid. It wouldn't make any difference if it was frozen or not as long as she cooked it in a pressure cooker. As she unwrapped the freezer paper, she fixed her gaze on her neighbor. "Are you sorry you got caught up in my mess, Wylie?"

Wylie jammed his hands into the pockets of his jeans. "No. I just feel helpless because there isn't anything I can do except be your friend and help out with the dogs. Are you okay, Lucy?"

Lucy rummaged in the bottom of one of the cabinets for the pressure cooker. "No, I'm not all right. I feel like some kind of freak. What if this thing in my head never goes away? What if . . . what if . . . Jonathan really does come for Christmas? How am I going to handle that? He's going to want . . . *you know*," she said, throwing her arms in the air. "They want me to trap him. I don't exactly have a problem with that depending on how long it takes to put everything into motion. It's the between time that is bothering me. And, all those insurance policies. I'm worth more dead than I am alive. The truth is, I'm scared out of my wits."

Wylie felt like his heart was being ripped out of his chest. "Listen, throw that meat in the pot and let's go out and play in the snow. I haven't done that in years, and I bet you haven't either." Seeing Lucy's frown of indecision, he took charge of the meat. He snapped the lid on the pot with the air of a professional. "Now, let's get dressed and have some fun."

Lucy laughed as Wylie escorted her to the coatrack. She was dressed within seconds and out the door in minutes. Then tried to run in the deep snow but kept falling. "Snow angels! Snow angels!" Lucy laughed.

Wylie dived into the snow in the front yard and started to move his hands and legs. "My God! The last time I did this I was six years old!" Lucy followed suit, laughing and giggling. "The trick is," Wylie shouted, "to get up without disturbing the angel imprint."

In the end it was impossible not to disturb the imprint, the snow was just too deep.

"Let's build a snowman. A big one. I think the snow is wet enough to roll the balls." They huffed and puffed as she rolled a giant ball for the base. Breathless with the exertion, Lucy found herself leaning against Wylie. She was so close she could smell his aftershave, feel his warm breath on her cheek. She knew in that instant she was committed to this man forever and ever. She *heard* it then. *God, how I love this woman. I feel like slinging her over my shoulder and carrying her off to my lair.*

Lucy leaned even closer. "Guess what, Wylie, you don't have to put me over your shoulder. I'll go with you willingly. So there!" She took off running but didn't get far because Wylie tackled her. They both went facedown in the snow. Their arms around each other, they rolled down the front lawn. When they reached the road, Wylie smacked his cold lips on hers so fast she saw stars. A long time later she said, "I'd tell you to do that again, but right now I feel like I'm on fire. Can we do it again later?"

"Does the Pope pray? Well, yeah. I'm available twenty-four/seven!"

"I'll write that down," Lucy giggled as she struggled to her feet. "I guess you know Jake is watching us from the front window."

Wylie laughed. "Those parapsychologists are a curious lot."

Together they trudged through the snow to the front door. "I have hot chocolate, kiddies," Jake said, as he held out two steaming cups.

Back in the kitchen, their wet clothes in the dryer, Wylie harked back to Lucy's confession about being scared out of her wits.

"Coop and I could move in with you. We could say my heat went out or something like that. Hell, if you need bodies to fill up the house, I can have a few of my friends move in, too. Nothing like having to step over a bunch of bodies everywhere to quell . . . *you know*. I'll do the vegetables while you braise the meat," he said, changing the subject abruptly.

"Okay," Lucy said agreeably. "You have to go back to work tomorrow, don't you?"

"Yes, I do. Jake will be here, though. I'll try to make it an early day. I have two paralegals and a partner who can cover for me. I don't have to be in court, so that's a plus. It will work out, Lucy."

Lucy adjusted the flame on the burner as the roast sizzled in the hot oil. "Do you ever get burned out, Wylie? Do you ever question yourself, the system, your clients?"

"Every damn day," Wylie said cheerfully. "My second choice after law was forestry. I think I would have made a hell of a forest ranger. Did you have a second choice?"

"Not really. I didn't really know what I wanted to be. My brother always wanted to be a lawyer. Our parents were lawyers, so I guess it was natural. For a little window of time, when I was first in college, I wanted to be this one-of-a-kind athlete. I was a distance runner, and I qualified for the Olympic trials, but then my mother got sick, and I had to bow out. Only after my mother died did I go to law school. I'm still not sure why. Maybe it was because I wanted to prove myself in the same arena my mother operated in. It's hard to give up a dream, but you know what they say, everything happens for a reason. What would have been your game plan if you had become a ranger and found yourself face-to-face with a grizzly?"

Wylie threw back his head and guffawed. "To run like hell!"

He was *so* cute. Lucy laughed out loud.

Wylie rinsed the carrots, onions, celery, and potatoes he'd peeled, then put them in a large yellow bowl. "You remind me of a girl I used to know my first year in college. Her name was Angie and she was homecoming queen. Typical blond, blue-eyed nymph. Every single guy on campus wanted her. I had the inside track, though, because I had a car. It was a bucket of bolts, and it didn't run. The guys in the dorm and I worked on it every spare minute we had. Among ourselves, we christened it the Sex Machine. It was a convertible and strictly for picking up chicks. Back then our hormones were raging. I paid fifty bucks for it from some shyster, and he overcharged me by forty-nine bucks. It had some good tires on it, though. We painted it robin's-egg blue. To match Angie's eyes. Let me tell you, that was one spiffy-looking vehicle."

Lucy's eyes twinkled. "Is this a sad story?"

Wylie shrugged. "The day of her maiden voyage, I called Angie and said I'd come by her dorm to pick her up. I think every student on the floor was outside when I picked her up. It was a perfect spring day, not a cloud in the sky. Everyone ooohed and aaahed when she climbed in. Do you know what she said to me?"

"I don't have a clue," Lucy said.

"Well, what would you have said?"

"This *is* a sad story. I guess I would have said, 'Where are we going?' "

"Nope. She said . . . she said, 'Put the top up! I don't want to mess up my hair!' "

Lucy pretended horror, her hands going to her lips. "No!"

"Yes! The Sex Machine didn't have a top. Well, it did, but it was in tatters, and it didn't work. It was a convertible! When I told her it didn't work, she got out of the car and left me sitting there. I couldn't even drive away because the damn car wouldn't start. The guys had to push it back to the garage off campus where we kept it. That was the end of my inside track with Angie

Motolo. I was suicidal for a whole day."

Lucy clamped the top onto the cooker and set the pressure gauge. She dusted her hands dramatically. "That is a sad story. What happened to Angie Motolo?"

"She married the trombone player in the school band and is now a hostess on one of those shopping channels. I called in one night to buy some socket wrenches and they put me on the air with her. Usually the hostesses get chatty with the customers, so I told her who I was. She said she didn't remember me or the robin's-egg blue convertible. They hustled me off the air real quick. Her loss." Wylie grinned.

Lucy burst out laughing and couldn't stop. Wylie clapped her on the back, but she kept on laughing and choking. Later, he couldn't clearly remember how it happened, but he was kissing her, and she was kissing him back.

With gusto.

A long time later, Wylie held her at arm's length and looked into her eyes. "Tell me it was okay to do that."

Her head reeling, Lucy said, "It was okay for you to do that. I'm not engaged any longer," she said, wiggling her ring finger. "And to think you live next door and we never met."

"Yeah, that's mind-bending all right. My mind is going in all directions here, Lucy Baker," Wylie said hoarsely.

"So is mine, Wylie," Lucy gasped.

"Why don't we try doing that again and see what happens?"

"I think that's a very good idea, Wylie." Lucy moved closer, her eyes glazed.

"Ahhh," was all Wylie could say, before he found warm, moist lips covering his own.

8

It was a quarter to eight when Lucy flipped on the outside light and opened the door to admit the biggest man she'd ever seen in her entire life, ex–Navy SEAL Mitch Logan. Lucy smiled, Mitch smiled, and the dogs went ballistic as they tried to climb all over him, sensing a friend. Wylie whistled, and the dogs calmed almost immediately, except for Lulu, who was crawling up Mitch's pant leg. With hands as big as ham hocks, the big man scooped her up and rubbed his cheek against her little head. He tweaked the bow on top of her head before he grinned from ear to ear. "She's a girl, right?"

"That she is, and she's been leading these two," Lucy said, pointing to the retriever and the Lab, "around by their noses. Come in, come in, it's cold out there," she said shutting the door. "Dinner's ready. We were just waiting for you to arrive. I'm Lucy Baker," she said, extending her hand.

Lucy watched as the men acted like college freshmen as they slapped one another on the back, hugged, said it was way too long between visits. She listened to the male banter and suddenly felt like everything in her life was going to be all right. She hoped she wasn't wrong.

Lucy finished setting the table while Mitch washed up, the dogs right beside him. "The dogs love Mitch because they know he likes animals," Jake said. "He has a whole team of K-9 dogs he uses in his business. They're in demand, big-time."

This is nice, Lucy thought as she placed bowls on the table. She stood back to look at the mound of food she'd prepared — the six-pound roast, sliced to perfection, garlic mashed potatoes, fresh string beans with slivers of julienne carrots, mushroom gravy, yeast rolls, soft golden butter, and a large garden salad. A small bowl of mango chutney garnished the platter next to the meat. The blackberry cobbler would be just cool enough when it was time for dessert.

"No business while we're eating," Jake said. "We don't want to insult Lucy with shop talk after she slaved over this wonderful repast all afternoon."

It was a dinner Lucy enjoyed, dealing mostly with the three men's college antics. The blue convertible, however, was the main topic of conversation. Lucy felt a tad jealous of the faceless Angie Motolo as the guys ribbed Wylie, who soaked it all up with a wide grin. While they joked back and forth, Lucy struggled and strained to see if any of their thoughts would come through. She lowered her hands to her lap and crossed her fingers. Maybe *it* was finally gone.

Jake took charge the moment he finished his cobbler and accepted a refill in his coffee cup. Lucy cleared the table, but she listened intently as the men talked. She could feel Mitch Logan's eyes on her. She knew he was taking her measure and wondered if she was coming up short or not. And then she heard him. *She looks frazzled. What the hell kind of guy is she mixed up with?* She was so stunned, she dropped a handful of silverware. All three men stared at her.

Flustered, Lucy bent down to pick up the silverware. "I am frazzled. The truth is I am scared out of my wits. I don't know what kind of man Jonathan or Leo Banks is. I'm learning real fast, though. Let's just say somehow, some way, he managed to bewitch me, okay?" This last she said angrily. She was damn sick and tired of defending herself.

The big man held up his hand. "Whoa, there, Miss Lucy. I want you to back up a moment and think about what you just said. The word *scared* is not in my vocabulary, and I want you to erase it from yours. From here on in, I want you spittin' mad. Not scared, mad. That . . . ah . . . that little thing in your head can be used to your advantage. Don't be frightened of it. I think somebody," he said, pointing upward, "wants you to have that particular ability right now at this point in time. Otherwise, you wouldn't be experiencing what you're experiencing. That's how you have to look at it for now. You're alive, you're young, you're healthy, and we're going to make this all come out right. And, no, it does not spook me that you can read my mind. I'd like some more coffee please."

"Well, when you put it like that, I guess you have a point," Lucy acquiesced as she reached for the coffeepot. It *was* going to be all right. She could feel it in her bones.

Jake slid the minirecorder into the middle of the table and turned it on. Mitch Logan listened intently as the FBI agents talked about the security at the house in Watchung. When Jake turned the recorder off, three sets of eyes stared at Mitch Logan.

"I think I can handle this. I know exactly what they're talking about. Mr. Whatever-his-name-is must have some pretty powerful friends to install that kind of security. The last time I saw anything even remotely resembling what the agents were talking about was in a drug lord's compound in El Salvador. I was a SEAL then. Makes you wonder what that guy has stashed in his house."

"What about all the snow?" Wylie asked.

"Snow, rain, sand, makes no difference. I have everything I'll need in the back of my truck. If you don't mind, I'd like to call a guy I know who lives in Sparta, right here in New Jersey. He retired from Delta Force and works for me from time to time. I'd like him to meet us at the house. I checked the map before I left, and he's sixty minutes away. That okay with you guys?" Everyone nodded. "Good, then it's a go. He's waiting for my call. Now, if it's okay with all of you, I'd like to turn in. I get up at four, and it's been a long day."

Five minutes later, Lucy was holding the door open for her guests. "Do you feel better now?" Wylie whispered.

"A lot better. I'd really feel wonderful if Jonathan wasn't coming for Christmas. Good night, Wylie. I'll see you in the morning."

"You don't mind keeping all the dogs, do you?"

"Not at all." She knew Wylie wanted to kiss her. She wanted him to kiss her, too, but Jake and Mitch were waiting. "Tomorrow's another day," she said, and smiled.

The house seemed exceptionally quiet when she closed and locked the door behind her guests. She immediately armed the security system. Someone like Jonathan could probably disarm the system in a heartbeat. *Someone like Jonathan.* How weird the thought was. Lucy gave herself a mental shake to drive it away. Well, she had a backup. If Sadie couldn't shred an intruder's skin down to the bone, Coop would use his brute force, knock him down, and sit on him while Lulu chewed him to pieces. The thought was so amusing, Lucy burst out laughing.

She was still laughing when she entered her bedroom to see all three dogs sound asleep on her bed. There was barely enough room for her from the looks of things.

Lucy brushed her teeth and fixed her hair into a ponytail before she went back downstairs to check the dying fire and turn off the lights. She stood for a moment watching the last of the flames in the huge fireplace, wondering what was going to happen to her nice, quiet life now that

Wylie was in the mix. A river of heat raged through her body when she remembered how she'd returned his kiss. She'd never kissed Jonathan like that. She'd never felt anything like what she'd felt with Wylie when she was with Jonathan.

Lucy sat down and hugged her knees, the warmth from the fireplace embracing her. She wondered what the men next door were doing. Were they talking about her? Probably. She thought about Mitch Logan in his red-and-black plaid lumberjack flannel shirt. From the tip of his military buzz cut to the tips of his toes, he looked every bit as fearful and as awesome as Jake said he was. And, he wasn't the least bit concerned that she could read his mind. *Amazing,* she thought.

She needed a game plan where Jonathan was concerned. In a courtroom, she could hold her own with the best of them. When it came to affairs of the heart she was a dud, and she knew it. Was Jonathan planning on killing her, as the agents implied? The man had used her. And she had allowed it, which didn't say much for her. She hated thinking about her ex-fiancé. Thoughts about his handsome good looks, his lean, muscled body, and the times they'd made love had become hateful memories. She cringed, shame enveloping her when she thought about the things she'd done with that lean, muscled body. Things Jonathan would expect when he arrived for Christmas. "Like hell!" she snarled.

Lucy knew deep down that Jonathan had picked up on something in her voice. She knew him well enough to be aware of the little nuances in his voice. She wished now that she had said something to Wylie or Jake about how afraid of the man she was. On the other hand, maybe they knew. No, men were dense about things like that. The dogs would have to be her security, her balance, her protectors. Better not to think of such things. Better to get up and go to bed.

Lucy's hand was on the newel post as she prepared to head up to the second floor when the phone rang. She shrugged as she made her way back to the kitchen, where she'd left her cordless. "Hello," she said cheerfully, thinking it was Wylie on the other end of the phone. To her dismay, she heard Jonathan's rich chuckle reverberating in her ear.

"Oh, darling, I'm glad I caught you. I thought you might have turned in already. I think I had too much wine at dinner, and for some reason I can't seem to compute the time difference. How are you? Do you miss me?"

How can I miss a low-down skunk? "You're right, Jonathan, I was halfway up the stairs, on my way to bed, when the phone rang." *Too much wine, my foot.* Jonathan never, ever lost control. He only drank more wine than he should when he knew he was in bed and would get at least five hours of sleep. Usually after making love. Maybe he was with some other woman. The thought pleased her. *He's worried about the IRS,* she thought. *That's the reason for this call.* "I'm fine, Jonathan, how are you? Of course I miss you. I'm counting the days till you get here. Where are you, Jonathan?"

"I'm still in Zurich. I'll be heading for Cairo shortly. You've been on my mind, darling. All I've been doing is thinking about you instead of business. I know you're worried about your IRS meeting. I'm sure it's some minor nitpicking item they're homing in on."

Lucy sucked in her breath. *You bastard.* "Actually, I put it out of my mind, Jonathan. The one thing I don't do, and have never done, is mess around with my tax records. As a lawyer, I'm trained to keep impeccable records. My brother and I check each other's returns to make sure neither one of us inadvertently forgets to put something in. I was just antsy seeing the letter. It will be fine. I don't want you worrying about me, Jonathan. They did not indicate that this was an audit. Let's not waste our time talking about those pests at the IRS. Let's talk about *us*. Tell me what you're doing and when can I expect to see you?" *Never* would be the appropriate response to her question.

Jonathan's laughter didn't sound genuine. Lucy found herself shivering. She cradled the phone on her neck and shoulder so she could hug her arms against her chest. *Just hang up already, Jonathan. I hate talking to you. I hate you. You're making my skin crawl.* Still, she had to play the game so she could return to her nice, normal life. And, the only way she could do that was to help the FBI trap the man she'd promised to marry.

"You sound like you miss me, Lucy. I'm doing my best to clear the decks, darling. If all goes well, I might be able to finagle a few extra days to make it a full two weeks instead of ten days. What do you think of that?"

Lucy wished she could tell him exactly what she thought of that statement. Her mind raced. Two weeks was fourteen days.

That would mean he would arrive on her doorstep somewhere around the . . . what? The seventeenth or the eighteenth of December, give or take a day either way, assuming he would leave to go back to whatever rock he lived under on January 2.

Lucy struggled to work enthusiasm and excitement into her voice. "Fourteen whole days! Jonathan, this will be a first for you . . . *us*," she purred. "As soon as this pesky snow starts to melt, I'm going to go shopping for a whole new wardrobe."

Jonathan chuckled again. It sounded just as forced as before. "You know what they say, less is more." Lucy felt light-headed at the insinuation. "Do you know what else, darling? I was sitting here thinking I'd like to take you dancing. I want to feel you next to me, your body pressed tight against mine as we glide across the floor with other people watching us, knowing we're going to make love when the night is over. I'm getting hard just thinking about it."

Lucy blinked at the sound of the words and the meaning. She wanted to gag. "Hmmm," was all she could get past her tight lips. Let him think whatever he wanted to think.

"Does that mean we're on the same wavelength?" Not bothering to wait for her response, he said, "Of course it does. When you go shopping, be sure to pick up some dancing slippers and a slinky, sexy dress. Get a red one. I love you in red."

He must be thinking about someone else. She didn't own anything, even underwear or pajamas, that were red. Red, in her opinion, was a harlot color. Did Jonathan know that? Her arm, wrist, and hand ached the way she had the receiver pressed to her ear. *Why isn't he hanging up?* She couldn't take one more minute of this.

A stifled yelp escaped her lips. "Oh, my goodness, Sadie just threw up. I have to hang up now, Jonathan." Just as she was about to end the call, she heard him mutter something that sounded like, "On the rug?"

Jonathan snapped the cell phone shut, his eyes speculative as he stared out the window of his hotel room. It would be dawn in a few minutes. A new day. He felt the pulse in his wrist. Too fast. Way too fast. He needed to calm down and think about the conversation he'd just had with his fiancée. Really think.

Jonathan moved then, across the elaborate suite of rooms to the room service tray that had arrived just as his call to Lucy went through. There was nothing like a jolt of pure Colombian coffee to jump-start the morning. Just what he needed, caffeine. He gulped at the hot, dark brew.

Jonathan licked at lips that felt dry. Lucy was suspicious. Of what? The IRS letter? There was no way she could know about the brokerage accounts or the house in Watchung or the amended tax returns. Or could she? She had to know or suspect something. Why else did she sound so . . . so *wary* when he called her, like she was choosing her words, thinking, weighing what she was going to say. Damn, the feds had probably paid her a visit.

As always, when Jonathan was under pressure, he sat down at the ornate desk and turned on his laptop. Blizzards of files and numbers raced across the screen. His holdings. His security. The totally different life he was about to embark on come the new year. A life he'd prepared for with his own sweat, blood, and yes, even a few tears. With the money he'd secreted around the world, he could take his place among the rich and famous, with Lucy at his side.

He'd chosen Lucy from a hundred other women because she knew the law and had credibility. After they were married, he'd suggest some of the famous salons in Paris.

Perhaps a little plastic surgery. A haute couture wardrobe, and she would be worthy of holding on to his arm. Her French was so-so, and he would insist she become fluent.

Why was he having all these thoughts when the very real possibility that he would have to kill Lucy banged around inside his head?

If his instincts were right, and they'd never failed him before, maybe he should cut his losses where Lucy was concerned and sever his relationship with the lawyer. Damn, if the *federales* were onto him, he was going to have to do some clever shape-shifting in order to enter the good old US of A.

It was getting lighter outside the windows. Jonathan walked over, opened the draperies, and stared down at the city. Damn, it was snowing again. He hated the cold. He really did. The French Riviera was the place to be at this time of year. Any time of the year for that matter.

Jonathan flipped open his encrypted cell phone and proceeded to punch in a number he knew from memory. His voice firm and cool, he canceled his proposed meeting in Cairo, saying urgent business demanded he return to the United States.

The promise of a rescheduled meeting and a discount calmed the voice on the other end of the line.

Jonathan's next call was to Swissair. Better to fly commercial than have his pilot bring the Gulfstream to Lucerne. He thought then about his latest acquisition, a Bell Jet Ranger helicopter. He couldn't wait to play with that particular new toy. Payment for a job well-done. He smiled, but the smile didn't reach his eyes. His immediate business taken care of, he could concentrate all his efforts on what he was going to do about Lucy Baker.

If there was one thing in life that Jonathan St. Clair, aka Leo Banks, hated, it was a switch in plans that had been synchronized down to the last sync. That's when things went wrong, ordinary, little things that brought men like him to their knees.

Well, that wasn't going to happen to him. He'd worked too long, too hard, to secure the good life that was about to become his.

Jonathan poured the last of the coffee from the silver pot. As Jonathan gazed out on the swirling snow, he pictured Lucy in his mind and wondered if he would miss her if his instincts were on target.

9

Lucy rolled over to feel little puffs of breath on her neck. She opened one eye, then the other. Lulu was curled into a tight ball on her shoulder, half under the covers and half out. The little pink bow jiggled each time she exhaled. Lucy smiled as she reached out to stroke the tiny head. Lulu immediately bounded up, ready to play. Coop and Sadie were on the bed an instant later. All of them tussled for a minute or two before Lucy swung her legs over the side of the bed.

"Okay, troops, time to go out and do your thing. Oh, oh," she said, padding down the carpeted steps. "Looks like it snowed during the night." Two minutes later, Lucy eyeballed the mountain of snow on top of the hot tub. At least another six inches must have fallen. That had to mean Wylie wouldn't be heading for Manhattan. The thought pleased her.

Lucy unlocked and slid the sliding glass door to the side. Coop bounded through, his bark high and shrill. Sadie was right be-hind him, nipping at his tail as they raced to the back of the yard. Lulu stuck one tiny little paw into the snow on the deck, then backed inside, the pink bow jiggling furiously. "Okay, little one, let me get yesterday's paper." Not trusting the Yorkie, Lucy scooped her up and carried her to the family room, where she grabbed the sports section of the paper. She spread the paper and Lulu piddled, then ran to the door to watch her new best friends cavorting in the snow.

In the kitchen, Lucy made coffee. What would all this new snow mean to the guys' trip to Watchung? For some reason she didn't think it would make a difference to Mitch Logan. Jake, however, looked like a creature of comfort. Wylie would be game for anything if he didn't go into work. That left her. Well, she had a ski suit and rubber boots, so that meant she was up to the trek if the men thought it advisable.

Mitch had said he drove up in a truck, so he was prepared. Wylie's Land Rover had four-wheel drive. By the time the coffee dripped all the way, Lucy had herself convinced the trip would go on schedule.

Was the trip a good idea or a bad one? She simply didn't know. What she did know was that she wanted this whole mess to be over and done with.

The phone rang just as Lucy added cream to her coffee. Her voice was wary when she uttered a greeting.

"Luce, it's Steven. I'm just calling to tell you the city is shut down pretty tight. No one was expecting this much snow. I'm not even going to attempt to go to the office. I think I'm going to hang out at home, drink a few beers, and watch some videos. How are things with you, sis?"

"Same old, same old. Sadie loves the snow. She's out there right now having a grand old time. I just got up as a matter of fact. Anything new?"

"Lucy, why don't you just come out and ask me if I'm seeing anyone new. Actually, I am. Her name is Belle Andrews. She's a lawyer at Justice. Long legs. Looks good in a bikini, and she likes me. Oh, did I mention she can cook? She can. She thinks I'm handsome, and she likes to run her fingers through my curly hair. Did I leave anything out?"

Lucy laughed. "Does she have any outstanding marks on that beautiful body?"

"A real strawberry mark by her belly button. Is that more than you wanted to know? Hey, anything on Jonathan? How are the wedding plans going?"

Lucy sucked in her breath. "The wedding is off, Steven. I'm going to tell Jonathan when he arrives for Christmas. It's not something I'm comfortable saying over the telephone."

Steven whooped his pleasure. "Glad you're seeing the light of day, Lucy. That guy was all wrong for you. I, for one, am relieved. Guess that means you have to go on the prowl again."

Lucy's voice turned indignant. "I have never, nor will I, go on the prowl. There is this really nice guy next door. All I have to do is walk up to the fence, and I can see and talk to him. You'd like him, Steven. Maybe we can get together. I can meet all of you in the city, and we can do dinner one night if this freaky weather ever clears up. I can't wait to meet the ravishing Belle."

"Okay, sounds like a plan. This neighbor of yours, does he have a name?"

"Of course he has a name but you don't need to know it. I don't want you running any checks on him. He is what he is, a nice guy, a lawyer. I'll call you next week, okay?"

"You got it, sis. Why don't you go out and play in the snow with Sadie?"

Lucy laughed again. "Great idea. I did that yesterday. Maybe I'll do it again today. See ya, Steven."

Lucy wished she was a kid again, when life was simple. In those days she ate, played, ate, played until she was exhausted, then slept. There were no worries, no angst, no betrayals unless you counted the time Janet Williams told Bill Kelly she called him stinky because he needed deodorant. She'd made snow angels with Betty Lou Saylan, had ice-skated on Desty's pond with Betty Lou. She should call Betty Lou, who now lived in a little town in Virginia. And, she would, just as soon as her life returned to normal. Maybe she'd even take a drive to see her. Old friendships were the best even when they were reduced to semiannual phone calls and the extra special Hallmark Christmas card along with a "family" letter describing the year's activities. Yes, she would get in touch with Betty Lou.

It was nine-thirty when Lucy showered, dressed, and made her bed, which the dogs immediately messed up by playing tug-of-war with the comforter. Wylie should have called by now to announce their plans. Was the trip on or off? Lucy stared at her reflection in the stainless-steel Sub-Zero refrigerator while she waited for a fresh pot of coffee to brew. She was dressed for a day in the snowy mountains. She'd layered her clothing underneath the plum-colored, fleece-lined sweat suit. Warm cashmere leggings covered her legs. At the moment she was wearing slippers, but if the trip was on, she'd change into her rubber boots. Knowing her hair was going to get mussed up inside the hood of her parka, she'd simply piled it on top of her head with tortoiseshell combs to hold it in place. If Wylie did not call soon, she would have to start peeling off her carefully assembled cocoon of clothing.

Outside, the thermometer on the deck said it was a freezing twenty-nine degrees. Just thinking about the cold made Lucy shiver. With nothing else to do while she waited for Wylie and his friends, Lucy emptied the dishwasher and folded the towels in the dryer. She hated emptying the dishwasher, but it was something to do. Maybe she should call Wylie's house. Then again, maybe she shouldn't.

She couldn't help thinking about Jonathan's phone call the night before. She wished she knew if her telephone was bugged. Did the federal agents listen in on her calls? Would they ask if she'd heard from Jonathan? Did she dare lie? To what end? She shook her head wearily. Maybe she needed to switch mental gears and think about Thanksgiving. For a moment, she couldn't remember how many days she had to get a turkey.

Lucy was jolted from her thoughts when all three dogs let loose with earsplitting barks as they raced in tandem to the front door. She sighed in relief as she made her way through the dining room to the front door. When she opened it, Wylie announced that they had come for breakfast.

"In that case, I hope you brought it," Lucy said curtly. "I can offer toast and jam, but that's about it."

"We'll take it," Jake said happily. "I'm also up for heated leftovers."

Mitch took his seat at the table and stared up at Lucy. "Are you up for our trip to the mountain, Miss Lucy?" The giant of a man was always so formal and so polite. A smile tugged at the corners of her mouth. She loved the way "Miss Lucy" sounded rolling off his tongue. She was almost positive he'd had a Southern upbringing. Later, she would ask.

Lucy nodded. "With the new snow, I wasn't sure if we were going or not." She pointed to the sweat suit she was wearing. "I'm ready to go." She dropped bread into the four-slice toaster that she had retrieved from its home in the cabinet and poured coffee. She rinsed the empty pot and made a second. "By the way, Jonathan called again last night just as I was locking up. Maybe it's just me, but I think he knows something is going on."

"Something *is* going on. We're going to find out what the man is up to and why the feds are on your case. We spent the last hour loading all my gear in Wylie's cargo hold. We can't take my truck because there's only room for one passenger," Mitch said as he rolled up the sleeves of his thick, woolen shirt. Today, the colors were blue and black. His wide-wale corduroys matched the blue in the lumberjack shirt. He wore the same buff-colored Timberland boots Jake and Wylie had on. To Lucy's eyes he still looked as big as a grizzly bear. He also looked like her savior. She hoped she was right.

As the three men gulped and munched, Lucy elaborated further on Jonathan's phone call. The trio said nothing, only nodding from time to time until she wound down at last.

It was finally time to go. Lucy let the dogs out one last time, cleared the table, and slipped into her ski jacket. She was as ready as she would ever be.

Wylie drove, Lucy in the passenger seat. Mitch and Jake in the backseat. It took them twenty minutes to make their way out of the development to Park Avenue, which had been plowed and sanded. Still, driving was treacherous, four-wheel drive or not. Another hour was spent trying to reach Route 22, which would take them to Watchung and Jonathan St. Clair's house.

The men talked about football and cars as Lucy stewed and fretted in the front seat, wondering what they would find when they arrived at the house that had her name on the deed.

They used up another thirty-five minutes on the highway by driving past the property because the driveway hadn't been plowed. Wylie drove until he found an exit and turned around. This time they all looked for the marker, hoping the Land Rover would make it up the steep, twisting driveway to the very top of a hill.

"The snow's making the driveway look bigger and longer than it is," Mitch said. "I think you can get as far as those electronic gates, Wylie. We pile out, and I do my thing. Let's see what this baby can do." The engine of the Land Rover whined and strained as it fought its way through the deep snow. Twice, the four-by-four bucked, then stalled, slipping backward.

"Miss Lucy, come around to this side and drive. The three of us will push you up to the crest. Low gear." Lucy felt like cheering when the Land Rover came to a halt on level ground near the fortresslike gates.

Hands on hips, Mitch looked around. He pulled his navy wool hat down over his ears. "Impressive," was all he said.

"Makes you kind of wonder what's behind those awesome-looking gates," Jake said.

Awesome was definitely the right word, Lucy thought. Iron spikes, ten inches tall, stood up from the iron grille of the fence and gates. Thick shards of glass were embedded in the concrete between the spikes. Put there, Lucy assumed, in case anyone was foolish or daring enough to climb over the fence. She risked a glance at Wylie, whose face was totally unreadable. Lucy felt sick to her stomach. What *was* he thinking? She strained to pick up his thoughts, but nothing came through. She crossed her fingers inside her warm mittens that he wasn't thinking she was part of whatever was going on at this house.

"Let's get to it, gentlemen," Mitch said, opening the cargo hold to remove his equipment. "Let's see how serious this dude is about his privacy."

Lucy watched as the trio hauled out mysterious-looking gadgets and equipment. What they were for, she had no idea. James Bond would probably know. Shivering, hugging her arms to her chest, she watched as the three men plowed through the snow with their futuristic-looking tools.

"The windows of the house are multiple-pane glass. They have a Mylar film inside. To you guys that means anyone outside the house with a laser listening device wouldn't be able to hear a thing inside. I'm thinking this is a safe house of some kind." Mitch swung a long tool and pointed it toward the Tudor-style house. "The walls of the house are lined with copper. That's so nothing can be picked up from monitoring devices on the outside. I saw something like this in Venezuela. This is drug lord surveillance," he said, sweeping the grounds with something that looked like a metal detector. "This guy must have some big bucks. The security he's got here is worthy of the White House or Colombia. The Colombians never stint on security and back it up with trained commandos. Now why does a guy who brokers business deals need something like this in his backyard?" Mitch asked. He didn't expect a response. Instead, he walked through the grounds in the deep snow, pushing first one gadget, then another, and yet others until green lights glowed coolly on the equipment all of them carried.

"Okay. The green lights tell me I've located all the sensors. Now all I have to do is disarm them. I want you all to stand in the driveway behind the car in case one of these little beauties decides to go off. Boom!" he said playfully.

Thirty-five minutes later, Mitch looked at the green buttons that were slowly turning from yellow to red. "Red is the safe zone," he said cheerfully. "Relax, guys, I know what I'm doing. I did it for fifteen years, and I have citations saying I'm the best of the best. This is puppy-dog stuff. The real test is going to be disarming the gate and the next round of embedded security. Then comes the house." Wylie and Jake looked skeptical.

Mitch was in back of the Land Rover, stowing his gear and replacing it with different tools and gadgets. Everything glowed and vibrated. "What is all that stuff?" Lucy asked, in a hushed whisper.

"Tools of the trade, Miss Lucy. We live in a different world today and need such things. These things," he said, motioning to the packed cargo hold, "are all government issue. Updated equipment we used when I was a SEAL and Drew was with Delta Force. Oh, oh, looks like we have company. I'm thinking it's my buddy, but just to be on the safe side, don't move. Don't even blink." Mitch's hand, she noticed, was inside the blue-and-black lumberjack shirt. *Shoulder holster,* she thought. *This is all just a bad dream.* She pinched herself to make sure. It was all too real she decided when she felt the pain in her arm where she'd pinched herself.

No one moved when they heard a car door slam shut. All of them relaxed when a voice called out. "Yo, Mitch, you up there? It's me, Drew."

Mitch's gloved hand fell to his side as he maneuvered his way to the driveway. Lucy saw a tall man wearing a backpack coming up the driveway. A suntanned man who looked like Charles Atlas, the bodybuilder. He was handsome, probably in his late thirties, possibly his early forties, with a buzz cut like Mitch's. He wore jeans, probably over long underwear, boots, a long-sleeved shirt, and a hunter green down vest. When he removed his sunglasses, Lucy saw he had bright, summer blue eyes.

Introductions were made, hands shaken,

then Lucy was outside of the loop as the men traded gear, poked and probed each other's tools, and talked in low voices. The minutes crawled by. Lucy climbed into the Land Rover and turned on the engine. The heat kicked on almost immediately. She sighed with relief. She leaned back and stared out the window at the house the feds said belonged to her. Why did Jonathan need all this security?

Then she heard it. If she had been standing next to the men outside the truck, the words couldn't have been any clearer. She was hearing Mitch's thoughts.

And then Wiley's thoughts. She was sure they were Wiley's thoughts. *She can't be involved in this. There's no way. She's scared out of her wits. Hell, I'm scared out of my wits, and I don't even know the stupid guy.*

Then the newcomer, a man who didn't even know her. *There's something weird going on here. The word* trap *comes to mind. This is New Jersey, for God's sake. Stuff like this doesn't happen around here. No stakeouts. Where the hell are the feds when you need them?*

Jake's thoughts were different. *A nice juicy cheeseburger, with onion rings on the side. Maybe a double malt. French fries with loads of ketchup when this is over.*

Lucy sighed. If, and it was a big if, Jonathan was responsible for this security, this house, and everything the feds said, what did the word *safe* really mean? If Jonathan had the kind of money they alluded to, he would be able to find her anywhere.

Minutes crawled by. Minutes that turned into an hour. The sun that had been bright just minutes ago was gone, the day turning gray and ominous. Lucy rolled down the window. The air felt heavy with the threat of more snow to come. She shrugged as she watched the gray overcast sweep across the sky. The weather was just as freaky as what was happening to her. She wiggled around in her seat to see what the four men were doing. Mitch and Drew both had cell phones to their ears. That told her they were stymied. They must be calling other experts, hoping for clues as to how to disarm the sophisticated systems in place. Wylie and Jake looked like they were frozen to the ground. Jake's nose was as red as a cherry. Wylie ran in place to keep warm. She knew they were chilled to the bone.

Wylie looked in her direction, saw the rolled-down window, and ran over. He leaned into the warm car, little puffs of steam escaping from between his lips.

"What's wrong?" Lucy asked.

"Mitch said he hasn't seen anything like this before. Drew agreed. They said this stuff is updated practically on a daily basis. I think they're checking with members of their old units. Drew said he knows a spook at the CIA who might be able to help. This gadgetry is way beyond anything I've ever heard about." Wylie shook his head and walked back to join the men.

Lucy cracked the driver's-side window before she settled down to snooze. That was when she heard the sounds on the windshield. Snow was silent. This was hard-driving sleet slamming against the windshield. Sleet meant the roads would freeze up. Suddenly she felt frightened and didn't know why.

What *were* they doing out there? Just seconds ago she was thinking about taking a nap. Suddenly she was too angry and frightened to sleep. Her adrenaline pumping, Lucy hopped out of the truck, her head down to avoid the stinging sleet as she slogged her way over to the men by the gate. "Why don't we just climb over the damn thing?" she shouted to be heard over the wind and sleet.

"That's exactly what we're getting ready to do, Miss Lucy," Mitch shouted back.

"We're betting the guts of this security gate are on the other side, inside that stone gatehouse, and the owner has a special encrypted card that he just flashes when he wants to go in and out of this gate. It's obvious we don't have one of those particular cards, so we're going to blow the system. Wylie is going over first and will blow it. I want you to stand back."

Card. Lucy's memory stirred. "Wait a minute. What kind of card are you talking about?"

"You know the kind you swipe through a lock or show it faceup to a small screen. Sometimes they go by eyes or thumbprints for ID. It's okay, we know what we're doing, Miss Lucy."

"Wait. Please wait. I think I might have the card. Jonathan gave me a card several months ago. Early in the summer. He said it was for international shopping, you know, for when we went to Europe. Okay, okay, so I was stupid. To me it was just a weird-looking credit card," she said defensively at the skeptical looks on the men's faces. "I put it in my wallet and forgot about it till just now. You can make whatever you want out of that. If you give me a minute, I'll get it for you."

Minutes later, when Lucy handed over

the card, Mitch looked at it, then at her. His gaze was so intense, Lucy felt like he had nailed her to the ground. He handed it to Drew Warner, who walked up to the gate and simply waved the card in front of the monitor. The gates slid open with barely a sound. Lucy felt queasy and light-headed as she followed the men through the gate.

Wylie reached for her hand. He bent over, and shouted into her ear, "Smile, it adds to your face value. Look, we're inside, and that's all that matters."

Lucy nodded as she watched Drew and Mitch roam the property inside the gate. Even through the stinging sleet, she could see small dots of green, yellow, and red on the equipment they carried. Wylie led her to an overhang by a small round-arched back door. The narrow eave deflected some of the sleet. Jake joined them a few minutes later.

There, close to the house, Lucy found she didn't have to shout at the top of her lungs to be heard. "I swear, I forgot about the card, I actually believed it was what Jonathan said it was, an international credit card. Since I never had one, how could I know if it was real or not? I was taking everything Jonathan said back then at face value. The card did say GLOBAL on the front of it. It looked like a damn credit card, Wylie." If she hadn't been so cold, she would have burst into tears of frustration. *Why is this happening to me?*

"If he tried to keep this house secret, why would he have given the card to you?" Jake asked. "How were you supposed to get into the house? All it does is open the gate."

"I don't know, Jake," Lucy wailed at the outright suspicion in his voice. "I don't know anything about how or what Jonathan did. You have to believe me."

Jake took off his gloves and blew on his fingers. "No offense, Lucy, but your fiancé must have thought you were really stupid."

"Yes, I guess he really did," Lucy snapped. "And, I just proved to everyone how really stupid I am. He bamboozled me, okay. I take full responsibility for my own stupidity, but I am not involved in anything he did or said."

Wylie put his arm around her shoulder and pulled her close. "We're going to figure this all out, Lucy. Don't go off the deep end now."

The trio remained under the narrow overhang shivering, their teeth rattling with cold for another forty minutes — at which point Mitch and Drew returned their gear to the truck and brought back different equipment. Another forty minutes passed as they explored for trip wires, then deactivated the alarm system and locks.

At last they were all inside the garage. Mitch fumbled for a light switch. All of them reared back at the huge black Chevy Suburban sitting squarely in the middle of the six-car garage. For some reason it looked obscene to Lucy. Obscene *and* frightening. Lucy wondered about the other six cars the FBI agents had mentioned. Nothing had been said about anything as prosaic as a Chevy Suburban.

Another twenty-five minutes passed while Drew checked out the Suburban and Mitch worked the keypad outside a door that led into the main body of the house. Eventually they were inside the house, all of them standing in the kitchen. Jake pressed a wall switch, and the gray room sprang to light. Outside, sleet hammered against the windows, sounding like nails being shot from a nail gun. Wylie looked around for a thermostat and turned it up to ninety degrees. Immediately a warm rush of air spewed from the baseboard grates.

Lucy looked around the huge kitchen.

This was not a kitchen Martha Stewart would love. While state-of-the-art, there was nothing warm and cozy about the room. The word *institutional* came to mind. Every appliance was Sub-Zero, and stainless steel. Even the sink. The floor was dove gray granite. The hanging pot rack over the center island was loaded down with shiny stainless-steel pots and pans. *Never used,* Lucy thought as she looked up at the contraption. She could see the glue marks on the pots where the price stickers had once been. Out of curiosity, she opened the refrigerator. It was empty. She opened the freezer, and it was full. She reached for a package of frozen ground coffee and a container of half-and-half. "I'll make some coffee," she said curtly. "We all need to warm up."

Mitch nodded as he walked away, Drew Warner on his heels. Jake and Wylie stayed with Lucy in the kitchen. Her voice was a whisper when she said, "I don't think anyone lives here or has ever lived here." Lucy pointed to the glue marks on the pots hanging overhead. The tears she'd been holding in check escaped and rolled down her cheeks. "What *is* this place?"

Wylie grimaced. Jake looked at the pots. "I don't know, Lucy. Mitch said he thought it was a safe house. What that means exactly, I don't know. It's getting warmer; let's check out the rest of the place. C'mon, it's going to be all right. We have professionals helping us now. Right, Jake?"

"Absolutely," Jake said as he removed his topcoat and muffler. "Actually, it's getting downright toasty in here."

A short hallway led them to an immense room that seemed to be, aside from the kitchen, the entire first floor. Lucy blinked. It was a round room. Lucy was reminded of a soccer ball. How could a square house have a round room? And it was white, so white it was dazzling.

A round white brick fireplace sat squarely in the middle of the room, the venting hood going all the way up to the ceiling and probably through the roof. Lucy couldn't remember if she'd seen a chimney when she was outside or not. She tried to calculate the size of the pit and finally likened it to two circular hot tubs. Six huge cherry logs with strips of kindling laid between them were ready to be ignited. A circle of deep, white, velvet couches surrounded the strange-looking fireplace. No matter where you sat, you would have a view of the fire. There were no tables, no plants, no pictures on the wall — no knickknacks of any kind. The floor was hardwood, probably oak, and strangely enough it wasn't the least bit dusty. She wondered if the house was hermetically sealed. The thought sent chills up and down her arms.

The wraparound windows were cloaked in heavy white brocade shot through with silver thread, the only concession to color. Was silver a color? *Is there a silver color in a Crayola box?* she thought inanely. She decided silver wasn't a color. And the world would go on with the knowledge Lucy Baker deemed silver not to be a color. She must be losing her mind.

Lucy peered down into the pit and frowned. For some reason she didn't expect to see ashes. But there they were. Someone had been there, and that someone, at some point, had built a fire. A few of the bricks on the bottom were scorched and black. Little piles of ash rested under the neat pile of wood.

"It smells like . . . wallpaper paste," Jake said thoughtfully. "Maybe it's a paint smell. Maybe just a new house smell. What do you think, Mitch?"

"I think it's a paint smell combined with the fact the house has been closed up. This is definitely either a safe house or a stopping-off place for people on the run. I'm going to check out the rest of the house. Don't open those drapes," he cautioned.

"Check this out, Mitch!" Drew called from the front foyer, which was out of sight of the round room. They all ran through the arched doorway to a small foyer littered with mail. "The guy has one of those chutes like banks use at their drive-throughs. When the mail gets to here, the cylinder just opens, dumps the mail, and returns to the mailbox, probably someplace at the bottom of the driveway. I must have missed it on our way in. There's nothing here but catalogs and junk mail. Everything is addressed to 'Lucille Baker' or 'Resident.' "

If Wylie hadn't been holding on to Lucy's arm, she would have fallen. To prove what Drew was saying, Lucy stooped down and picked up a Crate and Barrel catalog. Sure enough, her name was on the label. She started to feel sick all over again.

"It's just a catalog, Lucy. It doesn't mean anything," Wylie said.

"Like hell it doesn't mean anything. This junk says I live here. Me — Lucy Baker — I get mail at this address. No wonder the feds are on my back. God, how I hate that man for doing this to me!"

Wylie shrugged. "Have it your way,

Lucy. To me, it means nothing. There's not one piece of personal mail, not one bill of any kind. That says a lot in my book."

Her eyes hard, her voice grim, Lucy said, "Try telling that to the feds the next time they show up. Hell, they're probably watching and spying on us right now."

"Now what?" Jake asked.

Mitch fixed his gaze on Jake. "Drew and I are going to investigate the upstairs and the attic while you guys pour us that coffee. It should be ready by now."

Five minutes later, just as Lucy was starting to pour coffee into the cups, Mitch called them upstairs. They ran, jostling one another in their haste to see what Mitch had found.

"What?" they said in unison at the doorway to a small room, no more than eight-by-ten in size.

Drew looked at them with a strange expression on his face. "I saw a room like this in Somalia that belonged to some badassed dudes."

"Yeah, and what's that supposed to mean?" Wylie asked, his voice on the shaky side.

His eyes hard as flints, Drew looked from one to the other.

"It's called a dead room."

10

"And a dead room would be . . . what?" Wylie growled. "We're just ordinary people here in case you haven't noticed. There doesn't appear to be anyone dead in this room, so I have to assume it means something else entirely."

Lucy's jaw dropped as she gazed around the small room. Something lumpy with the look of Styrofoam had been sprayed onto the walls and ceiling. The door was padded with strange-looking quilted material that resembled shiny plastic. The floor was intertwined wire-and-rubber matting. A scary-looking room in her opinion. As she tried to absorb what she was seeing, she could hear Mitch and Drew explaining to Jake and Wylie what they were analyzing on the computer table. Since she didn't understand the high-tech talk, she only heard snatches that left her even more clueless than before. Underwater parabolic eavesdroppers, fish-eye camera, microphones, a video console for the fish-eye camera, hard laser microphones. What she finally deduced from their conversation was that the room enabled whoever was in it to have conversations that were truly secure.

"What's that?" Lucy asked, pointing to the center of the table.

"I'm glad you asked," Mitch grimaced. "They're the latest in technology. The mikes and headphones enable people to talk on the phones face-to-face, have conference calls secure in the knowledge that whatever they say stays safe in this room. That's why it's called a dead room."

"Why would someone need something like that?" Jake asked.

"I don't have any answers, Jake. You could try asking the feds or the guy himself. There isn't anything more we can do here. So, let's check out the basement, drink our coffee, and head for home. The big question is, do you want all this stuff we dismantled activated or what?"

"No!"

"Okay, Miss Lucy, you're the boss. We will lock the door and reset the house alarm, though. You don't want strange people crawling around in here. You have the card to the gate so if you want to come back, you can just swipe it. I'll write down the code to the alarm system. You can come and go as you please. A word of warning, Miss Lucy. Somewhere, someplace, the person who installed all this hardware is going to know it's been compromised. They probably knew the minute we started dismantling the system. And before you can ask, the people who did this are experts. Your guy probably brought them in from other countries. It's not the kind of security you want your neighbors or your local security people to know about."

Drew fixed his gaze on Lucy and Wylie. "You might want to give some serious thought to relocating or else have the feds give you some kind of protection. From the looks of things, there's been some serious stuff happening here. It's anyone's guess if it is still going on. The federal agents were right when they told you it was dangerous, and you could get killed. Think about it."

Like I can think about anything else. Lucy nodded.

Mitch shrugged, his eyes worried. "Let's have that coffee before we head back to your house."

"I'll take mine to go. I've got some pretty steep roads to travel. I'll be lucky to make it home by midnight," Drew said.

In the kitchen, Lucy poured a mug of

coffee for Drew. "Thanks."

"Be careful," Drew said, as he shook hands all around before heading out the door with his coffee. He called over his shoulder. "Call me if you need me."

Mitch gulped at his black coffee. "Drew is right, Miss Lucy. You stumbled onto something that could get you killed. My suggestion to you is get in touch with the *feebs,* lay it out, bring them back here if necessary, and clean your skirts. Do that as soon as you can. Then relocate."

As Lucy sipped at the scalding coffee, she strained to *hear* the men's thoughts. Under the circumstances, she expected to hear a jumble, but nothing was coming through. Her shoulders slumped.

Wylie turned the thermostat to sixty-five before he placed his empty coffee cup in the sink.

Mitch set the alarm in the garage, and then they exited. The garage door closed with a loud bang. The little group, their heads down, ran as fast as they could through the deep snow and stinging sleet to the car outside the gates. Breathless, they piled into the vehicle. Wiley turned the key in the ignition and pushed the heater as high as it would go. Then he hopped out and scraped the ice from the front and back windshields. From his pocket he withdrew an aerosol can of deicer and sprayed both windshields. The wipers slid smoothly across the windshield as he slipped the SUV into reverse. They literally slid down the driveway and out to the main road.

What would normally have been a thirty-five-minute ride took them almost three hours before they pulled into Wylie's driveway. Wylie's head slumped down on the steering wheel the moment he turned off the ignition. "I need a drink!" he mumbled. "Hell, I need two drinks! I don't ever remember driving in road conditions like this in my whole life."

"Relax, you got us home safe and sound," Jake said cheerfully. "I'll personally make your drink."

"Good, because I have to make a meat loaf for Coop. Lucy, are you coming in or are you going home?" Wylie asked.

Meat loaf. The dogs. A drink. She was back in the world of normalcy. Safe and sane. There were no dead rooms in Wylie's house or in hers either. There were no security gates or things that would blow up if you stepped on them, no trip wires, no mail chutes here in this quiet neighborhood. "I'll go home and bring the dogs over. My larder is bare, so we'll have to raid yours. Have my drink ready when I get there," Lucy said, as she hopped out of the SUV.

The dogs knew she was home. She could hear them barking all the way in Wylie's yard. When she reached her own driveway she was surprised to see footprints in the snow. Someone must have been by earlier. Who? One of the kids from one of the side streets wanting to shovel her driveway? She shrugged as she fitted the key into the three locks on her front door, glad that she'd added the mega lock at the top of the door that went into the molding. As she swung the door open, she was greeted by three clamoring dogs.

Inside, she raced through the house, her gaze going every which way as she looked for accidents or a sign that someone was or had been in the house. She didn't see anything, so that meant the dogs were just barking because they really needed to go out. She turned on the floodlights on the deck as her hand went to the lock on the sliding glass door. There were footprints in the snow all over the deck. She started to shake as she bent down to take the dowel out of the sliding track. Even if someone had a key to the slider, the dowel wouldn't allow them to open the door. Whoever had been in her yard must have climbed over the fence or else was tall enough to reach up, over, then down to the latch on the other side of the fence. Who?

The door swished open. The dogs barreled outside, even Lulu, who immediately piddled on the deck. The moment she was finished, the Yorkie started to sniff at the indentations just the way the others were doing. Who? Who had been in the backyard? Not some youngster wanting to shovel the driveway. Who?

Coop looked up and threw back his head and howled. Lucy jumped at the sound. Sadie moved across the deck to the fence gate. Her nose in the snow, she walked back and forth, but she didn't bark. Did that mean she'd picked up the scent of someone she knew? *Who?*

"Who? Who? Who?" She sounded like an owl. She called to the dogs. They all bounded into the house. Lucy waited to see if they'd sniff out anything unusual. They didn't. That meant no one was in the house. Who in their right mind would enter a house where a dog like Coop barked? *Who?*

Jonathan, that's who.

Lucy felt an adrenaline rush at the

thought. She looked down at her watch. It was quarter to eight. Time enough for Jonathan to have gotten there from wherever he'd been when he had called last night. Lucy could feel her insides start to clench up at the implications of what she was thinking.

Quicker than lightning, she ran around the downstairs rooms, turning off all the lights. In the kitchen she snapped off the night-light over the stove. Total darkness washed over her. Sadie growled at the strange goings-on. Lulu yelped to be picked up, and Lucy obliged. Coop started to prowl, sniffing at the track of the sliding glass doors.

Lucy crept over to the little alcove off the kitchen where the pantry was located. No windows, no doors where a person could be seen. She started to shake. Hot tears of anger and frustration burned her eyes. *Weaklings and sissies cower in fear,* she told herself. *Top-notch lawyers with brains are trained to stand up to just about anything. Yeah, well, today was over the top. He's playing with my head, that's what he's doing. I know it because I know Jonathan. I should call the FBI right now and tell them what we found.*

"Maybe I should call the feds," Lucy

muttered. "But if I don't know if I should trust them, what's the point?" She thought about how nasty they'd been to her, how cold and uncaring. "The hell with it," she muttered again. She backtracked in her thoughts. If she told them she thought the footprints belonged to Jonathan, they'd probably laugh their heads off. They'd say she was just trying to wiggle out from under their scrutiny. She smacked her hands together. That thought alone convinced her it was not in her best interests to call the agents. Lucy dropped to her knees, Lulu clutched tight against her chest. "Listen up, you two," she said to Coop and Sadie. "We're going to Wylie's house. Straight across the yard." Her voice was so jittery and shaky that the dogs actually paid attention to what she was saying. Lulu licked at her chin.

She was still wearing her jacket. She slipped into her rubber boots, scuffling along as she herded the dogs to the front door. Key in hand, she took one last look around before opening the door to let Coop and Sadie out, then locked it. There were wings on her feet as she crossed the yard to Wylie's house. She didn't bother to knock, just let herself in. Wylie was watching her from the foyer when she turned around and snapped the dead bolt.

Lucy was breathless from the run in the deep snow across the yard. "Someone was in my backyard. They must have been by the front door, too. Coop pitched a fit, but not Sadie, so that means the scent she picked up was someone she knew. Lulu picked up on it, too. I'd appreciate it if you'd close your blinds, Wylie," Lucy said. She could have saved her breath because Wylie was already closing the vertical blinds. Mitch meandered into the foyer, Jake behind him. Both had beer bottles in their hands.

Wylie explained Lucy's nervousness as she kicked off her boots and shed her jacket.

Mitch was the first to speak. "When it snows like this, people have a tendency to look out their windows from time to time to see if it's still snowing, how deep it's getting. Call some of your neighbors and see if they saw anyone at your house, Miss Lucy."

Lucy hung up her ski jacket. "After being in that house, I think I'm spooking myself. I suppose it could have been a youngster wanting to shovel the driveway."

Mitch swigged from his near-empty bottle. "If that's the case, then the kid would have knocked on other doors in the neighborhood. It won't hurt to call around, Miss Lucy."

"While you're doing that, Lucy, I've got to finish the meat loaf for Coop. By the way, that's what we're having for dinner, with baked potatoes and canned corn. I have some cabbage if anyone wants to make coleslaw or fried cabbage. Then I have to go across the street to feed Rachel Muller's cat and change the litter box. I almost forgot I was supposed to do that. She's liable to call me tonight to ask how the cat is. It won't take me long."

Curiosity ringing in her voice, Lucy asked, "Where's Rachel? I thought I saw her this morning."

"She went to Delaware to spend Thanksgiving with her sister. Her brother was picking her up just as we were leaving. I've had a key to her house forever. She used to take the cat, but he's old now and doesn't travel well. On nice days she used to walk Coop while I was at work."

"Lulu is going to be mighty upset if you come home smelling of cat," Jake warned. "We might as well have something besides corn. I'll do the coleslaw."

They were chatting about mundane matters, hoping to wipe away the look of anxiety on Lucy's face.

"I think I'll have a beer. Jonathan could have been on a plane when he called me last night. If he was, he could very well be here. Maybe I should call one of the agents. I think I figured it out. Jonathan is trying to play with my head so I'll go off the deep end," Lucy said as she marched into the kitchen. "Jonathan knows I haven't made any real friends since I moved here. Aside from Nellie, that is. He also knows Nellie goes south for the winter, and so he figures I'm here alone. I'm sure that's what he's doing. When I walked away from my law practice, he said a *stable* person wouldn't do something like that. When I said I didn't want to be a judge and was going to turn down the offer, he made a really big deal about it, saying I was losing it, that I wasn't *stable,* that I was teetering on the edge. Believe it or not, I laughed in his face." Lucy gulped at the beer she was holding.

"And, Miss Lucy, he would do this . . . why?"

Lucy watched as Wylie pulled on his jacket and boots and made his way to the front door, Rachel Muller's key in his hand. An ordinary, kind thing to do for a neighbor. Jake was chopping cabbage, and

Mitch was pacing the kitchen. The dogs were tussling in the family room with a long, coiled, braided rope. Everything just then seemed normal.

"Why?" Lucy shrugged. "An unstable person, someone teetering on the edge, wouldn't make a good impression on the FBI now, would she? They're crawling all over me, trying to wear me down. They think I'm lying about the brokerage accounts and the house in Watchung. Remember what you were thinking when I came up with that card that opened the gate? I saw all of your faces. You were thinking, how convenient it was that all of a sudden I remembered I had it. You know you all thought I might be mixed up in whatever Jonathan has going on. I'm not," Lucy said wearily as she sat down next to Mitch.

Mitch locked his gaze on her. "And you think he's here now because of the footprints you saw in the snow."

Lucy nodded. "Yes."

"Call around the neighborhood and see what you can find out. Want another beer?"

"Yes, thank you, I would like another beer."

Wylie blew into the house like a wild

gust of wind, his arms loaded with groceries. His eyes were watering, and his cheeks were red from the stinging snow. "Rachel left all this stuff on the table for me along with a note. She won't be back till next Saturday. We are going to have a feast, lady and gentlemen. The cat is doing nicely, thank you."

Jake was the only one who seemed interested in the array of food.

"I saw Rudy clearing his driveway," Wylie continued, "so I asked him if anyone had been around asking to shovel driveways, and he said no. He said he was watching television in between blowing out his driveway. As a matter of fact, he said other than us and Rachel leaving, no one has been on the street all day. What he said was, there were no strange cars on the street."

A look of disgust washed over Lucy's face. "A kid wanting to shovel snow wouldn't arrive in a car. Nor would Jonathan if he was up to something and being sneaky about it. He could very easily have come in from the back, off Frances Road. He could have parked on Richard Road and walked up this street. We haven't been plowed out. Maybe he didn't want to get stuck. I'm telling you, it was Jonathan. Where's your phone book, Wylie?"

Wylie bent down to open one of the kitchen cabinets. He handed her the white pages. "We've eliminated three already, Nellie, Rachel, and Rudy. That leaves Carol, Joan, the new people on the corner, the Hendersons, and Tom and Alice."

They watched as Lucy dialed her neighbors, one by one. The conversations were short and succinct. No one had offered to shovel their driveways. No one had seen anyone around her house all day.

"Then who was at my house?" Lucy demanded when she hung up from the last call. "Did he just drop from the sky?"

Jake scooped his chopped cabbage into a bowl. "This could turn out to be one of those little mysteries in life that is never explained or solved. You're here, you're safe, the dogs are safe, and that's all that matters. We won't let anything happen to you, Lucy."

"What's the game plan, guys?" Mitch asked. "I'm going to be heading home in the morning. But I can always come back if you need me. If you just want to ask me something, call or e-mail me. I'm going to write up a report for you. You can hand it over to the *feebs* or you can just keep it. Your call. My firm does work for a bunch of different government agencies, and our credibility is above reproach. I think I'll start on the report right now, Wylie, if you show me where your computer is. After dinner, I'm going straight to bed. The plows will be working overtime tonight, but by five or so, the roads should be in good shape. I've got a business to run, and I hate being away more than a day or so. Did I mention that my bill will be in the mail?"

When Wylie and Mitch left the kitchen, Lucy plopped her elbows on the table, dropping her head into the palms of her hands. "I think I'm scared, Jake. I thought I knew Jonathan, but I don't know *this* Jonathan. My God, I was going to marry the man. I don't know what he's capable of. I wouldn't make a good spy. I guess I gave myself away a hundred different ways when I spoke to him. The one thing I do know about Jonathan is he is not a stupid man. Then there's this . . . this thing going on inside my head. I'm staying here tonight. I don't care if I have to sleep on the floor."

Jake sat down across from Lucy. "Fear is a healthy emotion, Lucy. I would probably be worried about you if you tried to blow all this off as inconsequential. My personal opinion is you have to open up to the feds. Don't hold anything back, or it will jump up and bite you. Truth always wins out in the end."

"No, Jake, truth does not always win out in the end. I'm a lawyer, I should know. If I had a nickel for every dishonest client who said they were telling the truth, I'd be rich. God, I'm tired. How about you?"

"I can't remember when I had as much fresh air as I've had today. I think I'm going to go to bed after dinner, too."

Lucy leaned across the table. "Jake, after seeing that house, what do you think Jonathan is up to?"

"Jeez, Lucy, I don't know. Like Drew said, the guy's a badass dude. He must be one hell of an actor for you to have been so bewitched."

"I swear to you, Jake, it never occurred to me that my ex-fiancé was anything other than what he professed to be. Maybe I was too busy with work and wrapped up in my own world to pick up the clues. Fool me once, shame on you; fool me twice, shame on me. He knows I'm onto him. I just wish I knew what all that stuff at the house means."

"If you put my feet to the fire and I had to venture a guess, I'd say your old friend Jonathan is bringing illegal people into this country, and that house is a stopover. A place that is safe and secure until they get to their final destination, wherever that might be. Money laundering is a billion-dollar business. Then there are the drugs. I think you can just about take your pick or go with all three."

"Aside from all that first-class security, there's something about that house that bothers me. I can't quite put my finger on it," Lucy said, frowning.

Jake nodded sympathetically.

Ninety minutes later, the kitchen was cleaned, the leftovers — of which there weren't many — were wrapped and stored in the refrigerator. Mitch and Jake both headed off to bed, saying good night.

Wylie turned to Lucy and put his hands on his hips. "It's just you and me, Lucy. I'm as tired as those guys, but I'm wired, too. Let's put another log on the fire, have a snort of brandy, then we can go to sleep. You can have my bed, I'll take the couch."

"No, Wylie. I'm not taking your bed. I sleep on my own couch fairly often. I'll just curl up with the dogs here by the fire. I'll be fine."

Wylie added two logs to the fire. Sparks showered upward. Lucy was reminded of the Fourth of July sparklers she and Steven used to wave around when they were kids.

While Wylie poured brandy into two balloon glasses, Lucy wiggled her fanny back and forth, the warmth from the fire racing up and down her back. How good it felt.

Glasses in hand, Wylie led her to the couch. They sat down next to each other, each of them more than a little aware of the other. Lucy strained to *hear* Wylie's thoughts. She almost fell off the couch when she *heard . . . what now, Romeo? Do I put my arm around her shoulder, do I kiss her? Maybe I should ask first. She'd laugh her head off if she knew I haven't been with a woman in over a year. What the hell is she thinking? Is she waiting for me to make a move?*

Lucy watched as Wylie gulped at the fiery liquid in his glass. When she saw his eyes start to water, she set her glass aside, moved to the right, throwing her right leg over his and yanking him toward her, all at the same time. "I think you need to kiss me *right now.*" The command came out in a sexy, throaty growl.

Wylie obliged. Talk about wishful thinking.

When they finally came up for air a long time later, the three dogs were on their haunches staring at them intently. Lucy burst out laughing.

Wylie stared at Lucy. "I liked that. Yeah, I

did. I mean, I really did. You're a great kisser. I haven't been kissed like that in oh . . ."

"A little over a year." Lucy giggled.

Wylie pretended outrage. "You read my mind. That's dirty pool."

Lucy laughed again. "I was getting impatient. You couldn't make up your mind. You know us lawyers, we have to make snap decisions. By the way, I liked it, too. Want to do it again?"

"Are you one of those women who likes to toy with a man's affections? I don't want to have my heart broken."

"You're serious, aren't you? That wasn't a fun question, was it?"

Wylie jumped up and walked over to the fireplace. He poked at logs that didn't need to be poked. He turned around, his eyes bright. "I was serious. I think I started to have feelings for you that first day I met you. Coop loves you, so that endeared you to me right off. I don't want to catch you on the rebound, Lucy. Been there, done that. I'm thinking if you aren't ready or if you don't share my feelings, then we should sit on separate chairs. Or . . . or something."

Lucy bounded off the couch, causing the dogs to move backward. "Do you think I just go around kissing guys who have nice dogs? Huh? Well, do you? Listen, there's a lot going on in my little world right now. The fact that I allowed myself to kiss you, and make no mistake, I kissed you, should be all the proof you need that I . . . that I . . . care about you."

She was right next to him, her body a hairbreadth away from his. She could smell the brandy on his breath. He opened his arms, and she stepped into them. She felt the hardness of him as she laid her head against his chest. Nothing had ever felt this right, this good. A sigh of pure happiness escaped her lips.

Wylie swayed dizzily, his gaze going to Coop, who seemed to be drooling in anticipation. His mouth worked silently. She likes meat loaf. The huge dog stared at his master a moment before he lay down, stretched out, his head dropping onto his paws. Wylie almost swooned. That was Coop's seal of approval.

"Want to go for it right here, or are you one of those women who needs a bed?" Damn, was that growling voice his?

"A bearskin rug would be nice."

"Uh-huh?" His eyes almost bugging out of his head, Wylie couldn't believe what he was seeing. A sweatshirt flying across the room, sweatpants dropping to the floor.

Lucy laughed as she unhooked her bra. "You better hurry or you won't be able to catch up."

Speed. She wanted speed. "Watch this!"

Lucy watched.

11

The man standing at the twentieth-floor window of the Woodbridge Hilton Hotel that was a mere seven minutes by car to Lucy's house bore absolutely no resemblance to the man known as Jonathan St. Clair. His identification, international driver's license, credit cards, and passport said his name was Spiros Andreadis, a Greek national. His credentials said he worked for a Swiss clock company. Thanks to shoe lifts, Spiros Andreadis was two inches taller than Jonathan St. Clair. His eyes were a startling blue opposed to Jonathan's hazel and now stood out sharply against his olive complexion. Spiros's hair was coal black and matched his mustache. Jonathan St. Clair sported sandy-colored hair, and his upper lip was clean-shaven.

The Greek's clothing, shoes, and all items in his possession shrieked that they were *not* made in America. His luggage, one bag, was sturdy, battered cowhide and bore travel stamps from all over the world.

His shoulders stiff, his stance angry,

Jonathan whirled away from the window. It was late, he should go to bed. The only problem was that he was too angry to go to bed. He'd spent close to two hours tramping through a virtual blizzard to reach Lucy after a dozen phone calls to her home and cell went unanswered, only to find she wasn't home. He was further irritated that he didn't have a key to her house. Lucy's explanation for why she wouldn't give him a key was simple, "Jonathan, I'm always home, why do you need a key?" What Lucy didn't know was he *did* have a key. Three visits ago, he'd been so miffed at her refusal to give him a key, he'd waited till she finished her fourth glass of wine and fell asleep, at which point he took the key from the peg by the back door and pressed it into some melted candle wax. The next day he'd gone to a drugstore and within ten minutes he had a bright, shiny key in his hand. For all the good it did him. Who knew Lucy would add a new lock, the kind that went into the molding at the top of the doorframe. She'd never stuck dowels in the sliding doors before, either. At least he didn't think she had. Right now he was too angry to think straight.

If she had been home and opened the

door, he would have killed her. "Always pay attention to your gut warnings," he muttered.

The last thing he'd expected when he walked off the plane was snow. He'd left tons of snow, ice, and cold in Zurich. He'd expected temperatures in the high thirties. It was, after all, only November. He also hadn't expected the phone call he'd received as he was going through customs. The moment he'd heard the voice on the other end of the line he knew what had happened. "The property was compromised several hours ago." His eyes murderous, Jonathan, aka Spiros Andreadis, snapped the encrypted cell phone shut and jammed it in his pocket. His instincts were on the money. The only question was, who had compromised the house and property in Watchung, Lucy or the FBI?

His original intention had been to go to the apartment he maintained in Manhattan. His second thought was to check into a New York hotel. Furious after the phone call, he'd rented a car and headed through the storm to New Jersey. It was a damn good thing he hadn't gone to the house in Watchung, which had been his third choice.

He had to fall back and regroup, something he'd never had to do in his line of business. It was not a pleasant thought.

He was back at the window, his expression still murderous. *Just how the hell much snow is out there anyway?* According to the Weather Channel and the desk clerk, it was going to snow through the night. He supposed he should feel lucky because, according to the clerk, all the airports were shut down. With the airports closed, anyone following him would be stuck at one airport or another. By the same token, he wouldn't be able to leave if the airports didn't open up soon. "Lucky, my ass," he muttered.

Jonathan flipped open his cell phone again and dialed Lucy's number. When her voice mail came on, he hung up. It was after midnight: where was she? He rang the number again and again, hanging up each time after the seventh ring. If she was sound asleep, the steady ringing should alert her or, at the very least, rouse the damn dog who slept on her bed.

The startling blue eyes narrowed. *Maybe she isn't home. Where do people go in the middle of a snowstorm? Nowhere, that's where.*

Jonathan continued to watch the falling snow. He wondered how the rental Lexus would do in all this snow. What he really needed was a powerful SUV, but the rental agency said none were available. He'd never driven a Lexus before that day. He didn't even know if it had front-wheel drive. What if he got stuck in the snow? Maybe it would be better to wait till morning. He could pass the time by ordering drinks from room service and dialing Lucy's number. *Where the hell is the woman I'm supposed to be marrying?*

Angry beyond words, Jonathan hooked his foot under one of the chairs in the hotel room and dragged it closer to the window. He sat down and stretched out his legs so they rested on top of the heating unit.

He'd made a mistake, and that mistake's name was Lucille Baker. Down through history, he'd been told, women were men's downfall. Sex, according to history, was the reason nothing went right in the world. A sound of pure misery escaped Jonathan's lips. Sex had nothing to do with his predicament. He didn't love Lucy Baker. She was just someone to use to help him set up his retirement and a new life. His original plan had been to get rid of her a year or so into the marriage. A divorce if she behaved herself and wouldn't come back to haunt him.

A nice clean kill à la Adam Ligar if she stepped out of line.

Where had it all gone wrong? He knew that *he* hadn't made a mistake because he was a perfectionist and an expert at covering his ass, so it had to be on Lucy's end. Left to her own devices she would never, ever, have stumbled onto his affairs. Somehow or other he'd come up on either the CIA's, or the FBI's radar screen. He'd gone to extraordinary lengths to protect himself once he knew they were onto him. Knowing how the government agencies worked, they had probably paid Lucy a visit and threatened all kinds of things. That would surely account for the change in her attitude. Lucy was no actress; he'd picked up on her nervous tone immediately. She was probably scared out of her wits. Then there was that little tidbit about the Internal Revenue Service appointment. He'd seen through that immediately, too.

Jonathan's feet hit the floor with a thud. He got up, called room service, and ordered a bottle of Chivas Regal and a bucket of ice. He then dialed Lucy's number again from his encrypted cell phone. Again he hung up on the seventh ring.

He started to pace because he was furious

and needed to do something to control his anger. He was angry because he knew Lucy was hiding out. It really infuriated him that she thought she was smarter than he was. He had to find her, and he had to find her soon. He closed his eyes — envisioning a net descending over him. Well, that wasn't going to happen. He continued his frantic pacing until there was a knock on the door. He accepted the tray and handed the waiter a fifty-dollar bill. "Keep the change."

Three drinks later, the edge was off his panic, his breathing had returned to normal, and he was beginning to feel drowsy. He was back on the chair watching the snow slap against the windows as he tried to plot out the coming hours.

Twenty minutes later, he sat up straight as the thought hit him like a thunderbolt. Nellie! The old lady Lucy worked for part-time. She went to Florida for the winter. Lucy had said there was a going-away dinner for her not too long ago. That meant Nellie's house was empty. All he had to do was break in and watch and wait for Lucy to return home. Satisfied with his plan, Jonathan walked over to the king-size bed and pulled down the covers. His last conscious thought before sleep overtook him was, *Get in my way and you get what you deserve.*

The dream was always the same, and that night it was no different. Usually it came just before he was due to wake up, enabling him to remember the details clearly . . .

He was a vagrant, a bum in filthy clothes with rags tied around shoes that he'd stolen from someone else. He needed the rags because the shoes he was wearing were too big. He dragged his feet as he picked through garbage Dumpsters for aluminum cans and anything else he could sell or barter. He wanted to cry that he'd been reduced to picking through garbage to survive. Until a year ago, Leo Banks had had a good life, a nice apartment, a car, a pension plan, and a small amount of money in a savings account. Small because he liked fine things and didn't deny himself. He knew the value of savings and set aside what he could so that he could still enjoy a good life. He was, after all, only twenty-five, with a goal of retiring at forty. He had plenty of time to save for retirement. To him, the savings account was more of an emergency fund.

In his dream, he wondered what happened to the $2800.

He was whistling as he rode the elevator to the seventeenth floor. He smiled and waved at the receptionist who, for some reason, was ignoring him on that fine spring morning. It didn't matter. Then he noticed that no one else was greeting him or giving him high fives. Puzzled, he walked down the hall to his office and stopped short when he saw two men in dark suits waiting for him. He could feel his stomach start to flip-flop as he saw one of the men pull a set of handcuffs out of his pocket. His face draining of all color, he listened to the charges of embezzlement, then he was read his rights as he was led away, protesting that he hadn't done anything wrong. The conversation on the ride to police headquarters consisted of two words from the men: "Shut up."

He walked up a pair of dirty steps, careful not to get his new suit dirty by brushing against the walls. His handcuffs were removed before he was shoved into a room and told to sit and wait.

It was some kind of crazy mistake. He hadn't embezzled any money from anyone. Obviously, he needed a lawyer. If ever there was a time to use his emergency fund, this was it. He hoped his $2800 was enough to cover the up-front money all lawyers charged when they agreed to take on a client.

As he stewed and fretted, he heard a commotion outside the room. He likened the sounds to what he imagined a bomb scare would sound like. Walking to the door, he opened it to see cops, detectives, and office personnel running in all directions. He didn't stop to think but moved with lightning speed. It took him only a second to slide out the door and cross the room to the dirty steps and dingy walls. He never looked back.

He half ran and half walked down the street till he found a long narrow alley that led to other darker, smellier alleys until he came to where a group of homeless people lived. The little community of vagrants stared at him, but no one stopped or questioned him. He found a wooden lettuce crate oozing rotted lettuce and sat down. He hugged his arms around his chest as he struggled to get his emotions in check. He tried to figure out what had happened to bring him there. He sat for hours, his new neighbors watching him. When he started to cry, a toothless old woman came over and started to croon to him. He cried harder as he sobbed out his story. The old woman motioned to the others, who gathered close with offers of scraps of food and some water. One old man even offered half a cigarette.

"We won't tell," someone said. Frightened out of his wits he listened as his new best friends told him where he could get free food and a free bed for the night. Days, his friends said, were spent scavenging for things to sell and barter. The old lady told him to take off his fancy clothes and brought him a pile of rags to put on. She said she would wrap up his clothes and shoes, and put them away. He was so numb that he agreed.

Days later when he came out of his stupor, he tested out his disguise by walking past the police station with a few of his new friends and generally hanging out until the two detectives who had arrested him showed up. He walked right past them, deliberately jostling them. Both looked right through him with no sign of recognition.

Safe.

This, then, was his new life. He knew if he tried to use his ATM card, he'd be picked up within minutes. He also knew he would never be able to go back to his apartment. His new car would be repossessed. He couldn't risk calling any of his friends because they wouldn't want to get involved. That he knew as surely as he knew he had to keep breathing in order to stay alive.

Days passed, then weeks, and finally months. Almost a year to the day of his arrest, he looked into the backpack he'd found in someone's trash can, and counted out his money. He had $647 dollars and a gun that was fully loaded. The gun was stolen, too. It was payback time. He'd had a whole year to figure out who set him up for the embezzlement charge — his manager's son-in-law. With that knowledge under his belt, he spent three whole months with the help of his homeless friends tracking Adam Ligar and his every movement until he had his routine down pat.

"Dolly!" he called to the old woman. "It's time to get my suit cleaned and my shoes polished. D day!" The old crone cackled as she hurried off to get the suit and take it to the cleaners. An old man named Billy hauled out some rags and polished Jonathan's shoes by spitting on them. It was a perfect shine.

He cleaned up at a gas station and tied his hair back into a ponytail. His beard was on the scruffy side, but it would do.

It was time.

The meeting with Adam Ligar was at a steakhouse called the Barb Wire. He'd called earlier, arranged the appointment by saying he was interested in hiring a new broker and business manager and only had a few hours but a ton of money to invest. Ligar couldn't agree fast enough.

He'd chosen the Barb Wire because it was a dim and noisy bar where no one paid attention to anyone else. He kept reminding himself he was the one with the gun. Besides, he'd been a broker in training and could walk the walk and talk the talk. Which was exactly what he was going to do.

Leo looked at the slick little weasel sitting across from him. "Tell me how you'll invest my $750,000 if I decide to go with your firm."

Dollar signs flashed in Ligar's eyes. "You look familiar, do I know you?"

Leo shrugged. "I do a lot of business with a lot of people. Anything is possible." The weasel frowned.

"This place is just too crowded and noisy. Let's take a walk up to the park. It's a nice night. We can talk as we go along. If I like what you have to say, I'll hand over a check on our way back," Leo said.

"This certainly is a weird way of doing

business, but okay. Every day is a learning experience," the weasel said. He shrugged as much as to say, what the hell. "I have some good municipal bonds, a couple of triple A's, and a good up-and-coming high-tech stock called Sotech."

"That's a dog. You'll have to do better than that. Give me something that's going to make me some money. I want to retire at an early age."

"Where'd you get the seven-fifty? You transferring from another house?"

"No. It's an inheritance, and I don't want to lose it. My *real* portfolio is at Merrill Lynch."

"You know what, you remind me of a guy who used to work at our firm. He was arrested for embezzling money out of dormant accounts."

Leo laughed. "What happened to him?"

Ligar shrugged. "Don't know. Police lost him after they arrested him. Hasn't been seen since."

It was Leo's turn to shrug. "So, is that it, a few triple A's and a few munis?"

"If you can give me a few more days, I might be able to come up with something. You have to admit this is pretty short notice."

Leo looked up at the dark sky. Stars twinkled overhead. He was happy to see that the park was almost empty. Mothers were home with the kids; the old people were safe in their houses. A few runners and joggers and a stray bum were the only people he could see, and they were off in the distance. Perfect.

"Let's sit down for a minute. I want to think about something," Leo said, pointing to a park bench far enough off the path that no joggers or runners would bother them or, for that matter, even notice them, but close to a pay phone.

The weasel was antsy. "This park isn't as safe as it looks. People get mugged and killed here on a weekly basis."

"Uh-huh. Okay, Adam, hand it over."

"Hand what over?" the broker squeaked, fear rattling his voice.

"Your wallet. I mean business. The cops never got me after I escaped, as you well know. I was innocent. You lousy creep, you set me up. You're the one who embezzled the money. You were always logging on to my computer and my files. Stealing from the family is a no-no. C'mon, I don't have all day." The gun flashed in the sliver of moonlight that slid out from its cloud cover.

"You son of a bitch! I knew you looked familiar. Put that stupid gun away, Leo, before it goes off. I didn't set you up."

"I don't think so. Oh, yeah, you set me up. I've had a whole year to do nothing but think. Give me your wallet and the keys to that fancy Mercedes. Do it now, Adam, or I'll blow your damn head off."

"Listen, Leo, let's talk about this. We can work something out." He sounded like a whiny little kid who had dropped his ice cream in the dirt.

Leo clicked off the safety. It sounded exceptionally loud. He loved it that his old colleague was whining and begging. The gun was all-powerful.

"Okay, okay."

Leo eyed the little pile of personal effects, which included Adam's passport, on the bench. You got an ATM card, Adam?"

"Doesn't everyone?"

"I don't. Thanks to you. What's the pin number? Don't even think about lying to me." Adam rattled it off. Leo made a mental note of it.

"Now, we're going over to that pay phone, where you'll call your wife and tell her something came up and you're going out of town for a few days. Tell her you'll call her later. Make up one of those lies you're so good at. What's your home number?"

"It's 207-2323." Adam's voice was even shakier by then, all sound of belligerence gone. Eyes wary, he watched Leo dial his home number. "What are you going to do? C'mon, Banks, let's make a deal here."

"Like that's really going to happen. Stop whining. It's not manly. Say what I told you to say."

To make his point, Leo jabbed the gun into Adam's side as he started to talk. "Dorothy, something's come up, and I have to go to the Caymans. I think I'll be gone for three days or so. I'll call when I know more. Everything's fine. It's a guy who has a boatload of money he wants to invest. I sort of fell into it. You gotta strike while the iron's hot in this business. That's what your father told me when he hired me. Yeah, I love you, too."

"Does Dorothy know about you hopping the blonde in payroll and that waitress at Starbucks?" Leo asked as he forced the hapless broker to return to the park bench.

Adam was openly sweating in the cool spring evening. "You know she doesn't. What do you want, Banks? Look, if it's money, my wife has plenty. I can get it for you. Leo, if you shoot me, you'll go to jail for the rest of your life."

"I want everything you've got. Everything you stole from me. What I don't want is your wife's money. How much money is in your wallet?"

"About five hundred dollars."

"How much in the account with the ATM card?"

"Maybe forty-four hundred."

"How much can you take in one day?"

"Two thousand."

"What's the limit on your credit cards?"

"They're all maxed out except the Citi card. My limit is $7500. My wife likes to shop." Sniveling, he wiped his nose on the sleeve of his jacket. His eyes were wet and pleading.

Backing away from the man who had changed his life, Leo Banks digested the information before squeezing the trigger and shooting Adam Ligar smack between the eyes. He looked around to see if anyone was within eyesight or earshot. No one. Being careful not to get any blood on his clothes, Leo took five minutes to roll Adam off the bench and into a deep grove of shrubbery, where he removed Adam's jacket and shoes. He whipped off the broker's Rolex and stuffed it in his pocket. Let the police think Ligar was just another homeless man until they made a proper ID. Leo laughed all the way back to the

Barb Wire, where he picked up Adam's Mercedes and drove off.

Leo spent the next two hours driving from one ATM machine to the next, taking out as much money as he could. When he hit the magic number of $2000, the maximum Adam's bank allowed in one twenty-four-hour period, he tossed the ATM card in the nearest trash can. His next stop was an all-night drugstore, where he bought packages of underwear, socks, and shaving gear.

He registered at the Algonquin, where he showered, shaved, and ordered the biggest steak on the hotel's menu. In the morning, he shopped until the stores called a halt and said his card was overdrawn. It was fair. The charges equaled out to the amount in his 401k. Then he found a less-than-scrupulous car dealership and sold Adam's fancy Mercedes for seven thousand dollars, well under its twenty-thousand-dollar value. A bonus from Adam to him for the year he'd lived the life of a homeless bum. He left the dealership with a smile on his face as he trotted over to Citibank and cashed the check.

Then he visited the establishment of an "entrepreneur" he had come across in his year on the streets and had a photograph taken and carefully substituted for Adam Ligar's photograph on Ligar's passport. Then, to cover his tracks somewhat, he took a cab to Kennedy, where he took the shuttle to Washington. He had a cabbie take him to the nearest travel agency, where he booked a flight to London for later that day. At six-fifteen, Leo Banks boarded his flight.

When he set foot on British soil he became Jonathan St. Clair, Spiros Andreadis, Nathan Willowby, Dunston Craig, and a host of other identities.

12

Lucy woke slowly, savoring the warmth of the cocoon she was wrapped in. She sighed happily as she remembered where she was and what had transpired earlier. She reveled now in the warmth coming from the body next to her. A smile started to build on her lips. "Hmmm," she murmured. "You feel *soooo* good." She waited for a reply and when none was forthcoming, she frowned. Maybe Wylie was a sound sleeper. A *real* sound sleeper. She wiggled her leg, then her thigh and hip.

"Woof!"

Lucy bolted upright, her face registering a hundred different emotions all at the same time. "Coop! Sadie! Lulu!" And then, "Wylieeee!"

He came on the run, spatula in hand. She could tell he'd already showered because his hair was still wet, and he was dressed in jeans that hugged his lean frame and a muscle shirt that was tattered around the sleeves. NOTRE DAME was stenciled across the front. He even had shoes on, while she was buck-ass naked with three dogs curled alongside of her on top of the blanket. The fire was blazing, she could feel the heat.

"There's nothing like the body warmth of a dog," Wylie said happily. A sappy grin plastered itself on his face. Seeing the look of chagrin on Lucy's face, he started to babble. "I had to get up early to make sure Mitch got off okay. I helped him put chains on his tires. That was a workout in itself. You know how I like to run every morning. Well, if you don't know, I do. Since this snow I haven't been able to run, and that makes me feel like I'm cheating my body. Why are you letting me babble like this?" He waved the spatula in the air as Coop tried to jump up to get a lick.

Lucy enjoyed his sudden discomfort. "Did . . . did Mitch see me sleeping here?" Lucy asked as she finally got her tongue in working order.

"Uh-huh. Jake saw you here, too, when he came downstairs. I don't know this for a pure fact, but I don't think they know I was sleeping there, too, by you, alongside of you." He shook his head again, the spatula doing double time, as was Coop. "What I mean is I don't think they have any idea we had sex. I can't be sure, but I don't think so."

"I'm naked under this blanket, Wylie."

Wylie hopped from one foot to the other. "Yeah, I know." He lowered the spatula, and Coop grabbed it. The three dogs raced down the hall.

"Don't make my eggs with that spatula," Lucy said as she struggled to wrap the blanket around her. "I'm going to take a shower now. What time is breakfast?" she asked coldly.

"Okay, I see that you're ticked off at me. Whatever it is I did, I'm sorry. Are you mad that Jake's here? Listen, I can tell him in no uncertain terms that we did not have sex last night. I'll do that if it's what you want. Why would he even care, assuming he does know? He's married, he can have all the sex he wants."

Lucy shot him an evil grin as she got to her feet. She stormed off, muttering that men loved to brag about their sexual conquests.

"Not me. I'm not one of those men who brag about my sexual conquests."

"Liar!" Jake said as he entered the room, demanding to know when breakfast was being served. "Morning, Lucy, did you sleep well?"

"Shut up, Jake!" Lucy snarled as she made her way up the steps, the blanket trailing behind her.

"So you two had sex last night, huh? How was it? Was it everything you thought it would be?" Jake asked gleefully.

"Shut up, Jake, and it's none of your business if I had sex last night or not, and where the hell were you when it was time to put the chains on Mitch's truck? You were sleeping, that's where you were, because I could hear you snoring all night long. If I was doing that, how could I be having sex? Breakfast is right now. Don't you ever think about anything but food?"

"Prickly this morning, aren't we?" Jake smirked.

In the kitchen, Wylie turned to look at his friend, his face full of menace. "If you say one word, even intimate that you think we had sex, I am going to kick your ass out in the snow and let you freeze to death. Lucy is a sensitive person, and right now she's going through a difficult time. Women don't like it when men discuss what goes on between them. It's supposed to be a secret."

Jake stared at Wylie with keen interest. "You certainly are knowledgeable when it comes to women. You led me to believe you were a lost cause. You are an interesting case, Wylie. I might even decide to study you someday. C'mon, c'mon, I'm starving here. Four eggs and a load of that nice pink ham. I'll make the toast."

Upstairs, Lucy listened at the heating vent in the bathroom through which Wylie's and Jake's voices carried clearly. For the first time in days she giggled. With happiness. When was Jake leaving? She wished it was right then, so she could drag Wylie back to bed. Their night had been the most satisfying sex she'd ever had in her life. Wild, crazy, and wonderful.

As Lucy washed her hair, her womanly wiles surfaced. Maybe she could entice Wylie to go down to Nellie's house or over to Rachel Muller's house. Jake liked to take naps. A sterling idea. After all, there wasn't really anything else to do on a day like this but watch television or read a book. Television, book, sex. Only a fool would choose the first two.

Life was suddenly looking good, but the smile left her face and her mood darkened. How could she be thinking about sex when her life was in danger? Maybe she was losing her mind. Or, more likely, she'd already lost it. Shower over, her hair wrapped in a turban, Lucy wrapped a towel around her body as she padded to the window to look outside. All she could see was a blanket of whiteness. It had to be the blizzard of the century. Maybe two centuries. One thing for certain, Wylie wouldn't be going to the city. Probably not for the rest of the week. She crossed her fingers that the power wouldn't go out.

Lucy dressed in the same clothes she'd worn the day before. Later, she'd go to her own house for fresh clothes.

Brushing out her wet hair, she strained to hear Jake and Wylie talking in the kitchen. She cautioned herself that eavesdroppers never heard anything good about themselves. She shrugged when she heard both men grousing about the snowstorm. Wylie's terminology was extremely colorful, while Jake fretted that they might run out of food before the storm blew itself out.

As Lucy descended the stairs she tried to come up with a casual plan to pretend she hadn't slept with Wylie the night before. Never having been in a situation quite like this where a guest was in residence the *morning after,* she was unprepared as to how to handle it. She was in for some ribbing, she could almost guarantee it. *Alleged* sex. Uh-huh. Always fall back on legalities.

She needn't have worried. Jake did little more than nod because he was too busy eating and watching the weather report on the counter television. Wylie looked like a professional chef as he stirred, whipped, and flipped. A huge smile on his face, the kind men wear after a night of *alleged* rousing sex, he motioned her to sit down. She scowled.

"They're calling this a blizzard," Jake said, between mouthfuls of food. "Yesterday they said this was the worst storm in fifty years." He pointed to the kitchen window with his fork to make his point. "This morning they're saying it's the worst storm in a century. I sure hope you guys have good, solid roofs on your houses. There's gotta be at least a foot of snow on your house, Lucy. Yours, too, Wylie. Yep, this is definitely a blizzard."

Wylie slid a plate across the table to Lucy. The scrambled eggs looked light and fluffy. The ham was pink and succulent. The toast was just the right color, and the butter was soft. Perfect!

"Sooner or later the power is going to go out. We've been lucky so far. How are you fixed for wood, Wylie?" Lucy asked.

"I have a good-sized stack on the deck," Wylie said, sitting down across from Lucy. "Everything is shut down, the airports, the turnpike, the parkway. Even the post office and banks, and, of course, the schools. I think we're looking at the rest of the week here. When it stops, it's going to take days to dig out. It's a bit of a reprieve for you, Lucy, as far as the feds go. I wish you'd call the FBI and tell them we suspect Jonathan was here yesterday. I know, I know, the footprints are gone. You need to document everything. Call and even if they pooh-pooh it away, it will make me feel better. Tomorrow is Thanksgiving. It's kind of sad when you think about it. Thanksgiving is when families are supposed to be together. I bet a lot of people whose travel plans fell through with the weather will be eating weenies and whatever is in their freezers. We're the lucky ones, Lucy, we're together with the dogs, and Jake is here. Personally, I'd like to see our table filled with friends and family, but if this is all we get, I'll take it."

Lucy nodded solemnly, pleased at how Wylie viewed the holiday she always considered so special.

"Now, Friday is normally part of that holiday, then the Christmas season kicks in. Marooned until next Monday. Woohoo! When are you leaving, Jake?" This all was said so happily, Lucy had to stifle the laugh that was bubbling up in her throat.

Lucy almost choked on the ham in her

mouth. She could hardly wait to hear Jake's answer.

"Well, it's like this. The airports are going to be backed up for days. I think I'll rent a car and drive back as soon as the roads open. Have I worn out my welcome already?"

Wylie didn't look the least bit embarrassed. "Of course not. Stay as long as you like. I was just curious. So, gang, what should we do today?"

Jake pondered the question, his dark eyebrows knitting until they met in the center of his forehead. "I'm going to go online and see if I can find out a little more about Lucy's predicament. I want to e-mail some colleagues. You know, just in case your power goes out. I hate wasting time. Not to worry, I'll be out of your way. How about you guys?"

"I'm going to work out for a while. I've been thinking about taking out the snowblower to clear Rachel's driveway." Wylie turned to look at Lucy. "Nellie has that big deep freezer in her garage. What do you think the chances are there might be a turkey in there or at least a very big chicken?"

"A very good chance. Nellie belongs to a food service that delivers sides of beef all cut up and packaged, plus all kinds of food. I think Rachel may belong to it, too. Nellie loves to cook and feeds half the neighborhood. You know that. You've been one of her recipients many times. When Rachel Muller was sick this past spring, Nellie cooked for her and her husband for two full weeks because Gerhard can't even boil water."

"Good! I'll use the snowblower on Nellie's driveway, too. See," Wylie said, waving his fork in the air, "now we have a plan. Jake, you clean up, I'm going to work out. How about you, Lucy?"

"What kind of equipment do you have in your workout room?"

"A treadmill, a cycle, a rowing machine, weight bench, a universal. Want to join me?"

"I'll take the treadmill. My ankle feels good enough now. If I start out slow, it should be okay. Lead the way," Lucy said, tossing her napkin on the table.

Wylie's workout room was just that, a workout room. Aside from the carpeted floor and the exercise equipment, a television sitting on a bracketed shelf attached to the wall, and a pile of books and legal pads in the corner, there was nothing else in the room, not even a chair.

Wylie turned on the television with a remote. Martha Stewart was preparing a wild rice/chestnut dressing for the turkey she was about to cook.

Lucy climbed on the treadmill, hooked on the heart monitor, set the grade, and began by warming up. She walked, then jogged before she broke into a run at 4.5.

Forty minutes later, she looked down at the distance button and saw that she had already gone four miles. Her normal routine was a ten-mile run. When the numbers changed to read five miles, she felt the first twinge in her ankle. She slowed a little, but the twinge turned into a sharp pain. She stumbled and was about to yank out the safety key when Wylie caught her; otherwise, she would have fallen. "What's wrong?"

"I think I overdid it. I should have quit at four miles. If you have an Ace bandage, I might be able to nip this in the bud."

Wylie raced off and returned with an elastic foot brace. Lucy sat down on the treadmill while Wylie pulled off her Nike. She pulled on the foot brace, stood up with Wylie's help, and tried putting pressure on her foot. She nodded. "It feels okay. I'll just give it a rest while you work out, or I can make some coffee."

Wylie smiled. "Stay, I like the company. You sure you're okay?"

"I'm okay. Listen, I'm sorry about my surly attitude earlier."

"Yeah, me too. I don't want you to feel embarrassed. We're all adults here."

Lucy nodded. "While I was taking a shower I was thinking we could either go to Rachel's or Lucy's house and . . . and . . ."

Wylie almost dropped the hundred-pound weight he was holding, onto his foot. His eyes took on a glazed look as sweat dripped down the front of the muscle shirt. "And . . ." he prodded.

Laughter bubbled up in Lucy's throat. "And . . . we could look for a turkey in their respective freezers."

"You're a smart-ass, Lucy Baker," Wylie said as he placed the weight on the end of the bar. "That's not what you were thinking at all, and you know it. You know you want to ravage and plunder this finely muscled, sinewy body of mine. Admit it!"

This time Lucy let the laughter escape her lips. "And you're a mind reader too. Keep pumping that iron. I like my men *hard*. Hey, what *are* those books over there in the corner? Are you researching something?"

"I'm working on my thesis. You aren't

the only one who is fed up with the legal profession. I want to teach, not practice law. By this time next year, if all goes well, I'll be teaching political science some-where."

"That's wonderful, Wylie. You never said a word, why?"

"You never asked. I'm not one of those guys who runs around yelling, hey, look at me, I'm going for my doctorate. Actually, I'm kind of shy."

Lucy laughed again. "Yeah, right. You weren't shy last night."

Wylie could feel his ears turn pink. "Correct me if I'm wrong here, but who was it who was gasping, hoo hoo hoo! You weren't exactly a shrinking violet. Hell, you were the whole damn bouquet."

Lucy grinned. She was loving this. The mornings after with Jonathan had always been so . . . stiff and cold. "That's a com-pliment, right?"

Wylie leered at her. "Damn straight it was a compliment. The best I can give. It was a great night, Lucy. I'd like to do it again. I could just kick myself that I never allowed Nellie to introduce us. Look at all the time we wasted."

"Everything happens for a reason, Wylie. Back then, it probably wouldn't have worked. Think of all the fun we can have *making up* for lost time."

Wylie groaned as he replaced the weights and rolled over onto his stomach. He propped his chin in his hands to stare up at Lucy. "This isn't fun and games with me, Lucy. I care about you. I really do. There's some baggage we have to clear away first before we can have a serious relationship. Just so you know, I get a little *schizy* about rebound relationships. I don't want to be the interim boyfriend. My parents are gonna love you."

Tears pricked at Lucy's eyes. She didn't trust herself to say anything. She reached out to him. Wylie took her in his arms and held her close. There was nothing sexual in the embrace, just warm comfort and a new bonding. "I think we belong together," Wylie whispered in her ear. Lucy nodded.

"When should I get the ring?" Wylie laughed, breaking the moment.

"The minute this snow stops and the stores reopen. Just a little one, Wylie, a carat," she teased.

"You got it," he teased back. "Okay, let's fortify ourselves with some coffee before we head down to Nellie's house. God, would you look at that snow!"

"You look at it. I'd rather look at your

handsome puss," Lucy said as she pushed him down the hallway to the kitchen.

Once the coffee was ready and they sat down at the kitchen table, Wylie turned serious. "We really didn't talk much about yesterday. How are you feeling about all that?"

Lucy knew Wylie wasn't referring to their night in front of the fire. "I don't know what to think. I think Mitch and his friend were as befuddled as I am. Why in the world does Jonathan need so much security? What *is* this all about? Do you think Jonathan was bringing people illegally into the country or bringing in drugs, and that's why he needed a safe house? I am never going to understand this, Wylie."

"If you want my opinion, and it's just my opinion, I think it's all about money. The amounts of money the feds told you about are not chicken feed. Always follow the money. I think this is about *very large sums of money.* Money laundering. I'd stake my bank account on it. Think about it, Lucy. He moves money, different amounts each time, say from England to France, to maybe Latvia, three places total. Normal transactions. No one is going to pay attention to three transactions. It's done twenty-four/seven. Then maybe on to the Channel Islands or maybe the Marshall Islands. Multiply that by say fifty transactions, different locations, different amounts, and you come up with *kazillions* of dollars. All he needs is one man in the wire transfer room on his payroll, and your guy is golden. God alone knows what his cut is. I bet he has safe houses all over the globe. That house in Watchung is just one of many. If he smells trouble, he's gone. I bet you 'Jonathan' has dozens of identities. You following me?"

"Yes. Yes, I am. You could be right, Wylie. It makes sense. He wouldn't want to give up his citizenship, but if he did, and he married me, he would always be able to come back here if he wanted to. Assuming no one was on his trail. Yes, I think you're right. The last thing he ever expected was for me to catch on. I wouldn't have, either, if those agents hadn't come up to me that day when I was running. In a million years I never would have believed any of this. Never. I feel so stupid," Lucy said vehemently.

Wylie's voice was soothing when he said, "There's no need for you to feel stupid, Lucy. The guy's a slick con. He worked overtime to cover everything up. It doesn't matter how you were alerted, you were, and now the playing field has shifted."

Lucy ran her hands through her still-damp hair. "For God's sake, Wylie, I'm a lawyer. I should have picked up on something. Now that I think back, there were all kinds of clues. I was blind. The worst thing is, I don't think I was ever in love with him, and yet I was going to marry him. I *think* I was going to marry him. Maybe I wasn't," she dithered. "I sure put off addressing those wedding invitations long enough. I am almost one hundred percent convinced I would not have gone through with it." There, she'd said the words aloud, and she meant them.

Wylie's chest puffed out. He smiled. "I don't think you would have gone through with it either. You know why. You told me the guy doesn't like dogs. You'd never get rid of Sadie, would you?"

"No more than you would get rid of Coop. You know what, Wylie, you're really a nice guy. I like you a lot. Bushels in fact. And, you make decent coffee, too. Your meat loaf ain't half-bad either."

Wylie's chest puffed out even farther. He couldn't wait to take this young woman home to meet his family. This was *the one*. He could feel it from the top of his head right down to his toes. At last he'd found the sock to mate to his shoe. His mother always said for every old shoe there's an old sock. It wasn't a very romantic saying, but he finally knew what she meant. He didn't know how he knew, but he knew that Lucy Baker would love him, warts and all, just as he would love her.

Wylie and Lucy both beamed when Jake entered the kitchen. "Are we doing lunch?" His voice was hopeful as his gaze roamed the neat, tidy kitchen.

"No, we're doing coffee. Wylie and I are going over to Rachel's and Nellie's houses to see what we can scrounge up. If you pick all the meat off that ham bone, I can make some split pea or bean soup for supper, or I can make us some pot pies. You decide while we go on the hunt for Thanksgiving dinner. I feel like a Pilgrim, don't you, Wylie?"

Wylie threw back his head and laughed until tears rolled down his cheeks. Lucy and Wylie dressed as warmly as they could, layering sweatshirts and parkas. The boots were the last to go on. Lucy fingered the keys to her house in the pocket of her jacket before she pulled on fuzzy, pink mittens. Adjusting the scarf around her neck and over the lower part of her face, she said, "Okay, I'm ready. I want to go to my house to get some clean clothes first. Rachel's house is closest to mine, so let's hit it after my house. If we find enough food, we might not have to go to Nellie's."

Wylie nodded as he opened the door. Snow and cold air *swooshed* into the foyer. It took both of them to pull the heavy oak door shut behind them.

It was ten-thirty when the couple exited the house.

"I'll go first," Wylie said. "Step into the footprints I leave. It will be easier. Jeez, this snow is up to my thighs."

It took them thirty minutes to fight their way through the snow and wind across the wide expanse of yard to Lucy's house. Both of them were exhausted when Lucy fitted the key into the lock with numb hands. The moment they were inside, Wylie stomped his feet before kicking off his boots to dump the snow out of them. His wool socks were cold and wet. So were Lucy's.

"I have socks," Lucy said. "Dry out our boots while I get my clothes and the socks. Check my thermostat, Wylie, and set the faucet in the laundry room sink to drip. I don't want my pipes to freeze up."

"My feet are like ice," Lucy said when she returned with the socks. "Let's put them in the dryer so they're warm when we put them on." The clothes in her hand went into a plastic bag she tied around her waist.

"We're crazy, you know that, right?" Wylie said five minutes later as he pulled on a pair of Lucy's socks. "I hope you have spares because the same thing is going to happen when we get to Rachel's house and then, if necessary, Nellie's."

"You're right. Wait here." Lucy ran back upstairs and returned with a bundle of rolled-up socks. She added them to the plastic bag.

"Okay, heat's fine, water's dripping. Let's go."

Lucy opened the door, the arctic chill, driving snow, and the fierce wind drove her backward. Wylie stiff-armed her as they fought together to close the door and lock it.

"Same drill, Lucy, walk in my footprints. I'm going in a straight line, catercorner to Rachel's house. Stay close," Wylie shouted, to be heard over the ferocious wind.

Easier said than done, Lucy thought as she struggled to step into the indentations Wylie made in the snow. The problem was, he had long-legged strides, and by the time she was ready to plop her left foot down, she fell down instead. Wylie picked her up seven times before they made it across the street to Rachel Muller's house. Both of them were breathing like racehorses when Wylie finally made it to the overhang of the walk-through door leading into the garage. Inside, they both fell to their knees, struggling to breathe normally.

"This is crazy, Wylie. Why can't we just eat hot dogs tomorrow? Thanksgiving is about giving thanks, not about food. God, I wish I was sunning my butt in Florida or some tropical paradise."

Wylie groaned. "C'mon, we have to get in the house. I'll turn the heat up to warm us. We'll change socks and dry out our boots before we head out again."

Lucy started to laugh then and couldn't stop as Wylie led her into the kitchen.

"What's so funny?" Wylie demanded as he cranked up the thermostat.

"Remember when I told you I thought we could come here or Nellie's house and make out away from Jake? Boy, was that ever wishful thinking."

Wylie flopped down on one of the kitchen chairs. He was still breathing hard as he struggled to get out of his ski jacket. "If you told me right now you wanted to hit the sheets, I'd have to tell you no can do."

"Don't give it another thought. I don't

have the strength to take off my clothes. This is so damn crazy. Tell me again why we're here."

"Because nobody eats hot dogs on Thanksgiving. I'm trying to be a good host here, Lucy, even if we're stealing food from our beloved neighbors. Ask yourself if you want to see Jake waste away to nothing. Then there's Coop. He'll go ballistic if he doesn't get his meat loaf. I live for that dog."

"Ahhh." Lucy sighed. "It's getting warmer. Tell you what, Wylie. Find a towel, and I'll rub your feet if you rub mine. Then we'll put on warm socks."

"Okay, but I can't get up. It took us twenty minutes to cross the street, but I've had four-hour workouts that didn't leave me this drained. You must be exhausted. I'd come over there and sit with you, but I can't move."

"Stay where you are. I am beyond exhausted. Let's just sit here. Don't talk. Dream. Do anything but move or talk. Whatever you do, don't go to sleep."

"Okay."

Then Lucy broke her own order. "We don't even know if Rachel has a turkey or a chicken in her freezer. What if this was for nothing, Wylie?"

"I'll kill myself. If there is one, let's not go to Nellie's house, okay? God, I hate snow, this snow in particular. Hey, I'm starting to sweat."

"Shut up, Wylie. I told you not to talk. If you keep talking, you won't have to kill yourself, I'll kill you."

"Oooh, I love it when you talk like that." Wylie slid off the chair and rolled over to where Lucy was sitting. "If we get married, do you think we'll fight? Will we ever go to bed angry with each other? How many kids do you want? We should get a cat, too, and maybe a bird. A real menagerie."

"Yeah, okay. You sure do talk a lot."

"That's why I am going to make an outstanding teacher. Come on, Lucy, we can't stay here. Let's get this show on the road. I want to go home and take a nap."

"*Wuss*," Lucy said, staggering to her feet. She peeled off her jacket, tossed it on the floor, and ripped off her cold, wet socks. She tossed dry socks from her sack at Wylie and told him to empty out their boots.

Together, they checked Rachel Muller's deep freezer in the garage. "Oooh, tell me this isn't the mother lode," Wylie said, moving freezer packages. "And she labels everything, too, with the date."

Lucy watched as Wylie withdrew two ten-pound capons and set them on the floor. Five packages of ground sirloin came out next. "What else do you want? She has a ton of frozen vegetables, even sugared sweet potatoes with marshmallows. Told you this was the mother lode," he said as he piled up packages of frozen vegetables.

Lucy looked at the pile of food. "We can eat off the chickens for a day or so with leftovers. The ground sirloin is for Coop. Let's take a pork loin. We can always come back if we run out. Take some bread and those Sara Lee cakes. It might take a while for delivery trucks to make it to the supermarkets. We'll be okay because we still haven't explored Nellie's freezer. God, I am so glad we don't have to trudge all the way down there. I don't think I could make it."

Wylie pointed to the pile of food on the floor. Frozen food was heavy. "How are we going to get this home?"

"I guess we have to bag it and tie it around our necks or our waists. Hey, look, there's a sled hanging on the wall. Rachel's grandson comes to visit, so I guess the sled is for him."

"Nah, we don't have anything to tie it on with. Besides, it will be more trouble to pull the sled than it will be to drag the sacks. We'll double some garbage bags and just drag them behind us. Unless you have a better idea."

"Nope. Let's do it."

"It should be easier going home since we made tracks coming here."

"Yeah, well, those tracks are probably full of snow by now," Lucy grumbled.

Back inside Rachel's house, Lucy dressed, rummaged for plastic sacks for the food as Wylie turned the thermostat down to seventy and let the faucet in the kitchen sink drip. Within ten minutes they were ready for the trek home, with each of them dragging one of the sacks of food.

"You're right, Lucy, I feel like a damn Pilgrim on the hunt. I'd beat my chest, but I'm too damn tired."

Lucy knew Wylie was talking, but his voice was carried away on the wind. Her head down, she concentrated on stepping into the tracks he made. She lost track of time and was so exhausted she bumped into him when he came to an abrupt stop. She was colder than she'd ever been in her life. She couldn't feel her feet inside the high rubber boots. All she knew was they were full of snow. "What's wrong?" she managed to gasp.

"I don't know how to tell you this, but I overshot my house. We're at Nellie's house."

"Nellie's house!" Lucy screamed. "Nellie's house!" she screamed again.

"Lucy, I can't see in front of my face. Yeah, Nellie's house. It looks like we're in her driveway. I know it's her house because I can see that metal sun sculpture she has nailed to the garage door under the overhang. You know what else. Someone is here because there are footprints going around to the back."

"Who cares? It's probably Nellie's grandson. More than likely he got stranded at the train station and made it here. He lives in South Plainfield. Let's go, Wylie. Get your bearings and move. I can't believe we're at Nellie's house. Weren't you a Boy Scout?"

"No, I wasn't a Boy Scout. I was too busy mowing lawns, shoveling snow, and delivering papers. God, I hate snow — or did I say that already! I feel like a damn packhorse," Wylie said as he turned around and moved across the virgin snow toward his own house. Lucy followed him blindly.

If it hadn't been snowing so heavily, or if the wind hadn't suddenly ratcheted up, one or the other of them might have seen the curtain on the upstairs bedroom window move as a man peered out of it.

13

At seven o'clock that morning Jonathan St. Clair let his gaze sweep the hotel room he'd been staying in. He grimaced at the cowhide suitcase, thinking of the cheap European clothes inside. He fumbled around inside until his fingers touched the canvas fanny pack that held numerous passports, matching IDs, and a stack of CD-Rs. The laptop glared up at him. Take it or not take it. Better to leave it, but first he had to dismantle it, just in case he wasn't able to return to the hotel.

Working with an economy of motion, Jonathan ripped out the motherboard and stuffed it into his fanny pack. Now, he was ready to go.

Just minutes ago, he'd used the laptop to access MapQuest to get directions to Lucy's house. But instead of listing Lucy's address, he'd substituted the words, Golden Acres Shopping Center. He copied down the information, then deleted the request.

Jonathan walked back over to the window. Suddenly, he felt nervous, uneasy.

He didn't like the feeling. Not at all. He felt bile rising in his throat, the heavy breakfast threatening to erupt. Was he losing his edge? "Three strikes and you're out," he muttered.

Never a serene person, he realized he was fast coming up on strike three.

First it was Lucy and her strange behavior. The second was his decision to put his business on hold and fly to the States. Third was this unprecedented snowstorm and the house in Watchung that was compromised. Maybe he was on strike four and too stupid to recognize it. He shivered with the draft coming in around the windows. So much for hermetically sealed windows.

Jonathan shivered, not with cold but a mixture of fear and apprehension.

According to MapQuest, it was a little over four miles to the shopping center near to where Lucy lived. Knock off a quarter of a mile, and it was still almost four miles. Would he survive in the weather outside? Not unless he had a pair of boots. He shivered again as he imagined being brought down for lack of a pair of storm boots. Well, that wasn't going to happen.

His heavy wool coat over his arm, Jonathan marched to the door and thrust it open. He half expected to see the maids working in the hallway, but it was empty. That meant no one would be getting clean sheets.

The elevator was full when he stepped in and rode to the lobby. He wasn't surprised to see the milling crowds of people, some sleeping on the leather furniture or in the wooden chairs in the lobby restaurant. He took his time as he meandered around looking at people's feet, then at his own. Most of the men were wearing either Brooks Brothers tasseled loafers or wing tips like he was wearing.

Jonathan walked to the back entrance, hoping to see a door labeled MAINTE-NANCE. When he found it, he knocked softly and opened the door. The room was empty. Seeing no boots, he backed off and walked toward the glass doors that led out to the snow-filled parking lot, where hundreds of cars were parked every which way, all covered with mountains of snow. He didn't know if it was his imagination or not, but it looked like the snow was abating somewhat.

He saw the maintenance workers then. Some with shovels, some with snowblowers. All were fighting a losing battle. All the men he could see wore high, rubber boots. Now, all he had to do was get a pair of those boots. Eventually, one or more of them would take a break, come indoors, and go to the maintenance room, where he would be waiting.

Jonathan backtracked and boldly walked toward the maintenance room, where he opened the door and walked inside as though he belonged there. As far as he could tell, no one paid him any attention. He held his breath to see if anyone followed him into the room demanding to know what he was doing. His sigh was mighty when nothing happened. He looked at his watch — 7:30.

He waited.

It was nine o'clock when the door finally opened and two weary men stepped into the room. Jonathan watched from his position behind a tall metal cabinet as both men shed their plastic outerwear, winter clothing, and heavy, rubber boots. The taller of the two men rummaged in a bag on the floor and brought out a huge Thermos of coffee. He poured for both of them. Neither man said a word as they gulped at the hot drink. When they finished their coffee, the same man reached again into the canvas bag and brought out an ordinary-looking kitchen timer. Jonathan could hear the clicks on the timer as the man turned it on. He waited five minutes, then another five minutes before he stepped out from behind the metal cabinet. Both men were sound asleep, both snoring loudly. Cautiously, he removed both men's boots, stepped into one pair, folding down the others and stuffing them into the canvas bag along with his wing tips. He looked back at the men. Neither had moved. He was almost to the door when he remembered he needed a hat. He ran back and snatched a wool cap off the table. His nose wrinkled at the cheap scent that wafted past his nose as he drew the hat down as far as it would go over his ears.

Three minutes later he was outside, trying to make his way to the driveway that led to the road. He had memorized the MapQuest directions and knew exactly where he was going. All he needed was to get to his destination.

By the time Jonathan worked his way to the front of the hotel and the downward-sloping driveway, he was already exhausted. The boots were impossibly heavy, and, before he knew what was happening, he was on his rear end, sliding down the partially cleared drive. When he finally used the heels of the boots to bring himself to a skidding stop, snow had ballooned up and around him, going up his sleeves and down his boots. Overhead, the stinging flakes beat against his face as it covered him better than any blanket. He looked over his shoulder and saw the handles of the green canvas bag at the top of the driveway. He had no conscious memory of dropping the bag. It looked, from what he could see, like it was in a drift. If the snow continued the way it was, it would be covered completely in another hour. It would be sheer torture to try and make his way back to the top of the driveway. So he would lose his wing tips. He made the decision to leave the bag.

Somehow, Jonathan managed to get to his feet. As far as the eye could see, there was nothing but a vast wasteland of snow. There was no sign of humanity, no cars, no trucks, no sign of life. He knew, as he climbed over a steep snowdrift, that to his right was the Metro train station. All he had to do was make it to the traffic light, cross over, and he would be on Wood Avenue. A steep hill if he chose to go that way. Or, he could make a left on Route 27 and walk to the town of Metuchen, where he would then follow Central Avenue to Edison. There he would make another left on Park Avenue and take that directly to the development where Lucy lived.

His head down, Jonathan trudged on, opting to take Route 27 in the hope snowplows had been through earlier.

Time lost all meaning as Jonathan urged his body and his feet to cooperate.

He talked to himself when the images of warm waterfalls and tropical breezes failed to help him. He cursed and vented, his lips blue with cold.

It was eleven-thirty by his watch when he came to an intersection.

Jonathan had yet to see a human being or a vehicle. He kept slogging forward, past Saint Joe's School for Boys on the left, private homes on the right. He trudged up a small hill and saw a huge sign that said CHARLIE BROWN'S RESTAURANT.

The scarf around his neck was full of ice and bone cold on his neck. He knew he was in trouble when he started to feel light-headed. Would he die out there?

He heard the sound, saw dim yellow lights through the swirling snow, and knew instantly that it was a snowplow. He didn't stop but kept moving. The plow turned right. There was supposed to be a traffic light, but it was out. It had to be Park Avenue.

Jonathan turned and followed the plow. It was easier going. Maybe he wouldn't die after all. Still, it took him another twenty minutes to trudge to the gas station on the corner of Stephenville Parkway and Park Avenue. He walked the half block, falling twice, face-first into the snow. He managed to get to his feet knowing he was close to Nellie's house. Just a little farther. He literally staggered to the corner of David Court and turned right. He fell again, got up, and fell back down. He rolled and rolled, over and over, until he came to the first house on David Court. Using the last of his strength, he struggled to his feet, forged his way up the driveway and around to the side door of the garage. With his elbow, he smashed one of the small panes of glass, slid his hand inside, and undid the lock. He literally fell through the open door.

The boots were the first thing to come off before he entered the kitchen. He felt drunk when he lurched his way to the thermostat to turn it up. When he went back to the garage to close and lock the door he thought he heard voices. *I must be delirious.*

Back inside Nellie's house, he looked around. Other than the furnishings, the house had the exact same layout as Lucy's. He started to shed his clothes as he made his way to the first-floor bathroom, where he turned on the shower. Thank God there was hot water. His body burned and tingled as he stood under the steaming spray. Maybe he should use cold water, tepid water. Like hell.

He still wasn't sure if he was going to die or not. He told himself at that point he didn't even care. All he wanted was to be warm again.

When the hot water ran cold, Jonathan stepped from the shower and put on Nellie's flannel bathrobe, hanging on the back of the door. He shuffled out of the steamy bathroom in search of liquor. He found a bottle of cognac and a bottle of apricot brandy in one of the kitchen cabinets. He couldn't get the bottle to his lips fast enough. When his throat and stomach protested, he capped the bottle.

The house was cozy warm as he made his way to the second floor, the brandy bottle clutched tightly in his hand. He'd read somewhere that old people liked to use electric blankets. He hoped Nellie was one of those people. She was. He turned the blanket to high before he pulled down the covers. While he waited for the bed to warm up, he rummaged in Nellie's drawers and found a pair of flannel pajamas. Nellie must be fat, he decided as he climbed into them. One leg into the pajama bottom, he jerked to awareness and hobbled to the bedroom window when he heard what he thought was Lucy's voice. And then another voice carried on the wind. A man's voice. Lucy and a man, literally outside this house. A devilish smile ripped across his face. He yanked at the pajama bottom as he made his way to the bed. "Glad to know where I can find you, Lucy. See you later . . ."

Jonathan fell into the bed. He had the presence of mind to turn off the blanket before he pulled the covers up to his chin. His last conscious thought was that he wasn't going to die after all. The watch on his wrist said the time was 1:12.

Jake and the dogs were waiting in the foyer when Lucy opened the door. Wind and snow spiraled through. Coop reared up and started to howl. Sadie followed suit. Lulu danced around in a circle, yapping and growling.

"We must look like something from another planet," Wylie said. "It's us!" he said to the howling dogs as he dropped his sack of food. The moment he ripped off his dark hat, the dogs stopped their racket.

"You look . . . frozen," Jake said.

"Guess what, Jake, we *are* frozen. You're in charge of this food," Wylie said, pointing to the sacks of food that were dripping melted snow onto the floor. "Lucy and I are going to get into some warm clothes and sit by the fire. I don't know when I've ever been this exhausted."

Lucy just shook her head as she stepped out of her boots and weaved her way to the steps. "I'm going to take a warm bath. I'd appreciate it, Jake, if you'd make a blazing fire. I'm going to wrap myself in a blanket and take a nap."

"Me, too," Wylie said. "You're in charge, Jake."

"Hey, Lucy, the FBI called. They want you to call them back. The agent said it was urgent. I left the number by the phone in the family room. And, before you can ask, they said they got Wylie's number from the phone book. I guess they assumed you would be here. Those guys don't miss a trick. I didn't confirm or deny but said if I saw you, I'd give you the message."

Lucy's response was to raise her middle finger high over her head. Jake chuckled as he picked up the sacks of food, a happy smile on his face. He wasn't going to starve after all.

It was seven o'clock, and time to wake up his hosts, when Jake set the table. The timer for the oven pinged, confirming his intention. Ah, his Bisquick biscuits were done. They were a rich golden color. Perfect. The pot on top of the stove held chili, the only thing he really knew how to cook. He hoped he hadn't made it too hot. He himself loved hot, the hotter the better. Who was he kidding? He loved food, anything that was chewable. He'd chopped onions and grated cheese to sprinkle on top of the robust meal. He'd even baked the pie he'd found pushed back behind bags of soup bones in the freezer. The expiration date on the box said the pie had expired six months ago. He ignored the date and cooked it anyway. Pie was pie, and it was frozen, so how could it be bad?

He'd played housekeeper all afternoon while his hosts slept. He'd replenished the fire three or four times, cleaned the hallway, set the capons in cold water in the laundry room sink to thaw, put everything else away, then watched the snow fall outside.

Jake walked over to the sliding glass doors, where he turned on the deck lights. Damn, it was still snowing. Perhaps not as heavily, but it was still coming down.

He went into the family room, where he bent down to wake up his hosts. "Rise and shine, boys and girls, dinner is ready. It's seven-thirty, and it is still snowing. Chop-chop. I slaved all afternoon in the kitchen, and I don't want it to get cold."

Lucy stretched inside the quilt she was wrapped in. She felt blissfully warm and contented. "Seven-thirty at night!"

"Uh-huh. You've been asleep for over five hours. It's supposed to snow through the night and finally stop by midmorning tomorrow."

"What did you cook, Jake? Hey, I thought you didn't know how to cook," Wylie grumbled as he kicked his quilt aside.

Jake flapped his arms to get them to move. "My one and only specialty, red-hot chili. We have biscuits and pie and, of course, fresh coffee. Let's go, let's go. I'm starving."

Lucy was on her hands and knees trying to get upright. Every muscle and bone in her body protested. Jake reached out a hand to pull her to her feet. She winced in pain as she limped her way to the downstairs bathroom.

Jake braced his feet solidly on the floor before he held out his hand to Wylie.

"Son of a bitch," Wylie seethed. "I hurt, Jake."

"Stop whining and get your ass upstairs

and cleaned up. Work the kinks out."

Wylie eyed the stairway and knew he couldn't make his legs go up them. "I'll just wait for Lucy to come out. So the FBI called . . ."

"Yeah, and they sounded . . . pissed that neither you nor Lucy was here. They did say it was urgent, Wylie. I think Lucy should call them after dinner."

"Yeah, well, that's Lucy's decision," Wylie said as he staggered, with Jake's help, toward the downstairs bathroom. His eyes shut, he leaned wearily against the wall and waited for Lucy to come out.

Lucy pushed her chair away from the table. "That was really good, Jake. I ate way too much. Where did you learn to make biscuits?"

"I followed the directions on the box. It wasn't like I had anything else to do. You guys were wiped out, and I didn't know how long you'd sleep. How about some pie?"

Lucy shook her head, as Wylie said, "A small piece and some more coffee. Lucy's right, Jake. The chili was hot and delicious. Thanks for taking over."

Jake bustled about the kitchen but talked as he worked. "Lucy, are you going to call that guy at the FBI?"

"In the morning. What could he possibly have to tell me that's urgent? The morning is time enough, and besides, it's almost ten o'clock. They're just guessing that I'm here. Somebody probably alerted them that we were in Watchung. Like that's urgent. I've read enough novels about the FBI to know everything they do or say is urgent with them. I told you before, I don't trust them. I think I just overreacted yesterday. There's no way Jonathan could get here in this storm. If I had to take a wild guess as to the 'urgent' call, I'd say they probably have information that he's on a flight here or his flight is grounded. I'll start to worry when there's something more for me to sink my teeth into." Lucy grinned suddenly. "Let's not forget these three killer dogs who are guarding us. As I said, morning is time enough."

"Lucy, this might be a good time for me to start testing you if you're up to it. I'd like you to develop your powers of ESP so you can call on them if you ever find yourself in a dangerous situation.

"Do you remember when I first got here, I told you both about the Pentagon's secret projects. They wanted to investigate extrasensory phenomena to see if the sheer power of the human mind could be harnessed to perform various acts of espionage. It was written up in the *New York Times* sometime during the mideighties. They spent millions of dollars, according to three different reports. I'm in the process of trying to track all this down. I don't know what it will mean other than to prove maybe you're one of those people whose mind can be harnessed. I don't think we're talking espionage here, but maybe something damn close to it. On the other hand, it could really have nothing to do with you, and your condition is just temporary, a freak occurrence that will dissipate in time."

"I don't want to be a freak of nature. I just want it to go away," Lucy said.

"No, Lucy, you don't want it to go away until this crisis is over. You and I are going to go in a quiet room, and I'm going to work with you. We'll see if we can rein your, ah, new talent, in to the point where you can control it and call upon it if you need to. I am almost certain, when your life returns to normal, your . . . talent will fade away. We should get a weather update before we start."

Wylie looked up from his pie. "Why?"

Jake shrugged.

When Coop and Sadie barreled through the laundry room and raced to the sliding doors Lucy bolted out of her chair. "You didn't close the blinds, Wiley," she admonished as she ran into the windowless laundry room.

"What the hell . . ." Wylie, too, was off his chair, running toward the sliding doors. Coop was growling and snarling as he raced back and forth, Sadie on his heels. Lulu cowered by Jake's feet, begging to be picked up. He obliged.

The little dog's trembling limbs brought Jake to attention. "Lock the damn doors, Wylie. *NOW!*" Wylie didn't have to be told twice. He slammed the latch into place and dropped the dowel standing in the corner into the track. He looked confused when he turned around to stare at Jake.

Lulu in one hand, the cordless phone in the other along with the sticky Post-it, Jake headed for the laundry room.

Lucy cowered in the corner beside the dryer, her hands cupped over her ears. *Damn snow . . . bitch . . . ruin my life . . .* Her face was whiter than the snow that was blanketing their immediate world.

Wylie and Jake both dropped to their knees. "What? What's wrong, Lucy? Did you *hear* something?" Jake demanded.

Coop was even wilder by then, running and leaping on the back of the couch and down on the other side as he tried to paw at the vertical blinds covering the sliding glass doors. Sadie sat up on her haunches, throwing her head back and howling, an ungodly sound.

Jake took command. "Get it together, Lucy, and call the number. I'm dialing it for you. You can do this. They said it was urgent." Jake identified himself, and said, "Agent Lawrence, I have Miss Baker for you. Hold please."

Lucy dropped the phone twice before she was able to bring it to her ear. Her whole body shook from head to toe when she said, "This is Lucy Baker."

"Where are you, Miss Baker?"

"What difference does that make? What is it that is so urgent?" She let her head rest against the wall as she listened, her eyes closed. Wylie and Jake both reared back when Lucy barked, "How do you know that? If you're trying to frighten me, you are certainly succeeding! No, I haven't heard from Jonathan. I'm not home, and I don't have my cell phone with me. I suppose Jonathan might figure out I'd be someplace close to home, but that's a bit of a stretch to my mind. However, he did call the day before when the storm was just beginning. He does get weather reports, and he does watch television while he's away, so there's a good chance he knows about our weather conditions. As you said on more than one occasion, he's not stupid. It's only logical for him to think I wouldn't go far. Unless Jonathan has magical powers, how could he possibly know which house I'm in? I don't know why the dogs are barking, Agent Lawrence. How could he possibly get to me? We have four feet of snow outside. It's a blizzard. I thought you were FBI. If you knew it was Jonathan, then why didn't you pick him up? How many damn times do I have to tell you, I don't know anything about Jonathan's activities. I don't give a damn what you think, Agent Lawrence."

Wylie sat down on the floor across from Lucy. She was getting mad. *Good,* he thought. Better she should be mad than a cowering basket case. Color was coming back to her cheeks, too. The dogs were still barking and howling.

"Yes, we did go to the house in Watchung. My friends knew some men who have expertise in security systems. They dismantled the systems and turned them off. They don't work now. You said it was my house. Why shouldn't I go there? I wanted to see what I own. There was nothing in the house except some high-tech equipment. And there was a Chevy Suburban SUV in the garage, a car you never mentioned in your catalog of fancy vehicles. It was a waste of time and energy going there. Go check it out yourself. I'll give you the code to the house alarm and there's a card for the gate. Everything else is off. Why didn't I call you? Why should I? The last time we spoke, you said, when you left, that you would be in touch. To me that means you were supposed to call me, not the other way around. Well, goddammit, Agent Lawrence, if you are so sure of your facts, why aren't you here protecting me? I'm a taxpayer. Well, if you can't get here, how do you expect Jonathan to get here? I don't believe you, Agent Lawrence. How could Jonathan be here, and what do you mean by *here?* I'm not home, so where is here?"

The trio looked at one another. Wylie thought the phone conversation was over and reached for the phone. Lucy shook her head.

"Fine. Yes, I understand. Well, dammit, get a horse and sleigh and come and get me." Lucy pressed the button to end the call. Jake and Wylie looked at her expectantly.

"They think Jonathan is here. Like in the neighborhood or somewhere close. They said they tracked him when he left Zurich, but they lost him in New York. He's using another name and some kind of disguise. Real cloak-and-dagger stuff. They had him right up till he went through customs, and that's when they lost him. They think he's coming for me. What *are* those dogs barking at?"

Wylie locked his gaze with hers. "Either someone is out there moving around, or some kind of animal is invading Coop's turf. I don't know, Lucy."

"I *heard* him. I know it was him. If I *heard* him, that has to mean Agent Lawrence is right, and he's close. My God, he might be in the backyard."

"What did you hear, Lucy?" Jake asked.

"I heard the words *damn snow*, the word *bitch*, and then the words *ruin my life*. Maybe it was Dick Palmer, the guy who lives across the street. He's always fighting with Marion. He talks like that. He's always calling Marion a bitch and saying she ruined his life. I think that's how they communicate. You know, by fighting with one another. Everyone on the street knows what a miserable person he is. He hates being home. I don't know why those two stay married. It could have been Dick. It could have been Jonathan, too. I don't know. Nothing else is coming through. I'm trying, but there's nothing there. If Agent Lawrence is right, we're sitting ducks."

"The guy would have to be Superman to get through that snow. Look what it did to us, and we only crossed the yard. How could he get here from New York? Everything is shut down tight. The airports are closed. The train station is closed. For sure there are no cabs out and about. The police are citing people who try to go on the roads. I heard that on the five o'clock news," Wylie almost shouted.

"Look, I do not know how he got here, but he could be here, and you two know it. Explain those tracks at my house. Well?"

Wylie threw his hands in the air. "I have a gun. I'm not much of a shot, but if push comes to shove, I know how to take off the safety and I know I could plug someone if he broke into my house. I have two baseball bats, too. Think about it, Lucy, the guy can't have a weapon. He could never get one through the airports. Not even a knife. Yeah, I suppose he could have bought one in New York, but how likely is that?"

"I have a gun, too, at my house. Jonathan knows I have it. Maybe it was he who left those footprints, and he was trying to get it. To kill me with my own gun. Oh, God! Why is this happening to me? I didn't ruin his damn life, he ruined it himself. Did you close all the blinds, Wylie?"

"Yeah. Listen. How's this for an idea? Let's all go to Rachel's house."

"Why? He doesn't know where you live, Wylie. He doesn't know anything about you other than that you are a neighbor whose dog I was watching. You could live in any one of the twelve houses on the block. Why go to Rachel's house?"

Wylie shrugged. "It was a thought. You know, confusion, throw the guy a curve, that kind of thing. I guess you're right. If he doesn't know where I live, there's no point to moving out. I'm going upstairs to get the gun, though. Do you want me to go to your house and get yours?"

Before Lucy could respond, Jake said, "Yeah, Wylie, get her gun. Bring yours down here. I know how to shoot. Actually, I'm a fair marksman."

"Okay, where's the gun, Lucy? Is it loaded?"

"Of course it's loaded. Why have a gun if you don't keep it loaded? It's not like I have children living in my house. It's in my night table drawer. The table on the right side of the bed. There are a few extra clips, too, so bring those. Are you sure you don't mind going out again?"

"Hell, yes, I mind, but I'm going to do it anyway. In case nobody noticed, the dogs are quiet now. It was probably only a stray animal, maybe a possum or a squirrel, whose weird scent set them off. Sit tight, I'll be back."

Lucy wondered if Wylie really believed what he was saying or if he said the words for her benefit. She made no move to leave the corner of the laundry room. Sadie trotted into the room and sat down on her lap. Coop sat alongside them both. She stroked their silky heads as Jake followed Wylie out to the foyer.

"My gun is in the top dresser drawer under my socks. I'm going to take it with me," Wylie said as he donned his ski jacket and hat.

"Don't shoot yourself in the foot, Wylie. How long should I give you before I go out looking for you?" Jake asked.

"Forty minutes," Wylie responded grimly. "Not a minute longer."

"Gotcha."

14

The moment Jake slammed and locked the front door behind Wylie, Lucy started to pace, her eyes glued to the watch on her wrist. Jake noticed that she carefully avoided walking past any of the windows in case her shadow could be seen from outside. At least, that's what he surmised.

Lucy circled the dining room, the kitchen, and then the foyer. "Do you think Jonathan is here, Jake?"

"Yes," he said. There was no point in kidding himself or Lucy. "Yes, I do," he said again.

Lucy twisted the watch on her wrist as though by moving it back and forth, the time would go faster. "You know what, Jake? I do, too."

"Well, there's three of us and one of him. We have two guns. I want you to think about something else, Lucy. Remember how difficult it was and how cold and exhausted you and Wylie were, and all you did was walk back and forth across the yards. If he's here, he's on foot. The police are citing people and giving them five-hundred-dollar tickets if they're caught out on the roads with a vehicle. Your guy doesn't sound like the mountaineer type. You gave me the impression he's a bit of a dandy. Don't go giving him too much credit, Lucy."

"Then why were the dogs going nuts like that? Who made those footprints at my house? He's here. Hey, with all we now know, he could have weaseled himself into someone's house by saying he was stranded. No one would turn him away in this weather. He'd flash wads of money to make it harder to turn him away. Jonathan loves money and assumes everyone else does, too."

Jake brought his arm up to see the numerals on his watch. "Wylie should be on his way back by now. Come on, Lucy, nothing is going to happen to my buddy. You like him, don't you?"

"Yes, I do, Jake. I like him a lot. I just wish I hadn't gotten him involved — you, too — in this mess. I feel like such a fool. I am really having a hard time accepting how stupid I was where Jonathan is concerned."

Jake walked to the window and parted the vertical blinds to peep out. "The bad news is, it's still snowing, but the good news is I see Wylie. He's near that little grove of cedars that separates your property from his. Don't be so hard on yourself, Lucy. At one time or another, most of us have done things we wished we hadn't. You found out in time, and we're going to make it right."

"Why does he feel he has to kill me, Jake?"

"We don't know for sure that he does want to harm you. That was a statement the FBI threw out to scare you. We don't know if it's true or not. If it is, my guess would be he thinks you're onto him and will try to trap him for the authorities. He wants to keep his good life. A stretch in the slammer doesn't fit in with his game plan. That's the best I can come up with."

Lucy threw herself into Wylie's arms the moment the door opened. She looked up at him and gave a shaky laugh. "You have icicles on your eyebrows. What took you so long? I was so worried." Lucy jabbered, as Wylie took off his jacket and sat down on the small bench across from the front door. She struggled to pull off his boots.

Jake trotted off and returned with clean socks and the bottoms to a pair of flannel pajamas. Lucy backed off and watched as Wylie dropped his pants and shed his wet socks. He wasn't a boxer man. It pleased her. She took a full minute to appreciate his hard, muscled thighs. She grinned wickedly when he caught her eye.

"Don't even think about it," he groaned.

"Okay," Lucy said agreeably.

Wylie reached over to his jacket, took Lucy's gun out of his pocket, and handed it to her. Then he took out his own. "I'm going to bed," Jake said, looking at the guns. "I'll be upstairs if that makes a difference. Are you guys going to sleep down here?"

"Yes," they said in unison, as Wylie reached for the gun in Lucy's hand and made sure the safety was on both hers and his before he returned the .22 to Lucy.

Lucy led Wylie to the sofa in front of the fire and handed him the quilt he'd used earlier that day. After adding a log to the fire, she sat down next to him. Wylie wrapped the quilt around them both. The guns on the coffee table glared up at them. Wylie reached down and opened a copy of *Time* magazine, which he spread on top of the guns before he cuddled next to Lucy. Within seconds, the dogs were on the couch with them, burrowing in the quilt for comfortable positions.

"Go to sleep, Wylie, you look exhausted.

I've got the guns and the dogs, and I'll wake you if anything goes awry. The phone is here, too, and Jake is upstairs. I'd give up everything in the world that I hold dear if I could go back and avoid getting you involved in my problems."

Lucy smiled when she heard Wylie's light snoring. She stroked Coop's head. "He's a real okay guy, this master of yours," she whispered to the dog. She leaned back into the softness of the couch and stared into the fire.

As Lucy stroked Wylie's dark hair, aware of how wonderful he felt next to her, she thought that maybe some good would come of all this intrigue and angst she was going through. Meeting Wylie and falling for him, and she was falling for him, was the icing on the ugly cake named Jonathan St. Clair.

She had an analytical mind, at least where the law was concerned. Maybe she should think about this whole mess as though a client had dumped it in her lap. She nodded to herself. *Go back to the beginning. Way back.*

Lucy knew she was ordinary, not spectacularly beautiful, but she wasn't ugly either, nor did she have the best figure in the world. She knew how to apply makeup, fix her hair, and cover what she perceived as her flaws. What was it that had attracted Jonathan to her? Her capabilities, her professional success, her personality, what? She'd been flattered, that much she did remember, when he'd singled her out. Flattered by his attentions because he was so handsome, so virile, she'd thrown caution to the winds and plunged into an affair with him.

It had taken some juggling, what with working eighty-hour weeks and staying true to her clients, as well as maintaining her legal winning streak. It didn't hurt that Jonathan traveled and was away more than he was in New York. When he did return, their get-togethers were that much more intense. More often than not they spent the two or three days in bed, only getting up to eat or have some wine.

She realized that what she had loved was the sex, not necessarily the man. But the magnificent engagement ring and his marriage proposal had helped to convince her that marriage to Jonathan would be fine. When the passion and sex were gone, what would their marriage be like? How many times had she asked herself that question? She hated the word *divorce*. But there it was. When she'd expressed these thoughts to her fiancé, he'd pooh-poohed them away, saying their love for each other would last a lifetime. Then he'd pour her more wine and, like a fool, she'd guzzle it, and they'd hop in the sack.

She'd had doubts from the beginning, she just hadn't acted on them. She'd been so happy to have a sexy man in her life who had appeared to want to commit himself to her.

What had they talked about? Had there ever been any meaningful, profound discussions? None that she could recall. Somehow or other, Jonathan had always managed to relegate any serious discussion to another time.

What a fool she'd been.

Red flags should have gone up when she asked him *exactly* what he did, and he evaded the question, simply saying he brokered business deals and received a commission for his efforts plus a generous expense account. There were never any precise details or even little anecdotes. He'd gone on to say she shouldn't worry her pretty little head about such things. He would take care of her in the style she deserved.

Her brother Steven hadn't liked Jonathan. She should have paid more attention to that, too, but she hadn't.

Then there was the sudden deluge of clients — less-than-savory characters — right after Jonathan came into her life. Clients who didn't balk at her outrageous fees and always offered a bonus when the acquittal verdict came in. Steven always chortled at their robust incomes. Now that she thought about it, Jonathan always seemed to phone her the evenings the verdicts came in. At first she hadn't paid much attention, but when Steven had commented, "your boyfriend acts like he knows these guys," she'd started to pay attention until she came to the same conclusion herself.

Bad actress that she was, she'd tried to pry something out of Jonathan, and all he'd done was look at her with cold, narrowed eyes. "What are you trying to say, Lucy?" was enough for her. She'd never brought up the subject again. She'd cut back, though, refusing to take on more cases or dumping them on Steven. When one prospective client pitched a fit right in the office when she turned him down, she knew for certain he was a referral from Jonathan. She'd never said a word to Jonathan, waiting for him to work his way around it. He did, and she'd looked him right in the eye and said she was too busy to take on any new clients no matter what they were willing to pay. Eventually, Steven came around to her way of thinking and refused to take cases they both thought were suspect. Of course, she could prove none of this. And that's why she hadn't told all this to the FBI agents when they'd asked about José Rafael and Manuel Aroya. For all she knew the people she'd turned away could have read or heard about her impressive winning record in the courtroom.

Maybe that's where she made her first mistake. Maybe her first mistake wasn't when she told Jonathan about the "upcoming IRS interview." Then again, maybe it was when she told Jonathan she was leaving the firm and turning down the judgeship.

Whatever it was, it no longer mattered. As Steven was fond of saying, the fat was in the fire.

Knowing and understanding all that, why did Jonathan want to kill her? Assuming, of course, that what the FBI agents said was true. Why didn't he just fade away, call off the wedding, and drop off the face of the earth? Surely he wasn't madly, passionately in love with her. No, it had to be more than that. Maybe he thought she knew something she didn't realize she knew. Like signing those documents the night he got her drunk? He was too cocky, too arrogant to believe the authorities were on his trail. Or was he?

He'd canceled the Thanksgiving trip, then moved up his Christmas trip. Now, if the FBI was correct, he'd changed his plans again and was back in the States. Figuratively, if not literally, in her backyard. She thought about the ruckus the dogs had made earlier. Maybe he *was* in the backyard. Maybe he had tried to get into her house.

Lucy's eyes snapped open. She hoped to God that she was safe here in Wiley's house. She didn't want any harm to come to him, Jake, or the dogs. She didn't want to die either. She wanted to have a relationship with Wiley and maybe, just maybe, marry him and have children, a little girl to dress up in a bonnet and starched pinafore, and black patent Mary Janes. Did they still make pinafores for little girls? A little girl she could push on a swing attached to the big apple tree in the backyard, a little girl she could teach to ride a bike and to play hopscotch. A little girl who would run to her shouting, "Mommy, Mommy!" A little girl to kneel with at the side of her bed to say her nightly prayer. A little girl who smelled like warm sunshine and fresh flowers. A little girl to love, to hug, to squeeze, and to kiss. A little boy to deck out in sneakers and blue jeans, a little boy who looked like his daddy. A little boy who skinned his knees and waited for that kiss and the Band-Aid that would make it all go away. A little boy who would throw his arms around her neck, and say, "I love you, Mommy, a bushel and a peck and a hug around the neck." A little boy with a red wagon filled with treasures. It would be the first thing she bought him. Every little boy needed a bright red wagon. Tears blurred in her eyes. Would she ever come out of this whole?

There were so many things she still wanted to do. She wanted to go to the seashore and paint pictures. She wanted to hang new wallpaper in her kitchen and paint the woodwork. She'd always wanted to swim with the dolphins. She wanted to go to the cemetery to visit her parents' graves.

She wanted to run the New York Marathon, too. Someday. Building a small front porch onto her house was another thing she wanted to do. She hated the stoop, hated the small overhang. She wanted a front porch so she could sit on it in nice weather in the evenings. Preferably with someone like a husband and that little boy and girl she wanted so desperately. Strange how until meeting Wylie she had never wanted children. Had she somehow realized that Jonathan was not the type to be a father? If that wasn't to be, then with Sadie and perhaps a neighbor stopping by just to chat with over a cup of coffee.

She wanted to belong to the neighborhood like Nellie, Rachel, and Wylie belonged. The neighbors counted on each other. She wanted them to count on her, too, just the way she wanted to be able to count on them. Plus a whole host of other things. Things she hadn't thought about until the FBI agents warned her of her own mortality. Now, suddenly, those things seemed like the most important things in the world.

"I hate you, Jonathan St. Clair. I damn well hate your miserable guts."

"Amen to that," Wylie said groggily. He sat up and rubbed the sleep from his eyes. His voice turned anxious when he asked, "Did something happen, Lucy?"

"No, Wylie, nothing happened. I was sitting here trying to figure out where I messed up. You know what I think. I think he picked me. Picked me, Wylie. I really think he thought he could mold me into whatever scheme I was to play a part in. I didn't play the game right, though. Somehow or other I screwed up and threw his plans into a tailspin. Now, if we could just figure out what those plans are, maybe we could make this all go away and get on with our lives. How do you feel, Wylie?"

"Like I was kicked by a mule a few times. Is it still snowing?"

"Yes. It's not supposed to stop until mid-morning tomorrow, Thanksgiving Day. Are you hungry? I think there's some pie left if Jake didn't finish it off before he went to bed."

"No. This is nice, sitting here with you and the dogs. I don't want to move. I can't believe I fell asleep, though."

Lucy cuddled closer. Wylie clasped her hand under the covers. "When this is over, Lucy, and it will be over, are you and I . . . what I mean is . . . ah, hell, you know what I'm trying to say here."

Lucy smiled in the glow from the fire. "Yes, but only if you swear on Coop that you're over Angie Motolo."

Wylie threw back his head and laughed so loud, Coop reared up and barked.

"Lady, you drive a hell of a bargain. I swear on Coop that I will never think about Angie Motolo again. But," he said, holding up his hand, "what do we do when we run across her at my class reunion?"

"I'll think about that when the time comes. How's that going to work with us living next door to each other? I don't want to give up my house. I'm psyched to build a front porch."

"I love front porches. I grew up with one. We used to sit out there on the floor on rainy days and play Monopoly and other board games. We had a swing. Are you going to have a swing?"

To Lucy's ears it sounded like the most important question in the world. "Yep, and I'm going to paint it Dartmouth green to go with my shutters."

"Will you be happy hanging out with a stuffy college professor?"

Lucy pretended to think. "Will you be happy hanging out with a smart-mouth lawyer who, in legal circles, is considered the best of the best?"

"Oh, yeahhhh," Wylie drawled. "What happens if I get a teaching job out of state?"

"Like a good, dutiful wife, I'll go where my husband goes."

"You're saying you'll marry me. I'm supposed to ask you first. Did I miss something here?"

For the first time in her life, Lucy was flustered. "But you said . . . I thought . . . are you saying you don't want to marry me?"

In the blink of an eye, Wylie was out of the covers and down on one knee on the floor. He reached for her hand. "I was kidding. Will you . . ."

Coop was off the couch, and on his hind legs, his front paws wrapped around Wylie's neck. He grabbed for the big dog and finished what he was going to say. "Will you marry me? This big *galoot* goes with the deal, and you have to promise to help me make his meat loaf every day. Swear to me on Sadie, or I withdraw my proposal."

Lucy eyed the man kneeling in front of her. She could read the anxiety in his eyes. She knew he was serious about Coop. "I accept your proposal and the restrictions. I will always cater to Coop's needs. How could you even think otherwise? I've come to love that dog. Are we going to have a prenup? I like them for other people but not for myself."

"That's how I feel. Jeez, we're a pair,

aren't we? Wait a minute. What about the dogs?"

"What about them? Sadie is mine and Coop is yours. There's no problem that I can see."

"Yeah, yeah, there's a problem. I want them to be *ours*."

Wylie's tone was light, almost teasing, but Lucy now knew him well enough to know the dogs were an important issue. "Okay, I like that. His and hers sound cold and calculating. I like them being ours. We can change their papers if you want."

"Coop doesn't have papers. I told you I found him. I hope that doesn't make a difference. I wouldn't trade Coop for all the pedigrees in the world."

"Okay. Boy, I'm glad that's settled. Hey, want a beer?"

"Well, sure, if you're going to fetch it. Bring some rawhides for these guys. I'm going to use the last of the wood to build up the fire. From here on in, we'll have to start busting up the furniture if we want a fire. I have a couple of boxes of those starter logs, but they don't throw off any heat."

"I'm not that much of a pioneer, Wylie. Just crank up the heat," she called over her shoulder as she made her way into the dark kitchen, the dogs right behind her.

Lucy found the rawhide chews in a yellow Happy Face cookie jar. She jammed them into the pocket of her sweatpants before uncapping two bottles of Michelob. Bottles in hand, she was about to leave the dark kitchen when she saw Coop start to slink on his belly, growling deep in his throat. Sadie followed suit while Lulu danced around in circles whining and whimpering.

Lucy froze in her tracks. Her eyes on the dogs, she called out, "Wylie, I think you better come out here."

"Don't tell me we're out of beer," Wylie exclaimed. He looked from Lucy to the dogs, who were slinking from one sliding glass door to the other before he ran back into the den, where he picked up both guns. He hoped he had the guts to use the lethal weapon in his hand if need be. In the kitchen, he took both bottles of beer from Lucy's hands and set them on the table.

"I'm not sure, but I think I saw pinpoints of light between the blinds. Like someone waving a flashlight around. Don't turn on any lights, Wylie. The dogs aren't barking and howling. What's that mean?" Lucy asked fearfully.

"I don't know. Coop is very territorial. If someone invaded his yard, he'd go ballistic the way he did before." He stood close to

Lucy, who was trembling. "Look, the lights are out, no one can see in. The doors are locked. We have two guns. *TWO!* If you're thinking I should go out there in the snow, think again. It wouldn't do us any good. Inside, now, that's a different story. This is my turf. We have the dogs and these weapons. I want you to go to the front window, Lucy, and look out to make sure it's still snowing. You can tell by the streetlight across the street. I don't want to risk turning on the deck lights to alert anyone. You know, just in case. What I don't like right now is that Coop's tail is down between his legs. So is Sadie's. The fur ball has a cropped tail, so who knows about her. For sure you don't mess with a dog when his tail drops down. Move, Lucy!"

In the end, Wylie had to nudge her. She did move then, running to the window. She was back in an instant. In a shaky voice, she said, "It's still snowing. I couldn't even see Rachel's house through the snow. What are we going to do, Wylie?"

"Nothing, Lucy. We're going to sit here and wait. This might be a good time for you to go off by yourself, maybe the laundry room, and try to see if you can *hear* anything. Really try, Lucy. Nothing is going to happen. I promise." Wylie patted her shoulder the way her father used to do when she was a little girl. The pat meant things would be all right.

Lucy licked at her dry lips. Her head bobbed up and down as she walked toward the laundry room. She wished she could explain to Wylie, to make him understand that she couldn't *turn on* what she heard. Still, if it made Wylie feel better, she would do it.

Lucy hated herself for cowering in the corner like some dimwit.

Warm air gushed from the vent under the laundry room sink and warmed Lucy's legs. She tried to make her mind go blank, to think about nothing but the mounds of snow outside the house. She envisioned deep, snow tracks, flashlights, falling snow. She did her best to conjure up a picture of Jonathan, with Coop and Sadie chasing him through the snow. Some of the tension eased in her shoulders with the vision. Nothing was coming through. She kept trying. Finally, she said, "I give up." She stomped her way to the kitchen in frustration.

Lucy was calm now, even embarrassed at the way she'd fallen apart. *I really have to get a handle on this,* she thought. *I cannot let that man invade my life like this. If I do, I'll be a drooling idiot and no good to anyone.*

Sadie nipped at Lucy's arm to remind

351

her of the rawhide chews she had in her pocket. She smiled.

Lucy was surprised to find Jake sitting with Wylie at the kitchen table. They'd turned on a light.

"Lucy, you said there was something that bothered you about the house in Watchung. What bothered you? Sit there, dammit and don't say another word until you know what it is. That's a damn order, Lucy. I'm through wasting time here," Jake said forcefully. He pounded the kitchen table to make his point.

Lucy dutifully, and meekly, sat down at the table and let her mind have free rein. Jake and Wylie watched her intently, like two precocious squirrels whose gazes were fixed on a pile of nuts.

Twenty minutes later, Lucy bounded off the chair. "I can't think with you two watching me. I don't know what it is. Listen, I was cold, angry, and worried about the storm. All that security blew my mind. It was probably nothing. Why don't we just go in the den and watch a video or something?"

"Why don't we *not* do something like that. I have an idea," Jake said. "Let's do a word association test. Maybe something will jog your memory. Are you up for it, Lucy?"

Lucy looked upward at Wylie, who

nodded in agreement. "Okay," she said.

"Good. Let me get a pad and pen, and I'll be right back."

"I'm just agreeing to this to humor Jake. My brain is tired, Wylie. I don't have any clues; there's nothing hidden in my head. God, I just want this to be over. And, by the way, I have cabin fever. I need to go outside. I need fresh air. I feel like I'm in a damn tomb."

"We all feel that way, Lucy. Try not to think about it. Before you know it, the roads will be plowed, and we'll be able to get in our cars and get out and about."

Lucy snorted. "Assuming we can find said cars. What makes you think they'll even start up. In Buffalo, during that storm in '77, the engines were nothing but blocks of ice."

"So we'll use our blow-dryers to melt the ice. You're whining, Lucy."

"I know, Wylie, and I hate myself for it. I can't seem to help it."

"Then you need to try harder," Jake said, sitting down across from Lucy. "Now here's how we're going to do this. I say a word, and you respond immediately. Don't stop to think. Blurt out the first thing that comes to your mind. For instance, I'm going to say one word now. You respond. Stove."

"Cook," Lucy said smartly.

"It might help if you lean back in the chair and close your eyes."

Lucy did as instructed. "All right, I'm ready."

"Alarm."

"Two, six, eight, nine. It's the code to my alarm system," Lucy said.

"House."

"Cozy."

"Snow."

"Danger," Lucy said.

"Dogs."

"Unconditional love," Lucy responded.

"Jonathan."

"Evil," Lucy shot back.

"Stainless steel."

"Institutions."

"Security gates."

"Secrets," Lucy said.

"Dead room."

"Mortuary."

"Round."

"Square."

"White."

"Virginal," Lucy quipped.

"Evil."

"Jonathan."

"Fear."

"Hide."

"Fireplace."

"Fire, logs, flames. I know that's three, but they popped into my head," Lucy said.

"Square."

"Round. White. Dirty."

"Dirty."

"Jonathan's fireplace. That's it. That's what bothered me. Who in their right mind would have a white fireplace? Certainly no one I know. There were ashes in it, and a few of the white bricks were dirty. No, no, that's wrong. Those bricks had smudges on them. There was no soot inside the hood. I clearly remember looking up inside it. Most fireplaces have a trapdoor on the floor where you just open it up and brush the ashes through it. I have a huge barrel in the crawl space under the house. That's where my ashes go. It has to be a barrel or a drum of some kind because oftentimes the embers are hot, and you don't want a fire under the house."

"She's right, Jake. I have a barrel under mine, too. I empty it out every spring."

"So, what are you trying to say, Lucy?"

"We were supposed to think that the fireplace was used. If we thought about it at all. I think we were supposed to be confused, or anyone else who entered that house, for that matter, at the round room. We all commented on it, don't you remember? Not only was it round, it was startling white. The fireplace or the fire pit, whatever you want to call it, was the focal point. But, once you saw it, recognized it for what it is, you didn't give it a second thought because your mind went to the roundness and the startling white. I remember someone saying we needed sunglasses. Am I crazy here?"

Jake tapped the pen in his hand on the tabletop. Wylie scratched his head, his expression perplexed.

"Well, will someone say something?" Lucy said.

"What you're thinking is, something is hidden underneath, is that it? My own trapdoor in my fireplace at home is on hinges. There's not a lot of room to sift the ashes through either side of it. I have to pry it open with the fire tongs and brush the ashes through. It's a messy job."

"Ours are the same way. That doesn't have to mean Jonathan St. Clair's is the same. It could be a flat steel plate with a ring to lift off. Just like a lid. What do we think is in there?" Wylie asked.

Two blank faces stared at him.

"Are you thinking money, records, drugs, an arms cache, what?" Wylie persisted.

The blank faces continued to stare at him.

"Maybe all of the above. Nah, this is about money. If this guy is as global as I think he is, he has to have a home base somewhere. Maybe that house is his home base and, as such, it's where he keeps his stash, whatever his stash is," Jake said.

Lucy spoke for the first time. "Do you want to know what I think?"

"Hell, yes," Wylie exploded.

"This is just my opinion, but I think Jonathan would never hide anything that could aid and comfort him. He'd keep it on his person. I'm talking about his bank records. Anything that could be hidden is on a computer. He carried it with him all the time. Sometimes, when he was in Europe, he would chain it to his wrist. He told me that himself. I think whatever is hidden, if I'm right, and it's there, is a record of the people he did business with. For want of a better term, his bargaining chip, if things ever went awry. A way for him to cut a deal. I think it was Agent Lawrence who, in one of our very first conversations, said we were talking about billions of dollars. That's billions with a *b*. In my head, that translates to drugs. What do you think? Am I off the wall here, or does this all make sense to either one of you?"

"Honey," Wylie said, bending over to

hug her, "I think you nailed it."

Lucy grinned from ear to ear. "We have to call the agents and tell them. Not that they can do anything right this moment, but they can call it in and have other agents look into it.

"Okay, having said all that, Jonathan just wants to kill me because . . ."

"You upset the little world he created for himself. It's a vengeance mentality thing with him. You have to pay for disrupting his world. It's that simple. A little while ago you said to keep it simple."

Lucy looked from one to the other. She suddenly felt nauseated. When Jake left, Lucy realized that the session was over. She looked at Wylie, a devilish glint in her eyes.

"You know what, Wylie, your dog is the only dog I know who has his own room. He's got two beds, boxes of toys, and he sleeps with you."

A grin stretched across Wylie's face. "It's called devotion. Now that he has new friends, I'm just someone who makes him meat loaf. I admit, I was a little jealous at first."

"Really! Me, too. Sadie was always glued to me. I guess it's a good thing. Hey, you want to mess around?"

Wylie's eyes almost bugged out of his head. "You mean like . . . *mess around?*"

"Uh-huh. Me, you, together. If you're too tired . . ."

"Tired! Who, me? I'm the guy who just had a nap. No sirree, I'm not the least bit tired. I'm up for . . . what I mean is I'm, ah, yeah, I'm *up*."

Lucy wiggled her eyebrows as she led Wylie over to the fire. "If you're sure you're really, you know, *up*, then let's get to it. Before the fire burns down."

Wylie was already pulling off his shirt. "I thought you were worried about Jake being in the house."

"Jake who?" Lucy purred.

Wylie's sweatpants dropped to the floor. "Yeah, Jake who?" His voice was so hoarse, he had a hard time believing the words came out of his mouth. "I'm ready," he said, diving onto the pile of quilts Lucy dragged over from the couch. "Let's do that *thing* we did the last time."

"Did you like *that?*" Lucy purred.

"Oh, man, did I ever. Hurry up, it's cold."

Then she was on top of him, his head clasped in both her hands. She kissed him until his ears turned beet red. Wylie groaned, convinced that kissing Lucy was one of life's greatest pleasures. He was stunned when she pulled away and stared down at him. "You ready, big guy?"

"Yeahhhh," Wylie said exuberantly.

"Then, let's do it. Remember now," Lucy said, breathing little kisses all over his face, "no screaming, no yelling, no kicking on the floor."

"I'm not making a promise *like that!*"

"Me either."

15

Special Agent Sylvia Connors stared out of the eighteenth-floor window of the Hyatt Hotel in New Brunswick, where she and her two fellow agents had been staying since the onset of the worst storm in a century. In the whole of her career, she'd never felt this hopeless.

She was cranky, out of sorts, and was rapidly becoming angry at her colleagues' callous attitude toward Lucy Baker. Attribute it to her background, training, expertise, whatever, she knew Lucy Baker had told them the truth. Mason and Lawrence thought otherwise.

Sylvia clenched her teeth as she picked up her conversation with her colleagues. "She's in grave danger. I'm telling you, she's Banks's victim. You two know squat about women."

"Get off it, Connors. She's in this up to her eyeballs. Did you really expect her to admit to anything? She's a lawyer, for God's sake. She loves that word *allegedly*. She was marrying the guy. We went along with you when you demanded a hand-writing expert to verify her signature. The proof came back positive. It's her damn signature. She's in it right down to her toes, so cut us some slack here."

"There are all kinds of ways to coerce a signature out of someone. Trickery is something Banks probably excels at. She probably thought she was signing something else the way a lot of people do when their intended or their spouse asks them to. I've done it, and don't tell me you haven't either. Your wife says, sign the tax form, and you sign it because she's the one who took everything to the accountant, then picked it up because you were too damn busy, and all she wants is the refund, and the sooner the better."

"Then that makes her a lousy lawyer in my opinion," Agent Lawrence said, speaking for the first time.

Sylvia eyed her two weary colleagues, knowing she looked as awful and as tired as they did. The three of them had been wearing the same clothes for almost three days. The storm had caught them all un-awares, and they'd been lucky to secure the suite of rooms, with Lawrence sleeping on the sofa, Mason on a rollaway, the bed falling to her. For that she was grateful.

They'd been sniping at one another for the past twenty-four hours, ever since the call came through alerting them to Banks's arrival at Kennedy Airport and the fact that he had disappeared. Mason punched his fist into the pillow he'd been sleeping on. His face was full of anger. "Tomorrow is Thanksgiving," Mason said. "My wife is going to have a fit when I don't make it home. We have a thirty-pound bird and are expecting twenty-two people."

Sylvia Connors sniffed. "I think your wife and kids will be eating that bird by themselves. There are no open roads. And just to keep the record straight, we have a woman's life at stake here, and showing up for a turkey dinner seems kind of insignificant compared to that. I think Lucy Baker would agree."

Agent Mason had the grace to look embarrassed.

Agent Lawrence frowned as he clicked on his cell phone. "It's dead," he said, disgust ringing in his voice. "And the charger is in the car, probably frozen. Mason's went out last night. How's yours, Connors?"

"The battery is low, but it's still working. If I'm lucky, ten, maybe eight minutes of airtime. For now, we use the hotel phones."

Lawrence walked over to the window. His voice was almost a whisper, when he said, "It looks like the end of the world out there. What's that saying, 'not fit for man or beast'?"

"I assume the beast you're referring to is Leo Banks. No sane person would be out in that . . . that . . . *stuff*. When this case is wrapped up, I'm putting in for a transfer to San Diego. They have almost perfect weather," Mason said.

"Why are you so certain Baker is clean on this deal, Sylvia?" Agent Lawrence asked.

Senior to her two partners, Sylvia locked her gaze on Mason first, then Lawrence. "No cold, hard facts if that's what you mean. I agree that everything points to her as being his partner, but it's more than that. I saw the way her eyes kept going to that pile of wedding invitations. We destroyed her world. We barged in there and ripped it up one side and down the other. She had no clue. And, do you remember Conover telling us she was wearing this sparkler on her ring finger that was as big as a headlight? When we saw her, she wasn't wearing it. That means she took it off because of what she was told about her fiancé. I'll bet you lunch at Burger King that she hasn't put it back on, either. See, that's what you have to understand about women. Unless she can be certain we have the wrong man, unless we can prove without a doubt to her that the guy she was planning on marrying is not a global crook, that ring is never going to see the light of day again.

"In addition, an engagement ring is a commitment. Lucy Baker is no longer committed. The commitment ceased the day Conover and his partner talked to her. Bottom line, she's telling us the truth, and we have to protect her."

Both agents stared at Sylvia, aware of her past record and her climb up the ranks. She had more citations than the two of them put together, and that's why she was the leader of their team. Both men shrugged. It was as much as she was going to get from either one of them.

"Assuming you're right," Mason said grudgingly, "how the hell did he get here from New York. Everything is shut down tight. Where is he holed up?"

Connors ran her fingers through her thick hair. She realized she needed a haircut. "If I knew that, I'd tell you. I'm assuming a hotel or motel somewhere. There are a hundred or so from Newark down to

Edison. The only thing that gives me even the littlest bit of comfort is that Lucy Baker is at Wylie Wilson's house. There's another man there, too, some academic. And, let's not forget the dogs. Dogs are a powerful deterrent to someone with evil intentions."

"We're powerless to do more than we're doing, which is nothing," Lawrence grumbled. "The switchboard here at the hotel is swamped. I've been trying for hours to get an outside line. There's no way to check the hotels and motels. If we knew which hotel or motel he was staying at, we might be able to figure out how he could get to Baker's house from there. We're five to seven miles away. He could be less than a mile away. If he's desperate, he might take a chance on foot. Tell me what you want me to do, Connors, and if I can do it, I will. If you're right, I don't want to see her harmed or killed. I'd like a notch in my belt by apprehending him. Hell, who wouldn't?"

Sylvia Connors looked down at her Ferragamo shoes, then over at the other agents' feet. Both wore tasseled loafers. Their clothing was winter clothing but not blizzard attire. There was nowhere they could pick up suitable outerwear, not at that point in time. Three raging cases of pneumonia coming up.

"The weather report said the snow was to stop around midmorning. I have an idea. Mason, I want you to go down to the desk, ask for the manager, tell him when the snowplow comes through, we want to be on it. See if you can make arrangements for the driver to drop us off at a spot where the Edison plows can pick us up. They have to pay attention to the request, we're FBI. If necessary, we'll commandeer the plow."

Lawrence looked across at Sylvia, a new respect showing in his gaze. "Good idea. Guess that's why they pay you the big bucks."

Sylvia Connors snorted. Overworked and underpaid was more like it. "It's the only thing I can think of. Just keep trying for outside lines and check the hotels and motels. Check the ones closest to where Baker lives. Better yet, go down to the manager's office and, unless there is some kind of emergency, take over the phones. I don't think they'll give you any trouble. If they do, come and get me. Since it's my turn at the shower, I'll be doing that while you do what you have to do." *God, I hope there's some hot water,* Sylvia thought as she made her way to the bathroom.

Inside, after she locked the door, she sat down on the edge of the tub and dropped her head into her hands. She was worried witless about Lucy Baker. And, right then, there was nothing she could do about it. Not until the storm abated. She hoped that wouldn't be too late.

She'd tried hard during the initial meetings with the lawyer to be cool and professional, almost to the point of not caring. It was a facade, though, because her stomach had churned, her heart had pounded, and her head throbbed. Because . . . once, light-years ago, she'd been in a similar situation.

During her senior year at Northwestern University, she'd worked at a bank part-time as a teller. Within a month of starting work, she'd met Daniel Westport, a suave, preppy young man going for his master's. So, he'd said. Like everything else he'd told her, it was a lie. His name wasn't even Daniel Westport, and he wasn't a student. The truth was, he'd said a lot of things. Things she'd loved hearing. His only flaw as she saw it back then was his obsession with the banking profession. He'd ply her with wine until her tongue loosened, and she'd answer all his questions without a second thought.

Until the day the bank was robbed while she was working. The three robbers wore ski masks. Everything had been synchronized down to the last sync. They knew where all the security buttons were, knew the backgrounds of the employees, knew where the vault was. In short, they knew everything because she'd told him, albeit unwittingly, never suspecting a thing. What she'd never been able to put behind her was the senseless killing of the guard by the front door, an older man due to retire in less than six months.

Until the police showed up at her apartment and started asking questions, she'd been just like Lucy Baker, she didn't know anything, didn't suspect a thing, never knew her fiancé had a past, or that he'd changed his name. She'd been in love.

She left her job at the bank and started to waitress at a cocktail lounge. The tips were better, and she wasn't home in the evenings. As hard as she tried, she couldn't regain the old feeling she'd had with Daniel. He sensed it, and he also sensed her aversion to being touched by him. She did her best to break it off, even moved from her apartment to one with two other young women.

Daniel had started to stalk her. She

bought a gun, enrolled in martial arts classes, but she was still fearful. The day she couldn't take it anymore she went to the police and told them she suspected Daniel was the brains behind the robbery, but that she didn't know if he was the one who killed the guard or not. She didn't stint on what she considered her involvement either.

Two attempts on her life later, she'd cut and run, Daniel on her trail. One of the detectives, a fatherly man, had been watching over her, on his own time, unbeknownst to her until that fateful day. Five more minutes and she would have been dead, a victim of a random shooting. That fatherly detective with honed instincts had fired off a shot and killed Daniel. Now when she thought about it, she didn't know who was more stunned, the detective or herself. She learned later that it was the first time the detective had ever fired his gun. He'd called her girlie when he put his arms around her. Even now, she remembered how he'd trembled and yet he'd tried to calm her down, turning her face away from the man he'd killed who had been intent on ending her life.

Five minutes.

Every year, from that day on, no matter

where she was, no matter what she was involved in, she flew back home and took Detective Janson to dinner on December 17.

Not only did she owe her life to Detective Donald Janson, she owed her career to him as well. He was the one who persuaded her to apply to the FBI when she graduated from Northwestern third in her class. Every time there was an award ceremony, he was in the front row, cheering her on. As an orphan, it meant the world to her.

Right that instant, she'd give anything to have enough minutes on her cell phone to call him. She'd tried earlier to get through the switchboard, but was unsuccessful. She just wanted to talk over the case with him, to see if he had any insights she might have missed.

Donald Janson was the one who taught her to go by her gut instincts. That's half of all investigative work. Screw the manual, screw procedure, go with your gut instinct. Later, you can worry about the manual and procedure.

It wasn't that she ignored the manual and procedure. She stayed true, playing by the rules but always with a clear understanding that if her gut instinct reared up, that's what she paid attention to.

It was in high gear now. She knew that

Lucy Baker was *that* close to having her life snuffed out.

"Not if I can help it," she muttered as she stepped under the shower. The water wasn't hot, it wasn't warm, but it wasn't freezing cold either. She hoped she could work up a lather with the hotel shampoo.

The only thing that consoled Special Agent Sylvia Connors, even a little bit, as she stood under the shower was, if she couldn't get to Lucy Baker, neither could Leo Banks. "Wherever you are, Leo Banks, I'm coming after you, so watch out," she murmured to the cool spray beating on her body. "I'll find you, too. You can count on it."

Spiros Andreadis, aka Jonathan St. Clair, aka Leo Banks, prowled through Nellie Ebersole's house searching for clothing. He'd slept for five hours and woke when it was dark. His body ached from head to toe. The medicine cabinet held a variety of headache tablets. He gulped three Advils and washed them down with ice-cold water. He didn't feel one bit better. On top of his aches and pains, he had a thundering headache.

Hoping food would ease the pounding in his head, he rummaged till he found a pound cake in the freezer and a package of freeze-dried coffee. He devoured the whole cake, which he spread with strawberry jam that he found in a kitchen cabinet, and consumed the contents of the four-cup coffeepot. An apple pie was thawing on the kitchen counter. For later.

Nellie Ebersole was a neat, tidy person, he would give her that. Everything appeared to be geometrically aligned. The hall closet held an array of winter clothing, two long coats, three short coats, a lined raincoat, four umbrellas hanging on special hooks. On the floor, next to a rack holding clogs and rubber boots, was a basket that held neatly folded scarves, wool hats, leather gloves, and wool gloves. He could wear the hat and scarf, but the gloves and boots were too small for him. The top shelf held boxes of catalogs for her popcorn ball business. He took a minute to admire the bright colors before he shut the door. He moved on to the guest bedroom and struck pay dirt. The scent of mothballs was strong. It became overpowering when he opened the closet door to see what he surmised was Nellie's deceased husband's clothes. He tried to breathe through his mouth while he rummaged. The man must have been big, tall like himself but with a huge waist. *Okay, that's why leather makers manufactured belts.* Lucky for him Nellie hadn't been able to part with her husband's belongings. Maybe knowing they were there gave her comfort. *Now, where in the hell did that thought come from?* he wondered.

There were shoes, ankle-high boots, sneakers, sandals, slippers, and a pair of dark green knee-high Wellingtons. He knew just by looking at them that they would fit. He smacked his hands together in glee.

The dresser drawers gave up everything he needed, warm, wool socks, underwear, and tee shirts. One drawer held nothing but thermal underwear. Jonathan's fist shot into the air.

A smaller drawer held a box of cigars and three packs of cigarettes, one pack opened. Obviously, the faceless, nameless Mr. Ebersole had been a smoker. He wondered when the man had died. How stale was the tobacco? Like he cared? When he made his next pot of coffee he'd either smoke the cigarettes or the cigars. Whatever he was in the mood for at the time. Not that that mattered either.

Because he was a thorough person, Jonathan kept opening and closing drawers. He poked and prodded at the deceased man's belongings. He couldn't believe his luck when he moved a thick argyle-patterned sweater to see a gun along with the paperwork that meant Nellie's husband came by the gun legally. A box of clips sat next to the gun. *Everybody has guns these days,* he thought smugly. *What is this world coming to?* The gun felt comfortable in his hand. Familiar and comfortable.

Jonathan kept searching but found nothing else that interested him. He looked around at the house he was inhabiting. It was all so . . . so *middle-class.*

Jonathan took a full minute to wonder if it would bother him to wear a dead man's clothes. He decided it wasn't going to bother him at all, just as it wasn't going to bother him to use the man's gun to kill someone. It wouldn't bother him to use his smokes either.

He continued rummaging through the small house for other things that might benefit him. He walked back down the steps to a small room off the dining room that Nellie obviously used as an office for her popcorn ball business. Everything in the room was neat and tidy, as well as colorful. The deep wine-colored chair was ergonomic as well as comfortable. The file cabinets lining the room were every color of the rainbow. Above the file cabinets hung framed pictures of popcorn balls wrapped in brilliant-colored cellophane. Cheerful, he decided. *Old people must like bright colors.* He himself was a beige/navy blue kind of person. Conservative.

Because he had nothing else to do at the moment, Jonathan riffled through Nellie's files. His eyebrows shot upward a few times when he saw what a lucrative little business the old lady ran from her home. No overhead. She contracted out the making of the popcorn, contracted out the wrapping and shipping, paid Lucy a small salary, and still banked — after taxes — over a hundred thousand a year. He looked at her income tax records and saw that she also collected $1400 a month in social security benefits plus six hundred a month from her husband's pension and another $1600 a month from her own pension fund.

Nellie Ebersole was solvent.

Jonathan was about to pick up the phone to dial Lucy's number when the cell phone in the breast pocket of the pajamas started to vibrate. He opted not to answer it. Instead, he followed through with his intention to dial Lucy's number. He let it ring seven times before he hung up. He then dialed her cell phone number and listened when a metallic voice said the person he was trying to call was either out of roaming range or the phone was turned off. "You can't avoid me forever, darling Lucy," he said softly as he turned on Nellie's computer.

A Mickey Mouse clock on the wall over the computer said it was eight-thirty. No time for fun and games. He had to get down to business. He bustled then, going upstairs to change into Nellie's husband's clothes. He was back downstairs in minutes, fully clothed, and out in the garage.

Goddamn snow! Was it ever going to stop?

Even though he had tucked the heavy corduroy trousers down over the Wellies, he could feel snow inside them. Snow stung and beat at him as he struggled to cross the yard to the house that sat between Nellie's and Lucy's houses. He tried to remember if Lucy had ever told him who lived in the middle house. When he couldn't remember, he decided she had never told him.

As he forced his body to move, he felt like he was swimming against the tide, caught in a pool of Jell-O. His already tired body started to protest again. He was at the edge of Nellie's property. He knew it was the edge because he was prevented from going farther by a chain-link fence as high as his waist. If he wanted to get on the other side of the fence, he had to lean over and fall into the snow. With the height and weight of the snow, it was the same as stepping over a log, or so he thought. He ordered his mind to comply and did his best to step over the fence. He fell facedown, snow going up the arms of the heavy jacket and down under its collar. He was exhausted when he finally managed to get to his feet. He froze in his tracks when he heard fierce barking from the dark house looming ahead of him. He didn't like dogs because he didn't trust them. What he was hearing was a deep, belly bark that made his nerves tingle.

The night was dark, and yet it was light, with the sea of white snow. For a moment he thought that he might be seen if someone looked out through the windows. He retreated and fell back over the fence. *Big mistake.*

Never panic. He needed to keep going, barking dog or not. When it dawned on him that he could barely see the nearest house through the swirling snow, he realized that he couldn't be seen. Why had he panicked?

When no answer surfaced, he went back over the fence and moved on, taking care to stay far enough away from the house so he wouldn't be seen. Now he could hear a chorus of barking dogs. More than one? Two? Maybe three? Would the owner let the dogs outside? Unlikely. He kept going, but he was trembling. He didn't like the feeling. He still kept going.

A long time later, he knew he had crossed the yard and was standing next to Lucy's wooden fence. All he had to do was lean over it, and he would be on the other side. Just like the chain-link fence. He bellied over, picked himself up, and crossed the yard to Lucy's deck. There were no tracks anywhere other than his own. That meant Lucy wasn't home. Sadie, her big dog, would have made a path of some kind. He was looking at virgin snow. He eyed the mountain of snow on top of the hot tub. He struggled with the door, but it was locked. He squinted to see if he could see between the slats of the vertical blinds. The house was pitch-black, with nothing to be seen except the glowing red dot on the alarm system. Wherever Lucy had gone, she'd armed the system before she left. So, he wasn't going to be able to get his hands on her gun. If there was one thing he didn't need right then, it was a nervous female with a gun. The thought infuriated him as he turned around and headed back the way he came.

The trip back was easier because he could walk in his tracks. He could still hear the barking dogs. Plural. Maybe Lucy was in that house. Her and Sadie. She'd said something about watching a neighbor's dog. One dog, not plural. Her dog and the neighbor's dog made for plural. That would certainly account for the loud barking. The really odd thing was, whoever lived in the house hadn't turned on the outside light to see if anything was out there to cause the dogs to bark. Strange.

Numb with cold, Jonathan stood perfectly still to see if any other lights would come on in the house. None did. Maybe whoever was inside *was* hiding. From him. Lucy and the neighbor. It wasn't a far-fetched thought. In fact, it made so much sense he started to tremble again. This time with rage.

Back in Nellie's house, Jonathan shed his wet clothes and boots, leaving a trail as he made his way to the bathroom for a hot shower. He stopped once, half-naked, to pick up his encrypted cell phone. He needed to charge it. Thank God he'd had the presence of mind to stick the small charger in his pocket before he left the Hilton. It still had enough juice to make a few short phone calls. Namely Lucy.

Under the steaming spray, a thought came to Jonathan. It was so simple he didn't know why it took a sojourn in the snow to think of it. Nellie kept files. Nellie, according to what Lucy had told him, was the matriarch of the street. That had to mean she would probably have all the homeowners along with their telephone numbers in a file someplace on her computer. All he had to do was find the file, and he could start calling on the neighbors, asking for Lucy. Damn, maybe he wasn't losing his edge after all. He knew he wouldn't have one bit of trouble accessing Nellie's files since he'd accessed them earlier. Lucy had laughed when she told him how computer illiterate Nellie was. They'd laughed again over Nellie's choice of password, which was popcorn.

Simple minds, simple solutions. He thought about all the firewalls and security he had on his own system. Understanding high tech was the only way to go, especially in his line of work.

Jonathan padded down to the guest room, stepping over the wet clothes he'd left behind to help himself to more of Mr. Ebersole's warm, dry clothing. As before, the smell of mothballs was overpowering.

Then he was in the kitchen making fresh coffee and heating the apple pie in the microwave oven. He ate all of the pie except for one slice that he saved for later. He carried his third cup of coffee into Nellie's small office. He leaned back on the ergonomic chair, propped his feet up on the desk like he belonged. He fired up one of the cigars he'd confiscated. A cloud of blue-gray smoke sailed upward as he puffed on the cigar to make it draw. It was no Havana, but it would do.

Jonathan puffed contentedly as the tenseness left his body, and he became more relaxed. The Mickey Mouse clock told him it was shortly after ten. The whole night loomed ahead of him.

A half hour later, Jonathan's feet hit the floor. It was time to meet the neighbors on David Court.

It was so easy it was almost laughable. The file was named simply, Neighborhood. Every person was listed, along with their address and phone number, and cell phone number if they had one. Thoughtful Nellie had even added a brief summary of each person, age and size. He surmised Nellie was a gift giver.

Within seconds, Jonathan whittled the list to Lucy's neighbor. One Wylie Wilson, attorney-at-law. Age thirty-nine, divorced, six-foot-three. Dog's name is Clueless Cooper. A golden Lab. Ninety-five pounds of animal, he read. He copied down the phone number and turned off the computer. Then a terrible thought struck him.

His fingerprints were all over Nellie Ebersole's house.

16

The pier glass said she looked beautiful. More important, she felt beautiful. The women, Nellie, Rachel, Wylie's sisters and mother, oohed and aahed as Nellie positioned the white veil on Lucy's head. The best part was, she felt like a bride. And she would be, in thirty minutes. Maybe thirty-five minutes if the minister was slow. Happiness sparkled in Lucy's eyes as she twirled around one last time for the benefit of everyone.

"Something old, something new, something borrowed, something blue. You have all those things, don't you?" Rachel Muller asked fretfully.

"I have everything, Rachel. A blue garter, my mother's pearl earrings, the diamond pendant, Wylie's wedding gift to me, and I borrowed an ankle bracelet from Wylie's sister. I'm good to go."

Wylie's mother, who wore a perpetual smile, cupped Lucy's face in both her tiny hands. "I know it's a little early, but I wanted to be the first to welcome you into our family." Her voice dropped to a mere whisper that only Lucy could hear. "My son loves you so much he aches with the feeling. A mother knows these things. Be as good to him as I know he will be to you."

Lucy choked up. Not trusting herself to speak, she bobbed her head up and down. She looked deep into her almost-mother-in-law's eyes. Esther Wilson smiled from ear to ear; so did Lucy. She was going to love belonging to this large, lusty family. She was already friends with the six sisters. She'd never been happier.

"Time to go," Nellie said. "The limo is here. The girls will hold your train until you get down the steps, then we'll pin it up. The judge got here a few minutes ago." The judge Nellie was referring to was Judge Logan Applebaum, and he was giving away the bride. It seemed fitting since Lucy's first job out of law school was clerking for him. Steven was the best man, and Wylie's sister Iris was her maid of honor.

It was going to be a small church wedding at St. Helena's on Grove Avenue, the reception a little larger. Family, neighbors, and a host of good friends. After the ceremony, the bride and groom would come back to the house, as the reception was in the backyard. Wylie had taken the fence down between his house, her house, and Nellie's house to accommodate the tents and assorted tables and chairs. Nellie and Wylie's sisters and mother had prepared all the food. Wylie's father and brothers had seen to the rainbow of flowers that were everywhere. They had also installed a portable dance floor and hired a DJ for later. After the reception, Lucy and Wylie were going to honeymoon in Hawaii for two full weeks.

The ride to the church was short. Lucy had to take deep breaths three different times to calm her jittery nerves. She had one foot out of the limo when she heard the bell. She didn't know they rang the church bells for weddings. How nice, she thought as she made her way across the concrete apron that led to the front door.

Inside, Lucy took a deep breath, the sound of the bells louder there. She reached for the judge's arm and took another deep breath. The moment the organist struck the first chord, she would walk through the door. The bells were louder now. The organist was right on cue. The doors opened just as the bell gave one last, loud peal. She gaped as she stared at the two people blocking the doorway.

Angie Motolo and Jonathan St. Clair!

Lucy woke, struggled with the quilt that was covering her. Half-asleep, her fist lashed out. "Your phone's ringing! How dare you invite Angie Motolo to our wedding! How dare you, Wylie! Didn't you hear me, your phone's ringing."

Wylie struggled to come out of his deep sleep, befuddled at why Lucy was shouting. "What the hell . . ."

"When a phone rings in the middle of the night it's usually bad news. Aren't you going to answer it? We can talk about Angie Motolo later, and don't think for one minute I'm going to forget about it either," Lucy babbled sleepily.

"Huh?" Wylie mumbled and growled under his breath as he struggled to reach the portable phone on the coffee table where he'd left it before they fell asleep. The room was dark except for the red, glowing embers of the dying fire. He groped for the phone in the darkness and finally found it.

Lucy scrunched herself into a tight ball to keep warm. She tried not to listen to Wylie's end of the conversation which was really nothing more than a few grunts of surprise. She was startled when he held out the phone to her. Without thinking, she reached for it, her eyes full of questions. "I think it's the feds," Wylie hissed.

"In the middle of the night?" She knew before she heard the voice on the other end of the phone that it wasn't the federal agents on the other end of the line. "This is Lucy Baker," she said in her sleep-filled voice.

"Darling, how are you? I've been listening and watching the news of your storm. You must be overwhelmed. I had a devil of a time getting through to you. Your home phone and cell don't seem to be working. So, I put my own agile brain to work and asked myself what I would do if I was in your position, and I decided I would probably gather all the neighbors under one roof, pool resources, and food for safety reasons. Tell me I guessed right, darling?"

There was no time for finesse, this was Jonathan on the phone. In the middle of the night. Raging anger raced through her. "Where are you calling me from, Jonathan? How did you know I was here and where did you get this number?" Wylie bounded up off their nest of quilts. Under other circumstances, Lucy might have laughed. Instead, fire and anger spewed from her eyes.

"I'm in Cairo. I told you where I was

going, don't you remember? Even halfway around the world, we still get stateside news. I became so alarmed at the storm news, I started calling the weather bureaus. As I understand it, there is no transportation, there are eight to nine feet of snow up the East Coast, snow is to the rooftops and the National Guard is being called in. The different bureaus used the word *paralyzed* repeatedly. I think that's what scared me. That's why I became so alarmed. Are you sure you're okay?"

"I'm fine, Jonathan. How considerate of you to worry about me. In a few hours I'll be preparing a Thanksgiving dinner with a little help from my neighbors. You didn't tell me how you got this number. It's the middle of the night, Jonathan."

"I called Information, and explained the reasons I needed everyone's number on the street. The young lady was most helpful. People do tend to pull together when disasters like this occur. You sound terribly grumpy, darling, so I'm going to hang up and let you get back to sleep now that I know you are with friends and neighbors. I just wanted you to know even though I'm half a world away, I'm checking on you because I love you. Take good care of yourself and all your neighbors. I'll see you soon, darling."

"How soon is soon, Jonathan?" Lucy asked flatly.

Lucy heard the chuckle and cringed. "Sooner than you think, my darling. Sweet dreams."

Lucy stared at the pinging phone. She was stunned to see that her hand was steady when she handed the phone back to Wylie. "He said he was in Cairo. He sounded like he was in the next room. He knows I'm here in your house. That call was a warning. He wants me to sweat. I'm telling you, Wylie, he thinks I betrayed him, and he's coming after me. He knows more about this storm than you and I know. He said the National Guard is being called in, and he said we had four or five feet of snow. How in the hell could he know that?"

Wylie shivered as he reached for his clothes. "Look, I don't know about you, but I'm done sleeping for the night. I'll make us some coffee and turn the heat up. I want to hear the news, too. I want you to think about every single word that man said to you and I want you to repeat it. Then we're calling those agents. No more *futzing* around."

Lucy reached for her own clothes and

pulled them on. Minutes later, she joined Wylie in the kitchen. The coffee was already dripping into the pot when Wylie held out his arms to her. She stepped into them. He cradled her head against his chest as he stroked her hair. "It's going to be okay, Lucy. There's no way he can get to you. The man is playing with your head."

"He's here, Wylie, I know it. The rest was all lies. I know he's here. The dogs know he's here. I don't know exactly where he is, but he's somewhere close by. And, you're right, he's trying to mess with my head. I'm going to call the agents now. I don't care if I do wake them up. What did I do with that number, do you know?"

Wylie trotted into the den to return with a slip of paper in his hand. Lucy drew a deep breath before she picked up the phone to dial the number from the slip of paper. She was stunned to hear Agent Lawrence say, "Our battery is low, please call the Hyatt in New Brunswick if you want to talk to Agents Lawrence, Connors, or Mason. Ask for extension 1702."

Lucy blinked and held out the phone to Wylie. "The agent said their battery is low. They're at the Hyatt in New Brunswick, extension 1702. Where's your phone book, Wylie?"

Wylie opened one of the kitchen cabinets and pulled out the thick book. Lucy flipped pages until she found the hotel listings. She punched in the numbers and was not surprised to hear a busy signal. She held out the phone so Wylie could hear the busy signal.

"Just keep hitting the redial. Sooner or later you'll get through. I hope," he muttered. "Damn, it's still snowing. It's up past the kitchen window now. I'm starting to feel like I'm sealed in a tomb."

Lucy raked her already messy hair with her left hand as her right hand kept hitting the redial. "Please don't say that."

"Okay, I won't say that. Let's get the weather." He turned on the television set and sat down with his coffee. He stared at the small screen, his heart pumping furiously. Instead of things getting better, they appeared to be getting worse. Now, the anchor was comparing this storm to the Blizzard of '77, which hit Buffalo, New York, killing twenty-nine people over a three-day period. His heart gave a little jump of fear when the television station started showing footage from that particular storm and making comparisons. "It's the drifts," he said inanely.

Lucy nodded as her thumb kept hitting

the redial. "At least they're still saying the snow will stop by midmorning. That's only six or seven hours away. Thank God, your heat is still on. If it goes out, then we will have to burn your furniture. Those starter logs of yours aren't going to help us one little bit."

Wylie stretched out his legs. "If I had my choice of picking someone to be marooned with, I'd pick you, Lucy." He leaned across the table, and whispered, "I guess you know I've fallen in love with you." He waited, not realizing he was holding his breath. Wasn't she going to say anything? Had he just made a fool of himself?

Lucy licked at her dry lips. "I was having this . . . wonderful dream when the phone rang. In my dream I thought the sound was the sound of church bells. I was marrying you in my dream. Nellie and Rachel helped me with my wedding gown. Your mother and your sisters were there. Your mother wanted me to assure her that I would be as good to you as you would be to me. She told me in my dream that you loved me so much you ached with the feeling. She said a mother knows these things. I told her yes, I would be good to you."

Wylie just stared at her.

"Then we went inside the church and the bells were still ringing. When the organist started 'The Wedding March,' the doors opened and . . . and . . ."

"And, what? What, Lucy?"

Lucy doubled over laughing. "There was Angie Motolo and Jonathan blocking my way into the church. I slugged them both!"

"Jesus."

"Yeah. Then I stepped over them," she fibbed. "Then I woke up. I guess the bell I was hearing in my dream was the phone ringing. Oh, my God, the phone is actually ringing. Extension 1702. This is FBI business, put me through immediately," Lucy said in her best courtroom voice, a voice that clearly said, I'm in charge.

"Special Agent Connors speaking."

"This is Lucy Baker, Special Agent Connors. I'm sorry for calling you at this hour but you did say I could get in touch with you at any hour of the night or day. Jonathan St. Clair just called me. He *said* he was in Cairo, but I think that's a lie. Earlier in the evening, the dogs went wild trying to get outside. I think it's safe to say no animal was lurking out there. Possibly a two-legged animal, but not a four-legged one. Then, a few hours later they were sniffing and snorting again, but they didn't bark and howl. I think he's close by, and the dogs are picking up his scent. I want you to know right now, right up front, that I have a gun."

"Can you see any footprints outside?" Connors asked.

"Visibility is zero. The snow is three-quarters of the way up the sliding doors. We can't see beyond. It's just a wall of snow. The point I'm trying to make here is, he's playing with my head. He found out I'm here at Wylie Wilson's house. He was warning me that he could get to me."

"That's exactly what he's doing, Miss Baker."

"Is there anything we can do or should do?"

"Not right now. What's the closest motel or hotel to your house?"

"There's nothing that's right around the corner if that's what you mean. The closest would be five miles in any direction. It's a guess, but I don't think it's more than that."

"There are no available vehicles to be found," Connors said, "and the authorities are arresting anyone stupid enough to venture outdoors. We're hoping to commandeer one of the snowplows or possibly a snowmobile as soon as the snow stops. We will do everything in our power to get to you. Sit tight. Is there anything else you want to tell me?"

"Like what, Special Agent Connors?"

"You must be thinking about this non-stop. I'm assuming you've gone over your relationship with this man a thousand different times. Maybe you remember something that didn't seem important to you earlier, but which, when added to the mix, helps to make sense of the whole. Anything like that."

"No. I'd tell you if there was. Are you saying you finally believe me?"

"Miss Baker, I believed you from the beginning. We had to see which way you'd go. Women in love do strange things."

"Well, I'm not in love. With Jonathan," she added hastily when she saw the stricken look on Wiley's face. "Wait a minute. Actually, Special Agent Connors, there is something I think you should know. Hear me out here. That house in Watchung . . . it's stark white and round. It's pretty hard to get past all that whiteness and the roundness. I think all that was deliberate so no one would think about anything other than those two things. I remember looking at the fireplace and thinking how odd it was that it was white.

It looked like it had been used, but the more I thought about it, the more I convinced myself it was just scattered ash. There's a trapdoor on the floor that you open and brush the ash through as opposed to shoveling it out. I have the same thing here in my own house. I think that's where Jonathan hid whatever he's hiding. I'm trying to help here. It's up to you to check it out."

"Okay, we'll check it out as soon as we can. In the meantime, we'll do our best to get to you as soon as possible. Don't do anything rash. Just be aware."

"All right. We'll save some dinner for you and your partners."

"That would be nice. The hotel here is just about out of food. We're going to try and get some additional cell phones. I'll call you with the number if we're successful. There is every possibility we'll be cut off from one another for a while. I don't want you to panic."

"I won't panic, Special Agent Connors. I told you, I have a gun, and the dogs. If you can't get here, Jonathan can't get here."

"We'll be in touch, Miss Baker."

Lucy handed Wylie the phone. "You heard my end of the conversation. Their cell phones are dead, but they're going to try to get others. The good news is they're going to commandeer a snowplow as soon as they can. If we're lucky, they might be able to get to us late in the afternoon."

Wylie reached across the table for Lucy's hand. "It's been a long time since I've been up at this hour. I'm going to be forty in a few months. Those days of partying and staying up late are long gone. Just so you know, I've become a creature of comfort and habit."

Lucy smiled as she scooted her chair closer to Wylie's. "I was never a party person. Maybe I take myself too seriously. At least my brother thinks so. Guess what, it's not a bad thing. At least I don't think it is. Did I tell you in my dream we were going to Hawaii for two weeks on our honeymoon?"

"No kidding! Can we afford Hawaii?"

Lucy giggled. "I didn't get that far in my dream. I guess so." Her voice turned fretful when she said, "Who is going to take care of the dogs?"

"My mom and dad will come and stay at my house. They love Coop, and Mom doesn't mind mixing up meat loaf every day. Not a problem. So, we're getting married. When?"

When indeed. "When I get a new wedding gown. When this thing in my head goes away. When this is all over. I think the big question is where we are going to live. I want to make sure we do it right, Wylie. Do you understand that?"

Wylie squeezed her hand. "Perfectly. In my off moments, I've been thinking of selling my half of the firm to my partner and devoting all my time to my thesis. If I do that, I think I could be done by August or September. That's not too long to wait, is it?"

Lucy looked up at Wylie. She loved this man, really, truly loved him. And yet she'd only known him a short while. She felt like she'd known him forever. She laughed out loud when Wylie said, "I feel like I've known you forever."

"Now who is reading whose mind. I was thinking the exact same thing just this minute. I'm so very happy, Wylie. I don't have the words to tell you. They say everything happens for a reason, and I guess you were the reason. The Jonathan thing. I'm not going to lie to you, I'm petrified at what that man can do. Yet, I'm happy. Explain that please."

Wylie looked befuddled, his hands rubbing at his bristly cheeks and chin. "We were meant for each other. That old shoe and old sock thing my mother always talks about. The whys, the hows, the whats simply don't matter."

Lucy leaned her head on Wylie's shoulder. He put his arm around her. "It's three-thirty in the morning in case you're interested."

Laughter gurgled in Lucy's throat. "I'm not interested. It's nice sitting here with you in the kitchen."

"When I was growing up, our kitchen was always the busiest room in the house. All of us kids did our homework at the kitchen table, and let me tell you, that took some juggling, especially with our milk and homemade cookies. We played board games on the same table. Mom was always cooking or baking. We had a picnic table and benches for a table because there were so many of us. The dog's bed was in the kitchen by the vent. The cat slept next to him. All the neighbor kids, all our friends, hung out at our house. Mom always made everyone feel welcome. She fed all of us and our friends. Stuff cooked in one pot to make it stretch. Was it like that for you?"

Lucy shook her head. "Not in the least. Remember, my parents were lawyers. We had a series of housekeepers. Summers, Steven and I were sent to camp. We had all these after-school activities to keep us busy. There was no time for neighborhood friends or playing outside. My only outlet was the track team. After college I was invited to the Olympic trials, but I had to decline when my mother got sick. I spent two years nursing her. Steven was younger, and we were pretty close. We became really close when we were teens. As to food at mealtime, my parents were rarely home at dinnertime. Usually it was just Steven and me. We used to have a Sunday supper where our parents would ask us for a summary of our week. Then we were dismissed. We weren't a warm and fuzzy family. And, we weren't allowed to have pets. Steven had a goldfish named Burt, but it died, and he never wanted another one. He used to talk to Burt for hours.

"We had to say, yes, ma'am, and yes, sir, to our parents. My parents never called me Lucy, it was always Lucille. Steven is the one who started calling me Lucy."

Wylie digested all this, his heart sad. "Didn't you have aunts and uncles or grandparents to pick up the slack?"

Lucy shook her head. "We did, but they were just like my parents. I wish you could have seen what our Christmases were like. The family came to the house on Christmas Eve, each of them brought us one present. Usually it was something we didn't want, need, or that was either too big or too small. Even as kids we knew they weren't interested in us. The really funny thing is, the wrapping looked like it cost more than the actual present. My mother dressed us up like we were going to be photographed for some magazine ad. We had to stand by the piano no one knew how to play and sing a carol. Steven could never remember the words, so I had to do most of the singing. I hated every minute of it. We didn't get to sit at the table with the grown-ups. We ate in the kitchen with bibs on so we wouldn't mess up our fancy clothes. Then we were dismissed.

"Every damn year, Steven and I would huddle upstairs and stay awake all night to see if, when we were younger, Santa would leave gifts. Then, as we got older, if our parents would leave gifts under this enormous fancy tree."

Wylie sucked in his breath. He hated what he was hearing. Hated that the woman sitting next to him, the woman he loved, had experienced even one moment of childhood angst. His voice was gruff, bordering on harsh. "And did they?"

"There were always presents but never what either one of us wanted or asked for.

We were never greedy. We'd each ask for one thing. It never happened. We got books, usually leather-bound classics, scarves, gloves. I think I was thirteen when I found out the housekeeper did the Christmas shopping as well as the wrapping. I almost think that was worse than finding out there was no Santa Claus. After a while, neither of us bothered, and we did our best to sleep through Christmas. Then when we went to college, we didn't bother going home for the holidays. We'd go off together somewhere, just the two of us, and make our own Christmas. Steven is just a year younger than I am, did you know that?"

"Jesus. Well, I knew your brother was younger but I didn't know it was just by a year. That's a good thing, Lucy. You could relate to one another growing up with no distance between you."

Lucy got up and walked over to the coffeepot. She reached for Wylie's cup. "I've been having these chaotic thoughts the past couple of days. I guess that happens when someone is out to harm you, especially when that someone was a person you planned on marrying. You, Wylie, are the only person I ever discussed my life with, aside from Steven. So, as long as I'm telling you all about me, I might as well tell you the rest. My guilt. For years I've said I was okay giving up my dream of going to the Olympics and competing to take care of my mother. After a while, I think I even started to believe it. The truth is, I resented it. I didn't want to do it. In fact, I hated doing it. But a daughter is supposed to do those things, so I did them.

"My mother was incredibly demanding during those two years. She absolutely refused to have a nurse, someone she considered a stranger, taking care of her. She had no idea what a stranger I was to her. She had no idea at all. She wore me down, beat me down, almost to the ground. Steven went off on her once for the way she treated me, and she looked right through him and didn't even respond. He'd come to the house to give me a break for a night out. He was going to sit with her, but she would have none of it. As sick as she was, she ranted and raved. Steven just left the room and closed the door and forcefully pushed me out the door. I went to the park and just sat for hours."

Wylie wanted to stop her, but he knew Lucy had to get it all out. All he could do was listen.

Lucy walked over to the table and set the

cup down with a steady hand. She remained standing, her gaze far away as she continued on. "I paid for that little outing. Big-time. That's when I started going to a shrink. Flash forward, he told me it was okay for me not to like my mother. Once I accepted that, I hired a nurse and a relief nurse. I did the things I was supposed to do and no more. When my mother died, I knew in my heart I had done everything humanly possible to make her comfortable. I didn't have to shower her with love because I had no love to give. I didn't grieve, nor did Steven. We were just relieved.

"Do you know what both my parents' goals in life were, Wylie?"

"No, Lucy, what was it?"

"They wanted to be judges. They wanted those black robes. They wanted the bench and the gavel. That's what their whole lives were about. Do you believe that?"

Wylie shrugged. "Is that why you turned down the appointment? Did you consider it sacrilegious or something?"

Lucy looked around, a vague expression on her face. "Or something. Well, that's my story. Pretty sad, huh?"

"Nah. Stuff like that happens more than you know. People have a hard time opening up and spilling their guts. What they don't understand is when they do that, the healing process begins. If you don't get it out, it festers like a boil that needs lancing. I'm proud of you, Lucy. Steven, too, though I don't know him.

"Listen, we're going to have a wonderful life. I promise. We're going to live in a college town that has sidewalks and big, old trees. We'll go to rallies, cheer on the school's team, interact with other professors and teachers. We'll help students get their start. You and I can sit in front of the fire and discuss our days. We can take turns cooking and walking the dogs. We'll rake leaves and burn them, and plant flowers. I love the smell of burning leaves. We'll pick pumpkins and put them on the front steps with candles inside. We used to do that at our house. Kids will drop by for extra help, we'll invite them in, and they'll become our friends and we'll mentor them. We'll have a big open house at Christmas with a grab bag so everyone gets a gift. We'll go out to some field and cut down the biggest tree there is. We'll lug it home on the truck and invite the kids to help decorate. Lots of kids don't go home for the holidays, like you and Steven and a lot of the foreign students. Home and hearth stuff, making a difference. It won't be an exciting roller-coaster kind of life, but it will be filled with love and contentment. That's how I see it anyway. It's what I want. I hope you do, too, Lucy."

"I do. My God, you have no idea how much I want that, crave it. It's what I need. Do you think we'll have fights?"

"Hell yes. Think about how sweet the making up will be."

Lucy laughed. "Do you have any idea how good you are for me? What's that saying, 'you're the wind beneath my wings'? Together we'll soar. So there."

Wylie kissed her, a long, lingering kiss that spoke of endless tomorrows, a kiss that she returned with just as much passion and promise.

"I love you, Lucy Baker," Wylie whispered in her ear.

"I love you, Wylie Wilson," Lucy whispered in return.

17

The three federal agents stared at the television screen in their room, their eyes wary and questioning. It was seven o'clock, and the light outside was blinding. Beyond the window, the world was a sea of white snow. Visibility, according to the commentator, had not improved. Still, they were predicting an end to the snow by midmorning. Just three hours away. Sylvia Connors didn't believe it for a minute. Neither did the others.

"This is only the second storm to be labeled a national disaster." The commentator on the television news station droned on, citing similarities to the first national disaster in Buffalo in 1977. It was obvious the man was tired, he had dark circles under his eyes and was dressed in the same clothing he'd been wearing for the past three days. "The army is being called in to augment the National Guard. Sad to say, ladies and gentlemen, there are going to be a lot of Thanksgiving tables with empty chairs this year."

The three agents turned away and

walked to the window as the anchor rattled on about how the snow, when it was finally removed, would have to be dumped in the Raritan River. A plea, he said, was going out to everyone who owned a snowmobile or four-wheel drive, to stand ready to donate them for rescue efforts. Everyone was urged to stay tuned after still another warning to stay indoors.

Agent Mason started to pace. "That guy used the word *paralyzed* six times in two minutes. How many times has he said twenty-nine people died in 1977? How many times did he say visibility has been zero for the past thirty-six hours, and how many times has he said wind gusts range from thirty to forty to sixty miles an hour at times? A hundred!" he said, answering himself. "How can that guy," he asked, jerking his head in the direction of the television, "possibly know or even estimate the damage at $200 million at this point in time? Sometimes I hate the media. They run with something and don't know when to stop."

"What do you think of Lucy Baker's phone call in the middle of the night?" Sylvia asked carefully. She was fed up with talking about the snow and the storm.

"Cairo, my ass," Lawrence said succinctly.

"We have proof he came into this country with phony papers. The guy is trying to scare her. I'm having some real trouble with the fact that he's even here at all. We never should have lost him. The guy's a pro, which means he's smarter than our guys. Why didn't he just cut his losses and lose himself abroad? What's here that he's risking getting caught?"

Mason nibbled on a hangnail that had been plaguing him for days. His hands were dry and chapped, his cuticles ragged. "The guy fits the profile of a person obsessed with himself. He's cocky and arrogant. He's in danger of losing it all, whatever 'it all' turns out to be. This he knows. He's blaming Lucy Baker for what's going on. So he has to eliminate her so he can go back to his own world. This guy is so arrogant, so self-absorbed, he doesn't think there's a chance in hell he'll get caught. I also think it's safe to say this storm is causing him some fretful moments. How is he going to get away? The exit is almost more important than the arrival and the mission."

"And . . ." Sylvia said.

Mason threw his hands in the air. "There is no *and*. That's it."

"Desperate men do desperate things.

He'll find a way. That's the first thing guys like that plan — not the mission but the escape," Lawrence said. "Look how long it's taken us to get this far. Three years. Like you said, the guy's a pro."

"So are we," Sylvia snapped.

"In a fair fight or race, the good guys usually win in the end. Unless the unknown comes into play. Then the playing field opens up wide. All you have to do is look outside. That's the unknown, the unexpected. It works more to his advantage than ours." Disgust registered on Lawrence's face. "Damn, I hate snow!"

Sylvia squeezed her eyes shut as she saw pictures of Lucy Baker, Wylie Wilson, and their houseguest, dead on the floor in Wilson's house. The picture was so horrendous, she bolted for the bathroom, but it didn't erase the vision or the knowledge of all the other murders Leo Banks had committed. Her shoulders drooped. Lucy and her friends were sitting ducks, and there was nothing she could do about it. Nothing. She squared her shoulders and walked back into the suite's living room. "How much longer before that snowplow gets here?"

"They said eight o'clock. It was iffy. When it gets here it gets here," Mason snapped irritably. He wasn't looking forward to braving the elements.

"Go back downstairs and see if you can find out anything. Find all three of us some boots and some heavier outerwear. Explain to the manager we'll reimburse everyone when this is over. Tell them to give me an outside line immediately and to keep it open. Don't look at me like that, Mason, do it!" Sylvia said, just as irritably.

When the door closed behind Mason, Sylvia looked over at Lawrence. "What do you think, Tom?"

Lawrence scratched at his head as he shrugged. "I don't know. Everything is getting jerked around by this damn storm. For whatever it's worth, I think he's close by, and I think he's made an attempt already but the storm foiled it. He knows where she is, even if she's with other people, so that makes his job easier. Where he is, I have no idea, but wherever he is, he has access to a phone, and yeah, he's trying to scare her. The guy she's with, Wilson, he's no lightweight either. Those two dogs would make me take a step backward. And, you said, she has a gun. The visiting guy doesn't appear to be any kind of threat, but you never know. You wanna run with this or what?"

Sylvia snorted. "Run where? Lucy said she thinks he's got something hidden under the fireplace. Any ideas?"

Lawrence's face registered despair, as well as disgust. "Nope. None. It's got to be something pretty awesome to warrant the kind of security he has installed there."

Connors's eyes narrowed. "Not so awesome if Wylie Wilson's friends dismantled it. I'm talking about the system, not what's inside."

"I think our pal was just trying to cover himself from the locals. They wouldn't know what to make of it. Goes with the profile. He's cocky, never thinking anyone other than the locals would home in on him. Maybe money, maybe drugs. And, Baker said there was only an SUV in the garage, a car we didn't even have in our inventory. What happened to the other vehicles? I think people went there and got them, his pals. Do I know why? No, I don't. What other explanation could there be for the other vehicles? One is left for St. Clair himself. Admit it, Connors, we're operating blind here. Half our case is assumptions. The guy is like quicksilver."

A scream ripped from Sylvia Connors's throat. In the blink of an eye, Lawrence had his gun in his hand as he pivoted to the right and to the left. "Jesus Christ, *what?*" he roared.

"Look, it's stopped snowing!"

Lawrence mopped at his forehead as he replaced his gun in his shoulder holster. "Christ, Connors, you almost gave me heart failure."

Connors looked sheepish. "Sorry, Tom. It really has stopped. Look for yourself. In your life, have you ever seen this much snow?"

Lawrence continued to mop at his forehead. "No, and I hope I never have to see this much snow again. Where the hell is Mason?"

As if in answer to his question, Agent Mason opened the door and dragged a hotel dolly into the room. On it were assorted jackets and parkas with hoods, a pile of gloves, scarves, and what looked like a small mountain of boots. "The plow is due in thirty minutes, the outside line is clear, and we owe a fortune for this gear. And, lady and gentleman, it has stopped snowing. They're singing in the bar downstairs. The booze is flowing, and it's all free. They ran out of food late last night, in case anyone is interested. There must be seven hundred people milling about. Everyone who made it on the train this far plus all the regular guests. It's a zoo down there."

Connors listened with half an ear as she dialed Wylie Wilson's house. "Mr. Wilson," she said, when she heard his voice, "this is Special Agent Connors. We're told that a plow should be here in about thirty minutes. That's not carved in stone, however. The good news is it has stopped snowing. I have no idea how long it will take us to get to your house but we wanted to tell you we're on our way. Hold a second, Mr. Wilson.

"Mason, did you get us some cell phones?"

Agent Mason offered up a snappy salute. "Yes, ma'am, Special Agent Connors, ma'am. I managed to snag three Nokias. They belong to the manager, the assistant manager, and the reservations clerk. They put a sticky on the side with the number on it, and they've been charged, so we're good to go. We either have to return them or pay for them." Mason handed one of the phones to Sylvia.

"Mr. Wilson, write down these cell phone numbers as I read them off to you. Please, repeat them back to me. Good. You'll see us when you see us.

"Then I guess we should avail ourselves

of some of this outerwear and head downstairs to wait for the plow. Does anyone know the temperature?"

Mason slipped his arms into a shearling-style jacket. "According to the television in the bar, it's around twenty-seven degrees. That's pretty damn cold if you want my opinion."

"Mine, too," Lawrence and Connors said in unison.

18

Less than three hundred feet from where Jonathan St. Clair sat smoking, Lucy rubbed oil on the capons she was getting ready to put into the oven. She used a heavy hand with the ground pepper.

Thanksgiving.

Lucy was washing her hands in the kitchen sink when she heard the thought. *Crash and burn, baby . . . This is a hiccup . . .* "Wylieeeee!"

It was Jake, his sandy hair standing on end, who responded to her call. "What's wrong? I passed Wylie in the hall upstairs. He was heading for the shower. You're white as this kitchen counter. Did something happen?"

Lucy told him what she'd *heard*. "Do you think that means he's close by, Jake?"

"There's no way of knowing, Lucy," Jake said quietly as he poured himself a cup of coffee. "The tests done on people that I read about were all in one location. Same medical building, same house, close proximity, that kind of thing. However, there are documented cases where a subject picked up on things a hundred miles away. I think there are six cases like that. My guess, and that's what it is, a guess, would be he's close."

Lucy's head bobbed up and down. "That's my guess, too. I feel him, Jake. I really do. He's close by. I can't explain how I know, I just know. The agents are on the way. Listen to the news, it's almost scary. No, that's wrong, it *is* scary. I wish there was something I could do, but this storm . . ."

"I hear you. You know, Lucy, I woke around five-thirty. My bed was so warm and toasty I didn't want to get up, so I just lay there thinking. I think my brain was going a mile a minute. I tried to dissect this whole thing, to put it into some kind of chronological order so it would make sense. I kept coming back to the same things every time. What would the man gain by marrying you? Why did he put the house and the brokerage accounts in your name, and why did he buy all that insurance? More important, how did he pull it all off? How did he get around the physical you should have taken for the insurance company? Why did he put that house in Watchung in your name? It's coming up to the first of the year, and in January, people start thinking about filing their income tax statements. How was he going to get away with that? Where do those brokerage statements go? And the paperwork pertaining to the house. I think all that stuff goes to the apartment you said he has in New York. I bet you a dollar he has someone pick up his mail once a week or something like that. Whoever picks it up is probably paid very well and knows how to keep their mouth shut. That person probably mails it to a drop box or someplace out of the country. It's so . . . detailed. Most crooks try to keep things simple, so they don't make mistakes."

Lucy made an unladylike sound in her throat. "It's pretty much like that in the law, too. Keep it simple, stupid. The more you plot, the more you scheme, the greater likelihood you're going to get caught and prosecuted for your efforts because, somewhere along the way, it gets hairy, and you make a mistake. Nothing about Jonathan was simple. He thrives on details. It's like a challenge to him.

"Do you want to know what I think, Jake? I think he was going to marry me and then . . . and then he was going to . . . kill me. Everything would then go to him legally. I also think he has setups like this all around the world. Jonathan is a global person, as the FBI pointed out. That's just another way of saying, he'd scratch me off his list and move on to another part of the world if this end of his venture went awry. He never thought I would find out what was going on."

"What's going on?" Wylie said, entering the kitchen, the dogs trailing behind him.

Lucy looked up at him and smiled. Her heart thumped in her chest at what she was feeling for this man towering over her. He'd shaved and was wearing jeans and a hunter green sweatshirt with DARTMOUTH on the back. Wylie loved collecting sweatshirts from different universities. They were his casual wardrobe, all old, all faded, but comfortable.

"We were discussing Jonathan, but we didn't come up with anything concrete. We're just guessing, at least I am. Gut feelings, that kind of thing. Maybe if and when the agents get here, they'll have some input. He's close by, Wylie. I can *smell* him."

"It's entirely possible," Jake said, "that he actually made it here and is in someone's house holding them hostage. Don't look at me like that. How else do you explain the dogs' strange behavior? He could have been prowling the neighborhood. Hell, you couldn't see your hand in front of your face when it was snowing. He could have tried to get into Lucy's house that first day. Anything, where that man is concerned, is a possibility."

"You two think about it while I get my clothes out of the dryer and take a shower. Wylie, turn the oven on in ten minutes," Lucy instructed.

"Yes, ma'am," Wylie said, saluting smartly before he blew her a smacking kiss that Lucy returned with the same gusto. Jake pretended to be embarrassed, to the delight of both of them.

Under the steaming shower, Lucy's thoughts turned somber. If Jonathan managed somehow to get to her, she'd never know what it would be like to be married to Wylie. She'd never have that little girl and boy, never get to meet his students, never see her brother Steven again. *If.* Like hell.

As the shower rained down on her, Lucy relaxed as she tried to get to that place in her head where she could *hear* a thought. *Lucy to Jonathan, Lucy to Jonathan,* she thought inanely. There was a buzzing sound in her ears and a *thrumming* sound in her head. She stopped rubbing shampoo into her hair and leaned back against the tile shower to take advantage of the moment. Then she *heard* it. *Harvey. Talk about stupid, dumb luck. Damn cold. Just wait it out. No crash and burn for you, buddy. So close. So very close. Return to fight another day. Wait it out. Relax. I'm going to get you, Lucy. I know you know I'm looking for you. I'll find you, too. Spend your days looking over your shoulder. You're the one who is going to crash and burn. Not me, never me.*

And then it was all gone, the buzzing in her ears, the *thrumming* sound inside her head. Gone. Lucy shivered against the cold tile. She immediately scooted under the hot spray and rinsed the shampoo from her hair. Her mind raced as she finished her shower and dressed in the Liz Claiborne plum-colored sweat suit she'd taken from the dryer. Her head was soaking wet, but she didn't bother to use Wylie's blow-dryer. Instead, she ran a brush through her hair, fluffed it with her fingers, and left the bathroom, but not before she hung up her wet towels and gathered up her dirty clothes to throw in Wylie's washer. When this was all over, she was going to burn these sweat suits and buy bright yellow ones. Maybe a pumpkin-colored one, too. She needed color in her life. Rich, vibrant colors.

Downstairs she took a deep breath and held her audience captive as she repeated what she'd *heard* in the shower.

Her voice jittery, Lucy asked, "Do you think it means what I think it means? That wherever he is, he's leaving because he's afraid he's going to get caught. Wasn't there a movie about a rabbit named Harvey or something?"

Both men stared at Lucy as though she'd lost her mind. Wylie shrugged. "What would a rabbit named Harvey have to do with anything?"

Lucy threw her hands in the air as she inched closer to Wylie. "He's leaving wherever he is, but he's coming back to fight another day. He wants me to crash and burn. Isn't that what pilots say when they fly those super airplanes? Wall Streeters and lawyers have been saying it for years. Jonathan is, among other things, a movie buff. He always prided himself on seeing first-run movies no matter what part of the world he was in. I don't know if it means anything or not. Probably not."

"Where the hell is he?" Jake suddenly boomed. Lucy and Wylie reared backward to gape at him.

Jake cursed under his breath as he waved his empty coffee cup about. "We should have figured this all out by now. Why haven't we?"

"Because Jonathan, or whatever his name is, has had lots of time to plan all this. We just fell into it. He knows what he's doing, and we don't. It's that simple," Wylie said.

"Well, we should know. We aren't stupid, for God's sake. The guy's a scumbag, a con, and he's starting to piss me off. Bigtime. Now, let's sit down here and talk."

Jonathan St. Clair looked at his appearance in the foyer mirror. No one would think he was anything other than a shuffling old man who had lost his bearings and was looking for warmth.

Dressed in Nellie's husband's oversize clothing with a little padding here and there really did make him look like an old man. He was also wearing one of Nellie's gray wigs he'd found in a drawer that he'd hacked and cut. He still sported the mustache he'd had earlier. The gray watch cap he pulled on his head held the wig in place, allowing just enough gray hair to show at the sides.

Jonathan felt confident that none of the neighbors who were busy with their snowblowers and shovels would pay any attention to him if he shuffled along with a destination in mind.

His plan was to go to the door, ring the bell, and push his way inside, gun in hand. Whatever happened after that was unknown. Hopefully, he would walk away leaving three dead people and as many dogs behind. He'd then clear the snow off the Rover with the four-wheel drive and capable of getting through this snow that was sitting in the driveway, at which point he'd get in, hot-wire it if he couldn't find the keys, and drive away slick as you please. He wasn't sure yet about his getaway. He rather thought he'd make his way to the Metro Park train station, switch up license plates from a stranded car or, if the trains were running, take the next train to New York, where he could lose himself. He could book a room in a small hotel, work out a disguise that would pass muster, and board the first flight he could get to wherever it was going. He had enough bogus identities to take him around the world. He'd made a clean getaway after he killed Adam Ligar, so there was no reason to think he wouldn't get away with it this time, too.

Jonathan hated the thought that he had to cut his losses where the house in

Watchung was concerned. All those beautiful, sparkling diamonds, all those bearer bonds, all those bars of gold he'd secreted under the fireplace. Sometimes, you just had to cut your losses and walk away. He consoled himself with the fact that he had other stashes in other places. Still, Lucy had to pay for this particular loss.

He wondered what she was doing, right now, this very minute. Was she cooking Thanksgiving dinner? Was she laughing and talking with the man she was with, Wylie? Were they drinking good wine or that swill Lucy bought in the supermarket? Like he really cared what she was doing. Just a few more minutes and everyone in that cracker box of a house would be toast. Jonathan opened the garage door and looked around. He waited a few minutes, his ears tuned to any kind of activity. Minutes ago he'd heard a snowblower. Two men and a boy had been shoveling and shouting to one another. Now there was only silence. He moved then, slowly, the rubber boots that were too big almost coming off his feet in the deep snow. He used his knees to propel himself forward just as he heard a garage door open. Ah, the man with the snowblower was finished and going back into the garage. From what he could see, he had the road all to himself. Even so, it was slow going as he made his way to the house next door.

Wylie was blue with cold when he stomped his way into the small foyer. He was also covered with snow. Coop and Sadie had to be rubbed down with towels. Both dogs were shaking as Lucy led them to the fire where Lulu was prancing and yipping her delight that her new best friends were back in the fold.

"I cleared a narrow path to the road for the agents if they manage to get here. A few of your neighbors were doing the same thing. I'm going upstairs to take a hot shower! Hey, where's Jake?"

"In the study talking to his wife. Do you want me to make you a cup of hot tea?"

Wylie, who was halfway up the stairs, turned and called down, "I'm going to stand under the shower till it runs cold. Wait till I come down. Are the dogs okay?"

"They'll be fine as soon as they warm up," Lucy shouted, wondering if Wylie heard her. She shrugged as she made her way to the kitchen. She looked around. What was she doing before Wylie came in? Taking the garbage out to the garage, that's what she had been doing. She made a mental note to buy a trash compacter.

The bag was too heavy to carry, so she dragged it to the garage. The moment she opened the door she got a whiff of old garbage. She looked down at the five trash bags. She knew without a doubt the smell would invade the house if she didn't remove it. Since Wylie had shoveled a path to the road she could drag the bags down the path and dump them at the side of the road. If nothing else, the contents would freeze and kill the odor.

Lucy walked back into the house for her parka. First, though, she checked on the dogs. They were all sleeping side by side. Jake was still on the phone, and she could hear the water running upstairs. Wylie was as good as his word, using up all the hot water. She peeked into the oven. Everything was roasting nicely.

Lucy made her way to the garage, where she dragged all of the trash bags to the front door. Before she opened the door she tied the strings to the parka hood, put on boots and mittens. Using her feet she shoved the bags out the door and then closed it. The cold air was sharper than razor wire, the wind and swirling snow almost blinding her as she dragged the bags to the end of the shoveled path. Maybe, she thought, this wasn't such a good idea after all.

Huffing and puffing, Lucy was pushing and sliding the third bag to the end of the shoveled path when she saw the old man who seemed to be waving to her. Who was he? Did he need help? Maybe he was visiting someone on the street? He looked like he was in distress. She shouted, "What's wrong?" just as the man approached the end of the path that Wylie had shoveled.

Two things happened instantaneously. She heard Coop's and Sadie's shrill barks, and she tripped over the garbage bags just as the man's hand reached out to grab her.

The voice was menacing when he said, "Pick up your feet and move, goddammit! Into the house. I have a gun, and I'll use it."

"Jonathan!" Lucy gasped in horror.

"In the flesh! Unless you want to die right here, move!"

Oh, God! Oh, God! Why hadn't she *heard* him? Instead of moving, she took a deep breath and screamed Wylie's name. A second later she felt Jonathan's hand clamp over her mouth. Scared out of her wits at Jonathan's intentions she allowed herself to be dragged up the path to the front door. She could hear Coop body-slamming the door. Where was Wylie? Was Jake still on the phone? The dogs' shrill barking should have alerted both men by now. In her struggle, Lucy looked over her shoulder. She couldn't see a soul. She knew anyone looking out their window would think the old man was helping her or vice versa.

They were almost to the door when it blew open. Wylie in a bathrobe, water dripping from his head and face stood transfixed. Jake appeared out of nowhere.

Jonathan released his hold on Lucy and pushed her through the door. She literally slid across the wet tile floor.

Jake bent down to help Lucy to her feet, never taking his eyes off the man who had burst through the door. Seeing the gun in Jonathan's hand, he said, "Whoa! Whoa! Take it easy."

One hand in Coop's collar, the other in Sadie's collar, Wylie did his best to restrain both animals. Lucy knew Wylie was keeping the dogs from attacking Jonathan who wouldn't think twice about shooting them. That left Lulu, who danced and pranced and yipped but well out of Jonathan's way, the crazy pink polka-dotted bow jiggling furiously. Jake bent down to pick up the yapping dog. He whispered something to the quivering little dog and she quieted immediately.

"Back up, all of you. Into the den. That goes for the dogs, too. If any of you make a move, I'll shoot! Better yet, put those damn dogs in the garage. Do it now!" Jonathan shouted louder than necessary. "The rat goes in there, too," he said, waving the gun in Lulu's direction. He stepped back to make sure neither man nor dog got too close. Then, the gun steady in his hand, he shrugged out of the heavy oversize jacket and let it drop to the floor. The gun never wavered. His stance was steady and firm. Even from where she was standing, Lucy could see how his eyes were glittering. Right then she wanted to kill him with her bare hands.

No one argued with Jonathan's order.

Lucy bit down on her lip as she tried to harness her new ability. Concentrate, she told herself. Shift into neutral. This isn't happening. It's all a bad dream. She heard it then but it wasn't Jonathan. It sounded like . . . it sounded like Agent Connors. *Almost there . . . c'mon, c'mon, move this damn thing . . . the house . . . barking . . .* What did that mean, almost there? Did there mean here? This house? The dogs were barking. Were the agents close enough to hear the dogs? She heard the faint sound of the snowplow then and almost fainted. If so,

431

that meant three agents with guns.

"Don't do it, Wylie! Don't lock the dogs up. Your days, Jonathan, of telling me what to do are over. If you're going to do it, do it *now!*" Lucy snarled, hoping to divert his attention so either Wylie or Jake could tackle him.

Wylie had his hand on the knob of the door to the garage when Lulu leaped out of Jake's arms. The Yorkie was a five-pound dynamo as she flew back to the den and attacked Jonathan from the rear, leaping up to latch on to the back of his pants, which were far too big. Her teeth in the material, she tugged and tugged until his trousers started to slip down toward his knees. Off-balance now, he was taken by surprise and was whirling and twirling trying to shake off the tenacious little dog. Lulu held on for dear life but was losing the polka-dotted bow she was so proud of.

"Get this goddamn dog off me!" Jonathan roared, just as Coop jerked free of Wylie's hold.

One hundred pounds of solid dog moved at the speed of light, but the retriever didn't go for Jonathan's throat; he went to his back and ripped Lulu from her precarious perch. Wylie moved even faster and kicked the gun out of Jonathan's hand.

Jake picked it up as the two men squared off, the dogs howling and barking. Both men were at a disadvantage, Wylie in a robe and Jonathan with his sagging trousers. Lucy squeezed her eyes shut, then opened them in time to see Wylie sitting on Jonathan's chest while Jake held the gun pointed directly at Jonathan's head.

Lulu, furious at being left out of all the excitement, marched over to the prone man and bit his ear. Lucy bent down and picked her up. "We have to tie him up. With wire. With something he can't get out of. Let's put him in the garage so he can freeze. Do it quick, Wylie, I can't stand looking at him." She was half-crying, half-sobbing. God, where were those agents?

Jonathan struggled, but Wylie held his position. "You twitch again, you son of a bitch, and you're dead!" Jonathan ignored him as he tried to buck Wylie off his chest. Wylie's clenched fist smashed dead center in his Adam's apple. "The wire's on the shelf in the garage, Lucy. Get it."

"Okay. I see it. There's a whole spool, enough to wrap him up like a mummy."

"Coop, sit on this guy. If he moves, rip out what's left of his throat."

Coop sat.

Five minutes later, Leo Banks, alias

Jonathan St. Clair, was trussed and ready to go in the garage. "Wylie, can he talk?" Lucy asked.

"I doubt it. Why?"

"Why? I want to know the why of it all. I deserve to know why he did this to me."

"Because he could, Lucy. The important thing is he didn't get away with it. I crushed his larynx. He should be in a hospital, but we aren't going to worry about that right now. The FBI can deal with him if they ever get here. It's okay, Lucy, we got him. You're never going to have to worry about this guy again." Wylie opened the door and pushed Banks through. Then he took a second strand of wire and looped it through the garage door handle. He looked at the others and grinned. "If he so much as jiggles, he's going to go up and down like a yo-yo." He slammed the door shut and smacked his hands together. "Damn, I do good work! You can put that gun away now, Jake."

"Why didn't I *hear* him, Jake? I *heard* the agents. Why? Do you think it's gone, my talent or whatever we're calling it?"

"I don't know, Lucy, but I seriously doubt it. My guess would be that St. Clair simply wasn't thinking. He was operating by rote if that makes sense. He was simply doing what he thought he had to do and wasn't thinking about it. Time will tell."

"I hate it that *that man* is in your garage. I heard those agents a little while ago. Where are they?"

The doorbell rang at that exact moment. Jake answered it. The agents blew into the house, guns drawn. They looked around, puzzled expressions on their faces. "Thank God you're all right. The damn plow stopped dead at the corner. It took us a good fifteen minutes to trudge our way up here," Agent Connors said. "Listen up, we have a plan."

Lucy started to laugh and couldn't stop. "C'mere, Agent Connors," she said leading the woman to the door leading to the garage. She flipped on the light switch. "Allow me to introduce Leo Banks." Lucy stepped aside so the other two agents could see their quarry. "He's all yours."

Lucy left the men to explain the situation to the FBI agents. She returned to the kitchen and her Thanksgiving dinner. She thought about setting the table in the dining room but decided on the kitchen. For some strange reason people were always more comfortable eating in the kitchen.

As she was stirring the gravy the Chinese

fire drill inside her head returned. Lucy stopped what she was doing and turned up the volume on the television set sitting on the counter so the sound would drown out her thoughts.

Suddenly, her kitchen was full of people. Good people, all of them. Dinner was ready to be served but not just yet. She stared at the trio of agents. There had been a point in time when she'd considered them her enemy. Now she viewed them as her saviors. Not that she was discounting Wylie's and Jake's efforts. Three wise men. No, two wise men and one very wise, compassionate woman. She suddenly felt safer than she'd felt in days. "Can I get you some coffee and brandy? You're just in time for dinner. You have no idea, no idea at all of how glad we are to see you."

"Yes, Miss Baker, I'll take a brandy and a cup of hot coffee," Sylvia said. "I was terribly worried about you three," she said simply. "I'm on duty, but at this point in time I don't much care. I have never been so cold in my whole life. Something smells wonderful. We all have a lot to be thankful for on this day."

Lucy didn't trust herself to speak, so she just nodded.

And then it was time to say grace and

get down to the serious business of eating dinner. They all bowed their heads as Lucy said grace. The familiar words warmed her heart. She looked around her table. Everyone was smiling. Really smiling. Her thoughts totally clear, she waited for the bowl of mashed potatoes to be passed to her.

She felt Wiley's knee touch hers under the table. She grinned from ear to ear. *Now,* everything was perfect.

A long time later, a group of new agents appeared via snowplow and carted Leo Banks away. The agents all shook hands. Sylvia Connors wrapped her arms around Lucy and whispered, "The guy's a hunk. Don't you dare let him get away. If you invite me to your wedding, I'll be sure to come."

I knew she was aces. These other clods . . . just men . . . They don't know the first thing about women . . . I hope she's happy . . . The dogs are super. Makes me want to get one.

So she still had her talent. That was okay. She'd learn to work around it. Lucy nodded at the agent in agreement.

Lucy and Wylie, their arms around each other's waists, stood watching until the agents were down at the end of the street before they closed the door.

"I thought they'd never leave," Wylie said reaching for her.

"Hmmm, let's do what we do best, Wylie."

"And what might that be, Lucy Baker?"

Lucy crooked her finger before she reached for his shirt collar to drag him behind her to the stairs. "You talk too much, Wylie Wilson. Actions are better than words."

"Lucy Baker, you are a woman after my own heart," Wylie bellowed as he galloped up the steps behind her.

Epilogue

Lucy stared at her reflection in the pier glass, remembering the dream she'd had months earlier. She looked like a bride, and she felt like a bride. She crossed her fingers that nothing would go awry, not today or any other day. *Please,* she prayed silently, *let me be happy. Please.*

"You look beautiful, Lucy," Wylie's mother, Esther, said warmly as she kissed her almost-new-daughter-in-law's cheek. She brought her ear closer to Lucy's ear, and whispered, "Please be as good to my son as I know he'll be to you. My son loves you so much he aches with the feeling." Lucy's eyes widened in surprise, and Esther laughed. "Wylie told me about your dream, and he told me to say that to you." She hugged Lucy, careful not to disturb the satin gown or the veil hanging to Lucy's shoulders.

They were every bit as wonderful as Wylie said they were. The sisters were petite versions of Wylie, each with Wylie's sense of humor. She had loved them on sight. And they seemed to love her in return. She felt a moment of sadness that they would be moving away, but Wylie said one of the advantages of having a large family was that someone was always visiting. The brothers, both tall and good-looking like Wylie, were replicas of his handsome father, which meant she would have beautiful children.

Lucy looked around at Rachel Muller, Nellie, and the other neighbors gathered in her bedroom, along with the female side of Wylie's family. "I wish I had the words to tell you how happy I am."

Wylie's mother laughed. "You don't need any words, dear. It shows on your face. Welcome to the family. I want lots of grandchildren, remember that."

Lucy flushed a rosy red. Then she grinned. "I'll keep it in mind."

"I'm glad you decided on a backyard wedding. The flowers are in bloom, and we decorated everything. It's more intimate if you know what I mean. And the dogs can attend. Wylie took the fences down last week, so we have three yards for the overflow. It's perfect, Lucy, and the weatherman cooperated." Nellie looked at Esther and the sisters, and asked, "We really do have enough food, right?"

"More than enough, and I even made a meat loaf for Coop. All they have to do is say, I do, then we can party up a storm. I heard the DJ warming up a little while ago," Esther said happily.

Steven opened the bedroom door and stared at his sister. "Jeez, you look . . . great! The minister is ready. Wylie's about to collapse, and the guests are assembled, all 150 of them. It's time, Lucy."

Lucy rushed over to her brother. "I'm glad you're giving me away, Steven. I'm glad you're my brother. We need to say nice things to each other more often."

"Okay."

"Your neighbor, Mrs. Henderson, has her little organ all ready to play 'The Wedding March.' You ready, Lucy? Everyone is ready. Can we do it now? I'm nervous, can you tell?"

"I never would have guessed." Lucy smiled as the women moved past her to go downstairs to take their seats. She reached for the basket of flowers that Nellie had arranged from her garden when she looked down to see Lulu decked out in a jeweled collar and matching ribbon in her hair. She tried to claw her way up Lucy's gown. The hell with protocol. She reached down for the little dog and plopped her in the middle of the basket of flowers. "Okay, little brother, I'm ready. Are you sure Wylie is okay?"

"Hell no, he's not okay. He's in a stupor. Coop won't leave his side. Someone tied a blue ribbon around his neck, and he does not like it one little bit."

"Who? The dog or Wylie?"

Steven laughed. "I hear our cue. Just be happy, Lucy. That's all I want for you."

Lulu yipped as Lucy started down the steps and continued to yip right up to the moment the bride took her place in front of the minister, at which point she settled down in the middle of the flower basket and went to sleep.

Lucy looked through her veil at Wylie, her heart swelling with love. This was forever and ever.

Ten minutes later, the minister said, "I now pronounce you husband and wife. You may now kiss the bride!" Wylie obliged with gusto. "I love you, Mrs. Wilson!"

"I love you, Mr. Wilson."

Mrs. Henderson hit the keyboard with the same amount of gusto, and everyone shouted their congratulations as the happy couple made their way outside to mingle with their guests.

"I think everyone is here that we invited," Wylie said happily. "It's nice to have friends like this."

"I didn't see the agents. Did they make it?"

"Yes, Mason and Lawrence brought their wives, and Connors got some tall dude who looks like he climbs mountains for a living. Oh, look, here they come."

Introductions were made, and everyone kissed the bride. The men shook hands.

Sylvia Connors drew Lucy to the side and handed her a small flat gift wrapped in shiny white paper and topped with a huge silver bow. Her eyes sparkled when she said, "I wonder if you'd mind opening this now, Lucy."

Lucy reached for the package, and said, "Is that your guy? He sure is big! Is he the one?"

Special Agent Connors flushed and nodded. "Yes, he's the one. He belongs to our hiking club. His name is Sven. He's Norwegian. Will you hurry up already and open the present."

The shiny white paper and silver bow fell to the ground as Lucy gaped at the picture she was holding. "Oh, my God! Oh, my God! Wylieeee! Look, it's . . . it's Jonathan."

The picture wasn't all that good but the

message was clear. Leo Banks wearing handcuffs and a baggy, orange suit glared at the camera at his arraignment.

"One of my colleagues took the picture. I wanted you to start off your new life knowing the man who caused you such grief will be locked up for the rest of his natural life. Have a good life, Lucy."

Tears gathered in Lucy's eyes as she hugged the agent. "Thank you." She handed the picture back to the agent along with the wrapping.

"Not to worry, I bought you some eight-hundred-thread-count sheets. This," she said indicating the picture, "isn't your wedding present." The agent laughed as she walked away with her new beau.

"Wow!" was all Wylie could say.

If I wasn't married, and if Wylie hadn't gotten there first, I'd snatch her up in a heartbeat.

Lucy stopped in her tracks and looked around. Jake was grinning from ear to ear. Lucy flushed and winked. Jake laughed out loud, then moved away, his beautiful wife clutching his arm. He knew she'd just read his mind.

"What's so funny?" Wylie asked.

"Nothing. Hey, who's that little cutie over there with the four kids? Is she a relative you forgot to tell me about?"

Wylie looked everywhere but at the cutie and at Lucy. Finally, when Lucy pinched his arm, he said, "Oh . . . she's . . ."

"Angie Motolo?"

"Ah . . . yeah, yeah. My mother said I should invite her."

"I'm glad you did, Wylie. Even if she did break your heart. It mended, and now I have it."

Wylie beamed. "Yeah, my mother said something like that. God, I love you!"

"I love you more!" Lucy said.

"Jeez, our first fight."

Coop reared back and howled. Sadie did the same thing. Lulu leaped out of the flower basket and they raced off.

"There goes our family," Wylie said happily. "Ooops, I forgot to tell you, Lulu is staying with us for the summer. Jake and his wife are going to Denmark for some kind of special something or other. That little girl is ours till they get back."

"Perfect. Just perfect," Lucy said, as she linked arms with her brand-new husband. Stars in their eyes, they strolled off to greet all their guests.

About the Author

FERN MICHAELS is the *USA Today* and *New York Times* bestselling author of *Pretty Woman, Crown Jewel, The Real Deal, Late Bloomer, Trading Places, No Place Like Home, Kentucky Sunrise, Plain Jane,* and dozens of other novels. She is also the author of a novella entitled *Family Blessings.* There are seventy million copies of her books in print. She lives in South Carolina.

An avid animal lover, Ms. Michaels was devastated when she heard about a local police dog getting killed in the line of duty. She immediately had every dog in the police force outfitted for bulletproof vests, and has performed the same service for canines in other parts of the country. Ms. Michaels shares her own home with five dogs, including Flash, a rescue dog named after the K9 in her novel *Plain Jane.*

Visit her website at
www.fernmichaels.com